PENGUIN BOOKS

SEX AND POWER

Rita Banerji was raised all over India (in about thirteen towns and cities) and then moved to the United States, where she lived for eleven years, studying and working in the fields of ecology and the environment. She is currently based in Calcutta, where she works as a freelance writer and photographer. Her works have been published in *The London Magazine*, *New Orleans Review*, *The Word Worth Magazine* and *The Reveiw-Asia Magazine*.

Rita Banerji is the founder and chief administrator of the online campaign The 50 Million Missing, at www.50millionmissing.in, which is soon to be set up as an NGO in India.

[illegible]

[illegible]

[illegible]

[illegible]

Sex and Power

Defining History, Shaping Societies

Rita Banerji

PENGUIN BOOKS
An imprint of Penguin Random House

PENGUIN BOOKS

USA | Canada | UK | Ireland | Australia
New Zealand | India | South Africa | China | Singapore

Penguin Books is part of the Penguin Random House group of companies whose addresses can be found at global.penguinrandomhouse.com

Published by Penguin Random House India Pvt. Ltd
4th Floor, Capital Tower 1, MG Road,
Gurugram 122 002, Haryana, India

Penguin Random House India

First published by Penguin Books India 2008

10 9 8 7 6 5 4 3 2

The views and opinions expressed in this book are the author's own and the facts are as reported by her which have been verified to the extent possible, and the publishers are not in any way liable for the same.

ISBN 9780143064718

Typeset in Sabon MT by Eleven Arts, New Delhi
Printed at Repro India Limited

www.penguin.co.in

FSC www.fsc.org MIX Paper from responsible sources FSC® C047271

This is a legitimate digitally printed version of the book and therefore might not have certain extra finishing on the cover.

With much shame
to the millions of daughters
that India discarded
most unlovingly

CONTENTS

ACKNOWLEDGEMENTS

Many, many thanks to friends and family for the help they offered as I wrote this book: for comments and suggestions; for a place to stay; and for helping out with all the little crises—such endless printouts and motherboard crashes. I would particularly like to thank Jörg Balsiger, Vandana Sabharwal Baines, Asim Majumdar, Martine Marlard, Rupa and Dinesh Sharma, and Indira Banerji. I would also like to thank Dipali Singh and Jaishree Ram Mohan, of Penguin, for their detailed and very patient feedback, and David Davidar and V.K. Karthika, who thought this book worth publishing and commissioned it without my having written a single page. I am much indebted to Sebastian Barker, who in 2003 had asked me to write, for the *London Magazine*, an article from which I got the idea for this book. I owe much to my professor of religion at Mount Holyoke College, Dr Indira Viswanathan Peterson, who was the first person ever to give me an uncensored explanation of the lingam–yoni—as incredible as it had seemed to me at the time. My god-daughter, Adaire Robinson, who has been my loyal one-person cheering team, dreams dreams for me I dare not dream, and I thank her for bringing me her youthful hope and enthusiasm, even though I know she most probably will not be allowed to read this book till she turns eighteen. And finally, my heartfelt gratitude to the '50 Million Missing' team, Manvendra Bhangui, Hervé Blandin, Simone Borghesi, Caroline Martin and Lars-Gunnar Svärd, as well as all our nearly 2000 supporters for their belief in and consistent support of the online campaign www.50millionmissing.in, which was born of my research for this book. I would specially like to acknowledge M.A. Wuebker not just for her support but for also being for me such an inspiration of humanity and womanhood.

INTRODUCTION

Languorously sensual and of exquisite form, men and women in stone on ancient Indian temple walls engage in explicit and imaginative love-making, in an array of intriguing poses. The atmosphere they evoke is of such immediacy that even now, more than a thousand years since they were first conceived, they retain the power to speak unabashedly and eloquently of the carnal passions of the human race.

A man caresses his delighted lover's naked breasts with a lotus bud.[1] Another exchanges a coquettish glance with his lover as he attempts to seduce her with a glass of wine.[2] And yet another kneels before his lover and performs cunnilingus while she languidly gazes down at him and snips off his hair.[3] One couple prefers intercourse in the standing position—the woman with her leg draped around the man's hips, her arms entwined around his neck.[4] Another couple in coitus understandably requires assistance. Both are in a cross-legged sitting position, the man below, upside down and balanced on his head, the woman upright, held in position on top by two supporting female attendants.[5] A temptress attempts to tantalize, brazenly calling attention to her vulva by framing it with her hands.[6]

Every year, thousands of visitors from India and abroad contemplate these temples and respond in ways that are just as varied—from awe and disbelief to voyeurism and bewilderment, sometimes, even disgust. But while the world regards these monuments like oddities on the Indian landscape, quite a few Indians wish it would divert its attention towards other equally splendid but more asexual aspects of Indian history. Aiming their indignation at foreigners and intellectuals, they remonstrate: 'Why should people be so obsessed with these sculptures when India has so much more to offer?'

The answer could not be more self-evident. For how many civilizations of the world have been so inspired as to portray human sexuality with such artistry, elegance and candour, not just as a primal passion, but also a refined science and a cultivated art form? But even more significantly, what makes these temple sculptures particularly fascinating is how their very existence poses a challenge to the moral climate of contemporary Hinduism.

Even though these temples are a product of Hindu culture, no architect in India today would dare construct a temple or for that matter any public building along similar erotic lines. It would be considered sacrilegious—a disregard for public sentiment—and in all likelihood, given India's recent socio-political climate, could catapult the masses into a state of violent agitation.

So it is little wonder that a section of Indians find these relics more than just a bit disconcerting. These temples are an embarrassment, incongruous with nurtured concepts of Hindu religious sanctimony. And they are much too palpable to wish away. Hence many modern Indians would rather have them understated than re-examined and reworked into the fundamentals of their social fabric. In fact, Mahatma Gandhi, the messiah of celibacy, had wanted organized bands of his devotees to storm these historic temples and obliterate the offensive sculptures.[7]

On the other hand, these temples have enthralled scholars and intellectuals, many of whom have attempted to understand the philosophy behind the eroticism of these sacred monuments. They have mused over myths and lore, such as the one that avers that the sculptures were meant to stun the vestal sensitivities of the virgin goddess of lightning so that she would not strike the temples.[8] However, some scholars are dismissive of such colourful proposals, and assert that these sculptures propound no complex ideologies as such, but only reflect on that society's mundane regard for sex.[9]

However shocking the use of such explicit erotica in temples may be for some people, it would still be a mistake to regard these temples as anomalies of time or the remnants of some passing quixotic phase in Indian history. These sculptures, in fact, represent a trend that lasted for more than a millennium.

Between 100 BC and AD 1500, such temples were built all over India, the walls decorated with some of the most blatant depictions of sex ever to adorn a place of worship.[10]

Yet, whatever these temples may or may not say of their times, they do make a statement on the mindset of today's societies. After all, art serves as a double-sided mirror, embodying as much the creator as it does the beholder.

And so it follows that the question we should really be asking is not what these monuments say of their time, but how they speak to the social, the sacred and the moral ethos of our times. What we need to ask is why sex is such an odious subject in our contemporary world that we are dumbfounded by these historical sculptures? Why was the depiction of erotica on temple walls permissible a thousand years ago but not today? What causes this shift over time in a society's perception of sexual permissibility and moral precepts? And what role does religion play in this change? These are some questions that will be examined in this book.

THE MALIGNED SERPENT

The wall of contempt between the sexual and the sacred is not limited to modern Hinduism. Most dominant world religions today regard sex as blasphemous and obscene, something to be ostracized from the spiritual realm. At best, they might acknowledge it at arm's length like a filthy, malevolent creature that must be tolerated so that the wedded can procreate.

Sex is the pariah dog that roams the streets. The pagan outside the sacred walls. A dirty, titillating, though still indispensable contrivance. The lure of sex remains that of the maligned serpent, flashing the illicit fruits of temptation, draped over television screens and luscious magazine covers, or cloaked in humour to slickly engage an aroused audience in a covert act of sin. It is always devoid of the reverence, the faith, the dignity and the sanctification ascribed to the lofty altar of God.

However, there is no denying that sex underlies human existence. And if human life is sacred, how can sex not be? Why should sex not be enwrapped in holy robes and set up on the altar alongside faith, love and God?

The question is not rhetorical, for it is extremely pertinent to many of the cataclysmic issues challenging the world today. These include AIDS, contraception, population explosion, abortion, homosexuality, gender disparity, unwed parents, teenage pregnancies, sex education and sex work. The warped vision that dissociates the sacred aspects of life from the sexual acutely compounds many of today's social problems and even instigates some of them.

The moral edicts pronounced by religious institutions on sex or sex-related issues continue, even in the twenty-first century, to have either a direct or surreptitious grip on the way most societies think and function. With the exception of a dozen or so nations, the affiliation between governance and religiosity continues even today. It is a pronounced connection for most countries, including those with secular constitutions that proclaim the separation of religion and state.

Legal systems universally assume religion to be above the law, as evidenced by the practice of having witnesses testify under the oath of a religious digest. In most nations, the laws that continue to define social boundaries with regard to homosexuality, marriage, divorce, pornography, dress code, nudity, adultery, prostitution and abortion are direct religious injunctions.

In most modern democracies, homosexuality remains a criminal offence. Nor is there any recourse for the legal union of same-sex partners who want the social rights and privileges enjoyed by heterosexual couples.[11] While marital rape is legal in many countries, in some Muslim nations, women who are raped are often tried for adultery. Women in several parts of the world where Catholicism has a stronghold do not have the option of abortion, even if their lives are in danger.[12] Despite HIV and population growth rates exploding to epidemic levels, governments and societies all over the third world remain squeamish about making sex an open, natural and healthy issue that can contribute to social learning and discussion.[13]

IN DEFENCE OF SEX

The dilemma of sex, it must be admitted, has proved to be a challenging one, even for biologists, prompting them to dub it as the 'queen of evolutionary problems'.[14] Scientists have hypothesized that the earliest life forms on earth, such as bacteria, reproduced asexually (by producing clones of themselves), an opinion that religious texts seem to be in concurrence with, judging from the creation myths. Apparently, even Eve was cloned from one of Adam's ribs.[15] But somewhere over the course of evolution, sex became the favoured means of procreation for most organisms, including plants. What confounds biologists is why evolution would favour sex when it expends so much more energy than the asexual method.[16]

In sexual reproduction, an inordinate amount of energy is spent on searching for, selecting, attracting and competing for a suitable mate. In fact it can consume so much energy that some organisms like the salmon and certain cacti are able to do it only once in a lifetime, and die immediately after giving birth.

Though numerous theories regarding the question 'why sex?'[17] are constantly being put to the test, the general consensus is that sex is far more conducive to the survival and fitness of the species. It appears that sex, in the actual union of sperm and egg, serves as a gene repair workshop, eliminating harmful combinations of genes and allowing for the selection of recombinations that enable the species to be better adapted to its environment.

Staunch advocates of celibacy, who in contrast with biologists remain unconcerned about issues of species survival, point out that unlike other animals humans still have the choice to abstain[18] and that sex is a lifestyle option for the human species. This is a valid point, but it still needs to be pointed out that what is not an option, even for humans, is the sex drive or libido. Nature, the irrepressible architect, has designed the human body, and the bodies of all sexual animals, in such a way that the libido, with other physiological drives such as hunger, thirst, sleep, rest and excretion, is an inbuilt feature of every individual's constitution.

But what makes the sex drive a particularly crucial component of the constitution of the human species is that unlike other animals, humans do not have an oestrous cycle, the seasonal period of sexual arousal in animals that coincides with the ovulation cycle in females, when they are most likely to conceive. This is, in fact, the only time that female animals get sexually aroused, a state of being that some display very colourfully—in certain ape species, the vagina, buttocks or breasts swell up and turn bright red, blue or pink. But what this also means is that for most animal species, the females are sexually aroused only for short durations of time during any given year. The female gorilla, for example, gets sexually excited for just a few days a month till she gets pregnant and then will not have sex for another four to five years after she gives birth. So even if a male gorilla has a large group of females in his harem, he still is able to have sex only a few times a year.[19]

In the case of humans, however, there is no preprogrammed switch for sexual arousal that turns off seasonally. Testosterone, the sex hormone that controls arousal for both men and women, is as much a twenty-four-hour, involuntary aspect of our existence as are the hormones that control digestion, metabolism and all our other biological systems. Testosterone could stimulate sexual desire anywhere and at any time of the year. While reproduction is an evolutionary function of sexual arousal in most animals, it is not so for humans, despite the Vatican's insistence that God provided humans with sex for the sole purpose of making babies.[20]

Still another biological feature that bedevils human sexuality is that, unlike other animals where the system functions in isolation and the sex drive responds directly to the seasonal, clockwork switching on and off of hormones, the human sex drive is cross-wired to almost every other function of the body—to thoughts, sounds, smells, images, memories, movements, emotions, touch and taste. Through an intricate web of nerves and impulses, anything conceivable can trigger off the libido, thus making the very rhythm of living an element of human sexuality.

Yet, in its final evaluation of what constitutes 'purity' before god, religion does not regard any other bodily instinct as harshly as it does sex. Gluttony may be a sin, but eating is not, and certainly not hunger. Sloth is a vice but rest is not, and nor is weariness. The act of sex itself is not only regarded as the 'original sin', but also condemned as impure, along with desire and promiscuity. Undeniably, no other biological function has been more powerfully attacked by religious institutions than human sexuality has been. Worse still, no other institution has had as absolute a hold over the human mind and perceptions as religion has and it is this power that has often determined how societies deal with matters of sex and sexuality.

It is therefore imperative to ask what allows religion to have this power over the fundamentals of society—our customs, beliefs and laws, and why organized religion has chosen to specifically target sex so brutally.

SEX: THE ULTIMATE POWER WEAPON

Early royal dynasties often claimed to be descendants of the gods and subsequently affiliated themselves closely with religious institutions. It was an ingenious move, for it allowed royalty to govern with an authority that was recognized as divine and thus indisputable. Ultimately, it was not the royal throne but the supreme religion that was the tool of autocratic governance.

This power of religion, however, is not incidental or accidental. It has been built over time, as has been the institution itself, through a very effective exploitation of primal human fears. These are the fears of the unknown, the uncertainties about life events such as birth, death and illnesses, factors that appear to be beyond human comprehension and control, and threaten the primeval instinct for survival. Religion thus became a repository for uncontested mortal fears, a mode for societies to deal with the precariousness of existence.[21]

The supreme power that religion has over the masses, however, has transpired not from its being a guarantor of knowing what the future holds, but from its being the inducer of a state of ecstasy that has no place for doubt. This is what causes the believer to relinquish all personal power and resistance and submit to the absolute will of a divine authority, whatever fate it chooses to bestow. This is the bedrock of faith; it is also why Karl Marx called religion the 'opium' of humanity.[22]

Religious institutions have exploited this power by not only tapping into humanity's lack of perception of its own insecurities, but also by seizing a firm command over the human mind by perpetuating the fear instinct.

Through a system of myths that entailed the concept of a vengeful hell, as well as an inviolable code of morality—taboos and laws—that was to be feared and obeyed and whose desecration or even refutation would be dealt with by draconian punishments, religious institutions were able to construct a powerful technique of social control that acted like a leash on some of humanity's deepest and most instinctive needs. The crime of the violators and their punishments would be made public to deter others from those transgressions and to reinforce the social code. Public stoning to death or hanging, still implemented in some countries, were some of the arm-bending tactics used for the systematic conditioning of fear and conformity in societies governed by religious decree. Through prolonged conditioning by the use of such fear-based tactics, in time, many religion-based codes of morality became acculturated into the social ethos.[23]

Some of these moral codes, derived from centuries-old laws, have become imprinted deep enough in the collective human psyche to become something of a reflex response. Once an ancient law, which at one time threatened dire consequences, loses its bite, it settles very artfully into norms and attitudes that survive over generations. This occurs subtly, not necessarily through direct or punishing reinforcements, but simply through learning by observation and mimicry. It becomes the invisible process of socialization.[24] It even surfaces in people who may regard themselves as non-religious. Its morality becomes, as the German philosopher Nietzsche observed, 'a herd instinct',[25] an irrational process of living.

Codes of morality, depending on the particular religion, have routinely imposed varying restrictions on basic human drives such as eating, drinking and sleeping, for these drives are undeniably some of the most potent instincts in living beings. What is puzzling, however, is that it is the sex drive in particular that has been singled out over all other drives that are natural and integral to human biology, and utterly vilified. Why would sex alone be declared as immoral but not eating, drinking, breathing, sleeping and excreting as well? The answer is in that one feature which makes sex different from all other biological drives.

While the sex drive may be essential to the survival of the species as a whole, it is not, as the other drives are, inextricably linked to an individual's survival. So where an individual would perish without food, water, rest or excretion, for an indefinite period, he or she could very well survive a lifetime without sex. This is precisely what makes sex such an efficient yet non-lethal tool for the control of societies. Using any other biological instinct as a social control device would have threatened individual survival and inevitably instigated rebellion and resistance.

There is another more alarming aspect to human sexuality that could prove to be extremely disruptive to the process of institutionalization. The very process of institutionalization, even when it involves entire populations, has an inbuilt mechanism of group control that Irving Janis has termed as 'group think'.[26]

Group control is indispensable to the very survival of an institution and to the constant reinforcement of its legitimacy.

A critical strategy of the 'group think' process is to control the members through de-individuation,[27] a systematic stripping away of individuality. By compelling everyone to conform to a set standard of being, the institution is guaranteed a homogeneous cohesiveness that enables it to function more forcefully and effectively.

Human sexuality thus becomes a prime target of the de-individuation process because it is a unique expression of individuality. Sexuality as a concept is often thought of as a provocative exhibition of one's libido, or what in common parlance is termed as 'sexy'. However, sexuality is much more than that and is, in fact, an irrevocable form of expression for every individual, whether he or she seeks to express it or not. It is endorsed in his or her unique 'chemistry' and thus response—of attraction, repulsion or neutrality—to every other individual.

The power of sexuality is that it is far more than simply the mechanics of human physiology. Sexuality transposes the flesh into abstraction and causes it to become a vigorous tool of self-expression. It assumes a person's distinctiveness and becomes his or her unique identity. It is complex and encompasses many aspects, such as gender, sexual orientation, clothing, mannerisms, facial expressions, speech, preferences, thoughts, ideas, dreams, ideals, fallibilities, unconscious habits and interactions. It defies the rigid boundaries that institutions impose on people and emerges in a surge of expressions that are constantly and fluidly changing, trailing a person's path of growth and assuming it.

Sexuality, therefore, is synonymous with individuality. And it is individualities that hamper an institution's agenda, eddies that constantly threaten the cohesiveness of an institution by challenging its authority and undermining the processes that require homogeneity and conformity so that the members are easier to assimilate and herd together (hence the use of the term 'flock'). Sexuality thus is a potent anti-institution missile—nature's own defence against the artificial process of circumvallation. It, therefore, becomes imperative from the point of view of institutional control that human beings be stripped of their sexuality.

Religious institutions control sexuality not just by blacklisting sex, but also by tempering other aspects of sexual identity. They impose uniforms, robes and habits, and a dress code on those it can influence. In the manner of Delilah, for example, they target sexuality's crown—the hair. A sacrifice is demanded of Buddhist monks and nuns, who must keep shaven heads, while Christian nuns and Muslim women conceal their hair under veils. Even the social compulsion to clothe the natural body undoubtedly has its origins in the Garden of Eden where Adam and Eve made the first vain attempt to cover their shameful nakedness with fig leaves.

Ironically, religious institutions also discovered that there was yet another effective means of using sex as a tool of community control. Instead of banning it outright, they could offer it as a bonus to those who are more compliant with the institutions' sacred laws. Sex could be an incentive for people to fall into order.

Religions all over the world thus awarded sex as a privilege of 'marriage', one of religion's sub-institutions. By making sex available without guilt only to the married, the potentially free-roaming individual was lured into the trap of the structure and boundaries of the institution's social order. Logistically, marriage is the cement that binds one individual to another and to a whole network of kin and familial relationships. The individual is no longer a freewheeling, unrestricted, potential obstruction to the management of society and becomes what Nietzsche observed to be a 'function' of the 'herd'.[28]

In addition, by strategically making marriage synonymous with the concepts of 'love' and 'family', religious institutions have successfully established marriage as a desirable social goal. In western Europe, even though marriage is often reported to be going out of fashion, in Sweden, the nation with the most radical stand on the institution, 60 per cent of its people opt for marriage.[29] It is as though only the institution of marriage can confer sanctity and legitimacy on a conjugal relationship, which cannot be otherwise attained.

ORIGINS OF NEW SINS AND SHAME

However, despite safeguards, no power or the moral system it once implemented has been known to last eternally. History confirms that moral systems are in perpetual flux, and the manner in which societies have dealt with the issue of sex and associated practices and laws has constantly transformed over time. For instance, modern-day Italy with its Catholic world view was once home to the highly sensual, Dionysian pre-Christian culture. And Islamized as Egypt is today, under the Ptolemy dynasties sexual permissiveness, including incest among siblings, was once a royal privilege, the royalty themselves being regarded as descendants of god.

Nietzsche argued that the change of moral ethos in a society reflected an adjustment in the functioning of the system.[30] He contended that, ultimately, all moral systems were illogical and tyrannical. Moral values, whether good or evil, were arbitrarily assigned to human activities often against the dictates of logic and even human nature. The purpose of such systems, he said, was to always serve a certain need and to assert the powers of the 'creators' of moral laws.[31] Thus, according to this viewpoint, the line between the profane and the sacred, of what is to be taboo or customary, even for sexual morality, would be determined by how particular values served as a community control tool for the institutions in power.

Nietzsche also identified two primary types of morality based on the section of society they originated from. He called one 'master morality' and the other 'slave morality'.[32] Though he most probably meant it as an observation on human psychology, namely, the tendency of some people to create their own value systems and of others to mindlessly obey or rebel against an existing system, his theory lends itself well to understanding how paradoxical codes of moralities can arise in the same community over time and sometimes even coexist.

'Master morality' usually originates in the ruling or socially dominant classes. These classes are the creators of new moral systems in society as they generally possess the power and the luxury to do so. The 'master' assigns the moral value of 'good' to whatever quality he associates with himself, or that he feels strengthens his position or creates a good public image for him. The 'master morality' is, therefore, a form of 'self-glorification' for the dominant class. The master does not require public approval of its value system for he is its 'creator'. More so, the function of this system is to maintain the status quo of the master class by contravening change and the emergence of 'modern ideas' through a profound reverence for age and tradition and an emphasis on duties to one's own kind.[33]

'Slave morality', on the other hand, is a reactionary response of the underdog class to the master's values. It is a value system that foments among the repressed classes. These are generally the manipulated and/or governed people, or those who may also be scorned, underprivileged or marginalized. The slave class exists in a state of relentless struggle with its environment, and its internal system of morality is motivated by its attempt to survive and an innate desire for dignity. Often, however, slave morality is defined not so much by independent and internal reflection, as it is by a reactionary, often hate-filled response to the master's moral values.[34] According to Nietzsche, there is a 'hidden revengefulness' and a 'repressed envy' disguised as a desire for justice, and often even the self-righteousness of being 'good' versus the master's 'evil', in the formulation of the slave morality. Ultimately, the slave morality too craves the power of the master but feels frustrated by its impotency.[35]

SACRED MASTER, SEX SLAVE: CYCLES OF MORALITY

The central argument of this book is an adaptation of Nietzsche's slave–master morality theory. The proposal here is that in any society, at a given period in time, the mainstream moral ethos is determined by the factions that dominate that community at that particular time. The moral dictates serve the interests of the dominating camp and are used as its weapon for the assertion of its power and superiority. The new moral system is almost always imposed very effectively through the all-powerful religious institutions. It is subsequently followed by radical changes in mainstream social philosophies as well as customs and social practices. However, over time, there is an invariable shift in the power politics of the community, which could be caused by any number of factors: economics, class struggles, invasions, wars or civil strife. What follows is an establishment of a new dominant power and a corresponding shift in the society's mainstream moral values. That is not to say that other minor systems of moralities do not exist; they do, alongside the predominant ethos, but on a more restrained basis and confined primarily to the minor communities. However, the dominant class is not necessarily always the ruling class. Nietzche himself had often been accused of stubbornly trying to keep his theory 'intact' by refusing to 'pervert' it by applying the more complex dynamics of human societies. For instance, his theory does not account for erratic situations such as when rulers are ineffective, or if there is a massive revolt by the slaves or the repressed classes.[36] In fact, sometimes when the balance of social power shifts, the new master class could very well be a previous slave class that has overthrown the ruling class. In this case, there is almost always a momentous change in the societal moral scenario.

What is interesting in a situation like this is how with the reversal of class power a previous underclass morality, whose primary aim was to justify the existence of the underdog class and boost its own survival and self-esteem, would readjust to the new power equation in society. As the dominant community, it no longer needs to justify itself. Its moral values and customs might remain unchanged, but it now asserts them as superior and inviolable, something which is reflected in the mainstream society's acceptance and, perhaps, even adoption of this moral system.

It is the primary intent of this book to examine this interpretation of the slave–master dynamics in relation to how it applies to the transformations in a community's religious philosophies, moral edicts and social attitude towards sex. For this purpose, India, particularly in the context of Hinduism, is used as a case study.

Two factors make Hinduism an interesting venue for exploring the proposed morality theory, the first simply being the immense scope of study. Being the oldest living religion in practice, of about a 5000-year standing, Hinduism has had a much more protracted time frame than other religions to evolve. As such, it provides an immense database for study and observation of ideological changes over time.

The other is that there are clearly conflicting attitudes towards sex in modern India. The mind-boggling discrepancy between the earlier periods of Hindu life (when figures in the act of intercourse were sculpted on to temple walls) and modern India (where a kiss on the lips on the movie screen causes the censor board to emerge scowling with hammer and axe) indicates a society that has evidently undergone significant changes in its moral outlook on life.

THE CHRONICLE OF SEX: AN INDIAN TALE

This book identifies at least five distinct periods of major changes in the moral traditions of Indian society. These periods scale a total of about 5000 years, with each period ushering in a distinct and radically different role for sex and sexuality in the context of religious philosophies, moral values and social customs. Also evaluated for each of these periods is the corresponding transformation in the social power structure of internal and external group dynamics. The new moral order is generally seen to be a reflection on the priorities and needs of the new dominating or master class.

A startling pattern that emerges in the study of India shows that the sexual philosophy in each historical period is a direct rebuttal of the previous one, creating an intriguing 'yo-yo' effect. So, for example, where sex was a part of religious ceremonies in one period, it was completely banned from religion in the period that immediately followed and was regarded as sinful. And where sex was regarded as an obstruction to the obtainment of salvation in one period, it was embraced as a means to salvation in the succeeding period. In view of this observation this book also seeks to understand the factors within each period that precipitated change, and whether in fact, in accordance with the proposed master–slave morality hypothesis, the newer philosophies were a form of backlash or social rebellion that worked against the moral order and power structure of the preceding period.

The five periods delineated in this book are as follows. Though some of them may overlap, they are chronological in their order of appearance in Hindu mainstream society.

1. From 3000 BC to 500 BC (The Vedic Period):
Sex as a sacred duty

In the Vedic religion, which was the religion of the dominant community in this period, sex was regarded as the sacred duty of every man—the word 'man' here being gender-specific. Being a fiercely patriarchal community, the Vedics believed that every man had an obligation to his forefathers to perpetuate the lineage through the procurement of sons. Sex was regarded as a sacred ceremony where the man offered his semen as oblation to the gods. Consequently, the Vedics were intensely preoccupied with virility, and the social and religious attitudes towards sex, at least for men, were quite unrestrained. There were open references to the need for sex, and effusive use of sexual metaphors in sacred texts, as well as the use of sex in religious ceremonies. The Vedic sexual obsession, however, was expressly male-centric. It formed the core of the culture's identity and how the Vedics perceived themselves.

A secondary community that existed in this period and was subjugated by the Vedics also appears to have had sex as the central feature of its philosophy though in a manner quite different from the Vedics. These were the indigenous communities that had existed at least since 3000 BC. Between 2000 BC and 1700 BC, before the arrival of the Vedics, these indigenous communities had established one of the oldest and finest urban megalopolises—the Indus Valley civilization. Archaeological data indicates that the indigenous people perceived sexuality as a divine aspect of the universe, which was inclusive of all existence, including plants, animals and the rest of the natural world. Contrary to Vedic male-centrism, the indigenous cultures were particularly reverent of female sexuality—both in humans and in nature—and possibly regarded it as a supreme manifestation of the divine.

2. From 500 BC to AD 100 (The Buddhist Period): Sex as a prison

This period was marked by the rise of Buddhism, which not only emerged as a popular new religion but also caused a complete turnaround in the manner in which sex was socially perceived. Sex now became the symbolic shackle that kept society from realizing its highest spiritual goal of nirvana, the state where the individual is finally freed from the cycles of rebirth. It was proposed that sex imprisoned the individual in the body by keeping the body addicted to the pleasures of life and attached to personal relationships. Celibacy was thus widely accepted as the supreme path to salvation and freedom from suffering.

3. From AD 100 to AD 1500 (The Golden Period): Sex as salvation

In this period, sex was again given a philosophical reinterpretation in what was a complete reversal of the Buddhist notions—and it became known as the principal vehicle to salvation. Overcoming the social barriers placed by the preceding period, new cults emerged in this period in both Hinduism and Buddhism, which propounded complex and more evolved theories to re-establish the relationship between sex and the sacred. In many cults, sex itself was regarded as an experience of the divine. There was an extremely candid and almost celebratory approach to sex, which was discernible in all venues of life: the arts, music, dance, literature, sculpture, philosophy and even medicine.

4. From 1200 to 1947 (The Colonial Period): Sex as shame

This was the period when India was colonized first by Islamic warlords and later by intensely Christianized European nations. Hinduism borrowed heavily from the religiously defined prudish ethics of its colonial masters and in the course of time sex became an issue of shame. All matters regarding sex or sexuality were now considered vile and sinful, and had to disappear under the veil—their presence was banned from the public sphere. Notably, sex could no longer be blatantly associated with the divine. For this reason, the sexual symbolisms retained in some Hindu religious practices were reinterpreted in ways that outright rejected any implications of sex.

5. From the Twentieth Century Onwards (The Democratic Period): Sex as a paradox

It has been only sixty years since India shed its colonial shackles, enough time for it to accommodate to the notion of freedom. Yet it will be a while before the post-colonial dust settles and a distinct pattern of social trends, hierarchies and power structures emerges that will define this new period of democracy in India's history. It is this power structure that will ultimately and overwhelmingly dictate democratic India's sexual sensibilities and the overarching moral ethos.

At present, however, the direction this will take is difficult to gauge. A brief overview of India's modern chaos reveals that sex has rather an ambivalent status in society. If we were to follow the pendulum or 'yo-yo' momentum of the sexual ethos in Indian society from one historical period to another, we would expect that after the extreme puritanism of the colonial period democratic

India will, by default, adopt an excessively permissive approach to sex in the next few centuries. This speculation seems to be vastly justified by India's vigorous, out-of-control reproductive habits—India is expected to outdo China as the world's most populous nation by the year 2030. Besides, India is also soon to be home to the world's largest HIV-positive population, a virus that typically accompanies widespread sexual promiscuity.

Yet, paradoxically, India's vast majority still prefers to show a sexually prudish face to the world—one that it inherited from its colonial past. Indeed, it is puzzling how the nation reconciles its projected conservative persona with the sexual statistics of its social reality.

Perhaps one of the most striking symbolisms of this paradox is the lingam–yoni, possibly one of the most blatant depictions of sex in formal worship. It is also an icon that non-Indians often regard with utter disbelief. After all, not only does the word Shiva lingam mean 'the Lord Shiva's penis', but it is also sculpted in a particularly suggestive tubular shape. It stands erect on an ovoid, petal-shaped base called the yoni or 'vagina' (the shape actually corresponding to a vulva's), which is representative of Shiva's female consort, Shakti. However, most Indians will vehemently deny any sexual implication in this icon, insisting that it is nothing but a symbol of the divine.

Contemporary India's nonchalant acceptance of genitalia as symbols of the sacred is very curious. More interestingly, one wonders what it is about the Indian psyche that continues to uphold the lingam–yoni as one of India's most venerated symbols while it also simultaneously, and most bewilderingly, reviles sex as profane.

There are two theories that could shed light on this seeming moral paradox—theories that could also be used to speculate on what the emerging sexual trends might be in the foreseeable future of modern India. These were propounded by the Swiss psychiatrist Carl Jung and the Austrian neuropsychologist Sigmund Freud. Though they had their own speculations on religious symbols and their relevance to a culture's reality, their conclusions were—not unexpectedly—at odds. That, of course, makes the riddle of the lingam–yoni all the more interesting.

Freud's theory was that religious symbols and myths represent certain customs that were once observed by a particular community in the past, but were now taboo. He argued that these taboo practices were generally associated with the natural sex drive,[37] and over time had been forcefully repressed for they had come to be regarded as shameful, sometimes even unspeakable. However, because of the repression of the unconscious sexual desire associated with the practice, the community experiences tremendous psychological conflicts.[38] These conflicts might even verge on mass 'neurosis'.[39] Freud believed that religious rituals involving symbols sometimes verged on a type of 'universal obsessional neurosis' as the practitioners focused obsessively on the associated rituals to avoid the unconscious temptations of the repressed instincts. He held that the compulsive performance of or focus on 'sacred' rituals in cultures was driven by a deep collective sense of guilt and anxiety.[40]

To Jung these cultural and religious symbols represented concepts that were far more complex[41] than what Freud suggested and would also be undefined or at best vaguely articulated. In fact, the interpretation of the concepts too would vary according to the intuitive comprehension and the unique perception of the individual regarding it. Hence they are also open to multiple and creative interpretations.[42] Jung theorized that cultural symbols and icons were actually the abstract representations of concepts buried deep in the collective human subconscious. Besides icons, these concepts were also expressed in dreams, mythologies and in creative ventures by people. Jung called these buried concepts 'archetypes', and proposed—rather controversially[43]—that there was an obvious universality to their existence.[44] In other words, just as certain emotions and instinctive behavioural patterns are known to be integral to the human species and inherited by each individual at birth,[45] so too are these archetypes.[46]

Jung's point was that the archetypes represent a basic blueprint for the collective evolution of the human psyche. The archetypes in essence are fundamental concepts that developed in the primordial human brain and represented the basic human ability to assess and process its biological and emotional instincts—not only the sexual ones (as Freud would suggest) but also how humans relate to their environment. Some of the earliest expressions of archetypes can be deciphered in cave paintings that date back to the Palaeolithic civilizations.[47] The archetypes, however, do not deliver complete ideas or complex philosophies. They simply provide the potential for the evolution of complex thought, a basic framework of concepts that need to be developed through proper conditioning of the external, cultural environment.[48,49]

What makes archetypes particularly interesting is that they, in effect, herald the dawn of human consciousness or the concept of 'self'. They could be said to be the human brain's primitive scheme of registering the fundamentals of its own process in the form of elementary concepts. Contrary to the hypothesis that symbols are perhaps how the prehistoric human tried to explain his environment, Jung's argument was that it was much more than that. For these symbols also represent how the primal human mind explored and understood *itself*. These archetypes, therefore, laid the foundation for that feature which distinguishes the human species from all others—namely, consciousness, an awareness of its own existence and, more importantly, the urge to verbally express it.[50]

Jung's proposal was that archetypes, even as they occupied the subconscious levels of human existence, were propelled by the pursuit of specific goals. Like biological instincts or even genes, the archetype by design is driven by a need to express itself, and does so whenever the external environment is conducive to its needs.[51] The problem, however, arises when the archetype is perceived at a certain subconscious level, but is not being consciously comprehended or externalized.

In Jung's opinion, in situations like this, when a society is unable to or has not yet begun to consciously experience or verbally express an archetype, but recognizes it at a subconscious level, the archetype is compelled to manifest socially as an icon or a symbol,[52] such as the lingam–yoni. Since the archetypal concept cannot transform itself to the language of the culture, it is actualized as a symbol in the hallucinogenic image of the brain's unconscious.

However, like Freud's theory, Jung's too seems to come with a warning, which is that if a community is unable to intellectually come to terms with the archetype unfolding in its conscious reality, this can manifest as a conflict on the scale of collective neurosis.[53] Neurosis is usually expressed in social behaviour such as anxiety, avoidance and inhibitions.[54] Nonetheless, unlike Freud, who emphasized the perversity of the unconscious in its role of repression, Jung preferred to think of it as a place of creativity. In fact, Jung believed that the unconscious held immense, almost unlimited, creative potential for the collective evolution of society,[55] and that cultural symbols or icons that people venerated were the promise of this hidden potential.

Thus, according to these two interpretations of the lingam–yoni, there are two possible scenarios for the development of the sexual and moral ethos of twenty-first-century India. The Freudian model points to a dark, repressive social environment marked by a destructive perversity and a massive psychological conflict. The Jungian interpretation, however, provides a far more cheerful prospect. It speaks of the possibilities of a revolutionary breakthrough in the collective psyche of society and the emergence of a more wholesome and balanced approach to life and all its facets, including sex. The final chapter of this book speculates on which of these possibilities could typify the Indian sexual ethos in the next few centuries.

PART I

THE VEDIC PERIOD

SEX AS A SACRED DUTY

One could hypothetically say that most dominant religions of the world today have asexual origins, that is, they have been conceived and given birth to singly by an individual, usually a man.

Hinduism, therefore, could be seen as an exception in that it was conceived, evidentially, from the union of two opposing cultural forces whose differing philosophies and practices later fused to generate the matter and soul of what is today deemed as Hindu practice. One of the cultures, called the Vedic, was dominated by male sexuality whereas the other parent culture, the indigenous one, identified supremely with female sexuality. It is perhaps then apt that the very journey of Hinduism should mimic the complexity and the mysticism of all sexually conceived creatures.

It was not till much after its conception, till after roughly 2000 years of incubation in India's womb, that Hinduism was actually born and named. Its birth too, following its monumental scale of existence, was not an event that could have been borne by a single individual or marked by a specific time, and it stretched out over an agonizing period of numerous centuries, in a labour induced by the Muslim colonization of India. And yet the birth of Hinduism was as inevitable, as natural and as traumatic as the movement of life from the womb into the open. In form, Hinduism bore the features of both its original parent cultures, but like all living entities it embarked on its individualized path of growth and self-propelled evolution, transforming ceaselessly over the centuries.

HINDUISM'S FAMILY TREE

Of Hinduism's parent cultures, the goddess-worshipping culture was the existent one, already indigenous to the Indian subcontinent. Also referred to as the Indus Valley civilization, it was at its peak from about 2500 BC to 1700 BC and culminated in a highly evolved urban megalopolis in the valley along the Indus river in the north-western part of India.

Hinduism's other parent culture, a patriarchal, male-worshipping culture, arrived on the subcontinent in circa 1700 BC as aggressive, invading tribes, through the north-west frontiers of what now comprises Afghanistan and Pakistan. These people, who are said to have originated somewhere in Central Asia or Eastern Europe, are often referred to as the Aryans in Indian history books.[1] However, given the infamy that Hitler bestowed upon the term 'Aryan', here they will be referred to as the Vedics in reference to their religious texts, the Vedas, which were central to their way of life. The Vedics, who were habitual warriors, triumphed over the existent Indus culture, and emerged as the dominating force in this era.

The two cultures, much in the manner of the proverbial Mars and Venus, had conflicting identities and ideologies; but even as the Vedic tribes subjugated the Indus people as well as other indigenous groups, the two cultures inevitably converged.

The Vedic Ancestry

The Vedics were a nomadic, cattle-herding tribe. They are thought to have had a fairer colouring and a taller and broader physiognomy than the indigenous populations. They also had the sharper facial features of the Caucasian race. In contrast the indigenous people are said to have been dark-skinned with flatter aboriginal-style features, with broad nose bridges and thick lips. The Vedics, who were extremely contemptuous of the natives, often referred to them as the 'bull-lipped' and 'noseless'.[2]

Vedic culture was also far more undeveloped and rustic than the indigenous one. Where the indigenous culture had already peaked in large, permanent brick settlements in the Indus Valley, with planned townships and a remarkably sophisticated and organized urban lifestyle, the Vedics still had a rather wild and wandering existence. They herded their cattle as they rode alongside on horseback, and set up temporary encampments, where they lived in mud-walled huts with bamboo and reed roofs.[3]

The advancement of the indigenous civilization is also evident in terms of an existent script, which was an integral part of their daily life and appears to have been extensively used for various records. The Vedics, on the other hand, were largely unlettered and depended on oral tradition for chronicling their history. Their religious verses called the Vedas were not transcribed into written text till about 800 BC, supposedly almost a millennium after the original compositions.

The early Vedic mindset was still so primeval that the very concept of settled life was incomprehensible to these people. When they raided the Indus towns, setting them ablaze and razing them to the ground, it never occurred to them to use the settlements for their own habitation. They regarded the fortressed towns with disdain as *krishna garbha* or 'the womb of the black people'.[4]

Indeed, the Vedics demonstrated all the characteristics typical of populations that are homogeneous and insular. They were suspicious and fearful of the new and the unknown, which prompted aggressiveness towards the local people. The unfamiliar tongues of the Indus people made them the 'rudely speaking' ones, and their different faith made them the people 'without belief'.[5] The Vedics in their insularity lacked the mental sophistication to comprehend the new in terms of life itself and find a rational means of dealing with it. If it was different, it was vile and threatening, and had to be destroyed.

So it is no surprise that warfare was the very premise of the Vedic philosophy of life. It was the basis of their social interactions as well as their religion, for they looked upon their gods as their military partners in the wars against their enemies. The horse, which was a necessary aspect of their nomadic life, proved to be an effective and swift vehicle in their campaign of bloodshed and annihilation. The sphere in which the Vedics were far more advanced than the Indus people was in the development of weapons. They later learned to make weapons of iron, called *krishna ayas* or 'black metal', which were much more lethal and efficient than the earlier weapons.[6]

An exceedingly tyrannical and aggressive philosophy is evident even in the Vedic social structure, which was patriarchal and highly stratified. Male power was regarded as supreme and absolute in relation to female power, both among men and the gods. The caste system which ranked men, as also the gods, into hierarchical divisions, established the priests as the most superior and powerful class that controlled all of society. Next was the warrior class, which included the early tribal chieftains, who later took on the designations of kings and nobles. The third class was that of the traders, while finally, there were the slaves, the powerless and disparaged labour class, consisting mostly of indigenous peoples, many of whom were captured in war.

The gods of the Vedic religion were personifications of the natural elements that controlled the vulnerable nomadic existence of the Vedic people. Among them were the gods of the sun, the storms, lightning and wind. Though the Vedic pantheon had goddesses too, its most revered and powerful divinities were always male. However, there also was a concept of a single Creator, often called the One, who was held to be above and beyond the gods and humans alike. Unlike the Indus people whose gods were deified, the Vedics rejected idol worship, often quite vehemently, and instead focused on rituals.

Central to the Vedic rituals of worship was the fire sacrifice. A provisional altar was constructed, usually with stones or bricks, and the ceremony began, centred on the lighting of a fire in the altar—an invocation to the fire god—into which the priest poured various oblations, while reciting hymns from the Vedas. These were the most powerful moments for the priest, for the Vedics believed that it was at this time that the priest could contact the immortal powers of other gods through the fire god, and harness these divine forces for the use of human society.

The Indigenous Ancestry

While the invading Vedics remained nomadic for much of the first millennium BC, sections of the indigenous population had already adopted a settled lifestyle as early as 3500 BC and, as archaeological finds in Baluchistan suggest, had even begun to use the plough for farming.[7]

However, the zenith of the indigenous advance towards urbanization came with the Indus Valley civilization, one of India's oldest and most extensive megalopolises that included several cities and towns covering 1.3 million square kilometres,[8] and that is thought to have lasted in its peak form from 2500 BC to about 1700 BC. It boasted of some of the earliest and most meticulous urban planning known, and is testimony to a community that was highly evolved and sophisticated.

The Indus towns, unlike most cities, even modern ones, did not mushroom haphazardly, but were systematically planned and built. They were laid out in a grid pattern,[9] with the streets forming residential blocks, a layout that is seen only in newer cities like Washington and New York.

Another noteworthy feature of the planning of the Indus towns was the detailed attention paid to public sanitation—which included an extensive and separate network for the treatment and transport of domestic sewage,[10] covered brick drains along the main streets and a municipal garbage disposal system.[11] This kind of civic sense that incorporated health and sanitation into its urban module was astonishingly ahead of its time, considering that even as late as the nineteenth century, all of London's domestic sewage and factory pollutants were being emptied, untreated, directly into the river Thames, which not only killed all the fish but also caused a cholera epidemic in the city.[12] The Indus Valley inhabitants also developed specialized industries, which indicates a progressive community that was given to propagating innovative ideas and concepts. For instance, they did not just grow cotton, but they also spun and dyed their fabrics.[13] Their craftsmanship in metallurgy and pottery were of distinctive styles and designs.[14] The items produced were not just for the community's consumption but were also used in trade with other communities both within the Indian subcontinent and in lands as distant as Persia, Afghanistan and the Middle East.[15] While cotton was one of their popular export items and was much in demand in places like Babylonia,[16] the imports mainly consisted of metals and precious stones like gold, copper, silver and turquoise.[17] Trade was highly regularized and included a defined system of weights and measures.[18] This significantly points to the community's ability to interact cordially and comfortably with distant cultures through negotiation and mutual understanding, and not by demonstrating the primitive war instinct of domination and hoarding of resources characteristic of the Vedics.

This is also evident in the relative lack of preparation for warfare by the Indus people. Even though they had far more sophisticated methods of casting metal than the Vedics and knew techniques such as the lost-wax process (cire perdue),[19] they concentrated their metallurgy skills more on designing jewellery and idols than on producing weaponry. The weapons that have been excavated from Indus sites, such as axes, spears, and arrowheads, were rather flimsy and made of copper and bronze, which would have rendered them quite ineffectual in warfare. It is, therefore, possible that these were intended just for ceremonial use.[20] Furthermore, there is no evidence of the use of armour or shields,[21] which would have been necessary for feuding and battles.

This absence of a warmongering tendency implies that the Indus people most probably did not encounter many attacks from outside enemies nor did they face domestic uprisings and civil wars. An explanation for this might be found in a recent theory, backed by quite a few political analysts, including Spencer Weart, Bruce Russet and R.J. Rummel. Extensive research of the patterns of war between nations over the last century indicates that 'well-established democracies' have never been known to attack each other. The term 'well-established' seems to be significant here, for it indicates a stable democracy where the political dynamics ensure the safeguarding of a properly functioning egalitarian system with all the constitutional guarantees of citizens' rights. In other words, it denotes a democracy-style system which is less likely to be overthrown by a more autocratic one.

However, the tendency of 'stable democracies' to avoid war with each other does not necessarily relate to factors like trade, stability of economies or lack of competition since there are being fewer countries in a region. Rather, it has more to do with the political frameworks of these countries and the common ideologies of their people, including the culture and ethics. What ultimately maintains peace among these nations could include a combination of factors, such as a process of constitutional restraints that prevents the leader or leaders from hurtling the nation into battle, a sharing of similar ethical and philosophical values by the people of these nations, and a general perception of the possibility of greater mutual benefits for the nations, through trade and other venues than through bloodshed.[22]

Hence one can deduce that the nation states of the Indus Valley probably had some sort of a republican or neo-democratic form of governance, most likely administered by an elected ruler or a representative body of elected officials who governed in accordance with constitutional procedures and not by autocratic decree. It would also suggest an egalitarian system of law-making, where administrative policies and regulations were subject to some form of public consensus and discussions. Possibly, if the Indus nations had trade relations with neighbouring kingdom states, there might have been peace treaties. Numerous indigenous communities formed small, town-sized, independent nation states outside the geographic periphery of the Indus settlements that were not subject to Vedic warfare and are now known to have existed as republics,[23] which gives credence to the theory that the Indus nations must have had similar forms of government.

There does, however, appear to be evidence of a class system in Indus society, based on the varying sizes of the houses unearthed, with some large ones possibly indicating higher social positions. Nonetheless, even their poorer classes, who some assume might have been servants or slaves, lived in two-roomed brick houses.[24] There also appears to be no trace of a palace or residence that would indicate the presence of a monarch or a supreme governing authority. No central temple has been found either, unlike most ancient civilizations like the Egyptian, Aztec, Inca, Mesopotamian, which had a central temple, around which the city was built. It was usually through the ceremonies at the temple that the monarch asserted his divine power over the people.

In this context, the Indus society's multiracial composition is perhaps significant. Archaeological evidence suggests that the Indus sites were inhabited by various races including the Afroid, the proto-Australoid, the Mongoloid, a Mediterranean type and a Caucasoid sub-race.[25] It is believed that the latter two were also immigrant races, which drifted into the Indian subcontinent more than a millennium before the Vedics. Archaeological data also suggests that some of the Indus tribes may have had connections with or even origins in prehistoric Sumer, in what is now modern Iraq. A characteristic facial hairstyle in Sumerian men, where the upper lip is shaved but the beard retained in a short, trim form, is also seen in some Indus male representations.[26] Other artefacts that connect the Indus to the Sumerian and Babylonian civilizations are trefoil designs, the legend of Gilgamesh and the symbol of the ibex.[27]

However, by the time the Vedics arrived, all these tribes had managed to co-mingle, even as they coexisted, and the Indus civilization itself was possibly not only a fusion of various races, but also their cultures, practices and beliefs. The ability of such diverse people to exist in relative peace and voluntarily participate in a highly organized civic system also implies the evolution of a sophisticated social philosophy and advanced communication skills.

As the Indus script still remains undeciphered, much of our understanding of the religion and philosophies of these people is based on circumstantial evidence procured from artefacts and excavations. The Vedas too are a rich source, reflecting as they do the Vedic perception of their enemies.

Unlike the Vedics, the Indus people were idolaters. A vast number of Indus clay figures or imprints on seals found are nature icons such as tigers, crocodiles, elephants, bulls, snakes and trees,[28] which indicate that the Indus people practised animism, a tradition still sustained by existent indigenous tribes in India. Also central to the Indus tradition of worship were an omniscient Mother and a Divine Father figure. The Divine Father was often portrayed as a mendicant with an erect penis, in meditation, wearing a horned head dress and surrounded by animals.[29] The Vedas referred to him as the 'lord of the animals', and also the 1000-eyed Rudra.[30] Just as the Great Father was often portrayed as being in the company of animals, in artefacts, the Great Mother was frequently associated with vegetation. In some seals, sprigs of leaves were shown to be sprouting from her womb while her feet resembled the roots of a tree.[31]

Blood sacrifice might have also been a part of the Indus sacred rituals, as some of the seals show a figure standing before the mother goddess, holding up a knife and a cup in a gesture of offering.[32]

SEX AND THE CREATION THEORY

The role of sexuality in the Indus religion was, most likely, more elaborate than just the simple representation of a Divine Mother and a Divine Father figure. Sexuality, it appears, was fundamental to the very core of Indus spirituality—it extended to their notion of the sacred and their concepts of creation. Numerous fertility icons have been unearthed from Indus sites that include phallic-shaped and ring-like structures, believed to represent the penis and vulva, respectively. Many of the ring stones found in Taxila in the Indus Valley have nude figures of goddesses engraved on them.[33] Additionally, several figures of pregnant women and women with large breasts have also been found.

It can be hypothesized that the Indus concept of male and female sexuality and their connection to the sacred extended to all of existence. Not only was the Divine Father, the lord of the animals, often depicted with an erect penis, but the animal world he was inexplicably identified with consisted mainly of male and virile animals. Similarly, the Divine Mother, who was held synonymous with vegetation, was sometimes portrayed as emerging in human form, with breasts or a womb, from a tree.[34]

Even though the Indus 'ring' and phallic icons have never been discovered in conjunction, like the lingam–yoni idol of modern India, this concept of a sacred union, or of sex itself being fundamental to the power of the sacred, was expressed in the numerous seals that clearly portrayed the union of the Divine Mother and the Divine Father personalized as vegetation and animal powers, respectively.

A seal unearthed at Chanhudaro shows a naked female icon with the vulva exposed and a gaur with an aroused penis standing above her, about to copulate with her.[35] Other depictions were more indirect. For instance, in one continuous series of seals[36] that depict the Divine Mother as a tree and the Divine Father as a tiger placed below the tree, the final seals in the series clearly indicate sexual union. In one seal, a woman with animal characteristics—two horns, buffalo hooves and a tail—emerges from a tree. The tiger has acquired a leaf-like chest and paws, and his ears have turned to sprigs of leaves. In the final seal, the tiger and the woman merge to become one. From the waist up the fused form is represented as a woman, her arms stretched out sideways the way the Divine Father's were shown, and from the waist down it has the body of a tiger.

Another illustration of this divine coition appears in what were mandalas or geometric diagrams. For instance, the above-mentioned series of seals also incorporate a diagram that depicts a square with eight triangular petals.[37] Some of these mandalas were later adopted by the Vedics for their fertility rituals.

Numerous similar square seals have been found at Indus sites, bearing five- or sometimes six-pointed stars. In some of these seals, each of the triangular receptacles of the stars assumes the head of an animal. A confirmation of the sexual symbolism of these artefacts can be extracted from the myths and folk art of existent indigenous Indian tribes such as the Warli and the Bhils. In these cultures, triangles generally represent a gender: the ones with the upward pointing apex being male, and the ones with bases on top female.

The Warli believe that the triangles, when separate, are of mortal form with stick hands and legs. However, when they conjugate, that is, when the triangles fuse, the union represents the divine. The concept here is that sexual union itself is a representation of the sacred and its power. Interestingly, if these triangles are merged, so that the triangles overlap, they form five- or six-pronged stars, depending on whether or not the apex of one rests on the base of the other. This could possibly explain the five- and six-pointed stars on the Indus seals. In the Warli's depiction of the corn goddess, a headless man on a horse with five corn shoots emerging from his neck is often shown alongside the goddess.[38] Again, this could be a throwback to the Indus seals where the union of the Divine Mother and the Divine Father are shown in their respective plant and animal manifestations.

The Vedics, on the other hand, were iconoclasts and had an intense dislike for the Indus norm of idol worship, including the worship of the phallic icon. They even called upon their gods for assistance to help destroy the city of the 'phallus worshippers'.[39] However, this was not so much an expression of dislike for the phallic idol itself as it was for idol worship, for in the course of time, when the last Veda had been written, the Vedics had inducted the phallic icon into their religion, at least symbolically if not in form yet, and were composing sacred verses to glorify the 'golden penis' standing in the waters.

Indeed, sex was integral to the Vedics' own creation theories and the Vedas ascribed the very origin of creation to desire. The One, which was the Vedic religion's ultimate concept of the Singular Creator, held to be above all the gods, was the divine figure who first experienced desire. Then Desire, personified as a spark, placed a 'seed of fire' in the Golden Womb of the Creator, the One.[40] The world was then created from the divine union of an earth mother and a sky father.[41] Plant and animal life, on the other hand, were not divine personifications (as with the Indus people) but the products of the union of *prakriti* or matter, a female creative principle, and *purush* or man, a male creative principle.

Otherwise too, sex was very prominently placed in Vedic theology. Of the three (later a fourth was added) principal spiritual goals ordained for all Vedic men, one was *kama*, which, at least from the Vedic approach to the concept, was lust or satiation of the sex drive. The other two goals were *dharma* or sacred duty, generally determined in the context of the caste one was born to, and *artha* or wealth and material acquisition. Sacred texts were also unreservedly liberal in their use of sexual metaphors and innuendos.[42] In the Vedic fire sacrifice, the altar was considered male and the fire was female. The kindling of the fire in the altar was described as 'friction'. Similarly, during the reading of the sacred verses, when a priest separated two verses and brought two others together, the process was likened to sex, where a woman parted her legs and a man brought his together so that the ceremony would be profusely fruitful.[43] Vedic priests, who after a long period of sexual abstinence prepared the *soma* drink, one of the ingredients for the fire ceremonies that marked the end of their celibate period, would gleefully engage in raunchy jokes to lighten the drudgery of their labour. They spoke of a draught animal between two shafts as a man in bed with two women, and likened the movement of the pestle in the mortar to the 'pounding' of a penis into a vagina.[44] The priests would jauntily declare the cravings of their penises for 'two hairy lips', just as, in their view, the frog longed for rain after a long dry summer.[45] Also, many of the Vedic male gods were described as strapping virile horses or bulls bursting with 'seeds' and priests encouraged their patrons to give generous donations for their services, by petitioning for adequate 'seeds' to be put in the 'womb' for a productive ceremony.[46]

The Vedic scriptures, particularly the Atharva Veda, also offered various sexual remedies in the form of chants and herbal potions that claimed to boost a man's virility and increase his attractiveness to women. Besides, sexual jokes and even coition were integral to certain Vedic ceremonies. It was believed that sex or sexual jokes attracted the interest of the gods and entertained them and, therefore, drew them to the ceremony.

In both cultures, the Indus and the Vedic, sexuality was an integral part of the sacred world view and sex was akin to a religious experience. Yet, the context in which sex and sexuality played out in the two cultures through religious and social customs, and impacted on beliefs and taboos, varied greatly. This variation was largely due to the very different mindsets of the two cultures, one being male-oriented and the other female.

THE ALTAR TO VIRILITY

The Vedic patriarchal culture was defined by an extremely aggressive need to establish a social order that catered to male sexuality, both on earth and in the heavens—among humans and also among the gods. In fact, the entire Vedic spirituality hinged on the preservation of this cosmic masculine dominance.

Fundamental to this vision was the Vedic perception that regarded aggression and combat to be the natural state and aim of all entities. It pitted man against man, man against woman and man against nature. The entire cosmos was assumed to be in a perpetual state of war. For a society to function properly, men had to fight. The Vedic race had to fight to remain superior to the indigenous race and the Vedic man had to battle for manipulation of divine power, so their own women could not grab control. This conflict extended to nature as well. The way the Vedic man saw it, there was a dichotomy between humans and the supreme power of nature. He, therefore, had to constantly struggle to regain command over the unseen existence.

Through their creation myths, Vedic men established the superiority of their gender as well as of their fair-skinned race as unshakeable truths of existence. Humankind, according to the

Vedics, was created from the dismemberment of purusha, the primordial man.[47] The parts of the body above the waist were regarded as the 'pure' realm, and only the 'superior' creations arose from these body parts. Thus the upper-caste men and the male elements of nature grew from these parts: the Brahmin, who was of the purest Vedic race, from the mouth, while the sky and the sun—both male elements—from the head and the eye respectively. All parts of the body below the waist were regarded as impure, and, therefore, all the castes subordinate to the Brahmins were said to have been derived from there, their origins descending down the body according to their worth in the caste hierarchy. Women and the slave classes, mostly indigenous peoples, as well as natural elements regarded as 'female' such as the earth, were said to have been created from the feet, which were the lowest and, therefore, considered the most 'impure' part of the body.

Not only did the Vedic man spiritually institutionalize his racist and sexist vision of existence, but he also split nature along gender lines and imposed his system of hierarchy on all natural elements, thus authenticating male superiority as the ultimate law of nature. The only male power that the Vedic man had to contend with was that of the male gods. However, his notion of his gods' existence was not removed from the humdrum of his own earthly life. His gods may have lived in the heavens, and may as well have been immortal; however, the ultimate source of creation, the One, was believed to even transcend them. The Vedic man believed that, like him, the gods too were the creations of the great One[48] and emerged from the same womb as he,[49] both the handiwork of the great One.[50]

To establish his control over the cosmos, the Vedic man felt he needed to work in conjunction with the gods, so he could coax their powers in the direction he desired. The gods would first be invited to the sacrifice through chanting of hymns from the Vedas. They would then be pandered to and negotiated with.[51] It was a tricky relationship, for the Vedic man also saw himself as a competitor of the gods, vying with them for immortality, for power and for women. Unmarried women who got pregnant would often attribute their condition to one of the gods, and as such the Vedic man was convinced that the gods were trying to seduce his women. He believed that sometimes the gods would even be jealous of him and actually work against him.[52] However, as the gods were more powerful, the Vedic man felt he had to learn to be accommodating and to work with them patiently. He would flatter the gods, tell them they were all great and assure them that not one of them was small.[53] He would address the immortals as his good friends, and speak of how he 'rejoiced' in their 'friendship' and express his hope that they would allow for 'praises to flow back and forth' between them, men and gods.[54] To sustain his supposed position of authority in the scheme of existence, the Vedic man catered to the egos of his gods, bribed them with offerings,[55] negotiated deals and sometimes even manipulated their powers by pitting one powerful god against another.[56]

The power of the gods as well as their immortality, it was believed, was derived from their superior virility. Power, virility and immortality in Vedic thinking went hand in hand, each bolstering the other, each proof of the other, and that is why these were the three ambitions that the Vedic man hankered after most.

In fact, the most revered gods of the Vedics, and also the mightiest, were seen as testosterone powerhouses. These included Agni, the fire god; Indra, the king of the gods; and Soma, the god of the hallucinogenic, aphrodisiac drink used in religious ceremonies.

The fire god was characterized as sharp, insightful and impressively masculine,[57] with a beard, flame-like skin, yellow eyes and seven tongues.[58] He rode a chariot drawn by red horses, which could fly him from the earth to the heavens, so he could directly carry the requests of mortal men to the gods.[59] As the sun, he was sexually indefatigable, his reflection shining on the feminine waters. He impregnated them with his golden hues so that other fires were born on earth every day.[60] The fire god was the 'guardian of immortality'—since he was omniscient as a 'fixed light in the sky', and all mortals were compelled to regard him with awe.[61]

The god of soma, on the other hand, was the guarantor of male sexual prowess. He could bestow both virility and immortality upon the Vedic man, and provide him with protection against his enemies as well as the 'evil plans' of other gods. Apparently, after drinking soma, a man could become capable of uninterruptedly satisfying a hundred women at a time as well as destroying any known enemy. This is why Vedic men believed that the gods craved soma as much as men did.[62]

The most prodigious soma drinker was the king of the gods himself, Indra, who was hailed as a magnificent warrior. His thunderbolt, a club, an unmistakable phallic symbol, represented his fearsome skills in warfare. He was said to be robust, with abnormally long arms, and could annihilate his opponents by bombarding them with thunder and lightning. He was popular because he apparently often fought alongside the Vedic men, helping them destroy the stone cities of their indigenous enemies. Indra's excessive addiction to soma also made him prodigiously licentious, and he was known to have seduced thousands of women—not only the wives of other gods, but even those of mortal men and the sages. It was said that a cuckolded sage was so enraged that he branded Indra's body all over with a thousand vagina impressions.[63] In battles, Indra would consistently win, and then he would seize women on his enemies' side as war trophies. It was believed that when Indra's son, after drinking soma, got boastful about his prowess, Indra put him in his place by reminding him that he, the king of gods, was the only one who was ultimately indefatigable.[64]

The Vedic man, however, had to satisfy his desires for this immortal, virile power through lesser, earthly means. He would drink the hallucinogenic drink soma with ritual solemnity, convinced that the impressive images so produced in his mind represented the actual states of power that soma temporarily bestowed upon him. In one hymn, a man sings of being an eagle so gigantic that he appears to be as large as the gods themselves, with one of his wings alone simultaneously spanning the earth and the sky.[65] Other soma-intoxicated men envisioned such power that they apparently were able to lift the earth and place it where they willed.[66]

Convinced that he shared a common womb of origin with the gods, the Vedic man came to the conclusion that he too must have the potential for the same immortality as the gods. This, he further hypothesized, was possible through the procurement of sons. A son, in the Vedic man's understanding, was not simply another addition to the patriarchy's bloodline but an actual rebirth of himself, his exact replica. The son was a true-to-life reconstruction of a man in a woman's womb,[67] just as he himself was a replica of his dead forefathers who lived in the heavens. When the Vedic man contacted his forefathers in the heavens through the fire sacrifice, he was securing a line from the earth to the heavens that not only confirmed his interminability, but also guaranteed his seat in heaven alongside his ancestors and other immortals.[68]

Additionally, since virility was a direct indicator of immortality and power, Vedic men missed no opportunity to demonstrate their strength. In wars, they violently crushed the bones of their defeated opponents, flayed them alive, dismembered them, hacked off their penises and chopped up the testicles. The enemies who fled the battle were ridiculed as 'emasculates'.[69] This was an opportunity not simply to display a man's own sexual prowess, but also to strip the enemy of his. The same philosophy applied to men of his own tribe who were in competition for the same woman, for the aim of immortality was a very personal one. For instance, in one Vedic hymn, a man sings of how he would 'split' his competitor's penis on the woman's loins, just as reeds are split with a stone.[70] An opponent's woman bagged in war was a showcase trophy, so women were very often abducted during wars so that men could add to their harems and deprive their opponents of their women.[71]

DIVINE SEMEN

For the Vedics, the most significant measure of a man's power was his semen. Believed to be a concrete proof of virility, semen was treated like a precious resource. Vedic men, still a little confused about the workings of human biology, also hailed semen as the eternal source of life for men, women and the gods. It was, therefore, regarded as a prized commodity and sought by both the mortals and the immortals. While men carried their semen in their testicles, women, it was said, carried it in a 'pot' in their wombs. Semen, the well of strength and longevity for all beings, guaranteed men victory prizes, fame, virility and wealth.[72] In later texts, the Vedic god Agni would request the semen of the virile god Shiva (known as Rudra to the Vedics) for the other gods to drink. When Shiva released his semen, fragrant with the scent of jasmine and blue lotus, into Agni's palm, Agni drank it immediately and joyously proclaimed it as 'elixir'.[73]

Semen was also the definitive assessment of a man's worth. An impotent man was excommunicated from religious ceremonies, and among the very few rights that Vedic women had was the right to desert an impotent man. In fact, dead men were cremated in such a way that the genitals would not burn, in the belief that the dead man would be able to continue enjoying women in heaven too.[74]

Various herbs, potions and magic spells were employed to augment male virility and alleviate problems of impotence. One hymn addressed to a 'penis-erecting herb' appeals for the combined vitality of the horse, the mule, the he-goat, the ram and the bull to grace the person under treatment, such that his penis would be as stiff as a string stretched everlastingly on a bow. There were also hymns to establish virility though the sexual conquest of women, though the Vedic idea of seduction verged more on aggressive subjugation than romantic enthralment. Another hymn—meant to capture a desired woman—aimed at alienating her from her family and rendering her so 'powerless' that she would be entirely under the domination of her suitor. It spoke of shooting the woman in the 'heart' with an indomitable 'arrow' of desire, which would cause her such agony that eventually she would softly and meekly submit to her suitor.[75]

The Vedic man took careful stock of his individual semen, always with an eye to building his reserve, and when he did spend it, it was after a careful cost–benefit analysis based on the assumption of some high and worthwhile return. If a man ejaculated and spilt some semen on the ground, convention required him to pick it up with his ring finger and thumb and smear it across his chest and eyebrows, all the while reciting a prayer for the escaped semen to return to his body and replenish him with strength, virility and wealth.[76] A throwback of this old ideology lives on in a modern-day custom in India. Various sects still wear what are called 'caste marks', commonly a sign of an upper-caste man. These are special white markings of sandalwood paste made between the eyebrows and in the middle of the chest,[77] just where the semen was meant to be placed.

In the Vajapeya ceremony conducted by the Vedics to boost a king's virility and prowess, a drink, which was alleged to be of great effectiveness, would be consumed.[78] The gods, as the epitome of masculine power, were viewed as the most potent source of semen and the Vedic man often appealed to them to send them some.[79] They also prayed for help with their impotence, or to boost their sexual prowess.

One of the most sought-after fonts of semen was the hallucinogenic drink soma, which has also been personified as a god figure that could grant virility.[80] The god Soma was frequently likened to a 'tawny race horse, which bellowed like a bull' when he mated, the horse and the bull being popular images of potent virility in the Vedic texts.[81] Equally colourful are the Vedic hymns that describe the extraction of the soma juice from an indigenous plant, and its subsequent fermentation to make an intoxicating brew used in religious ceremonies. The pressing stones were referred to as 'bulls' who bellowed as they consumed soma and were aroused by its intoxicating effect. The stones would then call out to Indra, the king of the gods, to inform him that they had 'milked' the soma and discovered the 'honey'. Indra, upon drinking the soma, would acquire the stamina of a great, magnificent bull. It was assumed that even the pressing stones, because of their steady access to soma, lived long, never aged and never tired.[82] The priests engaged in the task of soma extraction and, excited about the end of their year-long vow of abstinence, would ecstatically sing of how, upon receiving a thousand soma-pressings, they too would be able to impregnate at least a hundred women to ensure their own immortality.[83]

As the gods were nature incarnate, there were various other ways in which it was believed they could deliver their divine semen on earth for men to receive. For instance, the god of the rain clouds, Parjanya, who bellowed like a bull 'bursting with seed', poured his semen upon earth like rain, impregnating cows, mares, women and vegetation.[84] The Vedic man regarded all these creatures to be holders of that divine semen that he was exclusively entitled to, so he got soma from the plant's semen, a son from the woman's semen and milk from the cow's.

Women, who the Vedas consistently refer to as cows, just as the men are bulls, were also regarded as a source of semen, as were the Vedic goddesses. Breast milk was often equated to soma, and believed to have its extraordinary powers.[85] Thus goddesses were frequently asked to offer the Vedic men their 'inexhaustible breasts' to 'suck' and receive all the nourishment possible, as well as the gifts that went with power, wealth and longevity.[86] The fire god was believed to possess tremendous virility because he was born of two women and had suckled them both.[87]

However, there were other ways a woman served as a semen channel for men. One of the most theatrical Vedic rituals in which the head queen procured the potent semen of the sun god for her husband was the Vedic horse sacrifice, the *ashvamedha*.[88] The horse for the Vedics was a symbol of victory as it was one of the reasons for the Vedic triumph over the indigenous peoples. The horse, therefore, was believed to be of divine origin and born of some of the most powerful male gods—the sun or fire god, and Indra. Invested with this might and swiftness, the horse was looked upon with admiration by ambitious men and lovelorn women.

During the ashvamedha a horse would be given the freedom to roam around the kingdom, and all the areas it traversed without being challenged by anyone were officially consolidated as the king's territory. This was how the monarchs periodically reinforced their sovereign powers over their subjects. Whoever stopped the horse to lay claim to a part of the kingdom had to battle the king's army. Finally, when the horse returned to the palace, it would be ceremonially strangled without the shedding of any blood, and the queens would circle it six times. Then the head queen would simulate sex with the dead horse, drawing its penis inside herself, entreating the horse to emit its semen into her. Presumably, it was thought that when the queen bore the king a son, the child would bear the invincible characteristics of the sacred horse.

Later, the horse would be chopped into pieces and cooked. The priests, on behalf of the king, would offer chunks of the flesh to various gods by name, along with a wish list for sons, power and wealth. The horse, it was believed, would fly to its celestial home, and carry with it the essence of everything that had touched it—the bridle, reins, pots, ladles, the places it had trotted on, the king, the queen and priests—and convey to the gods the wishes of the monarch. Various ingredients, besides soma, used as oblations in the fire sacrifice were also believed to be sources of semen. These included butter, honey and milk—it was said that butter, like soma, was the 'navel of immortality'.[89]

As semen was the source of power and longevity, people, particularly sages, were renowned for taking long vows of celibacy, which they believed stockpiled their semen reserve and bolstered their chances of achieving immortality. The sage Agastya had taken one such vow of celibacy and had asked his wife Lopamudra to assist him by vowing the same, for when they did finally unite, he explained, they would be able to 'win the race' to immortality. Lopamudra, however, was unable to contain her desires, and once, upon noticing Agastya's erection, assumed his willingness and seduced him. She was then judged by the scriptures as a senseless, unreasonable woman who had thwarted her husband's ambitions by draining him of precious semen.[90]

Of course, conversely, a man could voluntarily place his semen in a woman's womb, and the production of a son, his exact replica as the Vedic man saw it, was another means of attaining immortality. Though this meant a loss of semen, the Vedic man perceived this as a sacred offering at the altar of sex, a sacrifice that promised a bigger return than the loss. In a hymn composed towards the late Vedic period, a graphic description of this sacred ceremony likened the woman's genitals to a sacrificial altar, where the pubic hair was the smoke, the vulva was the flame and the phallus the fuel. The hymn's message was that if a man conducted the ceremony accurately, he would be able to extract semen from a woman and have a replica of himself immortalized in a son. However, if he failed at the ceremony, the woman would simply consume his semen, and he would gain nothing.[91]

The problem was that semen was also assumed to be a transferable resource. So it was said that a clever woman could retain the semen of one man in her womb and offer it to another man to produce his son and it would be the loss of the first lover. This was one of the primary reasons the Vedas considered women to be untrustworthy, as ruthless sinners who were malevolent in their deception of their husbands, and unrestrained in their lustfulness.[92]

WOMEN IN THE VEDIC SEX EQUATION

Women, it was presumed, were simply too greedy for semen. It was believed that if a man was not vigilant, the women with their 'hearts of jackals' would devour him as 'hideous wolves' would.[93] Apparently, all women wanted to rob the semen from their husbands and hoard it for themselves without offering the 'prize' of a son. The heavenly nymph Urvashi, who was likened to a wolf, was held by the scriptures as an example of this unscrupulousness in women. During the four years that Urvashi lived with her partner Pururavas, she would drink a little of his semen daily, and finally, when she had hoarded enough and was pregnant with a son, she abandoned Pururavas.[94] Even the female obsession with gold jewellery was seen as indicative of a greed for semen—women wanted to be bathed in the colour of gold, as it was regarded as yet another representation of semen. A piece of gold representing the 'semen virile' was also often offered as an oblation to the mighty gods in the sacrificial fire.[95] In fact, the word for gold, *hiranya*, is the same as the word for 'semen virile'.[96] This is why priests would pray that when the rain god sent semen down to earth to fertilize it, he should withhold it from women.[97] This intense misogyny in all probability was rooted in an unshakable fear that the Vedic man had of female sexuality. The female process of reproduction and women's exclusive ability at childbearing was a source of immense bewilderment for the Vedic man.

Menstrual blood was regarded as one of the most evil manifestations of a woman's power. It was believed that during the moon god's wedding his bride managed to capture him in her red and purple bridal gown and left a permanent imprint on him, which trapped him in her powers. It was, therefore, taboo for a man to have intercourse with his wife during her menses. The menstrual blood was a wild and evil animal, an incarnate of the wife's powers, one that could burn, bite, scratch, poison and even kill a man. The blood from the rupturing of the hymen was similarly considered dangerous and, after the wedding night, the blood-stained bridal dress would be handed over to the priest, who ripped it up and fed it to the ceremonial flames to rid the bride of her evil powers.[98]

The king of the gods, Indra, was exalted as he had evaded vaginal birth by emerging from the side of the abdomen after killing his mother because the vagina itself was viewed with suspicion as a dangerous place to pass through.[99] This antagonism towards women was also most likely a defensive response of the Vedic patriarchy that craved absolute power, yet found itself vulnerable in its total dependence on women for the continuity and preservation of the male lineage. Women, they believed, had the power to make any man immortal, if they wished to, by giving birth to a son who was his replica. But then, women were also supposed to possess the ability to withhold that boon if they so desired, by producing no children or just girls as many wilful and evil women managed to do. In fact, it was believed that if two women got their stores of semen together, they could conceive a child between them, and leave men out of the loop completely—indeed, the fire god was conceived by two mothers.[100]

Furthermore, the men also believed that it was through women, specifically the breast milk mothers offered their sons, that men received the foundation for their virility. Even the sun god, revered as one of the most powerful Vedic gods, needed his women—dawn and the waters—to be reborn each day, so he could sustain his immortality. For it was from these women that the sun god received his store of uncontestable semen.[101] It is remarkable how this concept has survived more than 2500 years into the twenty-first century. For example, in modern Indian films, heroes often challenge their rivals to duals with the taunt, 'If you have drunk your mother's milk then come on, fight!'

The Vedic man felt powerless and vulnerable in the face of what he perceived as a woman's reproductive might. He spoke of it as a 'mystery' and a 'secret hidden in the depths'. He begged to know in vain about its 'limits', 'the rules' and 'the goal' and wondered when it would grant him immortality, that is, in the form of a son, and all the gifts that accompany it, such as virility, fame and wealth.[102]

Women thus appeared as a challenge to the Vedic men, a threat to their patriarchal supremacy and esteem. It was a threat which they felt they continually had to contend with, and they did so with social rules, religious ideologies and stereotypes that they reinforced through their scriptures. Legends of the evil that women were capable of were immortalized in the stories of Lopamudra and Urvashi, the women who had swindled their husbands of semen. The Vedics further downplayed the power of feminine reproduction by using the concept of *nyuna* or deficiency to explain it. It was believed that the power of the sacrificial fire lay in the fact that it needed six items, but only five were offered—it was due to this deficiency that procreation could occur. Similarly, those with the ability to produce and create—such as women in making babies, and slaves in producing labour—were believed to be in some ways deficient and, therefore, created from the lowest and most impure part of the body, the feet.[103]

These social prejudices towards women, reinforced by the scriptures, were made into universal laws. Two of these laws were those of the divine order (*rit*) and the divine truth (*satya*). These two concepts, regarded as absolutes, legitimized the subdued and lowly position of women in Vedic society. It was proclaimed that women who asserted themselves and made their independent decisions according to their own wishes required men to control them. It was pronounced that these were the sort of women who would deceive their husbands with their wilfulness and disrupt the divine order of the cosmos. They actually subverted existence as it was meant to be, which led to the creation of hell.[104]

Conversely, male dominance, particularly that of the upper castes, was declared to be the prescribed 'divine order of the cosmos' and the uncontestable 'divine truth', and, therefore, upheld through sacred laws and social practices. For example, one of the social norms that reinforced patriarchy and was quite acceptable, at least at the beginning of the Vedic age, was incest. All through the Vedic hymns, there are frequent references to incestuous relationships. The fire god, the 'bull', mated with the 'mares' in the 'same stable' as his own, his mother's and sisters'.[105] Suryah, the daughter of the sun, was 'won' and shared by her twin brothers in a chariot race competition as they were irresistibly drawn to her beauty.[106] Pusan, the sun god's charioteer, was eulogized by the priests in a hymn as 'the lover of his sister', and his 'mother's suitor'.[107]

The later abolishment of men mating with their sisters or mother might have been a move to preserve the effectiveness of patriarchy, where the father needed to be the uncontested head of the family, asserting his right on his women as personal property. If a son started competing with his own father for the women in the same family, it would be disruptive to the patriarchal power structure. In a telling Vedic hymn of the twins Yama and Yami, Yami attempts to seduce her brother in their father's absence. She argues that the creator who put them in one womb intended them to be lovers, a reference to a time when such relationships must have been permissible in Vedic society. However, Yama refuses her for he believes that he would be violating his father's first right over her. He accuses Yami of the sort of betrayal that was expected only from a woman outside the family, but not from one's own family member.[108] This is also a reference to the Vedic perception of women in general of being licentious and disloyal. Therefore, even though the father's liaison with his daughter continued to be permissible, that of brother and sister later came to be looked upon as sin. It was also believed that such sinful unions between siblings led to stillbirths or diseased babies. Thus the Vedics might have begun to observe a pattern of congenital birth conditions linked to sibling relations,[109] which could have factored in their new incest taboos. But the fact that father–daughter unions were still allowed probably means that the Vedics had not fully realized that congenital diseases can surface through any form of inbreeding.

The father's sexual privilege over the daughter was regarded as an ordained aspect of the sacred order till quite late in the Vedic age. So even though Aditi, the daughter of the god Daksha,[110] as well as the mother of his children, was repelled by her father making love to her, she was compelled to accept it as a sacred law.[111] According to the inheritance laws of the late Vedic period, the only time a daughter could inherit her father's property was when she had the status of an 'appointed daughter', that is, one who bore the father's sons. The male child from that union assumed all the rights and responsibilities of a son, including the performance of the cremation ceremony for his grandfather upon his death.[112]

For many young girls, the father may have also been part of their early sexual initiation. This would seem so from Apala's story in the Rig Veda. Apala, a pre-pubescent girl, prayed to Indra for pubic hair, for she felt that her father was sexually disinterested in her because of her undeveloped body. She also prayed for hair on her father's head, possibly as proof of restoration of his virility.[113]

Apala presented a picture of docility that was considered ideal for the Vedic woman. Women in Vedic society were not only classified as property[114] but also appraised as such. The general social expectation of women was that they were to be docile, beautiful—with long fingers, long, flowing hair and large, rounded bottoms—and cheerful at all times. They also had to possess the ability to create for their husbands a perpetually stress-free environment. Additionally, the ideal women also brought wealth into the homes they entered as brides, in the form of sons, cattle, property and dowry.[115] Kakshivat in the Rig Veda is said to have become wealthy when he received ten chariots and 1060 cows, in addition to maids, as dowry.[116] Moreover, by the laws that were established well into the Vedic period, even if a husband was impoverished, adulterous and depraved, with not a single desirable quality, the wife was required to be faithful to him and venerate him 'as a god'.[117]

As sons were acquired assets for patriarchies, it was essential that the wife's reproductive capacity was exploited for maximum benefits, which meant that the earlier she started reproducing the more sons could be begotten from her. To ensure that a man enjoyed the full advantage of all the fertile periods of a woman, one of the Vedic rules for matrimony was that a girl was to be married off soon after her first period, and it was established that wasted fertile periods would accrue as a sin upon the father who did not follow this rule. Quite possibly, the custom of father–daughter incest might have evolved from this stipulation, for invariably the father might have felt compelled to avoid the burden of sin if he did not have the requisite funds for a dowry to enable him to marry off the daughter.

Another interesting feature in the Vedic moral values was that even though sibling incest and adultery by wives were sinful acts sexual intercourse itself did not figure in the inventory of sins. It appears that women openly prided themselves on their sexual prowess just as men did. Indrani, the wife of Indra, jealous of the intimacy her husband shared with another man, referred to as the 'virile monkey', bragged of how she was unrivalled in her love-making skills. She claimed that she could open her thighs wider, lift them higher—and thrust harder than anyone else.[118] It would seem that women in Vedic society had quite a bit of leeway compared to the extremely constrictive lifestyles that would be imposed on women in later ages. So, for instance, they too shared the men's enthusiasm for imbibing alcohol, were relatively free to move around, even travel out of town, and socialize with whom they willed.[119] In fact, there were certain inheritance and marriage laws that even made provisions for situations where a woman might be already pregnant at the time of her marriage though not necessarily by the man she eventually married.

However, even though there was a certain sexual permissiveness when it came to women, this freedom was not particularly appreciated by Vedic men, who rather viewed women as their sexual resources and rued how erratic and unmanageable women's lust made them. It was said that women had an inherent tendency towards adultery, and were always on the lookout for men to seduce, preferring men who were good-looking and also skilful at singing and dancing. It was said that it was their ravenous sexual appetites, their craving for power and their love of jewellery that caused women to pursue men other than their husbands.[120]

Nevertheless, married women, if suspected of adultery, were made to undergo confessionals at formal ceremonies where they would have to recite hymns and either plead guilty by revealing the names of their lovers or hold up as many blades of grass as transgressions.[121] Adulterous women were despised by the Vedic society as sinful and destined to be reborn as jackals,[122] but the attitude towards male adultery was far more permissive.

Essentially, the issue with men's adultery was not as much about morality as it was about their frustrated inability to wholly control female sexuality and reproduction. Men were warned against getting involved with adulterous women or allowing the attention to flatter their egos. For, they were told, all women were born temptresses, and they used cunning, malice and deceit to get their own way with men.[123] Men were also amiably cautioned about the foolishness of 'sowing' their 'seeds' in other's men's 'fields', which was how the wives were referred to, because then the 'fruits', that is, the progeny, could be claimed by the 'owner' of the 'field', and it would be a waste of seed for the adulterous man.[124]

The practice of polygamy was another means of entrenching male sexual dominance and privilege and keeping women subservient to it. Women confined to large harems endured enormous sexual frustration, as they were forced to compete for accessibility to one man: the husband. Priests who saw this as a good business opportunity would offer to conduct mystical ceremonies for frustrated wives and would chant hymns conveniently provided by the Vedas to 'quell' the rival wives.[125]

HARNESSING THE SLAVE

Like the women, the indigenous tribes and lowest castes too were tossed to the very bottom of the barrel in Vedic society. Not surprisingly, notwithstanding their show of masculine bravado in battles, Vedic men actually feared what they imagined to be the indigenous people's magical powers over matters of sexuality, life and death.

They believed that the indigenous races possessed evil powers and secretly indulged in 'black magic' to deprive the Vedics of their sexual prowess and their immortality. Through their pagan rituals and chants, the indigenous people were thought to have the ability to unleash various debilitating diseases on Vedic society, and to even kill the Vedics en masse. This betrays the fact that despite the Vedic bragging about victorious wars against their enemies, this might not have always been the case. Later Vedic texts spoke of the defeat of the gods by the demons because unlike the 'demons', the 'gods' had no forts as defence.[126] Forts were a common feature of Indus towns, and the Vedics always assumed their gods to be their collaborators in the wars they waged against their enemies.

The Vedic apprehension of the indigenous people is evident in the terms they used while referring to them: 'evil-doers', 'Brahmin-haters', 'wife-seducers', 'owl-sorcerers' and 'cuckoo-sorcerers' being some of the choice ones. An undisguised wrath and hatred permeate their sacred texts as Vedic men begged their gods for protection and for help to 'burn' and 'crush' their enemies, to blow them up like clay pots, to powder them in a millstone and to bury them into the earth, making sure that nothing good happened to those they despised so much.[127]

The Vedics concluded that it was the indigenous people's knowledge of forest herbs and potions, as well as their chants and rituals, that endowed them with a virility that could surpass their own. Not surprisingly, by the time the last of the Vedas was composed, the Vedics had incorporated many of these mystical herbs, potions and spells into their own ceremonies. It appears that the use of soma as a virility-enhancer may have been one of the herbal secrets that the Vedics stole from the natives, though they liked to think of it as a 'rescue'.[128]

Similarly, the Vedics also began to acknowledge some of the indigenous gods such as Rudra and Kama. These were gods who would have been seen as being particularly effective in dealing with virility issues. Rudra was the Vedic name for the indigenous god who appears to have had the Divine Father status in the Indus civilization. Most probably, because his iconic representation always showed him surrounded by wild animals, the Vedics also knew him as the lord of the forest animals. Evidently, he is the same god who in the later ages would be known by the name of Shiva. The god Rudra, according to Vedic portrayal, was the patron god of their enemies, whom they regarded as thieves and swindlers. He was also black-skinned, most probably in likeness to the people among whom he originated. The Vedics characterized him in the same way they described indigenous peoples: as 'fierce', 'dangerous' and 'destructive'.[129]

It appears that Rudra to the Vedics spelt trouble. One of their reasons for acknowledging him was most likely to keep his destructive tendencies at bay. Vedic hymns beseeched him tenderly to vent his death-inflicting famines, his fires and his poisonous creatures elsewhere.[130] However, just as the indigenous people were valuable to the Vedics as slaves and were incorporated into the community for the labour that could be extracted from them, Rudra too was adopted into the Vedic pantheon for the favours that he could offer them. He was believed to be a 'divine physician' who was very knowledgeable about useful forest herbs,[131] and he was testosterone-incarnate.

Although the Vedics had previously been hostile to the indigenous custom of phallus worshipping, within a few centuries they had also started adulating the phallus, one of the representations of Rudra—the Atharva Veda is effusive in its praise for the 'golden phallus standing in the waters'.[132] Rudra served as an important god in Vedic fertility rituals, and though initially the lingam appears to have been worshipped, not as an idol but rather as an abstract concept by the Vedics, a sculpted penis, symbolic of the lingam, was used for the ceremonial breaking of the hymen in brides.

Kama, the indigenous deity of erotic love and lust, was another borrowed divinity in the evolved Vedic pantheon. Believed to be a divine creature of exquisite beauty, Kama was quite helpful for casting love spells and the Vedics would specifically invoke him during magic rituals.[133] In fact, many of these love-spell ceremonies too were of indigenous extract and were once despised by the Vedics who found them incomprehensible, secretive and extremely threatening. However, in the latter half of the Vedic period, these rituals were enthusiastically incorporated into the Vedic religious texts, especially in the last of the Vedas, the Atharva Veda.

These hymns provided recipes for the making of potions and casting of spells for various love problems, as well as remedies for obtaining a mate, getting pregnant, disposing of a rival in love, protecting an unborn fetus, captivating a disinterested lover and increasing sexual stamina.[134]

Towards the latter part of this period, the Vedics also began to acknowledge certain indigenous goddesses. However, where they took their own goddesses for granted, viewing them as gentle, placid cows that would obligingly suckle them, they did not dare to assume the same of the native ones. They deeply feared the power of the indigenous goddesses and appealed to their egos, supplicating them as they did their own virile gods. In all possibility, the Vedic perception of the indigenous goddesses was reflective of the indigenous people's own attitudes towards and concepts of their divinities. As the Indus seals reveal, the goddess was worshipped as the Divine Mother, the ultimate in power, with even the Divine Father bowing to her and offering blood sacrifices.

The Vedics addressed the native goddesses as Nirriti, which means 'destruction', usually implying death and decay, and as Asuri, which means 'demoness'. These titles referred to the power over life that the Vedics believed the native goddesses possessed, as well as their ability to cast death spells on men and rob them of their chance of immortality.[135] Sometimes, the representation of the goddess was as a formidable, dark-skinned woman who roamed around stark naked and haunted people's lives.[136] 'Demoness', as the goddess was known, was also typical of how the Vedics referred to the women of certain indigenous forest tribes, describing them too as dark-skinned and evil. Some of the goddesses, it was believed, could take the form of tree spirits called yakshis and consume unsuspecting men, while others could manifest themselves as snakes or nagins, to feed on unborn children.[137]

Clearly, the cow-rearing Vedic, with the abilities of neither a hunter-gatherer nor a farmer, must have struggled hard with the insecurities of a nomadic existence. Being unfamiliar with the forests, they were most likely ignorant of how to protect themselves from the dangers of wild animals, including venomous snakes. All the more, the Vedics must have felt threatened by the ease, knowledge and familiarity that the indigenous people had with their environment. They not only incorporated the elements of nature into their lifestyle and philosophy, but also practised animism where they spiritually participated in the plant and animal world.

Many of these 'demon' goddesses were believed to live in the forest—regions unfamiliar to the Vedics—where they awaited the opportunity to prey on defenceless Vedic men travelling alone. Earlier, the Vedics would invoke the help of their masculine gods to send Nirriti as far away as possible. Clearly, what the Vedics feared was the supposed potency of the sexuality of these demon goddesses, which surpassed their own virility. For example, 'Long-tongue' was said to be a demoness who apparently would consume the entire stock of soma for the gods. Indra had to commission the handsome Sumitra and equip him with ten additional penises so he could court 'Long-tongue' and physically subdue her through intercourse with her ten vaginas—and it was while she was thus restrained that Indra killed her.[138] But obviously, even these planned assaults by the Vedic gods were not working in terms of the Vedics' perception of Nirriti's ability to cause damage, and so eventually they took to appealing to her directly.[139] Vermilion paste would be painted on to the roots of the trees—a practice which, remarkably, continues to live on today—as symbolic blood offerings to appease the goddess. It was said that it was only when they placated her that she would refrain from feeding on children and fetuses.

Vedic men travelling through forested areas would offer their humble salutations with much trepidation to the goddess, trying to humour her and convince her that, with all the fruits and berries available to her in the forest, human flesh would hardly suit her palate.[140] She was even known to confront men's ancestors as well as their virile gods, and when they tried to obliterate her, she would spring back to life, for she was indestructible. Perhaps the most mystical and fearful aspect of her power was her ability to contain both the cycles of life and death.[141] As Viraj, the goddess could penetrate all things large and small—the sacrificial fire, village and plants—and with the energy of her body could create or destroy at will. She controlled everything that lived and died on earth from the skies to the forests and she could grant prosperity to men just as easily as she could destroy at will. The Vedics were thus convinced that the demon goddess was a master 'illusionist'.[142] Fortunately for them, the demon goddess's powers were not all destructive. As Avi, the sheep-headed goddess, a deity worshipped by tribals in Orissa even today, she could clothe the trees with plenty of foliage for their sheep and cattle.[143]

The Vedics believed that if properly flattered the goddess could even bestow upon them her formidable energies. In one hymn, a goddess deified as a plant of a '1000 eyes' (perhaps the banyan tree) is invoked to place her powers in a bracelet so that the wearer of the bracelet would have the gift to see the invisible.[144] Many of the love spells in the later Vedic literature utilized the *sri yantra* or the instrument of the goddess. These were circular geometric diagrams that were regarded as the secret weapons of the goddess as they possessed her insurmountable powers over life and death.[145] The circle contained triangles representing male and female divine sexual energies and their union,[146] with the female triangles always shown as more numerous than the male ones. These were along the lines of the geometric motifs that were first observed in various Indus seals, again pointing to indigenous inputs. During the ceremony, a triangular iron pot called the *kunda* would be hung over the fire altar. The Vedic priests would wear red clothes and red flower garlands, and call upon 'the demoness of the red garment' and the 'reverent Rudra' her consort, to grace the altar and assist them.[147] Here, red most likely was symbolic of blood, or the goddess's power over fertility, whereas the red flower garlands symbolized the animal heads she had to be offered in a blood sacrifice to keep her satisfied. Given the Vedic alarm about menstrual blood in general, and their paranoid shunning of menstruating women, this undoubtedly was also an adaptation of indigenous customs.

The concept of the sexual union of the powerful goddess and her male consort as being procreative is clearly illustrated in the Indus seal and it was a notion obviously borrowed by Vedic rituals. Vedic scriptures that represented Rudra as an ascetic and a bard also speak of the bard copulating with a 'prostitute' to make the earth fruitful.[148]

Initially, while the Vedics still wandered around as nomads, their erratic lifestyle was geared towards only two major activities: one was communing with the gods, which was the job of the priest of the tribe, and the other one was warfare, which meant that the rest of the Vedics were warriors. However, as they got into a settled mode of living, they needed people with the requisite skills for other jobs—clearing land, planting, sowing, making pottery and trading—and so they inducted the indigenous population into the Vedic social structure. Some of these recruits might have been war captives. Although essential to the settlement and maintenance of Vedic society, these people were not only assigned to the lower castes, but were considered inferior human beings who did lowly work.

However, despite the religious borrowings, the Vedic man was extremely wary of the possibilities of racial mixing with the indigenous tribes, especially once they started cohabiting in settlements. One of the ways that the Vedics tried to ensure the purity and the superiority of their race was by making clear demarcations between the races, laying down rules of sexual permissibility. It was absolutely crucial that the race they deemed as inferior not be allowed to leak its racial make-up into their gene pool, or for that matter be allowed to usurp theirs. They would be furious when some of the indigenous people claimed to be as 'pure' as the Vedics when, in their view, they clearly were of a 'demonic' race.[149]

The caste system and the sexual boundaries established as social and moral laws for the intermingling of the castes were the mechanisms by which the Vedic society assessed racial purity and assigned human worth. The caste system was a categorical spiritualization of the Vedics' racist world view, for it was not only upheld as a social order, but as a natural law ordained by the divine force itself. The word for caste in Sanskrit is 'varna', which means colour, and castes were based on race and skin colour. The fairer the skin the greater was the assumed Vedic purity, and, therefore, the higher the caste designation. The highest caste, which was that of the Brahmins, was said to be of the purest strain. Various other gradients of skin tones that came about through the inevitable mixing of the lighter-skinned Vedics and the dark-skinned indigenous people were also accounted for in the caste system. There was possibly further differential placement of the indigenous tribes, who themselves were of diverse races, with some being Afroid, while others had Mongoloid features or lighter colouring.[150] Ultimately, the people with wheatish brown complexions, referred to as 'red',[151] were ranked second in the hierarchy, and assigned to the kingly and warrior caste. Those with yellow or sallow complexions were ranked third and designated to the merchant caste. And finally, the people with the darkest skin people—the 'blacks', mostly of aboriginal origins—were relegated to the lowest caste, that of the slaves who provided all the labour.[152]

True to its fundamental nature as a patriarchal society, the moral laws of inter-caste marriage upheld the Vedic men as sexually privileged over all the other races. In general, the upper-caste men, the priests and the warriors, had sexual access to women of all castes. This, according to the scriptures, was a privilege that Brahma, the Supreme Creator, had granted the upper-caste men, along with the gifts of time, speech and the constellations. The Brahmins, of course, always sat at the head of the table. Said to have been extracted from the Supreme Creator's own mouth, the Brahmin, the purest specimen of the superior Vedic race, alone was privileged to communicate with the gods, sometimes demonstrating his intimacy by sharing lively sexual banter with the divine.[153] Also being the substitute for the gods, the Brahmins were entitled to fertilize childless women. In fact, in the late Vedic age, the lawgivers actually instructed women who had impotent husbands to get themselves impregnated by priests.[154] This is a practice that continued well into the early twentieth century, when wandering Brahmins would stop at villages, and for food, lodging and maybe a fee, would 'marry' young, unwed girls. They would then spend a night with each of them, sometimes impregnating them in the process, and would finally leave the village with no obligation to return. For the parents of the girl, however, the 'marriage' would be seen as fortunate, as their daughter would now have the status of a Brahmin's wife.

However, the same sexual privileges did not extend to the upper-caste Vedic women. A woman, after all, was a sexual article for the use of men. She was the womb in which a man replicated himself. Therefore, it was absolutely taboo for a Vedic woman of any caste to sexually engage with a man of a lower caste, for that would subvert the caste hierarchy of male privilege. However, the Brahmin women's liaisons with the lowest caste, comprising the black-skinned aborigines, were considered as the worst humiliation of the Brahmin clans and were violently outlawed.

There were many other aspects of indigenous knowledge, besides magic potions, occult rituals, uncanny gods and the apparent secrets of virility, that most likely made the Vedic man feel inadequate and insecure about the native peoples. These could have centred on several cultivated skills like farming, metallurgy, pottery and the written script, skills that obviously stabilized the existence of the indigenous peoples and made them far less vulnerable to the vagaries of nature than the Vedics were in their nomadic lifestyle. It gave the Indus people and other scattered indigenous tribes the sort of control over their existence that perhaps the Vedics themselves desired. Therefore, despite their attempt at social and racial segregation, the Vedics ultimately incorporated sizeable aspects of the indigenous cultures into their lifestyle.

That Vedics most likely learnt farming through contact with the settled indigenous groups is supported by Dravidian extracts in Vedic literature. Dravidian is the term commonly used to refer to the family of languages and cultures of indigenous origins that occur mostly in the south in modern India. The borrowed lexicon included a great many words in agriculture, such as the words for plough, hoe, threshing floor, winnowing basket, mortar and pestle.[155] Similarly, the concept of a settled lifestyle and the setting up of villages too is obviously pre-Vedic: the word for village in Vedic literature is the indigenous word 'palli'.[156]

Likewise, there are also indigenous terms for metallurgy and trade in the Vedic language.

There are, in fact, some indicators that the Brahmi script itself, which was used by the Vedics, was most likely obtained from the native peoples. Some historians have argued, for instance, that though Sanskrit, the language of the Vedics, is supposed to have Indo-European roots, the sounds that are fundamental to its phonetics are closer to the Dravidian languages than to Indo-European languages.[157] Others have pointed out how orderly and scientific the Brahmi script is, in that the simple vowels, diphthongs and consonants form harmonized groups according to the bodily organ from which the sound is produced.[158] The script thus is widely at variance with the style of composition of the Vedic hymns. These hymns are sequentially haphazard and inconsistent in their styles. They frequently and unexpectedly jump from the literal to the metaphorical without context or introduction, and often lack clarity of sense to the extent of appearing befuddled. Clearly, the Brahmi script could have come only from a people who knew how to be extremely organized, methodical, rational and scientific in their approach, much like the Indus people were.

The scripts proved to be useful to the Vedics not just for recording their hymns, which until then they had to rely on their memory and oral traditions to preserve, but also for tabulating their prejudices into precise and detailed moral and social laws, and asserting their power over the lower castes and women much more effectively. It is possible that the Vedics might have desired the script so much that periodically they even disregarded their own racist sexual ethics. As the master class they had the privilege of moral transgression, if it suited their need to maintain an upper hand in society.

So it might seem puzzling that certain hymns indicate a certain desire for black babies. However, the Vedic reasoning was that a dark-skinned boy could be trained in the Vedas much better than the lighter-skinned ones, for where a fair-skinned son could memorize one of the Vedas, a dark-skinned one could learn three.[159] Initially, because of their familiarity with writing, some of the indigenous people may have furtively recorded the sacred verses they overheard, verses that they otherwise were prohibited by law from learning. While the Vedic students, in pursuing oral traditions, struggled to learn the hymns by reiteration, the indigenous people were quicker as they probably had a script for reference. To the Vedic men, this ability of the dark-skinned people may have seemed remarkable, and perhaps they thought this sharpness of memory was an inborn condition associated with dark skin. Since in Vedic society the priest was the keeper of the sacred hymns, it may have seemed desirable for them to have black babies. To procure white babies, the scriptures recommended that a husband and wife should eat rice boiled in milk with clarified butter, while for black babies the rice was to be boiled in water and then eaten with clarified butter.[160] Consequently, many Vedic priests had progeny with aboriginal women and some clans even recruited dark aboriginals directly into their priesthood order. In fact, the most legendary of all Vedic priests, Badarayana Ved Vyasa, the man who is credited with having compiled the written version of the Vedas, was also known as the black priest.[161]

JUNG AND THE PENILE ARCHETYPE

Towards the end of the Vedic period, the Vedic religion had incorporated many indigenous beliefs and practices, and even symbolisms. Conversely, large sections of the indigenous populations inducted into the Vedic society for purposes of labour or service, or through marriage, began to adhere to the Vedic caste system and its inbuilt logic of moral hierarchy. This merging of two antagonistic communities of near-conflicting ideologies, even if a disagreeable process—and most certainly unintended—did in fact set the base for what more than a millennium later would emerge as the Hindu religion.

One of the Vedic adoptions was, of course, the sacred penis, still an abstraction and not yet iconized. In later ages, it would resume the iconic phallic form associated with the Divine Father of the Indus cult, or Rudra of the Vedic religion, and come to be known as the Shiva lingam or Shiva's penis.

For the Vedics, however, the lingam was an ascertainment of a male-centric and utilitarian social philosophy. It represented the male ego, its desire for power and a very primitive instinct of territorial dominance defined by the sex drive. If the lingam as a religious symbol, in accordance with Jung's theory, is to be understood as an archetype representing the Vedic comprehension of the self as a collective human identity, at this stage, identity was exclusively corporeal. Everything in the Vedic perception of existence, even death, was defined and dealt with in terms of a tangible existence. The Vedic man prepared for a bodily afterlife, reserving a place in heaven next to his forefathers as if it were a seat at the theatre, or ensuring that his genitals were not cremated with his dead body, so that he could continue to enjoy sex in heaven.

In Vedic collective thinking, that unconscious element which separates the animal instinct from human perception, and forces the human element to examine itself reflectively as its own face in the mirror, had not yet emerged. The Vedic man had not even begun to realize a universal human identity, leave alone examine it in the context of a larger existence. His image of society was singularly masculine and pitifully infantile in its self-absorption. His understanding of life distanced him from everything that was not part of his own immediate existence as a male of a specific race; his concept of a human self was horrendously fractured along lines of gender, race, colour, occupation and even the natural world. Everything that the Vedic man saw as alien to himself was a threat to be crushed and subjugated. And yet, even in this agonizing perception of the ominous 'other'—the 'enemy' that Vedic man attempted to manipulate, dominate and violently crush—it was those very elements of the 'other' that Vedic man was compelled to reconcile with, failing to find them in his own culture. Perhaps it was here that the seed of the incipient stages of the human process of self-understanding lay.

PART II

THE BUDDHIST PERIOD

SEX AS A PRISON

All through the Vedic period, the Brahmins reigned over society unimpeded, their lives tranquil and undisturbed. As the 'purest strain' of the Vedic race, the loftiest caste and as priests and teachers of the scriptures, they had so far been able to manipulate the functioning of society by fashioning arbitrary rules and moral laws to suit their own ends. However, in the period that ensued around 500 BC, they could no longer hold on to their autocratic power. With an upheaval in certain social dynamics, the kingly class in this period displaced the Brahmins through a caste conflict and assumed supreme authority. Other castes, such as those of the merchants, also became increasingly influential.

With this transition came a revamping of various social rules. There were fresh perspectives on what constituted sin and shame, and revised laws of morality that would govern people's lives. The corporal, hedonistic culture of the Vedic age was philosophically challenged, and sex was no longer viewed as a privilege of the mighty, nor as a sacred duty or a facilitator of immortality. Instead, it acquired a severe notoriety as an evil propagator of agony.

These radically altered concepts of living were the dictum of the new messiah of this age: Gautama Buddha, the founder of

Buddhism. However, the moral makeover that society received in this age was preceded by some very significant developments in the Vedic community itself. These changes that created the climate for an alternative system of divine thought essentially redefined sacredness.

THE PRECIPITANTS OF A NEW SACREDNESS

Two new lifestyle adaptations were instrumental in this upheaval in the Vedic society. These were the formation of settlements and the cultivation of land.

The small village settlements of the nomadic Vedic communities progressively grew into larger towns and, eventually, between 600 BC and 300 BC, numerous kingdoms were established. Iron tools made it easier to clear large tracts of forested land all along the river Ganga in the extremely fertile, alluvial plains of northern India and enabled the Vedics, who till now were concentrated mostly in the north-west frontier, to invade the heartlands of the Indian subcontinent.

With settlements came a new concept of landownership. Though resource acquisition had always been the Vedic way of life and a potent measure of masculine power, in their nomadic days resources were generally limited and had to be movable—as cattle, women, sons, soma and, of course, semen. But in this period, other necessities like land, water, grain, labour and manufactured goods also counted as assets.

The economic opportunities of settled life enabled the materialistic ambitions of the Vedics in ways that their vagabond past never had. There were new measures for computing wealth and power. Where earlier war was the only means for wealth acquisition, this period afforded other sources, such as markets, trade, taxes and even marriage. This opened up infinite avenues for Vedic men to boost their sense of amplified prosperity and enabled them to reassert the supremacy of their patriarchal order.

The introduction of cash into the economy was particularly useful for the purpose of resource consolidation. Money reduced all goods and transactions—land, cattle, trade, women and slaves—to a single common denomination and copper and silver coins permitted an easy valuation of all things and also eased negotiations.

The kingdom economies that were thus established were quite diverse and, besides agriculture and cattle-rearing, included mining industries and factories for various manufactured goods. The king, the sole owner of the land and all its bounty, had a lot more to flaunt as evidence of his power than ever before. The Vedics also realized the need for a systematic and elaborate scheme of economic administration that would take into account all their invested capital and profits from produce, taxes, trade, labour and people. Methods were devised for the accounting of each resource in detail, and strategies were implemented for maximizing the output of each. The various administrative posts created were also a far cry from the simplistic job designations of the Vedic times. Extensive retinues of staff were hired just to handle the kingdom's finances: they included bookkeepers, tax collectors, governors, magistrates, comptrollers and auditors. Methodical as this may sound, the Vedic townships never acquired the sophistication of the Indus cities. Perhaps this was because Vedic public regulation was implemented not so much with an eye to civic sense or the living convenience of residents, as was the Indus planning, as to the calculative hoarding of resources for the kingly classes.

The resulting accrual of wealth by the kingly classes was one of the main factors that eventually subverted the Brahmin's position. Indeed, the displacement of the priest as the seat of power by the kingly class was a momentous change in the fundamental workings of Vedic society. The Brahmin, who in his role as priest, had so far claimed supreme authority because of his supposed affinity to the gods and his abilities to evoke divine assistance for the Vedic men's ambitions of virility, wealth and immortality, no longer held the same sway over the public. With the greater stability and material opportunities offered by a settled lifestyle,

Vedic men did not feel as vulnerable or dependent on the vagaries of nature and the fluctuating moods of the gods. Now the priest's ceremonies did not seem as indispensable to assuring victories in battles or conquests of kingdoms and acquisition of wealth.

The priest's secret knowledge, his moral dictates and his lone guardianship of sacred scriptures and ceremonies no longer bore the same credence in society. Material resources now were the primary determinant of power. Many of the kingly class, such as small-time warriors and noblemen, had managed to amass small and large territories through their skills in battle; they declared themselves kings and began to take pleasure in the idea of their own supremacy in society. They reasoned that if they could attain what they desired without a priest's guidance, surely they must be more powerful than the priest. Thus the Brahmin was now left to contend with a secondary station: that of adviser to the monarch.

This development caused much social tension between the priest and the king. Divested of his god-like status, the Brahmin found himself not just communally sidelined but also mired in economic uncertainty. Earlier on, the priest was regularly inundated with gifts from anxious worshippers because of his assumed power to communicate with the gods and thus make or break people's lives. The desperation of the priests becomes apparent from the scriptural injunctions that specified that a king was bound by moral duty to hire Brahmins, for if the Brahmins went hungry, the king's property as well as his life was doomed.[1] The king was advised, through the scriptures, to humbly seek the counsel of the head priests first thing in the morning to avoid the loss of his position. He was also instructed to present his gifts to the priest instead of the gods for better yields. The Brahmins further threatened that since they had the ability to dethrone a king, they could instigate the public against the monarch through methods suggested in the scriptures.[2]

Though the priest was not always content with playing second fiddle, he did recognize the need to reinforce the king's authority through his own position as the king's primary adviser, for now his gains were entwined with those of the king. After all, the priestly class too was the beneficiary of a wealthy royal treasury as the priest now received much of his income through the king's patronage. By using the scriptures, the priests declared that it was the moral duty of the king to tax the people, and contented themselves with fashioning divine laws that would now enable the king to better exploit the people and the resources of his kingdom.

With the scriptural sanction, and the assistance of the Brahmins, the king was now firmly established as the supreme authority and considered as fashioned by the creator god, Brahma himself, to watch over the universe. He was proclaimed to be a demi-god, superior to all mortals, with sacred powers that allowed him unrestrained control over the lives of all his subjects. A comprehensive law and justice system was established, enabling the king to inflict draconian punishments, which the gods had evidently created for him as tools with which to administer the public. It was declared that it was in the best interest of all lesser mortals to be mindful of their humble stations in life and serve the king, for he had the authorization of the gods to destroy a man and his whole family for any wrong that was committed.[3]

However, while the king had divine sanction for his unrestrained quest for power and wealth, it was not so for the priests. In the Vedic age, the priest was entitled to material pleasures and offerings from devotees. But now the people demanded a certain justification. This necessitated a good deal of scriptural reinterpretation of godly intentions. To tone down their reputation of greed, the priest proclaimed that it was not so much he that desired offerings from devotees, as it was the gods who obliged him to accept all material gifts on their behalf. And that he was being very generous in accepting all kinds of material gifts from land and jewellery to meat and perfumes, for if he did not do so, the gods would not entertain the devotees' requests.[4]

This new capitalism also began to influence the manner in which the Vedics negotiated with their gods, who apparently had turned into hard bargainers. Now there was a whole inventory of gifts that could be offered to the gods, along with a cost–benefit accounting of what a devotee could expect in exchange for each contribution. For instance, in offering land, it was said that the worshipper would obtain divine assistance in acquiring more land. For a bed, he would acquire a wife; for gold a long life; and for silver, beauty.[5] Sound economics, it would appear, was most appealing to the gods.

In keeping with this new spiritual outlook on life, 'economics' now evolved as a formal science. Its fundamentals were studied and theories formulated. Based on these, treatises called the *arthashastra*s were published, which contained the basic principles of a formal economic system for the administration of kingdoms, and offered laws and guidelines for business, taxation, revenue collection, accounting and budgeting. They also covered domestic and foreign trade, and the judicial system, including specified fines and punishments for the violation of individual laws, the fines being another method of revenue gathering.

'Artha' literally translates to wealth; but since it involves much more, it essentially means total material well-being. Therefore, the arthashastras accounted for everything that supported corporeal pleasure and all that related to the plush comforts of a worldly existence, including the regulations of governance, politics, laws, religion, slave labour and even family. From 650 BC onwards, numerous arthashastras were compiled—the most famous one was written by Kautilya, adviser to the ruler Chandragupta Maurya, and is placed around 321 BC.

The arthashastras established the king as the sole owner of land as well as the primary rent-collector. Ownership of land was a novel concept, which earlier had no bearing for the nomadic ancestors of the Vedics. But besides land, all public facilities in the kingdom, such as dams, bridges, water reservoirs and roads, were said to belong to the king, and people had to pay taxes for them regardless of whether these were built with money from the treasury or public funds.[6] Indeed, the single-minded goal of the administrative functioning of the kingdom was the acquisition of taxes. To further validate this goal, it was given a religious and moral edge, and buttressed by the support of the priests. It was stated as a matter of official policy in the arthashastras that the king was morally obliged and duty-bound to be a 'leech' on his people and feed off them consistently like a 'bee' or a parasite getting its sustenance.[7]

To enable the king's success in his parasitic obligations, the arthashastras provided numerous strategies that could be used to economically exploit the vulnerabilities of the subjects.[8] For instance, it was suggested that a temple to a deity could be erected overnight and made to appear like it were a miraculous happening and festivals could then be organized to collect money from the public. Or through craftiness, government agents could convince the people of the attack of evil or malevolent spirits, who could only be driven away through offerings to a deity or by buying certain remedies for protection. The king was also advised to use deceit, murder, blackmail and false accusations to extract income from the citizens, since the fees levied for crimes committed went directly into the royal treasury.[9]

Most taxes were in kind, though some, especially the penalties for crimes, were in cash. The king was entitled to 50 per cent of all land revenues and gold, and 17 per cent of everything else—crops, butter, meat, trees, fruit, vegetables, animal hide, bamboo, clay pots, stone items, and even luxuries like perfume and herbs.[10]

The slave or the labour class, though considered the least valued section of the Vedic society, was the foundation of its ravenous economy. As cultivators, craftsmen, artisans and entertainers, the slave classes bore the major brunt of the state's taxes. They lived in isolated quarters of the city, and had to contribute to the king's coffers with both cash and free labour such as construction work. They were also used as spies and as foot soldiers in wars as they were said to be good warriors.[11]

All avenues were explored to boost the monarch's monetary power. The judicial system, for instance, levied fees of specified denominations on various crimes and misdeeds, with the amounts calculated in minute details, often in conjunction with other forms of punishment like the injury or excision of a limb, tongue, genitals, eyes or nose, or banishment.[12] The money was to be paid by the accused to the king, even if the injury, loss or betrayal happened to a third party, as in the case of theft, murder or adultery.[13]

The profession of prostitution was another lucrative business for a kingdom. Brothels were entirely a state monopoly, owned, funded and run by the state, which amassed vast revenues from them. The state provided the jewellery, furnishing, musical instruments and other necessities to set up the establishment and invested in the complete training of the prostitutes in their requisite skills, which included singing, dancing, poetry recitation, painting, mind-reading, shampooing and love-making. Any woman of conspicuous beauty, from any family, not necessarily from a family of courtesans, and whether or not she desired to, had to be prepared to serve as a courtesan in a state brothel, a position to which she was appointed by the state. The state regarded these women as state property and financial investments, and hence any customer cheating or abusing the prostitutes would be punished.[14]

This new cash-powered system, though serving the interests of the king and to a certain extent the priests, extended to a lesser degree to the merchant classes. Though the merchant class may not have owned much land, except for the small, whimsical grants the king might have occasionally made to some of them, there were other measures, such as trade, money, material assets, slaves, women and sons, which the common man could still use to take stock of his social status.

Unlike the Vedic times though, now all the human commodities a man could own—slaves, women, sons and daughters—were assigned tangible economic values. Slaves could be bought, sold and traded, complete with a warranty period to test their worth, as well as that of their children. In fact, the abortion of a female slave's fetus was a punishable offence for it was an obvious loss of potential capital for the owner.[15]

A son was of the greatest value as a family's property could be inherited only through the male lineage. In case there were no sons, the property reverted to the king.[16] Daughters could inherit only the mother's jewellery and utensils, and that too only upon the father's death.[17] Therefore, the Vedic man's entire lifetime capital was literally invested in his sons. To ensure the production of a male heir, if a man himself could not produce one with his wife, the couple would try their luck with a male donor from among their relatives.

Conversely, where a son was an asset, the daughter was an economic liability and of no value to a man. In times of crises, such as in war, kings were advised to give up their daughters as hostages, as they were already a burden on him, and would only be an economic liability to the other party.[18] As women served various needs like childbirth and domesticity, they were listed as one of the properties of men, along with slaves, deposits and pledges. Being a commodity, a woman was not to initiate contracts or negotiations on her own, nor travel, or visit neighbours or even leave the house without her husband's permission.[19] This was quite a change from the Vedic period when women moved around freely, sometimes travelling to other towns, and formed their own associations, even though it was not to the liking of the Vedic patriarchy. However, now, even as a commodity, the woman's worth was only in her ability to produce sons. If she continually bore daughters, her husband could take on a second wife, and dispose of her with some monetary compensation or the return of her dowry.[20] Moreover, where earlier men obsessed incessantly with their wives' fidelity, now there were laws requiring women to be virgins at their wedding. Those who violated these laws had to pay a fine of fifty-four *pana*s, which was hiked to 200 panas if the woman tried to feign her virginity by smearing blood on the sheets of her bridal bed.[21] The Vedic man took account of all the fertile periods of his wife as potential investments in a son and was loathe to allow a fertile period to go to waste. However, to ensure the insemination gave a worthy return, that is, produced a son, men were advised to invest in their women, keeping them happy with supplies of clothes, food and ornaments.[22] If a widow decided to remarry, she would have to forgo her dowry and jewellery if she chose to marry a man outside her husband's family and clan.[23] Besides, marriages were also a form of a peace treaty made through a bargain between hostile neighbouring kingdoms, where women would be exchanged like gifts.[24] The laws further stipulated that even women captives could be used as a source of funds. If a woman was rescued by a man—from marauders, from drowning, in a forest or a famine—the man could claim payment for his services either in kind—as sex—or hold her captive till someone paid a ransom for her.[25]

BREAKDOWN OF THE VEDIC PATRIARCHY

As ownership of adjoining lands were consolidated by individuals warring for control over larger areas, town-sized princely states expanded into extensive kingdoms. Each monarch further attempted to consolidate his boundaries and establish his authority by enforcing specific laws and levying taxes on the inhabitants of his kingdom. This, however, led to a critical rupture in the cohesiveness of the Vedic patriarchy. There was now a major shift in how people established their social identity. Where the early nomadic Vedic tribes distinguished their identity from that of their indigenous enemies through pride in their ancestral race and religion, people now identified with each other more on the basis of the land they occupied or 'country' they belonged to.[26] With kingdoms constantly at war, and resources and livelihoods at stake, the king could no longer have a caste-based bonding with neighbouring kings, all of whom were enemies, and he had to depend on the allegiance of his subjects, across the caste boundaries, to protect his interests. This further eroded the notions of race and caste cohesiveness in the Vedic system. With settled life came agriculture and other industries that needed labour. It necessitated the induction of indigenous peoples into the Vedic social fold, even though if only as members of the lowest or slave caste. The restrictions and taboos on the slave caste were tighter than ever before, yet the upper-caste citizens of a kingdom depended on them as the labour force for the cohesive and integral functioning of the kingdom's economy and sustenance.

With the increased concentration and visibility of wealth, and greater amounts of resources at stake, there was mounting dissension not only between rival kings but also among members of royal clans and families. Parricide became a customary form of power usurpation and filicide was not uncommon. The *Arthashastra*, in fact, advised ambitious princes on various ploys to assassinate their fathers or incite a people's rebellion should their life or aspirations be threatened.[27]

Queens too were known to execute their husbands' murders by poisoning their food or scheming with their sons or other male relatives they may have desired, by arming these men with weapons and concealing them in their chambers before the king's visit, so they could assassinate him.[28] It is, therefore, not surprising that there were elaborate, almost paranoid, measures taken for the king's security. An extensive network of secret agents from various strata and professions—priests, prostitutes and peasants—were hired to work incognito and report sensitive information they gathered from the public to the palace officials.[29] The palace grounds were encircled with ramparts and moats and contained numerous concealed passageways and exits for the king's use during emergencies. The queens lived in separate chambers, indeed buildings, from the king, and before the king's visit, the queen's chambers would be thoroughly inspected, and all items such as food, perfumes and oils that might be used by the king during love-making would be tested beforehand for poison. The queen's contacts were closely monitored and she was permitted dealings with her family only during childbirth. However, during her pregnancy, rituals were performed to ensure that the desired son she gave birth to would not be a danger to the king. Once the prince grew up, spies would be employed to clandestinely test his loyalty to his father.[30]

The idea of a son's indebtedness to his father and forefathers and his obligatory worship of them had been the sine qua non of the dominant Vedic patriarchy. However, now this notion was being subversively challenged. Indeed, one famous dynasty of the kingdom of Magadha, around 460 BC, had five generations of parricide kings.[31]

However, despite the Vedic man's adulation of the powers of male virility, he could not rely on male bonding or trust his own kind when it came to personal safety. The king's personal bodyguards were all female archers, and only eunuchs were allowed to serve as his attendants, catering to his personal needs, such as bathing and dressing him and serving him his meals. Also, the king's innermost security circle comprised social rejects: dwarfs, hunchbacks and cave-dwellers.[32]

The Brahmin too became another of the Vedic patriarchy's vulnerabilities. The Brahmins, who had initially scripted and orchestrated the Vedic, patriarchy's power show and formulated its incontestable sacred laws, were now confronted with mounting social scepticism about their actual effectiveness in negotiating with the gods.

With a settled lifestyle and a steady availability of food and shelter, there was an inevitable increase in population and most likely in the average lifespan too. The result was the overcrowding of towns and unsanitary living conditions, which increased the risk of diseases. There were periodic outbreaks of epidemics that undoubtedly claimed many lives and caused widespread panic and civil unrest.[33] The kings, whose primary concern was the monetary loss from epidemics, attempted to combat them with purifications and occult ceremonies, such as burning effigies and milking cows in cremation grounds.[34] The priests' ceremonies, however, failed to guarantee men a virile, healthy old age, or freedom from disease and the constant fear of death. From these conditions of social insecurity and turmoil, a general mistrust of the Brahmins developed in the public mind.

The conflict must have seemed like a major threat to the power of the Brahmin clans for there was a desperate bid to prevent people from being overtly critical of the priests. Those who questioned the abilities of the Brahmins were warned that they could turn into donkeys, dogs or bugs.[35]

THE SEARCH FOR CHANGE

Notwithstanding the Brahminical attempts to protect their turf, a new post-Vedic phase emerged, which started questioning some of the fundamental concepts of the Vedas. Dissatisfied with the old religious injunctions and grand elaborations on existence, it sought more functional solutions to the bewildering problems of an evolving society. Many of these soul-searching inquiries were embodied in a collection of scriptures from this period called the Upanishads.

This state of philosophical chaos, however, resulted in a breakthrough in the collective consciousness of the emerging societies. The Vedics until now had been unable to reasonably conceptualize their own existence without obfuscating the boundaries between their reality, their desires, and the soma-induced hallucinated images of immortality. They had lived in a fantasized, and essentially escapist, world of gods and fairies, and men with superhuman abilities, too stupefied by their drunkenness, their egos and perhaps their insecurities to be able to take an objective view of themselves in the context of their environment.

And for the first time in Vedic history, the common man questioned his own existence in an objective manner. He desired to grasp the actual reality of his life in the context of a universe that was infinitely larger than him, and inconceivably complex. He needed to know: why was a person born and why did he or she live? And what happened to one after death?

There followed an intense period of collective social queries, discussions and arguments from which a whole new concept emerged in Vedic thinking: that of 'a soul'. It was theorized that an individual life had a material component, which was the body, and an unseen, inner component, which was the soul. Suffering, as from old age, disease, fear, hunger and death, was a condition of the body. But the soul was free of all these afflictions.

It was also speculated that the soul existed at two levels:[36] one was the universal soul, termed *Brahman*, which was immortal, undefined and constantly changing. It was the essence of all existence, and thereby also God. The other soul was the personal soul of individuals, and was termed *Atman*. This soul related to mortality, and was inert and confined. The individual soul was regarded as an integral aspect of the universal soul, the Brahman. The body, on the other hand, was the means by which all individual souls were trapped in the material world in an endless cycle of death and rebirth—*samsara*—in which the soul of an individual was transferred after death into another body, depending on what that individual's prior actions or karma were. The goal of each soul was salvation, that is, *moksha*, a state in which the body could be finally freed from the incessant cycles of rebirth. But this was possible only when individuals, through the accumulation of good karma, kept ascending to higher life forms, and eventually found their freedom from rebirth. When finally released from the material world, a soul that had attained *nirvana* found its peace in merging with the Brahman. Where earlier, according to the Vedas, a man had three spiritually ordained goals in life—duty (dharma), wealth (artha) and lust (kama)—now a fourth goal was added, that of salvation (moksha).[37]

However, salvation too came with conditions. First of all, it was available only to upper-caste Vedic men, specifically the Brahmins.[38] Secondly, it required the renunciation of the material world, a stipulation which in its harshness was a punishing contrast to the corporeal excesses of the early Vedic lifestyle. The salvation seeker had to renounce his home and family, and detach himself from all things of personal comfort. He was to own absolutely nothing, sometimes not even clothes, making do with leaves and bark, and he was to dwell in the forest, sleep on the ground or in caves, beg for his food and seek his salvation through penance.[39]

Still dictated to by the racial prejudices of the Vedic system, the lowest class was denied the pathway to salvation. The slave's only hope was to attain a higher birth in the upper caste in the next lifetime so that he too could access the road to salvation. However, to attain a higher birth, he had to be mindful of his lowly position in society, and fulfil his spiritually ordained duties, which included humbly serving the upper class.[40]

In a society agonizing over issues of disease, old age and death, salvation seemed like the divine solution. However, the methods recommending harsh asceticism seemed unfeasible to most and a large section of society, the slave class, was barred from even seeking this everlasting freedom. A feasible road to salvation, it seemed, was the most desperate and urgent call of that social period.

Gautama Siddhartha, later known as Buddha, was a young, ambitious man and, much like many others of his time, decided to meet this challenge. He relinquished his privileged lifestyle and family and went on to discover a pathway to salvation that would become very popular in his time and set the foundation of a new and different religion—Buddhism. Not only was Buddhism a radical departure from the very fundamentals of Vedic philosophy, but it was also a social revolution of the most radical kind.

BUDDHA, THE REVOLUTIONARY

The Buddha was born to the leader of an indigenous tribe called the Sakyas. The tribe existed on the fringes of Vedic society. Associated with dogs—considered to be wretched animals—and regarded as 'mere menials', the Sakyas were treated as outcastes by the Vedics.[41] Moreover, the Sakyas, unlike the autocratic Vedic societies, appear to have been a republic, a common form of governance among numerous indigenous groups.[42] These tribes functioned as unorthodox, neo-democracies, electing a leader through a system of votes to oversee the members, maintain order and dispense justice. Many of these tribal groups were opposed to Vedic rituals, including the caste system, and refused to acknowledge the superiority of the Brahmins. This is perhaps why the Vedics disliked and ostracized these groups.[43]

According to folklore, when Gautama was born, the sages had prophesied that he was destined to become a great spiritual path-breaker. His father, however, was not particularly enthralled with the prediction and attempted to steer him away from this unglamorous future, by inundating the young Gautama's life with sensual pleasures—luxuries, dancing girls and marriage to a young girl named Yasodhara. Gautama then had a son, who was named Rahula or 'The Fetter', perhaps in the hope that a child would keep Gautama bound to his family and princely lifestyle. However, that was not to be so and one night, the still youthful Gautama furtively walked out from the palace, abandoning all his family cares to seek his desire for salvation in complete freedom.

Initially, he tried the popular spartan method of his days, which was living in isolation in the forest, without much food and water. This method did not work and he found he was weak and unable to continue. He concluded that it was foolish to torment the body, and instead decided to attempt a new approach to salvation. His proposition was that the body had to be sufficiently cared for and provided with adequate food and rest, without indulging it, to ensure it was healthy enough to pursue the goal of salvation. He called this the middle path as opposed to the extreme and austere measures of asceticism.

NEW, REBELLIOUS IDEAS

Ordinary people, who dared not subject themselves to the harsh rigours of an inhumanly cold, hungry and lonely penance in the mountains, no longer had to go through the alternative but tedious journey of many births to ultimately free their souls. Buddha's method of salvation asserted that one could achieve salvation within a single lifetime and, furthermore, it was no longer necessary to torture oneself to do it. In fact, he was quite critical of self-mortification.[44]

However, besides rejecting asceticism, there were numerous other aspects of the contemporary Vedic society that Buddha's new-found movement denounced. First of all, salvation was now accessible to all people, irrespective of their station in life, and was no longer the privilege of just the upper castes as the Vedics had proclaimed. Secondly, the Buddha completely dispensed with the newfangled notion of the soul. He accepted neither the concept of Brahman, that is, a universal soul, or as the Vedics saw it, God, nor the existence of the personal soul. The Buddha argued that if there was a soul, freedom from rebirth would never be possible.[45] According to him, a human being comprised only a body, thoughts, sensations, comprehension and disposition.[46]

When a person achieved salvation or nirvana there occurred a total 'blotting out' or 'extinguishing' of all that represented the self, like a candle that is snuffed out.[47] However, nirvana occurred only upon death, and only in *tatgath*s. A tatgath was an enlightened soul, a living Buddha, one who through his meditations had attained wisdom and recognized that the body and all material existence were nothing more than an illusion. The living Buddha, therefore, effectively was a nirvana waiting to happen.

BUDDHISM: THE SLAVES' CIVIL DISOBEDIENCE

The sweeping popularity that Buddhism found among the public continued long after the Buddha's death. It attracted not just merchants, slaves and tribals, who must have been pleased to finally be accepted as equals into the folds of a mainstream and influential religion, but it was also patronized by kings and nobles. Kings were wary of the power struggle they faced with the priests within the Vedic religion, and perhaps found Buddhism less tedious. Buddhism was also embraced by many foreigners, among them Greeks, Scythians, Parthians, Kushans and Huns, some of whom had arrived earlier on the Indian subcontinent as rulers and colonizers, while others came as travellers or traders. The Greek king Menander, who from 155 BC to 30 BC had colonized a part of India, also converted to Buddhism. Usually foreigners, with origins outside the Vedic caste system, were regarded as outcastes.[48]

Later, Emperor Ashoka (r. 268 BC to 231 BC) of the famed Maurya dynasty, who was one of the first rulers to consolidate much of the Indian subcontinent under his governance, converted to Buddhism and propagated its spread not only within the subcontinent but to other countries as well, including Sri Lanka, Syria, Egypt, Macedonia and Greece.[49] Missionaries from the early Buddhist monastic orders in India also carried the Buddha's gospels to Burma (Myammar), Siam (Thailand), Tibet, China, Java and Japan,[50] countries where Buddhism became increasingly influential and was even adopted as the principal faith of the people.

Indeed, faced with the popularity of Buddhism, the Vedic priests found both their religious authority and their political clout dwindling. Their response quite expectedly was defensive and irate. They decried other religions along with Buddhism, calling them 'evil' and false, and declared that those heretics who did not respect the Vedas should be imprisoned and served the death sentence.[51] They announced that all those who rejected the Vedas were outlaws, the difference between the outcaste and outlaw being a technical one. The outcastes generally comprised tribals and foreigners, who were not included in the four-tiered caste structure of the Vedic society, and of individuals born of the union of upper-caste women and lower-caste men. They lived on the outskirts of society near the cremation grounds, or in isolation in the mountains or forests.[52] The outlaws, on the other hand, were individuals born into the upper-caste strata, who even married into their own caste, but did not honour the Vedas and rejected the traditional initiation ceremony. These individuals were stripped of their caste, not allowed any social or religious interaction with the upper castes and also forced to live on the fringes of towns and villages.[53] The Vedic priests even denounced Taxila, one of the largest monasteries and most important centres of Buddhist study, as impure.[54]

But the popularity of Buddhism soared. For Buddhism was a social insurgency as well, one of the earliest organized movements in India demanding equality and justice. However, preaching to a society that operated on the Vedic premise of people being unequal from birth, Buddha had to take a strong and confrontational stand on issues of race, caste and class. In publicly rejecting the caste system's method of human valuation, Buddha had challenged the spiritual laws of racism and declared the social boundaries that separated one human from another to be false and illusory.

Nonetheless, it appears that Buddha did not reject the caste system outright; he just gave it a new perspective. For instance, he disputed the superior status of Brahmins and emphasized that ultimately it was a person's deeds that defined him and resolved his fate after death. He further affirmed that all individuals, irrespective of caste, were capable of developing a supreme and enlightened mind if that was indeed their goal,[55] and rebuffed the idea that it was birth that determined one's caste. According to the Buddha, the titles of Brahmin and outcaste could be bestowed on anyone, irrespective of birth and lineage, and it was the hypocritical, deceitful person who ought to be called an outcaste, whereas anyone who was compassionate and wise could be called a Brahmin.[56] Where the Vedic priests used Sanskrit as a language of secrecy so that the common people who did not speak it would not be able to access their scriptures, the Buddha chose to preach in the vernacular of Magadhi so as to reach out to as many people as possible.[57]

The Buddha also called for a more even-handed society in terms of wealth distribution. He reasoned that it was due to a king's inequitable hoarding of wealth that poverty was created, and argued that poverty was at the root of crime. In fact, his demands were some of the earliest formulations of workers' rights that aimed at levelling social inequities and included fair labour conditions, work proportionate to an individual's strength, regular food provision, consistent wages, sick leave and official rest days.[58]

The Buddha's ideals about social and political governing are undoubtedly rooted in the environment he was raised in. The Buddha's tribe of origin, the Sakyas, was one of many self-styled republican states that existed on the periphery of the dominant Vedic society. In fact, the concept of republican style self-governance originated in India much before it did in Greece and Rome.[59] Referred to as *gana*s or *sangha*s, these republics tended to be small and independent and governed either by a ruling body of elected officials, or a clan or family nominated by the people to represent them. The social order followed a set of laws or rules that has been described in ancient texts as the *vairajya*, literally the 'kingless constitution'. The state assembly met in halls, specially built for this purpose. Large and open on all sides, these halls could accommodate up to 500 people at a time. Besides domestic issues, the assemblies discussed foreign affairs, and held audiences with ambassadors of other states. Conflicts and debates were resolved through a majority vote system, but laws could be passed only by the consent of the whole house. Freedom of expression and speech were rights that all citizens of the republic, even outside the state assembly, were entitled to, and any citizen could approach the law courts for a perceived injustice. There also seemed to be an attempt to prevent abuse of individual rights through subjective rulings of judges by the establishment of a guide book.[60] Thus the Buddha's call for a more just and democratic society was not so much a radical philosophy as a peripheral one, pushing its way into mainstream society.

With the changing social pressures of Buddhism, the communal boundaries that the Vedics had created to prevent racial mixing had also weakened, and the number of inter-caste relationships increased. Even Sanskrit, the secret language of the Vedics, the code of their scriptures and their tool of self-empowerment and superiority, was usurped by indigenous groups. This is evident in the hybridization of languages, where the indigenous cultures fused Sanskrit words and sounds with those of their own language.[61]

These transgressions must have infuriated the priest clans, who felt their artificially propped up racial and spiritual superiority weakening. Their response was to tighten the grip of the caste system and intensify the laws against intermarriage. The need for purity and protection of caste and lineage was emphasized and Brahmin sanctity was urgently buttressed. People were warned that the punishment for threatening or striking a priest, even with a blade of grass, was that they would be born to evil for twenty-one birth cycles and would have other people eat them in the nether world.[62]

The vulnerable position of the low slave caste in particular was reinforced through intimidation, that is, with more stringent rules and punishments, all in the name of sacred laws. A Shudra pretending to be a Brahmin would have his eyes gouged out; for approaching a Brahmin's kitchen, he would have his tongue rooted out; for claiming to know the Vedas better than a Brahmin, he would have boiling oil poured into his mouth and ears; for daring to sit on the seat of an upper caste, he would have his buttocks chopped off; and for verbally abusing a Brahmin, he would get the death sentence.[63]

In the light of increasing inter-caste liaisons, punishments were intensified for sexual violations of the caste hierarchy. Breaking the laws of caste boundaries was declared anti-religion or 'irreligion'. Mixing bloodlines, it was said, would destroy the foundation of both the social and the divine order.[64] The most abhorred alliance was that of a Brahmin woman with a slave man. They would be discarded as outcastes, and their children too would be assigned to the lowest and most despised subdivision of outcastes, 'the fierce untouchables'. The outcastes were driven out of towns and villages and compelled to live on the outskirts of society. They were to wander constantly since they had no right to a piece of land, even to build a home on. They were also to work in cremation grounds to burn dead bodies, and they had to act as the kingdom's executioners, two jobs which generally nobody wanted to do. Since they could not buy things from the town markets they had to make do with clothes they could scavenge from the unclaimed corpses they burned. They also had to beg for their food and eat in broken dishes. There were even stipulations on which animals they could domesticate; the cow being sacred was, of course, taboo to them, their choices being limited to the dog and the donkey, animals that were generally despised as being filthy.[65]

Upper-caste men who had sex with outcaste women themselves became outcastes. However, in the case of liaisons between upper-caste women and outcaste men, the transgressions were regarded as most heinous and the men would be killed while the women would be disfigured.[66] The priest's wife was absolutely out of bounds and men of other intermediary castes too were forewarned that if they had a secret rendezvous with the guru's wife they would contract a hideous skin disease. If discovered, the offender would be made to slice off his own penis and testicles, cup them in his two hands and walk towards the south-west, the supposed direction of ruin, till he fell dead.[67]

Even within the harem, the respect and marital privileges a wife commanded was determined by order of caste. A man was never to have his body tended to during bathing or dressing by the lower-caste wives,[68] though sexual intercourse was perfectly acceptable. Also, the inheritance of the sons was determined by the caste of their respective mothers.[69]

To preserve the concept of caste hierarchy and privilege, subcastes or *jati*s were formulated. It emerged as an extremely complex system with more than 3000 subdivisions. Each jati was determined merely by the castes of the involved parents, since each of them too could be of a caste mélange, and assigned a specific profession. These professions generally were regarded as menial and contemptible, and the higher the caste of the woman compared to her mate's, the lower the jati that would be assigned to their offspring and the more menial would be the associated occupation.

THE EXPULSION OF SEX

Despite its offering of a more accessible pathway to salvation, the demands of Buddhism were no less severe. Where the Vedic philosophy of life had been based on the indulgence of a corporeal existence and where satiation of desires was earmarked as one of life's four central goals, the Buddha kicked this sensory approach to life into the dust.

His logic was straightforward. If the body was the cause of a person's sufferings—as in death, old age and illness—one had to be rid of the body and its physical manifestations. According to the Buddha, the force that propelled the body repeatedly through rebirths was desire. He preached that the reality of our outer world as perceived by our bodily senses—by smell, touch, sight and sounds, for instance—was actually an illusion. Human beings however considered this as a permanent reality and sought it through sexual, material and emotional desires. Therefore, it was desire that kept people imprisoned in the material world and in their bodies.[70] This, according to the Buddha, necessitated the renunciation of sex, sensuality and a sensory existence if one sought to free the body from rebirths and be eternally liberated from suffering. As Buddhism became institutionalized, it adopted the social language of morality to ostracize behaviour that it deemed as obstructive to its ordained goals. Any activity that titillated the senses was 'vulgar' and 'degrading', and sex was now viewed as malicious a deed as killing and lying.[71] In Buddhist philosophy, even nakedness, which was said to awaken desire, became a shameful concept, something it was not before. Remarkably, sex had never actually been morally reprehensible for the Vedics, but then neither had murder, unless committed by a low-caste member against the upper caste; morality for the Vedics had more to do with the subversion of the caste hierarchy and patriarchal privileges.

Buddhism's stand on violence was perhaps one of its more indirect acknowledgements of the Vedic notion that humans had to be reborn to pay the dues of a vile karma from a previous life. Bloodshed and deceitfulness essentially went against the Buddhist belief of compassion for all living beings. Moreover, in Buddhism, sex, violence, war and materialism were perceived as activities that were indirectly motivated by some sort of earthly desires. Buddha's rejection of violence was, however, not absolute. As a prime advocate of social equality and justice, he was not opposed to the use of violent means as the final resort to achieve these goals. He believed that going to war for a just end and serving the death sentence to murderers were not contradictory to his non-violent teachings for these facets were a part of the struggle for truth and righteousness. Similarly, given the vast number of tribal devotees who were traditionally accustomed to a meat-eating diet, it is no surprise that Buddha actually defended the eating of meat. He declared that it was not meat-eating that made one unclean as the Vedics claimed, but human emotions like envy, malice, bigotry, and self-indulgence that were caused by desire.[72]

The life of the Buddhist initiate, even if not torturous, was certainly austere. It was, of course, mandatory for all monks to be celibate. The first five items on the list of major offences for monks were sex-related. Intentional ejaculation was forbidden. Monks were not allowed any physical contact with women—and even a mere touch was regarded as contact. Flirting, coaxing women into sex and matchmaking were excessively sinful. Fantasies or thoughts of sexual intercourse were also regarded as 'vulgar', and monks were not to allow them. They had to exercise restraint on all their tactile sense organs, which meant they were to eat only one meal a day, not indulge in any entertainment, particularly song, dance and music, nor adorn the body with ornaments, flowers, perfumes or cosmetics. They were not to sleep on large, comfortable beds, and were to constantly be on the move every seven to eight days. And though they could accept donations of food, they were forbidden from accepting gold, silver, women, slaves and animals.[73]

This spiritual disgrace of sex and sensuality had an across-the-board social impact. It coloured the general milieu of living and issues of moral acceptability to such an extent that it caused a major revaluation of concepts within the Vedic circles. With the increasing influence of Buddhism and obvious popular support for it, including that of upper-caste Vedics like kings and nobles, the Vedic priests felt a social pressure to adjust their philosophies to the moral ethos of the times. Where previously fire ceremonies were conducted to pray for immortality, for everlasting youthfulness and vigour, now the body was regarded as a 'vile' place for the person to live in, filled with excrement, 'polluted by passions' and burdened with old age and illness. But still driven by the old competitive attitude, the buzz in the privileged Vedic brotherhood now was that only when an individual abandoned his body could he finally 'win' that most treasured prize of salvation on earth and in heaven.[74] Those who remained attached to the 'darkness' of bodily pleasure and indulged in it were told that they would be reborn as animals.[75] Where Buddhism's idea of nirvana was a state of total non-existence—a void—and a complete snuffing out of the ego and individual identity, in the Vedic perception it was still an ego-driven contest, a prize sought and won by a heroic man.

Semen, once craved and hoarded as ambrosia, a divine resource, by Vedic men and gods alike, was now regarded as a 'dirty' fluid along with eleven other bodily excretions, including faeces, urine and snot.[76] Sex was no longer the mighty sacred fire ceremony where the offering of semen was made at the 'altar' of a woman's genitals, nor was the woman's womb a potent source of immortality, because both sex and giving birth were now 'polluting' activities.[77] Foods that were regarded as aphrodisiacs or psychedelic and growing from dirt, that is, under the ground, were prohibited; these included garlic, scallions, onion and mushrooms. Where breast milk may have been once consumed as an effective boost for a man's virility, it was now forbidden.[78] Vedic priests, who had sung like expectant frogs in anticipation of sex during soma ceremonies, were now expected to live austere lives, sleep on the ground, beg for their food[79] and be lifelong celibates.

Even kings, for whom the lustful indulgence of the senses was a noble privilege, were advised the 'middle path'. Though a king's daily routine accorded a certain amount of time to entertainment, which included music, dance performances and visits to the harem, the king was advised not to get addicted to the activities of the senses and avoid emotions like anger, malice, envy and resentment, much along the lines of Buddhist thinking. In Buddhist philosophy, all human passions, negative or positive, caused an unhealthy attachment to life. These as well as other sense-addictive vices as gambling, sex, drinking and hunting, it was said, were all the result of desire[80] and a lust for pleasure. Instead, the king was urged to substitute business for pleasure.

Where earlier battle conquests were jubilant confirmations of a man's worth in Vedic society and an affirmation of his virility, and patricide and inter-familial battles for the throne were key features of dynastic rule, now the inclination to war necessitated a certain validation—that had never been required before—in the light of the Buddhist-influenced social denunciation of violence. This justification presented itself in the immensely protracted form of the Bhagavad Gita, a prominent section of the highly regarded Hindu epic Mahabharata, which was written around this period. The Bhagavad Gita which assumes the form of a dialogue between the protagonist, Arjuna, and the Lord Krishna, who undertakes the role of Arjuna's charioteer, deals with the inner anguish of Arjuna for having to go to war against his own cousins and relatives in a familial battle for the throne. Arjuna bewails the 'great sin' that he and his brothers would commit by allowing their 'greed for kingship and pleasures' to drive them to war against their own family.[81] Finally, towards the end of the book-length sermon, Lord Krishna, through his divine intervention, was able to convince Arjuna that fighting his relatives was morally justifiable and thereby provided the Vedic society with the requisite spiritual defence for war.

EVOLUTION OF THE COLLECTIVE CONSCIOUSNESS

A vital and constructive change in society that did come about as a result of the Buddhist movement was a growth in the collective social consciousness.

Thus far, the Vedic perception of a human society, being ego-driven and self-obsessed, was woefully limited in its scope. The sense of what was human was thus not only extremely subjective, that is, they used their own clan as the central reference for all that existed, but it was also splintered along the lines of race, caste and colour. Consequently, the Vedics had been unable to look beyond these virtual walls of differences to recognize a distinct human identity.

Therefore, the Buddha's contribution to society was monumental in that it brought an element of wholeness and healing to the social perception of a common human condition. The Buddha introduced the idea of universal humanity into society's understanding of itself. He established that human experience in the context of the larger cosmos is the same, regardless of social divisions, and that ultimately the process of living, of experiences—including desire and emotions—was the same for all. Salvation was the concern of the entire human race and not just a select few. But most importantly, the Buddha established that there was a common path that could be undertaken by all to salvation regardless of the colour of skin, caste or profession.

The Buddha also brought to this collective social identity the acknowledgement of complex emotions and a recognition of a more developed and matured human psyche. This was, in fact, a breakthrough in the evolution of Indian society for it was the earliest attempt to comprehend the nature of the human being in its entirety as an objective process of self-reflection. It was like man looking into a mirror and recognizing the reflection he saw there, outside himself, as himself. This was the beginning of the common perception that, as a species, humans shared an existential identity, as well as common emotions, desires and goals. But the Buddha took this composite idea of a human self to a higher level—where he awakened it to its unconscious, untapped potential for universal love, caring, equality, justice, compassion and moderation, and, over and above all, a reverence for all beings, be they human or animal. These concepts would have been quite inaccessible to the Vedics' infantile vision of existence, which could not extend beyond some extremely narrow, primal instincts, namely, the urge towards resource acquisition and mates, insecurity-based competitiveness and aggression, and an instinctual need to dominate.

Perhaps one of the most constructive and extensive social impacts of Buddhism on this age was realized under the reign of Emperor Ashoka in the third century BC. After a particularly gruesome battle in Kalinga, the emperor was horrified by the extent of the fatalities and human devastation that his conquest had caused. Publicly expressing remorse, he renounced warfare and decided to convert to Buddhism. Ashoka governed on the principle of *dhamma*, a word that has been subject to much etymological scrutiny, but which essentially means living by a sense of inner conscience and relates to the Buddhist doctrine of each man being 'a lamp unto himself'.[82] The emperor's message to his people was for them to treat each other with decency and human compassion. He advised his subjects that as individuals they were to restrain their behaviour towards others through 'self-examination', by asking themselves if they were being brutal or angry or arrogant in their treatment of another.[83] Ashoka had these ethics written into law and inscribed on to monolithic rock pillars—now known as Ashoka's edicts—which were placed in the public arena. Periodically, the inscriptions would be read out aloud to gatherings, perhaps for the benefit of those who could not read, and as a reminder to the people of the ethics that were to guide their lives. The edicts instructed people to be kind to all living things, people and animals, and restrict the practice of animal slaughter to get food. There were laws prohibiting the hunting of wildlife and a majority of people voluntarily took to vegetarianism. The edicts even urged people to be good to Brahmins, who were otherwise quite despised in those times. In the spirit of universal compassion for all beings, Ashoka had built hospitals throughout the country, which had specialized wards for surgery, obstetrics and psychiatry, as well as veterinary centres for the treatment of sick and injured animals.[84]

One of the most crucial Ashokan edicts, number twelve, urged tolerance. It proclaimed that no religion was to be discriminated against or disparaged, for ultimately the spiritual growth of each individual depended on the honour that he could bestow upon another's religion. The truly secular tone of these edicts is further reflected in the fact that not one of the pillars speaks of any religion by name or association. Buddhism, the emperor's own religion, is also not mentioned anywhere.[85] Even though Ashoka propagated Buddhism in other countries outside India, he never discussed his religious beliefs in public and would converse on them only with other Buddhists.[86]

This was a momentous instance in Indian history for it was the first time that the Indian subcontinent was exposed to secular governance, not just as a thought or philosophy but actually as administrative policy: it was a phenomenon that at that time—almost 300 years before the birth of Christ—was unheard of in any other civilization in the world. The Ashokan pillar at Sarnath is exquisitely carved with majestic lions atop the capital. Its workmanship is suggestive of Persian and Greek influences,[87] which is reflective of Ashoka's keen interest in and receptivity to other cultures. In a befitting tribute to these edicts as some of the highest ideological markers in Indian history, India adopted the lions of Sarnath as its national emblem when it became a democracy in 1947.

WHY BUDDHISM FAILED IN INDIA

Though Buddhism had spread like wildfire, and much of the Indian subcontinent had also been under the reign of a Buddhist emperor for a period of time, the religion eventually survived only in small, isolated pockets in India. It failed, at least in India, to meet its promise to become the universal path to salvation for the common man.

Though many have faulted Islam for this ultimate demise, diaries of Chinese travellers' Fa-hsien and Xuanzang in the fifth and the seventh centries AD, who had come in search of Buddhist documents, reveal an erosion of Buddhist sects as well as the deterioration of Buddhist monasteries and institutions in India long before, at least 700 to 800 years before the arrival of Muslim colonists in India.[88]

One reason Buddhism declined in India is perhaps its uncompromising restraints on sex and general living, including its insistence on the renunciation of family life, which imposed on practitioners by early Buddhist sects as preconditions to the attainment of salvation. Thus one could be a Buddhist, and observe all the other prescribed tenets, such as truth, compassion and tolerance, but if one was unable to completely renounce the sensory life, one could not obtain nirvana within that lifetime. Where Buddhism survived outside India, it did so with massive reinterpretation and adaptations to people's regular needs. But perhaps because India was the cradle of Buddhism, the Buddhist orders in India might have felt a more compelling obligation to keep the Buddha's own philosophies about the religion alive.

Nevertheless, there were difficulties in this approach from the very start, which were already quite apparent then. Even during the Buddha's lifetime, droves of ordinary people who might have joined the monasteries in a hopeful attempt to learn about the path to salvation—which then was quite a novelty—had experienced terrible frustration. Novice monks were known to indulge in depraved behaviour that resulted from bottling up their sexual cravings. Some of them attempted to seek relief through intimate liaisons with animals. Others would take midnight walks in the open, outside the monastery, as they raved and ranted about meat, alcohol, perfumes, women and warriors, as a catharsis. Still others made their personal adjustments to render monastic living more bearable. One wealthy merchant built his own private chambers next to the monastery, complete with a kitchen, a larder stocked with his favourite food items and servants to cook his meals to his liking. Unhappy about the laxity of rules, the Buddha apparently had tried to warn eager initiates about the meagreness of the life that they were expected to lead. But as that tended to frighten off recruits, he eventually decided it was better to delay the warning till after they had been inducted into the order.[89]

But for many who could not adhere to the Buddha's sense-deprivation path, or were of the working lower castes, and as the primary earning members could not abandon their families, there still seemed no path to salvation available to them. The advice to them was to focus on their work and business, and follow certain basic teachings, including the avoidance of vices such as excessive spending, drinking and harbouring negative emotions like envy, greed and malice. The commoner was assured that even if he did not obtain salvation, his life of goodness would contribute positive merits towards the next one. And with a higher birth with each subsequent life, ultimately he too would get his salvation—even if not in one lifetime.[90]

But from a universal vantage point, there were also some very basic, technical flaws in the Buddha's suggested concept of salvation, the most significant being its absolute disregard for women. Despite its egalitarian emphasis on the equality of all men, Buddhism from its onset refused to account for a large section of society. The Buddha too had effectively failed to realize that any concept of salvation for humankind would not work unless it took all of humanity into consideration, not least of all women, who were at least half of it.

Initially, the Buddha was stubborn in his refusal to allow women into the order. Even his own aunt and stepmother—who beseeched him on several occasions, voluntarily shaving their heads, donning the characteristic saffron gowns of the ascetics and pursuing him on his journeys barefoot, fatigued and weeping—were turned down repeatedly.[91] He compared women to mildew in a field of rice, and proclaimed that if women were admitted, the order would rot away much before its time.[92]

He reviled women as inferior and lustful. Men, he declared, were weak and women were flirtatious and always preoccupied with seducing men and exploiting their weaknesses. Besides, according to the Buddha, women were much too dim-witted and vain to even access the knowledge required to attain nirvana. And so he preached that men ought to protect themselves from women, and regard them as dangerous entrapments and as enemies.[93]

Of course, the Buddha's social environment was predominantly patriarchal, and being a man himself, Buddha's thinking was fundamentally male-centred. Not only did he advocate salvation expressly for men, but since his method involved the denunciation of sex, it translated to a denunciation of women as well. Thus the encouragement of misogyny probably helped in creating a greater cohesiveness among the male followers of Buddhism, cementing the brotherhood.[94]

After much convincing the Buddha finally made a concession to nuns being included in the order. But the position of nuns was always to be subordinate to that of the monks and a nun was never to rebuke or contradict a monk. In terms of conversation, only a monk could address a nun and never vice versa and, regardless of whether the monk was a novice or however senior she was in the order, a nun was to always rise up for a monk and bow down to show him customary reverence.[95] In fact, when requested to allow monks and nuns to show each courtesy according to seniority, regardless of gender, the Buddha flatly refused, and even added that if a monk bowed to a nun, it would count as an offence.[96]

Not surprisingly, most Buddhist orders evolved along extremely male-centric lines, even though the state of Buddhahood or the attainment of enlightenment was meant to be a genderless one in keeping with the Buddha's instruction that all aspects of corporal identity were essentially illusory and non-absolute. Even the more progressive orders of the later Mahayana movement, which unlike the older sects incorporated women,[97] ascribed a male image to emergent Buddhas.[98] In fact, many contended that even if women could take the Buddhist vows and join the orders, they could never expect to attain perfect enlightenment.[99]

This broad reticence with regard to women is also apparent in Buddhist texts such as the *Jataka Tales*, where women are generally portrayed in an unsympathetic light,[100] and often shown to be sexually promiscuous.[101] Even though men too have a libido, apparently that of women's is far more intense and uncontrollable, which makes them inherently inferior.[102] Women's salvation in Buddhist parables frequently seems to culminate in violent and painful finales, while men are 'rescued' so that they can continue to live lust-free in virtue. In one such parable, the courtesan Vasavadatta fell in love with Upagutta, Buddha's disciple. When rejected by the disciple, Vasavadatta initiated an affair with a tribal chief, but got him murdered, so that she could get involved with a wealthier potential lover. Eventually, she was caught for her crime and punished—her ears, nose, hands and feet were chopped off and she was left to bleed to death. As she suffered the last excruciating hours of her life, Upagutta visited her and bluntly preached to her of the evils of lust, greed and vanity that, he explained, had caused her condition.[103]

In another parable called 'The Giddy Fish', the protagonist, a male fish, was lusting after a female fish and chasing her when he got trapped in a fisherman's net. The female fish, being a cunning female, managed to evade the net. Fortunately for the trapped fish, the Buddha, who understood fish language, and happened to be passing by, rescued him with the final lesson of renouncing the 'evil of lust'.[104]

What could possibly explain the Buddha's antagonism towards women? One rationalization is that he believed that women by virtue of their wombs are the cause of procreation and, therefore, the natural continuation of the cycles of rebirth. Indeed, the womb, even in later Buddhist literature, is often described as a 'foul place' of 'unbearable stench', which makes women unfit for ordination and enlightenment.[105] An eleventh-century Buddhist monk, in his book *The Jewel Ornament of Liberation*, spoke of how during pregnancy a fetus endured excruciating and mounting pain as it was 'boiled and fried in the womb's heat', like it was being cooked in a 'hot vessel' for months.[106] However, the Buddha must have also known that women could not be held singularly responsible for reproduction. Possibly, from the tone of some of his pronouncements, his view of women may have been influenced by Vedic thinking, which regarded women as innately lustful and responsible for deliberately tempting men into sex. Still, it is not clear why women were not permitted an equal standing in the Buddhist orders even when they were eventually taken in. After all, upon being persistently questioned by his faithful disciple Ananda,[107] on the behest of women eager to become initiates, the Buddha had acknowledged that women had the same capacity to attain nirvana as men did if they followed the prescribed path, which was one of worldly renunciation.[108] Some have argued that the Buddha was actually trying to accommodate women into his order and allowing them the space to practise without rousing the indignation of men in what was a terribly 'sexist society'.[109] The argument is not convincing because the Buddha openly flouted the caste-related conventions of his times, which undoubtedly upset quite a few social circles. Yet, despite their reluctant admittance, women generally were not encouraged to join the Buddhist sects, and instead their role in society was constricted to that of self-sacrificing motherhood. Their primary obligation in life was to raise and nurture their children, which was literally forced upon them, notwithstanding the despicable characteristics assigned to the womb. Yet, oddly, this same expectation was not placed on men, and much like the Buddha, if they so desired, men always had the choice to abandon their families in their pursuit of nirvana.[110] There are accounts of women forced into conventional marriage and child-rearing, when they deeply desired to pursue the Buddhist path of salvation. Many nuns who joined the Buddhist seminary faced tremendous social and familial opposition, and some had to flee so that they would not be forced into marriage. One woman was beaten to a pulp by her potential groom, while another feigned insanity and would wander the streets, eating food put out for dogs. Indeed, women in some other cultures as in Tibet, for instance, had far more leeway to become Buddhist nuns than did women in India.[111]

In the long run, the role of nuns in the growth of Buddhism was extremely trivialized and they were quite shabbily treated both within the Buddhist orders and by the lay followers. There are very few records, for instance, of Buddhist nuns, their specific contributions to the orders and their soteriologies. This disfavour was due to the eight fastidious rules, established by the founder, which greatly subordinated women's position in the order. Though Buddhist monasteries like the ones at Taxila and Nalanda, believed to be the crown jewels of Buddhism, became vast, impressive and prosperous centres of learning, they preferentially catered to male monks. The nuns had access to a negligible share of the resources offered by these wealthy centres, and some places did not even provide them with food. The Chinese pilgrim I Ching observed that the Buddhist nuns in India were much worse off than those in China. They were always poverty-stricken and compelled to beg for their food.[112]

The Buddha's attitude towards women could be indicative of unresolved issues that he had with sexuality, perhaps his own squeamishness about it from personal experiences, and perhaps the agony of his struggle in surmounting his natural sex drive. Some of the recorded literature on the Buddha's life as a young prince recall that, as handsome as he was, women who thronged the streets to greet him would throw themselves at him, rubbing their breasts against him, sometimes causing him to get aroused. But apparently, he always reminded himself that such pleasure was only momentary. Other accounts speak of an occasion, during a festival, when a troupe of female entertainers was sent to his private chambers. As they sang and danced for his pleasure, he remained unmoved. Finally exhausted, all the dancers fell asleep. Buddha watched them sleeping and thought to himself that the women who only a moment ago seemed so bewitching looked grotesque in their strange sleeping positions, with all the hidden flaws of their bodies showing, thus convincing him that women by 'nature' were indeed 'impure' and 'monstrous'.[113]

Tales of the Buddha's birth are couched in terms of immaculacy. He was conceived when a white elephant—an explicit sexual metaphor—entered the body of his 'pure' as a 'lily' mother,[114] implying that Buddha's conception was asexual. The vagina was also evaded during labour when the Buddha emerged chaste and without the afterbirth filth of blood and fluids, from the side of his mother's abdomen, killing her in the process. The Buddha was even believed to have tamed the wild earth goddesses, the tree spirits and the serpent deities of the indigenous people that the Vedics feared so much.[115]

Yet, despite Buddhism's wariness of women and their dismissal from its path to salvation, it preached a kindly and respectful treatment of women in lay society. Husbands were instructed to remain loyal to their wives and refrain from adultery. They were also told to permit their wives full control over the running of the household and to show appreciation with gifts of clothes and jewellery. Wives too were advised to be chaste and tender and take pride in their domestic tasks.[116] Essentially, Buddhism extended its philosophy of empathy and consideration for fellow beings to married couples as well. However, the trend was not replicated in the Vedic circles, where Buddhism's philosophy of the insignificance of women provided the opportunity for the subjugation of women to an even greater degree than ever before. Perhaps the difference in this approach may have been because Buddhism's hardcore philosophies applied specifically to its initiates and its religious orders, but to the rest of the outside world, which included women, it extended a more universal treatment of compassion for fellow beings. Hinduism did not make that same distinction between the religious sects and the more peripheral, secular society, for the sacred laws of the Vedas fully controlled all members of society. As dismal as the status of women was in earlier Vedic society, in the Buddhist period their condition deteriorated to one of the lowest points in Indian history. The period was marked by a raging misogyny.

At one time, despite the Vedic man's wariness of the power of female sexuality, there was a disguised awe of it, a furious attempt to court this power so it would enable men to have sons and thus replicate themselves in women's wombs to become immortal. However, in this Buddhist period the woman with her womb was considered to actually endanger men's ambitions of salvation, for in her womb she bore the life that further ensnarled him in the trap of rebirth and earthly attachments. Women now had no worth. They were labelled evil and lustful creatures who perpetuated sin. Since they had no concrete function, they were valueless, denigrated objects that men in their quest for salvation had to learn how to evade, overcome, dispose of and utilize as and how it best suited them.

In Taxila, a mainly Buddhist town, according to the records of Strabo,[117] a Greek geographer and historian, men from poor families would sell their daughters in the marketplace. To the accompaniment of a small musical instrument, in the same way that commodities were put up for sale, they would attract buyers. And when a potential customer showed interest he was permitted to inspect the girl thoroughly. Her clothing would be lifted and the back and front of her body fully exposed for examination; if the man liked what he saw, a mutually satisfactory deal was struck.[118]

The idea that women were promiscuous and deceitful gained currency. They were said to be lustful, lazy, power hungry, deceitful, malicious and vengeful by nature, and therefore not fit for education. Since the knowledge of the Vedas within the Vedic circles was still a prerequisite for people striving for salvation,[119] women were forcefully prevented from learning the Vedas.[120] This was another major setback for women, for it appears that even in the Vedic period they were allowed a certain degree of education, and some were considered learned scholars in specialized subjects, such as philosophy, grammar and theology.[121] Women were allowed to conduct certain Vedic ceremonies, but in the Buddhist period people were warned that if women were permitted to preside over ceremonies as priests, not only would the women be damned but the men for whom the rites were performed would incur misfortune.[122] Men were advised to keep guard on women at all times or they would bring great distress to the family with their promiscuous behaviour. Husbands were advised to ensure their wives were kept busy with plenty of housework so that their minds would not stray towards sex. The sacred scriptures warned that no woman could ever be allowed free will because of her sensory addictions and her tendency towards sexual wantonness. A woman, it was advised, must always be kept under the watchful eye of a man—first her father and then her husband. Likewise, when the father died, sons were cautioned about guarding their widowed mother.[123] One of the customs prevalent but not mentioned in the Vedas was *niyoga*, where a childless widow was permitted to conceive through a male relation in her husband's family. However, as soon as the woman was impregnated she was required to stop her relations with the man.[124] This possibly might have been a means to retain the woman—as she was property too—with the family, and prevent her from seeking a relationship outside it.

Men could also prostitute their wives, as well as arrange for a voyeuristic viewing of their spouses with other men if it so pleased them.[125] Where in the Vedic period, kings were generally allowed four wives at the most,[126] in the Buddhist period kings were believed to have built large harems, with a 'hundred' wives, hundred being a popular number to have. King Okkako was said to have had 16,000 women in his harem[127] and so did the king of Varanasi,[128] though possibly some of these numbers may have been exaggerations. Women were ranked in harems and subjected to the further humiliation of being promoted or demoted, as a means of psychological control. If a woman was disobedient, impertinent, or barren, she would be demoted in the harem and a newer wife would be given seniority.[129]

Greek travellers during this period observed that due to the frustration of harem life women often sought men outside it for the satisfaction of their needs, and sometimes even prostituted themselves for gifts.[130] In the Vedic age, an infidel wife could participate in a confessional ceremony in which she had to hold up blades of grass to show how many lovers she had and be thus pardoned for her infidelity, but in the Buddhist period she was to be torn to pieces by street dogs.[131]

Women were assigned a tolerable social image they were expected to measure up to. Besides being a good, cheerful and expert housekeeper who never exerted her independence, was sexually passive and refrained from running up household expenditures, a woman was also to worship her husband like a 'god' and 'master' even if he had no redeemable qualities. She was to tolerate his ill temper as well as his promiscuity and extramarital affairs. And she was to remain sexually faithful to her husband even after he died, by not remarrying. If she remarried as a widow, or had extramarital affairs while her husband was alive, she was warned that she would be reborn low on the karmic wheel and would contract terrible diseases.[132] Furthermore, as women were in general now regarded as pollutants and unsacred, they were banned from participating in religious ceremonies. During the early Vedic ages, women often took part in religious ceremonies alongside their husbands and there were specific ceremonies that women were allowed to conduct on their own such as the sati and the Rudra sacrifices for prosperity and fertility. But, now, even in death, they were denied libation. Priests would not accept food from women who were regarded as contaminated, including menstruating women, widows, women rumoured to be promiscuous, or those whose husbands had abandoned them.[133] Widows were often accused of having murdered their husbands because of their greed for money or lust for another man. A widow who lamented too loudly at her husband's funeral was assumed to be putting up an act after having poisoned her spouse.[134] Where earlier, in Vedic norms, widows could remarry, now widows, perhaps as retribution, or to ensure their faithfulness to their dead husbands, were burnt alive with their husbands' corpses and the custom of sati ensued. It became a rampant practice in the latter part of this period.[135] However, Buddhism itself never perpetuated sati and advocated that widows should be allowed to continue living their own lives.[136]

THE MIND AT ODDS WITH THE BODY

Unquestionably, the greatest shortcoming in the Buddha's attempt to define a collective human identity and, therefore, destiny was his insistence on exacerbating the gender split. The Buddha broke the caste barrier no doubt, in an emerging human consciousness, but eventually propagated a dichotomized, self-conflicted philosophy for the exclusive salvation of men. This was still an incompletely perceived human image and a flawed solution to a social quest.

But another aspect of existence that developed an unpleasant discordance in Buddhist philosophy was that of matter, with an undue emphasis on the mind–body duality. Buddha's antagonism to matter is particularly puzzling considering he acknowledged the body as a necessity for attaining nirvana. Even though he refused to define what the nirvana state actually is, he explained that when a person had become a Buddha, that is, enlightened while living so as to be able to achieve nirvana upon death, the body was much more buoyant, more radiant and had magical powers, including the ability to rise into the air.[137] The logic is convoluted: one needs the body to be free of the body for good. He said the body needed food and that an individual could overcome the stimulation and pleasure of the senses from eating. Why then could the body not be allowed its basic need of sex to be fulfilled while similarly controlling one's experience of pleasure from the act? And yet, the Buddha did in a way indulge his own senses. He liked his chambers to be elegant and perfumed and he even liked garlands of fragrant flowers to be strung up in his lavatory.[138]

Though the Buddha rejected the body's individualistic tendencies, upon enlightenment he proclaimed his own accomplishment as an individual. In fact, the Buddha's standing instructions to his followers were that upon his death he was to be given the traditional cremation of a 'universal monarch', and his remains were to be distributed among different groups of his followers who were then to enshrine the remains in semi-circular domed reliquaries called stupas.[139] It is quite astonishing, given Buddha's vehement negation of the human body, that he would pay such detailed attention to the preservation and enshrinement of his bodily remains.

Indeed, even as he rebuffed materialism he sought the patronage of business communities and royalty to keep his own order afloat. Nalanda, a leading Buddhist monastery and learning centre, which supported thousands of students, needed the income from the rent it collected from 200 villages to sustain itself. Buddhist monasteries were also generously supported by wealthy merchants; therefore, despite its emphasis on a non-materialistic world view, the Buddhist scriptures encouraged laymen to practise good business by dividing their money into four parts: one part for living on, two parts for reinvestment and expansion of business, and one to save.[140]

In any case, the overarching conclusion of the Buddhist period was that salvation was primarily a human quest, and that it could be achieved by all men, even those of the lowest caste, through celibacy and dissociation from women. Not surprisingly, this philosophy was most obvious in the evolution of the lingam—the archetype we follow in this book as a social marker for tracking changes in sexual ethics.

The lingam, which the Vedics had earlier borrowed from the indigenous cults, and revered as a non-figurative concept, was now worshipped in its symbolic form and for the first time since the Indus period it materialized as an idol. Unlike the phallic artefacts of the Indus Valley civilization though, which were vaguely shaped, the lingams that emerged now were sculpted as tall and well-defined erect phalluses, unambiguous in their physiological representation.[141] Moreover, the lingam often stood alone, attached to no vulva or yoni. Even some of the pillars erected by the Buddhist emperor Ashoka, as statements of the just order he sought to apply to his empire, became symbols of the Shiva lingam for local people, and they would worship them as such.[142]

Most telling, perhaps, are the mythologies spun in this period that accompany the lingam. Where earlier, Shiva, or Rudra as the Vedics called him, was synonymous with male sexual potency, he was now shown to be completely disinterested in his consort Parvati's sexual overtures. As the myth goes, Parvati, who desired Shiva immensely, tried to break his concentration with her feminine wiles, as Shiva sat atop the mountain in deep penance. When she was not able to entice him, she recruited Kama, the love god, to help draw Shiva's attention to her. Kama struck Shiva with one of his famous passion arrows just as Parvati approached him. It broke Shiva's concentration but also aroused his ire. He burnt Kama to ashes, thus reducing the god of love and passion to a bodiless, unseen state.[143] Kama, the love god whom the Vedic texts had described as being of an astoundingly beautiful form—with a golden complexion, black, curly hair, full-moon face, slim waist, hairy chest, well-formed nose, rounded, muscular buttocks and sweet-smelling breath[144]—and whose jasmine and mango blossom love arrows had helped many a man attain his desires of passion and lust, was as good as a charade without his body. Furthermore, Lord Shiva, the dark-skinned, austere mendicant representative of the lowest and most despised of outcastes, the ones that roamed the cremation grounds, was unshaken in his celibacy. He had the power to resist both the temptations of a woman and that of lust and was hailed as the supreme power. This version of Shiva was an idealized personification of the Buddhist path of salvation. Indeed, of the thirty-two characteristics attributed to the immanent Buddhas, one was that of an unseen penis.[145] Towards the end of this age Shiva was hailed as the most elevated of gods—superior even to the Vedic Brahma, the creator god.[146]

[illegible]

[illegible]

[illegible]

PART III

THE GOLDEN PERIOD

SEX AS SALVATION

The bleakness of the Buddhist era eventually gave way to a period that raged with fresh and irrepressible energy, and it sprung forth such innovative visions of life and art that it is sometimes regarded as the golden period of Indian history. Hinduism as an umbrella faith was still non-existent and what are now called Hindu sects were then essentially regarded as separate religions. Minor religions that might have skulked as peripheral sects in small tribal communities earlier now emerged to bombard mainstream society. The primary drive behind these movements was the search for a feasible pathway to salvation in the context of ordinary life, something that the traditional versions of Buddhism earlier failed to provide for. There was a social yearning for new methods of attaining nirvana that would willingly accommodate the sensory and often indispensable aspects of existence—including sex, and the sustenance of a family—in a manner that Buddhism would not permit.

Despite the stern injunction against a life of sensual pleasures, all through the Buddhist period, people discreetly indulged in certain transgressions. Aphrodisiacs and wines continued to be among the popular products imported into India, some from countries as distant as Greece.[1] And through the seasonal festival of Holi, the indigenous communities, from among whom Buddhism recruited many of its followers, would ceremonially mourn the fiery destruction of the love god Kama by an irate Shiva. Keeping alive Kama's image through ritualistic song and dance, the tribal myths spoke of the god of love as being 'immortal and indestructible'.[2] The songs and dances of the Holi festival had an explicitly sexual undertone to them and involved plenty of touching between men and women, sexual bantering and graphic mimicry of sex acts.[3] It was the undeniable expression of a community's need to reinstate love and lust as an integral process of living.

Even the austere, mendicant Shiva of the Buddhist age, whom Parvati had tried to seduce in vain, emerged with a new unreservedly lustful image in this period. In one instance, even with Parvati, his consort, by his side, he was unable to contain his lust for a beautiful, big-breasted, doe-eyed woman, and chased her like a 'rutting elephant' after a she-elephant in heat, spilling his semen all over the place.[4]

The collective repression of sexual desire perhaps prompted not only the reinstatement of sex in societal mores as a normal and acceptable practice in this period, but also its redefinition as an inextricable aspect of the sacred. Where Buddhism had virtually barred sex as vulgar and unholy from the sacred realm, the impetus of this period was to redeem it. In fact, in many sects that emerged now, sex itself was conceived to be a pathway to the sacred.

Besides sex, other teachings of Buddhist philosophy that were subverted in this age were those that denied the existence of God and forbade the practice of idol worship. Idol worship, in fact, was forbidden not just to the Buddhists but the Vedics as well. However, where the Buddha had completely dispensed with God as a concept, the notion of an omnipotent divine presence was restored in the rituals of worship through a more multifarious pantheon of gods than even that of the Vedics. Furthermore, these gods also assumed anthropomorphic forms, each with distinctive physical traits as that of hair, skin colour and physiology, which made them all the more human and lifelike to the worshippers. Even the Buddha, who never approved of idol worship, was deified and brought into the new pantheon of old tribal gods as an incarnation of the dark-skinned lord Vishnu.[5] Most cults and divine figures that emerged as prominent in this era appear to be a restoration of ancient indigenous religions and their gods.

The pre-Vedic indigenous cultures, as evident from artefacts of the Indus Valley civilization, did engage heavily in idol worship and seem to have regarded sexuality as a central principle of the divine. Along with the revival of these concepts, now both male and female sexualities were considered sacred and powerful in equal measure, and the goddesses no longer served as the shadow consorts to the gods like they had for the Vedics.

Interestingly, the gods and goddesses that dominated this age were also conceived in the phenotypic likeness of the indigenous people from whom they originated and had their dark skins. Among these were the gods Krishna, Shiva, Vishnu and the goddess Kali. Lord Shiva now fully supplanted the Vedics' Brahma as the Supreme God. Lord Krishna was believed to be of a mixed race and his wife, Rukmini was of indigenous origin from present-day Arunachal Pradesh.[6] Krishna had, in fact, previously been featured, though briefly, in the Rig Veda, where he was characterized as dark-skinned and belligerent. He was shown as repeatedly leading huge armies in violent clashes against the Vedic superhero god Indra, and was thus regarded with hostility by Vedic priests.[7] Now, Lord Krishna had large cults devoted entirely to his worship.

This colourful pageantry of gods resurrected in human form no longer lived in the distant skies, invisible and powerful like the Vedic gods, to be accessed only through fire rituals and soma-induced fantasies. The deities' relationship with humans now became more intimate and personal. Not only did the divine assume flesh-like human characteristics in clay and wood, but they also dwelled among the mortals, and lived the lifestyle of the average human. Interestingly, one of the central ceremonies for the consecration of the idol, the *pranapratishtha*, involves the infusion of the 'breath of life' into the idol.[8] Thus it was not only the gods who had the powers to bestow life, but humans too could reciprocate by facilitating the awakening of life within the gods. The earthly homes of the gods were the temples constructed in their honour; these were conspicuously huge, ostentatiously wealthy and magnificent structures that visually marked this millennium. Most were built of stone—red sandstone, grey granite or white marble—and despite time and neglect some are still standing today.

It is of enormous significance that the religious movements that emerged in this golden epoch and came to prevail over mainstream society actually had their roots in indigenous practices and rituals of the underdog communities whose cause the Buddha had upheld. These communities continued to be treated as peripheral by the Vedic religion that claimed that salvation was not preordained for them. In fact, numerous sects now dispensed with the notions of racial purity and caste privilege. Among them were the Shaivite sects that worshipped Shiva, one of the gods that the Sakyas, the tribe the Buddha originated from, honoured too.[9] Other sects went out of their way to blatantly flout the Vedic restrictions of the race-based caste system. There were indeed also some strong anti-Vedic feelings, and almost a defiant contempt for certain Vedic taboos. The Lingayats, for instance, practised post-puberty marriage and widow remarriage, much against the Vedic laws.[10] Therefore, the religious movements of this era were in a way akin to a massive uprising of people of the lower social strata, or in Nietzsche's term the slave class's push, for an equitable place in society. It was where the marginalized sought to redefine their self-worth and reinvent the process of spiritual endeavour, challenging the Vedic system's dehumanization of them.

Also making its impact on this period was what could be considered India's nascent feminist movement. The representation of women in religion, as well as the sexuality of women, repressed and denigrated for long under both Vedic and Buddhist cultures, now surfaced in powerful new cults of goddess worship.

WHEN THE SLAVE BECAME MASTER

The emergence of these radical new religious movements was preceded by significant changes in certain social patterns. One of these was a gradual and steady increase in the wealth and political clout of the lower classes. Moreover, following a trend begun in the Buddhist period, economic status now displaced the Vedic caste system as the primary determinant of social clout. With their financial ascent, the serving classes could now wedge themselves into the driver's seat and redefine the social and moral milieus of living. They were, consequently, able to promote their own cultures, beliefs and spiritual practices into mainstream society as an overriding aspect of the emergent vision of salvation.

Most labourers, such as those working on farms, artisans, those with specialized technical skills like potters, metallurgists, sculptors and builders, as well as entertainers such as actors, musicians and courtesans, who had been classified as the lowest or the labour class of Vedic society, were of indigenous origins.

While earlier they may have been from diverse tribal groups that may or may not have interacted with each other, they now had the opportunity to form cohesive communities as well as professional guilds in the organized sectors of 'towns' and 'cities'. Under the Vedic system, the lowest caste had segregated living quarters on the outer edges of towns. This controlled segregation actually contributed to the strengthening of the artisans' collective identity and facilitated the formation of guilds. At least eighteen such guilds existed including those of woodcarvers, metalworkers, stone architects, weavers, leatherworkers, potters, ivoryworkers, dyers, jewellers, fisherfolk, butchers, hunters, cooks, barbers, flower-sellers, sailors, basket-weavers and painters.[11]

The guilds had already begun to emerge in the late Buddhist period, but now they learned to coordinate themselves better. They formed their own settlements or villages and became a dominant and powerful feature of urban life. They evolved a republican style of self-governance, characteristic of the tribal communities they originated in and acquired quite a degree of economic and political autonomy and success.[12] They also became increasingly systematic and organized: they formed their own armies for defence, set up courts to settle disputes and elected a leader called the 'elder', who governed the functioning of the guild and its members with the assistance of a council of senior members.[13] All guilds had to be registered in the regions where they operated. They also organized workshops where they honed their art, their individual skills, and trained new artisans as apprentices. In the process, they were able to formalize and refine the knowledge and techniques of their respective crafts. The superb workmanship and distinctive formal styles that emerged in this period are evidenced by its coins, architectural splendour, engineering feats and stunning sculptures.

The guilds also formed cooperatives that would take on contractual work as a team. So, for instance, in the case of large projects like that of building a temple or palace, guilds of architects, engineers, bricklayers, sculptors and so on would undertake the assignment as a collective team. In this manner, they acquired such success as commercial entrepreneurs that they eventually were able to control market prices. Artisans also derived various other benefits from their membership in these guilds including perfecting their skills, economic security and enhanced social status. As the guilds flourished, they expanded their trade overseas to countries in North Africa, the Mediterranean and Asia, including China and Indonesia. They built large seafaring vessels that could accommodate 700 passengers at a time. Ultimately, many of these guilds became exceedingly wealthy and, with increased international trade, the domestic barter system had to be replaced with a cash-based economy. Coins in gold, silver and copper, depending on denomination, began to be used for most business transactions. The guilds, with their vast capital, were able to assume the role of community bankers, financiers and trustees and they also emerged as the largest employers in the kingdom. The artisan guilds, in fact, had begun to control a good deal of the kingdoms' economies, and consequently were able to have a strong say in social and political matters.[14]

Significantly, one of the biggest investments of this accrual of wealth was in the building of temples. Guilds contributed some of the largest donations towards temple building, and often participated in the actual construction.[15] It was inevitable that the gods to whom these temples were dedicated were the indigenous gods. The temples, which had huge complexes, were autonomous bodies and often also owned large tracts of land and village endowments, some of which were received as gifts from patron kings and nobility. Often, rulers would patronize the temples and the new sects as a way of keeping the masses from organizing social revolts and overthrowing the monarch.[16] Many wealthy merchants who earlier had converted to Buddhism and patronized Buddhist monasteries now began to fund the temples of these newly emerging sects, which honoured their own ancestral indigenous gods and tribal customs.[17] Serving as landlords, the temples received revenues from the villages not only in cash but also in kind as in oil, ghee, cloth, cows and even dancing girls.[18] The temples also became the earliest banks, financing trade guilds investing in inter-kingdom trade, which sometimes extended across four or five kingdoms, and giving loans for various village projects. The management committees of these temples comprised priests (generally indigenous and not Vedic Brahmins), trade guilds and the village assembly, and it appears that they had a structural and economic organization so vast and intricate that an eleventh-century Chola king had to deploy eleven of his officers to audit the finances of a certain temple.[19] The temples, besides being the town financial centres, had numerous other functions: they served as classrooms for the artisan trades and provided free room and board to hoards of guild students. The temples were also the cultural centres for the revival and establishment of indigenous arts, music, dance, theatre and sculpture, which were now established as formal disciplines, and studied, practised and developed further. The sanctum of the temple generally served as a theatre where cultural performances were held for the public. Other disciplines that were studied and developed at the temple schools were medicine, grammar, prose and metaphysics, just as they had been in Buddhist monasteries.[20]

Most importantly, these temples became community centres where the artisan communities gathered, held discussions and rallies and consolidated their political clout. The wealth and political power that became associated with these temples were instrumental in reviving indigenous traditions and establishing them as mainstream theologies with large, public followings.[21]

Not surprisingly, even the priests of many of these temples were from the artisan class. This dissociation of race, caste and profession was one of the most vital social developments of this period. Earlier, the Vedics designated caste according to purity of race and lightness of skin colour. Generally, only the 'whiter' Vedic race was permitted to occupy the superior priestly caste, but now wealth could be used to reassign caste bearings. The determinants of caste hierarchy now also included wealth. Even though this thwarted the original intentions of the Vedics to safeguard racial purity and power, the inherent valuation of people according to caste hierarchy, unfortunately, was much too deeply embedded in the social psyche and continued to be a defining status factor. Therefore, no matter what a person's economic or social status was, he would not be acknowledged as respectable or deemed worthy of certain positions if he did not have the appropriate caste to match it. Many people from the lower castes who had accumulated wealth and could afford to do so paid Vedic priests to construct new genealogies for them, often grand ones that linked the family to the regal sun and moon dynasties. Vedic Brahmins, who had long been fighting a losing power battle as well as unemployment, were perhaps only too glad to gain employment even if it was from the nouveau riche of the communities they had once disdained. Others from the lower castes paid to learn the scriptures and become priests or religious teachers, ambitions that in the Vedic age would have been perilous. As one Vedic rule book had it, a servant-class person who eavesdropped on the Vedic recitation was to have molten lead poured in his ears, his tongue rooted out if he recited the verses and his body chopped in two if he memorized them.[22] Besides learning the Vedas, those artisans who had the means to learn martial arts, also earlier forbidden to the lower castes in case it sowed wicked ideas of insurgency in their heads, could now join the kingly or warrior caste. Individuals or guilds could even raise their own armies and acquire their own kingdoms through usurpations, coups, assassinations and wars.

Though the trend appears to have already begun by the end of the Buddhist period, in this era, many individuals of low-caste origins became rulers of small, dispersed kingdoms. One of the most famous and influential dynasties of this period, the Gupta dynasty, could trace their lineages to tribal groups like the Nagas and the Lichchhavis.[23] There were even some kings who were the progeny of upper-caste women and lower-caste men, who traditionally would have been relegated to the status of outcastes and driven out of towns to live on the outskirts. King Marutta Avikshita, for instance, descended from a merchant-caste mother and a slave-caste father.[24] The Guhila dynasty of Mewar is said to have had its origins in the tribal Bhils, and the Candella dynasty in the tribal Gonds. This upward social mobility happened not just at a family level, but also at community levels, where entire guilds would upgrade their caste. Most Rajputs, for example, who constituted the royal families in present-day Rajasthan, were of non-Vedic, indigenous or mixed origins, and neither spoke Sanskrit nor observed Vedic customs.[25]

In fact, the new monarchs had a style of governance quite different from that of the self-serving kings of the Vedic lineages. Much like the Buddhist emperor Ashoka, who too was understood to be of low-caste descent, several monarchs of this period, as those of the Gupta dynasty and King Harsha of the seventh century AD, governed with an eye to the well-being of their subjects. Some like Harsha often travelled across the kingdom to personally listen to the grievances of the public,[26] while the Guptas, whose officials were said to be on friendly terms with the public and receptive to citizens' problems,[27] exercised a policy of tolerance for all religions,[28] ideologies that most probably are also rooted in the republican-style tribal communities. In fact, starting with the Buddhist period, there are clear indications in some literatures that in certain kingdoms people, some of whom gathered in the assembly style, would sometimes banish insufferable kings and their courtiers by majority vote.[29]

The advance of some artisan classes into positions of power opened up the way for others of the lower castes, for not only were they granted landownership, they were even bestowed the title of nobility or priesthood by the king as a gift for services rendered.[30]

However, despite the subversions of certain Buddhist and Vedic philosophies, the underlying approach to worship in this period was that of forbearance. Many Vedic and Buddhist practices were incorporated into ancient tribal traditions and it resulted in an extremely diverse and eclectic array of religious practices. Idol worship existed alongside the Vedic ritual of sun worship, for instance, and gods of various faiths would sometimes be worshipped at the same temple.

However, tolerance was not always the motivation for the accommodation of different religions. Kings of tribal or low-caste origin would compare themselves to Brahma and Indra and try to win the alliance of the Vedic Brahmins, still recognized as inherently superior, by showing support for the Vedic laws, and embellishing their indigenous religions with Vedic beliefs and rituals.[31] In fact, there appeared to be a tremendous eagerness among the indigenous rulers in the southern kingdoms to subscribe to the Vedic ways. So far, they had languished on the periphery of the grand Vedic empire, their languages referred to as 'goblin languages' by the Vedics in the north. Kings in south India would conduct vajapeya ceremonies and the ashvamedha, and assume titles like 'Great king of kings ruling according to dharma' even though these ceremonies and concepts like dharma were alien to their indigenous religions.[32]

Some of the inter-sect borrowings were extremely constructive from a social viewpoint. So from the functioning of the Buddhist monasteries, the new sects borrowed the know-how for centralized administration and the practice of using temples as centres for community congregation, education, social and political organization and trade and financing.

There was also a mindful and concerted social effort towards eclecticism, and certain religious scriptures of this period repeatedly and directly acknowledged all streams of religions, naming them as Vedic, tantric and mixed, and validated all forms of worship, such as that of idols, fire, sun, waters, self-reflection, as well as worship of the Vedic Brahman.[33] The sculptures and architectural elements in temples such as in the seventh-century AD Vaital and Shishreshvra confirm a blending of iconography from various sects, including the Shaivites, the Shakta or the goddess cults, the Buddhists and also the now reduced faction of Vedic worshippers.[34]

LOVE: THE PEOPLE'S MOVEMENT

The numerous cults that surfaced in the golden period continue to thrive in modern India under the common umbrella of

Hinduism. However, at that point, in the first millennium AD, they had emerged not as a single religion but diverse religions and were recognized as such. But what they all had in common was the goal of salvation through *bhakti* or devotion. This was devotion as in the lovelorn, single-minded hypnotic adulation of a chosen god. The new approach to salvation was, as Kalidasa, one of the most famous saints and poets of this period proclaimed, that type of devotion to a specific personalized god—Shiva in the case of Kalidasa—that would terminate the endless cycles of rebirth.[35] By the end of the golden period, around AD 1300, the bhakti movement had become consolidated and pervasive throughout the Indian subcontinent and would serve as the basis of modern Hinduism.

The bhakti movement in effect was a mass civil movement of the people to release the sacred from the exclusive domain of the priests and the upper castes, and make God socially accessible to all. It was one of the most critical ideological developments in Indian devotionalism that broke the barrier of priestly privilege that had thus far defined the Vedic religion. The bhakti cult discarded the need for Brahmin priests, secret rituals and complex texts, and dealt with the social issues of the lower castes.[36] The congregational form of worship, perhaps a borrowing from Buddhism, was very unlike the exclusive Vedic ceremonies, and actually fostered the strengthening of communal bonds among the lower castes. The cults emphasized the use of local language in their worship and rituals so as to be inclusive of all people,[37] unlike the Vedics, who used Sanskrit as a language of privilege and concealment to keep the sacred scriptures veiled from the lower caste. Furthermore, the bhakti cults generally embraced all castes and genders—the inclusion of women as disciples and saints was an important factor that gave these cults an edge even over Buddhism. Prominent bhakti saints like Ramananda (1400–70) accepted disciples from different walks of life, including outcastes and women.[38] Some scriptures even made pointed references to how the process of worship of the divine makes no distinction on the basis of caste, learning, race, family, origins, wealth or profession.[39] The *Bhagavat Purana*, an important text of this period, proclaimed that a low-caste man who practised devotion was irrefutably superior to the Brahmin who did not, and with his devotion the low-caste individual could attain salvation for his entire clan.[40] Many saints of this period were themselves from the lowest castes, and some were women. Notable among the saints were Kabirdas, who was a weaver; Raidas, who was a leather worker, one of the jobs considered to be the 'filthiest'; Chokha Mela, who too was a leather worker; Gora, who was a potter; Namdeo, who was a tailor; and Sawanta, a gardener. Among the women saints were Mirabai, Sakhubai, Muktabai, Janabai and Bahinabai.[41]

There was also a lively new momentum to the conceptualization of the sacred. Where Buddhism had seemed to suggest that life was like a bitter medicine to be tolerated till one could be rid of it, the approach now was to affirm the sacredness of life itself and all its processes, including the functions of the senses and sexuality. As some bhakti scriptures indicate, the devotees intensely communicated with their chosen god or goddess, wooing and yearning for them as they would for a 'lover'.[42] The god or goddess was the *ishta devta* or the beloved. One method of amorous adoration of one's beloved god was through the ceremony of *puja*, a key practice that flourished in this period and remains a defining element of modern Hinduism. In a puja, the beloved god in his or her human form would be wooed as a lover, through the arousal of the senses, a philosophy of seduction that was well propounded in this period by the kama sutras, the books of love-making. Sensuously evocative, the puja ceremonies entailed the offerings of beautiful clothes and jewellery, flower garlands, fragrant pastes, such as sandalwood, oil lamps, incense, different types of foods, anointments, massage and entertainment, in the form of songs and dances, for the gods.[43] Starting on a low key, the ceremonies would culminate in an orgasmic frenzy of music and dance, where the devotee would abandon his senses to the rhythm of the trance, the peak moment signifying the union of the devotee with his beloved. This was salvation for the bhakti cults, the consummation of this personal relationship with the divine. The liberation of the personal soul, though temporary, entailed a glorious merging with the divine soul. Some took this union so literally, especially during the early bhakti years, that laws had to be formulated, forbidding devotees from trying to copulate with the icons, and fining them if they did so.[44]

THE RESURRECTION OF THE LOVE GOD

Kama, the love god, who had been burnt to ashes by an infuriated Shiva in the legends of the Buddhist age, but whose memory was kept alive in the celebratory tribal songs of the Holi festival, regained his body in this period and was united with his consort, Rati (sexual pleasure). His return to life too would be celebrated during Holi, which coincides with the spring season, symbolic of rejuvenation and fertility. The celebrations were called *mojin kama* (playing with desire), and entailed songs with erotic lyrics and dances with unabashedly sexual gestures, as Kama would be burnt in a bonfire to re-enact how Shiva in his anger had destroyed the unfortunate love god. The following day Kama would be symbolically resurrected as people jubilantly doused each other with perfumed water and colourful powders in honour of his return. Krishna, who was regarded as an incarnation of Kama, was another god evoked in the Holi celebrations. His erotic relationship with his consort Radha was re-enacted in open-air public theatres, where the women who played Radha and her friends would sing to the men: 'I play Hori with you, O dark one'.[45] (Hori or holi is described as 'a type of indecent song' that is sung for the Holi festival.)[46]

The resurrection of Lord Kama essentially signalled the revival of the concept of kama, as expressed through love and lust, as a socially acceptable norm. While in the Vedic period kama was regarded as one of the four central goals in a man's life, what it primarily encompassed then was lust and reproduction. In this period, however, kama evolved as a much more complex concept which, besides lust, explored the notions of love, passion, desire and sensuality.

In fact, kama became a predominant philosophy of this era, influencing all aspects of life, including religion. The permissiveness regarding sex in society seems explosive in the aftermath of the sexual repression of the Buddhist era. In contrast to the Buddhist view of life as an excruciating process to be endured by repressing the senses, there was a vehement need in this period to affirm that salvation did not imply a total 'extinguishing' of life, as Buddha had preached, but could be found in life itself. The new perception was that the very process of living and its creative potential was the pathway to salvation.

Lord Kama came to be regarded as the divine inspiration for humanity. The concept of kama as love-making was said to have been propagated by the gods themselves. It was believed to be their gift to humankind,[47] so that people could bond with each other and with the divine. As salvation entailed a sense of physical and emotional union with God, the devotional songs of this era reflected an intense and sensual passion for God as lover. Manikkavachakar, a minister at an eighth-century court in Madurai, spoke of 'divine nuptials' with the lord who was as 'sweet' as 'honey' and 'nectar', while Nammalvar, a ninth-century Tamil poet and one of twelve legendary Vaishnavite saints called the Alvars, spoke of his soul as a beautiful, young woman restless and pining for her love, the lord.[48] The female saint Mirabai, who frequently referred to Lord Krishna as her husband, spoke of her love for him, comparing its intensity to an arrow that pierced her body, and lamenting that nothing could rid her of the agony. In her poems, she begs Krishna to come to her rescue swiftly and put out the flames of passion that consumed her body.[49]

Sexual intercourse even became part of certain rituals that were considered a pathway to salvation. In some sects symbolic sex with God or with his human representation accompanied certain ceremonies. At the Kamakhya temple in present-day Assam, for instance, there was a ceremony in which the goddess Kamakhya would be married to ascetics who were said to represent Shiva.[50] The *devadasi* tradition, in which families would offer their young daughters as wives to the gods, became a pervasive cultural practice in this era. Families would promise a girl child to specific deities, hoping to win the protection of the deity. When the girl was past puberty, she would be bathed, anointed and taken to the temple on a chosen day for the marriage ceremony, which would be conducted with much festivity and music, and the girl would be made to wear a *mangalsutra*, the gold chain signifying the married status of a woman. In the evening there would be a wedding feast for the community. Sometimes young women with distinct talents would be selected to be devadasis, an appointment socially regarded as prestigious. These women, besides being talented in song and dance, had to have certain physical attributes such as curvaceous hips, shapely eyes and soft, round faces, features that were said to render them beautiful enough to be wives of the gods. Religious texts such as the *Brahma Purana* gave descriptions of the characteristics of the chosen brides and the customs they were to observe. These wives of the gods were also considered extremely auspicious, or *sumangala*, as their husbands were immortal, and the women could, therefore, never be widowed.[51] Called devadasis or 'servants of the lord', these brides of god were duty-bound to serve their husbands by providing sex and entertainment at the altar, which included dance and music performances they were professionally trained for. These services were rendered to men as a sacred offering, and included priests and other temple clientele, as well as kings or travellers who used the temple as a rest house.

In certain sects, the rituals hinged on the copulation of gods and goddesses themselves, their coupling enacted by a human pair. Among the tribal Oraon, for instance, before the planting season, the earth goddess would be married to the sun god, with the village priest and his wife enacting the union through ritualized intercourse.[52] In tantric circles it was believed that if God's sexual needs were met and he was given access to a partner, he was more likely to be attentive to the devotee.[53] Many of these marriage ceremonies of sacred couples continue as traditions in India even today. In Bhubaneswar massive celebrations every year commemorate the marriage of Lingaraj to Gauri, one of the forms of Parvati, and in Puri Lord Jagannath or Krishna is wedded to Rukmini, a representation of goddess Durga.[54]

Other religious texts of this period like the *Shiva Puranas* attributed the power of creation to eros,[55] and thus extended the concept of the 'sacred' to something more than just intercourse: it now implied sexuality and sensuality as well. In certain cults of this age, particularly the goddess cults, where copulation was said to have been the precursor to creation,[56] the verbal expression of lust was regarded as a necessary part of goddess worship. In the Nikumbha puja and the Sabarotsava festival in Bengal, devotees wore flowers and leaves and danced with wild abandon as they sang and repeatedly chanted 'penis' or 'vagina'. The sexually charged performance, it was believed, pleased the Shakta goddess, a version of the present-day Durga,[57] and earned the devotees her favour. In fact, the chanting aloud of genitalia was permitted only to a select few who had been initiated into the Shakta cults.[58]

REPOSITIONING SEX IN SOCIETY

This open affirmation of the association between sex and the sacred had a resounding impact on the cultural practices and social attitudes of this period. There was now a certain permissibility in the communal perception and expression of sex that was almost an antithesis to the restrictions of the Buddhist period.

Love and lust were seen as celebratory aspects of life and celebrated as such in numerous public festivals that dealt with changing seasons and the fertility of nature, one being akin to the Western Valentine's Day. Referred to as the feast of love, it joyfully evoked the lord of love, Kama. Celebrated in the spring, this festival was marked by music, dancing and feasting, and offerings would be made to the god of love and his mistress Rati, the goddess of sexual desire. The sacred text *Shaiva Agama* instructed that the feast of love was to be celebrated with playing dyes and the use of sexually explicit language.[59]

Indeed, sensuality in this period became the quintessence of general living. There were architectural structures that were specifically designed to pander to love-making, customarily used in both public and private spaces. The homes of the middle class would have love chambers, rooms where the owner received his mistresses and courtesans. The decor of these chambers included erotic sculptures in wood and stone,[60] sensual paintings and images of Rati, carved on the doorways. The rooms were sprayed with fragrance, decorated with flowers and furnished with large, canopied beds, which according to one love-making manual of this period were always to be fitted with clean white sheets.[61] The love chamber was also furnished with various types of musical instruments, painting materials and books of sensual poetry and literature so that lovers could spend many leisurely hours entertaining themselves as they engaged in games of seduction. Some houses also had open-air bathing tanks, embellished with stone sculptures and floating lilies, meant for love sports. The sexologists of the time recommended special types of congresses in water.[62]

Palaces were much more lavish in their erotic decor and housed elaborate sculptures, paintings and engravings. For the nobles and the wealthier upper class, it was customary to own what was called 'a hill for sports'. This consisted of a hill, sometimes artificially created, with a mansion built on it. The mansions were splendid, with gold or ivory pillars, glass flooring, walls of crystal and a paradise-like environment, created by planting trees and luscious creepers indoors. A special feature of the mansion was a jewelled bench for love-making.[63]

Public art galleries were also meeting places for lovers. Impressively built with grand pillars, verandas and numerous square terraces, these buildings allowed for plenty of open spaces. The display halls, which were lit with chandeliers and mirrors, and perfumed with sweet-smelling fragrances, created a romantic environment for strolling through as lovers studied the pictures on exhibition, many of which dealt with erotic themes.[64] Even public gardens had special provisions for couples, with wooden pavilions constructed under bowers of vines or leaves where lovers could spend time. These love nests, which held special couches, were supplied with aphrodisiacs, ivory-handled fans and scented water to create a romantic ambience.[65]

In terms of social etiquette, it was permissible for people to revel openly in the pleasures of their sex life. Love bites were worn like trophies and souvenirs by young men and women, to be shown off later to friends as proof of their lover's passion.[66] Kings hired poets to write eulogies of their sex lives, which they inscribed on the walls of the temples they donated funds to.[67] Even on battlefields, special areas were designated to set up tents for courtesans, where men would be received and entertained for the course of a battle. Some literatures describe how soldiers who had survived a bloody battle during the day would, after the call of the bugle at sundown, go off with these beautiful women into the forests to bathe in the ponds.[68] Even priests and ascetics, in a departure from the Buddhist period, were entitled to bodily pleasures. One scripture for ascetics advised initiates that when they were free from their studies they ought to be enjoying women with firm bosoms and ample hips, whose passion during love-making was signalled by the closing of their eyes.[69] In fact, one of the popular themes in public art galleries as specified by a major treatise on painting, the *Naishadha-carita*, was the depiction of sages in amorous play with celestial nymphs.[70]

Unconventional sexual practices too were socially acknowledged without undue squeamishness. The kama sutras spoke without reservation of uncommon types of sexual customs among certain cultures, including group sex and sodomy. Sadomasochism was also acknowledged, described as marks of knives and pincers commonly visible on the breasts of young men and women in certain non-Vedic communities. The manuals provided candid examples as well of how such practices could go violently wrong, such as when the Chola king Chitrasena, in the throes of sexual passion, struck his wife so forcefully with a nail that she was killed. Another instance was when a general of the Pandya kingdom, while being entertained by the courtesan Chitralekha, hit her on the cheek with a borer and gouged out one of her eyes.[71]

The social acceptability of sex in this period is perhaps most evident in the esteem bestowed upon professional prostitutes. Devadasis, for instance, were highly respected members of society. Due to their talent in music, dance and love-making they were regarded as truly cultured citizens. Their role as the mortal wives of the gods was deemed so crucial to that milieu that even

Buddhism began to allow for the devadasi tradition in some of its temples.[72] The devadasis would be honoured at important social functions, and invited to exclusive parties and picnics by the upper echelons of society. Often they socialized directly with royalty, eating betel nuts with the queens for instance, an activity that indicated a very personal, intimate relationship, coveted by, but often denied to wives of other high-ranking officials.[73] The devadasis were also romantically sought after and courted by kings and wealthy merchants. During the dance and music soirees at the temple, the suitors would compete for the devadasi's attention, often causing much resentment among the wives and mistresses.[74] The social status of the devadasis is also revealed in their economic standing. Many were prosperous and owned land and personal property that were often gifted to them by their wealthy admirers. In fact, the construction of some temples was funded by the devadasis themselves. They lived lavishly, as substantiated by accounts of the grandiosity of one devadasi's house, which accommodated eight courtyards and had pillars of inlaid ivory.[75]

Professional prostitutes who worked outside the temple quarters were also held in high regard. Unlike the devadasis, prostitution for them was purely a professional enterprise, which according to the texts of this time was not immoral and could be undertaken both for income and for sexual pleasure.[76] Women in general were advised that if they acquired proficiency in the art of love-making, they were guaranteed to have an independent source of income, regardless of the country they lived in.[77]

Generally, it was understood that for the prostitutes their work was dharma or 'moral duty',[78] just as teaching was for priests, or administration for kings and fighting for warriors. This emphasized both the permissibility and the decorum of prostitution as a profession like any other in society and highlights the sacredness of duty, perceived as an elevated moral concept irrespective of the nature of the profession, akin to the dignity of labour. Also, unlike the Buddhist period where brothels were state-owned enterprises, prostitution now was an independent profession and a form of entrepreneurship for some women.

Prostitution as a career was certainly taken seriously and women were given sound advice on running their businesses efficiently. Scores of reference books were written on the art of prostitution and even the kama sutras, the household love-making manuals used by the bourgeois, had chapters dedicated to it. Prostitutes were advised on how to keep their customers interested, and warned never to work without remuneration so as to 'maintain her prestige'. They were instructed on the methods of maximizing profits, handling finances and balancing ledgers. It was recommended that they always select the higher-paying customers.[79] Men who failed to pay up or had gambled away their money were to be beaten up and thrown out by hired goons. Prostitutes were firmly advised against forming emotional attachments with clients and urged to keep the relationship purely professional.[80] They were also provided with interesting insights into the psychology of potential customers that could be useful in the handling of clients. The texts observed that potential male customers were generally wealthy, or vain or driven by fear and insecurity. The prostitutes were also advised to hire a pimp so that they could avoid diseased or violent clients.[81]

However, prostitutes too were of two classes: those who catered to all classes of society and the courtesans who catered only to the upper crust of society. The courtesans or *ganika*s, as they were known, were regarded as social celebrities. These women were renowned for their beauty, intelligence and expertise not only in the *kamashastra*s (the art and science of love-making) but also in the sixty-four associated arts. These included gymnastics, music, singing, dancing, dressmaking, logic, languages, sorcery and preparation of cosmetics and perfumes,[82] all prerequisites to the mastery of the kamashastras. They had freedom of movement to a much greater extent than most other women;[83] they were enterprising and negotiated their own fees.[84] Renowned for their beauty and talent, they were celebrities. Not unlike today's film stars, they were immensely wealthy, with flashy establishments and a team of personal staff, which included a hairdresser, a perfumer, a masseur and a musician. They occasionally made public appearances before excited fans and contributed to charity to maintain their glamorous image while the upper class clamoured to be seen in their company. Their potential customers and associates were carefully screened.[85]

SEX AS ART AND SCIENCE

This eminence of prostitutes was not unexpected as kama was the ethos of this age. Furthermore, exalted as the highest form of art and science, love-making was meticulously studied and practised as a science—known as kamashastra—and regarded as a requisite facet of civilized living. Prostitutes, particularly the courtesans, were sought after by the urban bourgeois as private instructors in the art.

Besides seeking the expertise of courtesans, people also studied love-making by using books. There were numerous guide books written on techniques and philosophies, including the kama sutras (anthologies of love-making) *Rati Rahasyam* (The Secrets to Orgasms) and *Ananga Ranga* (The Colours of the Love God), and the authors of these books would be awarded the title of 'acharya' or supreme teacher.[86] There were even study group clubs called *goshthi*s, among the elite, membership to which was viewed as a social distinction. Ambitious fathers who wanted their sons to develop social skills would send them to these gatherings. Among various other subjects of intellectual interest, they would discuss issues of sex and love.[87]

The sexology books, the kama sutras, meant for reference and study were illustrated manuals. The earliest of these books were said to have been written around the seventh century BC; by the first millennium AD, there had been numerous successive authors. The aboriginal origin of kamashastra is evident in that it was believed to be the creation of Mallanaga, the prophet of the demons—which is how the Vedics addressed the indigenous peoples—whereas the verses of the first kama sutra were said to have been revealed to and written down by Nandi, Shiva's bull.[88]

Therefore, the kama sutras were regarded as sacred scriptures containing revelations by God for the use of humankind and, as such, they also dictated the social and moral mores of society.

Though often addressing the average urban citizen, or the cultivated bourgeois and upper class, these books were meant for the use of all castes and classes. Instead of using the exclusive Sanskrit language, restricted to upper castes and classes, the authors of the kama sutras used the vernacular languages so that more people could access them. However, as the author of one of these books pointed out, members of any caste and class needed to be economically stable before they could cultivate this art, regardless of whether they made their income from gifts like Brahmins did, or through trade like merchants, or from service like the slave class.[89] Upper-class men could also take servant women as mistresses, as many were regarded as women of culture, who, being literate, were likely to be versed in the kama sutras.[90] In fact, young, unmarried upper-class girls, who were customarily schooled in this art at home, often studied the kamashastras with an older, experienced maid.[91] For poorer people, this knowledge was a source of extra income through lessons they gave to prostitutes. It also gained them admission into the homes of the wealthy because they were respected for being cultured and well versed in the kamashastras.[92]

The kama sutras were expansive and comprehensive studies, and were undoubtedly based on systematic physiological and psychological observations over a long period of time. They were perhaps some of the first sexology books to be written, almost 1500 years before the American scientists Masters and Johnson had studied many of the same questions in a laboratory setting in the 1960s. The kama sutras explored in great detail almost every sex-related issue, including sexuality, body types, courtship, seduction, psychology, sexual chemistry, foreplay, positions and orgasms. They also covered the impact of alchemy and the roles of medicine and astrology on sex lives.

The presentation of information in the books was extremely methodical, emphasizing classifications, patterns, probabilities and variability. People were classified into sex types based on the size of the penis or depth of the vagina, body form and temperament. Tables then presented the probable sexual compatibility between various sex-type combinations, including the expected intensity of orgasms.[93] Love play was said to have sixty-four elements,[94] and creative variations of each acivity were described. For instance, there were thirty-one suggested styles of foreplay, which included—among other techniques—touching, caressing, gazing and sex talk.[95]

The psychological dimension of sex and the attempt to understand it might appear absurd and overstated now, but in its time it was a novelty, an attempt at understanding the individual psyche—and yet another first in the breakthrough of the collective social consciousness. The kama sutra, in its psychological perspective on sex, went beyond the base emotions of anger, greed and lust to the more subtle nuances of the human mind. It asked questions, such as: what were the subtle feelings a person experienced towards another and what were the correct ways to recognize and respond to them? Excitement, the books observed, was when a woman wept or laughed upon seeing her lover after a long absence. And flirtation was when she fluttered her lashes or her eyes twinkled when she laughed and spoke.[96] Similarly, while kissing too was classified style-wise, its emotional, and not just sexual, dimensions were also explored. For instance, the kiss given to a lover who was distracted or upset was called 'the kiss of encouragement', the one bestowed on a lover's reflection in a mirror was one of 'tenderness', while to kiss a lover's fingers during a public outing or family gathering was to demonstrate care and intimacy.[97] Even more interestingly, these observations made allowances for cultural and individual differences, indicating that a lover's habits, customs and personal preferences might vary, and that it was important for individuals to accept these in their sexual relationships. The practice of oral sex and biting during love-making, for instance, were spoken of as being acceptable in some cultures, but not in others.[98]

Ayurveda, the formal institution of medicine established in this period, was an important extension of this social consideration for sex. Sex-related problems were specifically dealt with in medicine and various remedies devised in the form of herbs and ointments for all sorts of regular ailments. Besides pheromones, the Ayurvedic pharmacy developed lines of revitalizers or virility-enhancers, and had solutions for impotence, penis augmentation and the constriction or dilation of the vagina.[99] Curious and imaginative, many of these remedies were reflective of how closely the socially dominant communities—because of their indigenous origins—identified with the natural world, not only in the worship of various plants and animals, but in their use to alleviate their tribulations. For example, a recommended virility-enhancer was a he-goat's testicles boiled with milk and sugar.[100] Similarly, alchemy, with its established body of magical potions and charms, was regularly sought out by people to enhance their love lives. A peacock's eye wrapped in gold and tied to the right arm, in the spring season, was assumed to bring success in one's love endeavours,[101] while applying the oil of the yellow amaranth on the body or eating the powdered petals of the blue lotus with ghee and honey enhanced a person's magnetism in the eyes of the desired lover.[102]

Another trend that was a significant social preoccupation of this period was *shringar*—the beautification of the body in all its aspects, such as clothing, jewellery, make-up and beauty treatments. Literally, 'shringar' implied sensuality, sexual passion and eroticism,[103] and its power lay in stimulating desire. The word *alankrita* or adorned also implied 'mak[ing] ready or fit for a purpose'.[104] Shringar evolved into an art form, one that regarded the presentation of the body as a work of artistic expression, and a source of inspiration. Kama was not just about sex and aesthetics, but also about the beauty of ethics, inspiration, poetry, emotions, experience and expression. Copious works of sculpture and poetry were inspired simply by the act of women looking into mirrors as they dressed up. Even the arts were 'dressed up'. Indeed, the concept was applied to almost everything—poetry, dance forms, literary styles, sculpture and architecture. Poets often engaged in an ornate form of language involving puns, hyperbole, similes, antithesis and compound sentences to beautify their prose and enthral their listening audiences.[105]

However, surprisingly there were few variations in clothing styles. The basic garments were essentially the same for men and women: a lower see-through garment usually worn like a loin cloth, and an upper cloth, similarly diaphanous, sometimes draped across the chest and thrown over one shoulder, though both men and women often went bare-breasted. However, the scantiness of clothing was abundantly compensated by a spectacular array of jewellery. There were pieces for almost every conceivable part of the human body—from the top of the head, adorning the elaborate coiffeurs, to rings for different toes. There were even specifically designed necklaces that were meant to be worn to ornament naked breasts. People who could not afford gold ornaments usually wore silver, brass, glass or terracotta ones.[106]

Jewellery designs were exceedingly detailed, as were the various hairstyles, coiffeurs and hair ornaments. This was in sharp contrast to the simplicity of the clothing styles of this period. Most ornaments were made of precious metals like gold and silver, and various gems, including pearls. Each piece of ornament also had a name depending on the body part on which it was worn and the style of craftsmanship. Earrings, for example, ranged from the large, wheel-shaped *kundala* and the trumpet shaped *karnika* to the button-style *karnaphul*. Jewellery for other parts of the body included the *sitara*, a star-shaped gold or silver forehead ornament, the *haravsti*, a single-strand necklace of large pearls, the *kantha*, a short necklace consisting of pearls of graduating sizes, the *mekhala*, a seven-stringed girdle of gold chains interspersed with beads and precious stones, worn low at the waist, the *keyura*, a simple, flat armband, and the *kara* or heavy anklets.[107] The fashion dictates of this period seemed not to care much about swaddling the naked body with clothes, but were more enthusiastic about displaying the form and sensuality of the body's natural splendour by using minimal clothing and a profusion of jewellery.

The obsession with jewellery and hairdos appears to be a new development after the Vedic and Buddhist periods—artefacts from the Vedic period reveal only one piece of jewellery from the second century BC found at Taxila.[108] But more importantly, many of the sculptures from the Indus cultures as well as the Vedic scripts indicate a similar preoccupation of the Indus people with gold jewellery and hairstyles. This again is an indication of a resurgence of the indigenous groups into mainstream society and a restoration of their customs. It is possible that these cultures, as they existed on the fringes, might have continued to make ornaments throughout the Vedic and Buddhist periods, though in wood and clay, which then may have disintegrated over time.

Even soldiers in the golden period wore ornaments and make-up as they prepared to go to battle. Women would adorn themselves in their best clothes and jewellery and line the streets to see the armies off to war. It was believed that ornamentation actually imparted magical powers as well as luck, prosperity and protection on people and all things—including houses and streets.[109] When a bride and groom were donned from head to foot in jewellery, the bride was called *mangalakrita* 'made auspicious', and the groom *mangalamandanasri*. Coronation garments too were viewed as auspicious.[110] This most probably was an ancient indigenous belief, for the Vedics had observed that the tribals were often loaded with jewellery, which was supposed to give them supernatural powers.[111] It also guarded wearers against illnesses or helped to heal them; amulets were commonly worn for this purpose.[112]

During festivals, people would beautify themselves with ornaments, flowers and fine fabrics and decorate their streets and houses with paintings and coloured designs. According to the *shilpashastra*s, the formal guide books for architecture and sculpture, ornamentation of buildings brought prosperity and warded off evil and poverty. They listed eight auspicious carved objects to decorate the front door with: vines or creepers, water-filled pitchers, mirrors, elephants, horses, *gandharva* or forest spirits, the swastika and sculpted depictions of lovers. According to the kama sutras, attention to decor was an important aspect of civilized living, and a pleasant aesthetic environment created with flowers, rugs, cushions and small decorations would enhance the mood of love-making.[113]

Shringar was an important aspect of courting and unlike the Vedic times, when it was only a woman's job to adorn herself to keep her husband's libido alight, it was now a key important consideration for both sexes. It included hygiene, personality development, comeliness, ornamentation, clothing and aesthetic preferences—all as integral to the concept of fine living as to the notion of cultivated love-making.

Men aspiring to appear their best before their lovers were advised to brush their teeth and bathe regularly, as well as shave their underarms and use deodorants and mouth-fresheners.[114] In the evenings, men would dress up in silks and jewellery, and entertain their lovers in the company of friends, with music, entertainment and wine. Men would also organize group excursions to festivals or literary events or picnics for their lovers, as such social and cultural outings were regarded as proper and necessary to the development of a relationship.[115]

Both men and women also spent hours on their daily make-up, using a variety of products to enhance their looks. Herbs, roots and flowers were utilized for making an array of beauty products, such as creams, perfumes, eyeliners, lipstick and mascara.[116] Women also applied a certain type of red lac on their palms and the soles of their feet,[117] while henna was used for colouring and conditioning hair,[118] as it is today.

SEX AND THE CREATIVE DRIVE

Artists and artisans were another greatly revered section of society and were effusively patronized by the royal courts and ordinary citizens. Whenever they were commissioned for a certain project, they would first be honoured as guests at a special ceremony—perhaps to appeal for the blessings of the gods—before they started work. They were also well paid. One story narrates that a king was so pleased with a certain painter's creations that he gifted him ten villages. Renowned artists and artisans were also members of the royal assemblies of scholars, and would advise the king on matters relating to arts and aesthetics, and commissioned works for the palace and public places.[119] The evolution of the arts in this period—painting, sculpture, architecture, music and literature—was phenomenal and the formal styles that emerged were distinguished by the palpable influence of the sensually evocative social environment.

Besides the kama sutras, eroticism was a dominant theme in both the religious and the secular literatures in this period, some of which were explicit in their appraisal of sex and sexuality. Jayadeva's *Gitagovinda* in the twelfth century was an intensely sensual rendition of Lord Krishna's love affair with the much married Radha, and the public endorsement of this work is evident from the fact that over the next two centuries it gained widespread popularity in the Indian subcontinent, and was translated into many languages.[120] Like the other literary pieces of this period, *Gitagovinda* is resonant with sexual imagery that unrestrainedly evokes all the senses—sound, colour, aromas, touch and emotions—and is suffused with a melodic and seductive lyricism: 'My eyes close languidly as I feel the flesh quiver on his cheeks. My body is moist with sweat; he is shaking from the wine of lust . . . I murmur like a cuckoo; he masters love's secret rites. My hair is a tangle of wilted flowers; my breasts bear his nail marks.'[121]

In *Chandipucha Panchashika*, by Lakshmana Acharya, the magnificent beauty of the goddess Chandi's breasts are eulogized in fifty verses.[122] The sensual use of nature in imagery by numerous writers indicates a strong association between nature, spirituality and sexuality as perceived in this period.

Many writers like Bilhana also explored erotic themes in secular literature, indicating a general and unreserved embrace of sex in society. In Bilhana's *Chaura Panchashika* the hero while awaiting execution experiences a flashback of his entire life, set out in fifty verses, all giving detailed recollections of passionate sessions with his lover—the fragrances of saffron and musk on her body, her breath laced with camphor and betel nuts, their favourite positions of love-making, her expressions when she climaxed and her sexually aroused state whenever she woke up.[123] Perhaps because most writers were male, the feminine appears to be the primary muse in literature, although the description of male bodies could be just as sensual. One Vaishnava text gives a lengthy and extremely seductive portrayal of Krishna's physical appeal through the eyes of a woman: he has locks of curly, black fragrant hair, with bees droning around the flowers he wears as ear ornaments. His lips are red like the *bimba* fruit (Indian caper),[124] and his waist is like that of a lion's. He wears dazzling jewellery—bracelets, anklets and armlets.[125]

Similarly, sensual motifs were liberally used in the other arts—theatre, music, painting and sculpture. To speak of the sensuality of curved hips, draped in thin silks and jewelled belts, of breasts rubbed with smooth sandal paste and tresses bathed in perfume,[126] as the famous playwright Kalidasa did, was really to speak the language of the era. Even *raga*, a term used for the fundamental melodies in classical music, meant passion.

Theatre too in this period explored the motion of erotic love. Even the 'heroic' themes had erotic undercurrents.[127] Lust was candidly portrayed as an important element of personal relationships. In the play *Ratnavali* the narrator shows how the king, when he first encounters the heroine, is immediately aroused by her form, which he surveys in great detail: her large breasts, rounded hips and slender waist with three folds. Many theatrical works also treated sex-play as an engaging pastime. Sex was openly described in scripts as was the exhaustion of lovers after a particularly strenuous session. Perspiration, as large drops on the face during intercourse, was a common image, as were the nail and bite marks that women delighted in, the morning after, as 'marks of love'. Sexual role reversal, with women playing the dominant lover, was another favourite subject. Courtesans were sometimes portrayed as heroines, as in Charudatta's *Mrichchakatikam*, while the play *Malati-madhava* explored in intimate detail the sexual fantasies of unmarried girls from upper-class homes.[128]

The community staging of these plays was deemed perfectly respectable, and indicates an acceptance of sex as an issue of public interest and discourse. Among the most unabashed and public expressions of sexuality in this period were the erotic sculptures splashed all over temple walls. From about AD 100 to about 1500, a period of more than a millennium, there was an unabashed tendency to depict sex acts in temple architecture. Among these sculptures, which presented various positions in uninhibited detail, there were also portrayals of orgies, oral sex and bestiality. This trend was prevalent throughout the Indian subcontinent, and some of the relics are still standing in the states of Madhya Pradesh, Orissa, Gujarat, Maharashtra, Karnataka, Assam and Kashmir.[129]

Pairs of lovers, whether mounted on a temple wall or on the front door of a home, were such a common motif that there even was a term for it, *mithun*; if the portrayal was sexually explicit it was called *maithun*. The use of mithuns and maithuns, however, most likely dates back to pre-Vedic times when these were used as fertility symbols in tribal cultures. One of the earliest depictions of maithuns found in Daimabad, Ahmednagar district in western India, from around 700 BC is a crude caricature of two stick figures engaged in intercourse.[130] Also from around 700 BC are portrayals of couples having sex in five rock paintings discovered in Mysore's Kupgallu cave.[131] Though the ring-like vaginal and the phallic artefacts from the Indus period are not sculpted in conjunction, other portrayals (as discussed in Part I) clearly illustrated some sort of a sacred sexual union. For some reason, probably having to do with the Vedic sabotage and scattering of the indigenous cultures, many features associated with these cultures, including the mithuns, seem to have disappeared around 700 BC. However, these mithuns resurfaced again in a later period, between 300 BC and 120 BC, where the ring-stone artefacts clearly show a goddess figure with a male consort. Numerous terracotta plaques from about the same period depict couples engaged in sex. Among these are couples in the famously athletic positions, with the man below, balanced on his head, and the woman on top, that have become identified with the Indian temples of this period.[132] Various other features associated with the pre-Vedic indigenous cultures, such as the use of baked bricks in housing,[133] building of forts and reservoirs, and use of cesspits in sewage systems,[134] too began to reappear in some towns after 200 BC along with the mithuns, which once again indicates a resurgence of indigenous cultures and their ways and beliefs. It is unclear why this gap existed, but possibly some of the indigenous populations, including those that inhabited the towns of the Indus civilization, might have fled south and existed in smaller settlements. There is archaeological evidence, for instance, of a megalithic community in the south, at Mangadu, Kerala, that existed from 1000 BC to 100 BC, which covers the duration of this gap, and shares numerous features with the Indus Valley culture.[135]

By about AD 2, the representation of mithuns had become ritualistic and they began to appear on most temple constructions. No longer specific to tribal cults and ceremonies, the mithuns were held to be auspicious and their display was considered almost obligatory, regardless of religion and faith.[136]

For instance, mithuns were painted or sculpted on the walls of many Buddhist and Jain temples even though the fundamental ideologies of these religions rejected sensuality and sexuality. The Sanchi stupa is one example of a Buddhist monument with erotic depictions. In fact as the inscriptions suggest, some of the mithun carvings were donated by priests and nuns themselves.[137] However, we also see that the mainstream Buddhist leagues did not approve of these carvings.

Erotic depictions also appeared on mundane articles of personal use, mostly in urban centres; an ivory comb in Malwa of 50 BC bears a mithun motif and other similar commonplace artefacts with mithuns have been found.[138] Yet there was an obvious transformation in the forms of the mithuns sculpted after 100 BC. Till about this date, most sculptures were elementary and rustic in style, almost like caricatures, and perhaps were only symbolic of the male and female pairs they represented. The later ones, however, were more true to human form and also human experience with an emphasis on aesthetics and visual perception that strove for more than just symbolism. Not only were these sculptures lifelike in their rendition of the human body, capturing to perfection its contours and sometimes even depicting facial expressions in stone, but they also seemed to delight in human sensuality. The growth of artisan guilds and schools had allowed for extensive experimentation with new techniques in sculpting and some distinct, formal styles evolved. It is speculated that there was considerable Greek and Roman influence on the evolution of these styles, which would indicate an openness to learning through experience and contact with foreign cultures. In the aftermath of Alexander's invasion of north-west India, trade had steadily increased with the West and a great volume of Roman artefacts had flooded Indian markets.[139] There is also definite evidence from one trading centre of this period that local artists had imitated designs from imported Greek pottery,[140] and it is possible that sculptors did the same with their techniques. In fact, Buddhist sculptures, which are among some of the earliest examples of this new sculpting technique, depicted the Buddha and his disciples looking rather Apollo-like, with muscular physique and clothed in Roman togas.[141] Other figures were robed in the palliate, the Greek philosopher's wrap.[142] After Alexander's occupation of a part of northern India, numerous Greeks had settled down in India, adopted local religions and integrated into the caste system, and so the artisan guilds included some Greeks or their descendants. There are names of Greek artists on certain sculptural works, as in the decorations of King Kanishka's casket.[143] However, while Greek sculptures consisted mostly of statues, the Indian style showed a preference for relief carving with a three-dimensional effect when viewed from the front.[144] Indian sculptors also evolved a unique prototype and their human figures were stylized according to Indian body form and culture, including clothing, activities and ornamentation. For instance, Indian male representations were not muscularly well endowed, unlike those in Greece and Rome, where athletics and bodybuilding were obsessive pastimes.[145] Similarly, where the female bodies were quite ample and fulsome in Greek and Roman sculptures, in Indian sculptures they tended to be much slimmer and tauter.

The new Indian sculptures were clearly meant to be sensually evocative, as indicated by the portrayals of women in boudoirs, dressing up, doing their hair, gazing into a mirror or writing love letters, as well as those that showed couples drinking wine, or the portrayals of music and dance events. Some of these new-styled sculptures in temples now also illustrated the emotions involved in a couple's interaction. Couples were shown like never before, engaged in amorous embraces, flirting, kissing and engaging in foreplay. By AD 6, there was also a gradual movement towards the actual and realistic depiction of sexual intercourse in these temple sculptures.

These changes in sculptural techniques and in the subjects represented imply that there was an increasingly hedonistic acceptance of sex in society as also a more unabashed expression of it. This entailed a complete reversal of the taboos of the Buddhist period, but more importantly it also indicated a radical change in the concept of the sacred. Where the earlier representations of sexuality in religion reflected on ancient indigenous beliefs that associated fertility with the divine, divinity now included much more than just reproduction. Eroticism and sensuality in human relations were understood in greater depth and given their social acceptability, and were included in the sacred fold. A temple at Motap depicts an orgy in the presence of a goddess, with a music and dance concert going on simultaneously. Another temple at Pahavli bears a depiction of the god Ganesha with his consort, while a couple engages in sex, and musicians play on.[146] The dance and music repertoires performed by devadasis before the main altar in temples were sensual offerings to the gods as was the sex they provided within the temple complex. In fact, the temples themselves were believed to be sexual conceptions. The foundation ceremony of temples involved the impregnation of the earth's womb by a priest, and it was from this conjugation that the temple was said to be born.[147]

THE PSYCHOLOGICAL DIMENSION OF SEX

This age also developed a far more complex perception of sex than that of the ancient indigenous cultures, which related sex simply to the sacred powers of fertility. In all likelihood, this was the first time that the subject of sex was tackled from an ideological and psychological perspective as a human experience and a social issue.

Lust is not immoral, it was argued, but divine. How could it be immoral if it was a gift from the gods, the scriptures asked, as they went about setting the social rules for virtue, prosperity and sexual behaviour.[148] That such a point was categorically made indicates that it most likely was a repudiation of an older, Buddhist-influenced social attitude. It was candidly acknowledged that pleasure is obviously the most immediate goal of the sex drive.[149] Where the Vedic notion of kama was a woman dutifully offering her body to her husband to be able to bear his son, this goal was dismissed as archaic in the golden period. It was asserted that it was not for sons, but for the attainment of orgasms that both men and women had sex.[150]

It was also acknowledged that like with all animals, in humans too, the sex drive is inborn and does not need to be learned. But sex in humans was not just an instinct as in animals, and it was to understand these differences that people needed to study love-making both as an art and as a science.[151] This called for a radical redefinition of kama, and a more sophisticated vision of it. Now kama was no longer simply lust or sex, but was said to be the mind's complex aptitude to derive pleasure through the controlled stimulation of the senses of touch, taste, sight, smell and sound.[152] Thus an important component of sex was eros, which was the satisfaction of the five senses through training, learning and understanding.[153]

This systematic coaching of the body's five senses and awakening the brain's response to them was one of the stated principles of the science of love-making.[154] The kama sutras recommended that all students of the art of love-making should learn the sixty-four proficiencies, including vocal and instrumental music, dance with emphasis on body movements, expression and emotions, perfumery, cooking, winemaking, carpentry, language and riddles.[155] The emphasis, in effect, was on more than just training the five senses—it was also about improving physical and mental agility, as well as balance and posture, all of which would enable the brain to be acutely conscious of the sensations it was exposed to.

In the literary work *Nishadhacarita* by Shri Harsha, there is an elaborate description of the sex lives of the lover Nala and Damayanti. It was said that the couple engaged in sex night and day. The writer asserted that this did not sully them in any way, as their minds had been 'purified' by knowledge.[156] The implication was that, for Nala and Damayanti, sex was not an unthinking, animalistic act lasting for just a moment, but a deliberate one in full awareness of the body's own potential and the knowledge that allows for a prolonged and enjoyable exploration of it. This was a direct rebuttal of a basic Buddhist premise that the carnal experience impedes the attainment of the highest knowledge of nirvana by the mind. The concept that now emerged was that an enlightened mind also encompassed the most complete and non-destructive experience of physical pleasures.

There was also a heightened awareness of the cultural and personal dimensions of sex. With regard to sexual morality and ethics, there was a far more liberal and open approach than ever before. For instance, in the case of oral sex, where the Vedics believed that fellatio was immoral for a man because a woman's mouth was impure, one kama sutra author, Vatsyayana, argued that this was not so, as the woman's mouth was as clean as a new calf's mouth on its mother's teat. He also pointed out that while in some nations oral sex was not practised, in others it was perfectly normal. Individual choice, he emphasized, was the key, and ultimately it was up to people to follow their own inclinations and stay within the boundaries of what their partners too were comfortable with. Sexual morality was recognized as a relative concept that varied from culture to culture and mutual consideration for the needs of each partner would determine what was right in a given situation. The advice to people was to follow their own instincts and their customs, to respect their partner's wishes and to allow their fantasy free play.[157]

This psycho-sexual consideration in individual relationships extended to the choice of marriage partners as well. Marriage now was not simply about social fulfilment, but also about an individual's psychological growth, as well as emotional contact and connection with another individual. More radically, the idea of romance, of falling in love, was broached for the first time. So far, marriages essentially were social contracts to uphold caste and clan structures and procure heirs to perpetuate the family name. Some traditional forms of marriage even certified rape, kidnap and material transaction as means to a union. Marriage was also typically seen as a practical domestic arrangement for men to have their sexual and other needs met. However, in this period, the Gandharva form of marriage, where people chose their own partners, individuals they fell in love with or desired, was preferred over other types of marriages.[158] It was proclaimed that love is the goal of all human partnerships and that love marriages, even though they were not approved of by traditionalists, were better than all the other marriage arrangements.[159] It was argued that since love was the ultimate aim of every marriage, when partners chose each other out of mutual attraction, the relationship was already 'based on love'.[160] Young, unmarried couples who had already become sexually involved were urged to get married even if the man was still economically unstable; otherwise the girl would be forced by her family into a marriage not of her choice.[161]

As humdrum as the idea of romantic love may seem in the twenty-first century, and just as dreary the attempt of self-help gurus and agony aunts to uncover means to find an ideal partner, fourteen hundred years ago these ideas were quite a novelty, and not just in India but also in the rest of the world. In Europe marriages still were economic and social contracts and it would not be till at least another 700 years later, in AD 12, that the troubadours, the royal court poets, would introduce European society to the idea of romantic love and immortalize the legends of Romeo and Juliet, and Tristan and Isolde.

India wove a myriad folk tales of passion and pathos into its oral traditions: of Savitri hauling her husband, Satyavan, back to life from death's door, of the nymph Urvashi and the earthling Pururavas's yearning for each other across their irreconcilable worlds, of an unhappily married Radha stealing tender moments of fulfilment with her lover Krishna, and of Shiva, whose wife's death on being humiliated by her father enrages him so much that he dances with a fury that threatens to destroy the earth and alarms even the gods. These tales have survived over centuries through colourful narratives—village theatre, puppetry, poetry and song—and continue to engage people's imaginations even today.

With the acceptance of romantic love, marriage in India by the fifth century was no longer simply a tool for the procurement of sons. It was acknowledged as an emotional connection between two people that provided scope for the personal growth of each individual. The kama sutras observed that when a married couple shared common interests and pleasures, they 'enhance[d] each other's value'.[162]

This perception of an individual identity was yet another huge step in social development and the phenomenon of romantic love allowed for the concept of individuality to surface in the collective Indian consciousness. The idea that was gaining legitimacy was that people were not simply social constructs or functions of lineages and clans, but unique personalities, with their own psychological make-up and individual perspectives. Though caste and gender continued to typify a person's existence, an individual was recognized as being far more complex and unique. The nurturing of individualism occurred at many subtle levels in relationships.

Unlike the boorish Vedic era, when the concept of wooing a woman was limited to a man sexually earmarking her, courtship was an extremely important component of relationships in this period, attaining quite a degree of refinement. Men were advised to be attentive to the needs, interests and personality of the woman they desired and to try to understand her better through conversation.[163] They were advised to break the ice upon their first meeting with casual questions, and to attempt to gauge how the woman might actually feel about him before making a move—methods that are suggested even today, and are indicative of a sophisticated understanding of human psychology and individual behaviour.

Men and women also spent a good deal of time exploring each other's emotions by communicating their feelings through letters written on palm leaves and by talking 'endlessly', as well as sharing their dreams.[164] The sharing of dreams suggests that people were aware of an even deeper, more subconscious level of individual existence and its psychological play in relationships.

But perhaps the most crucial ramification of this burgeoning concept of individualism was the emphasis on fidelity and monogamy. Vedic societies were traditionally polygamous, and women in harems experienced tremendous emotional and sexual frustrations. Men were now urged not just to be monogamous but to assure their partners of their undivided love and their commitment.[165] The eighth-century author Damodaragupta, who was also the prime minister in the court of the king of Kashmir, wrote that when women felt unloved by their husbands and humiliated by their in-laws the emotional vacuum made them indifferent to customs and taboos as well as the honour of the family name, and compelled them to find other lovers.[166]

These avant-garde ideas—romantic love, individuality and monogamy—introduced a certain radical element into how people related to each other within society. Human relationships were no longer just an interaction of cohorts, of how a particular caste stood in relationship to others or how sect members were at variance with those of a rival sect. The individual now was an inescapable social parameter of how people construed their environment. And a person's individual behaviour, mannerisms, goals and philosophies had a much more significant role in determining social relationships. For now there was a more complex dimension to perceiving existence than just the consideration of 'us' versus 'them'; there was also 'I' and 'you'.

WOMEN ON THE WARPATH

Another important development that accompanied the changed attitude towards sexuality had to do with the social outlook on women. In an improvement over the earlier period, women now had some limited rights to worship and read sacred texts,[167] though it may have simply been a reinstatement of some of the rights they had in the Vedic period that were abolished during the Buddhist age.

There were even women writers, who usually wrote in Prakrit, and were sometimes consulted for a literary fee by their husbands or other male writers. Rajasekhara, a ninth-century scholar and dramatist, frequently quoted his wife, Avantisundari, referring to her views and suggestions. She too was a writer, and Rajasekhara had observed that there was no difference between the sexes when it came to the 'sensibility and sophistication' of writing styles. To make his point, he referred to numerous women writers, though mostly from the upper classes—royalty, or minister's daughters, and courtesans—whom he also commended for their vast knowledge of the scriptures. Many of these women scholars remain unexplored today, their works either lost or still undiscovered. Between 100 BC and AD 250 alone, at least 2381 works of poetry are known to have been composed by women.[168]

Widows too seem to have been socially better positioned now than in the Buddhist period. The custom of sati may have abated, for it appears that widows were now allowed to continue living. They might have even got some rights to property, which was widely acknowledged, especially between AD 900 and 1200.[169]

These changes in the status of women, however, were not as evident in the socio-political arena as they were in the redefinition of female sexuality and a greater allowance for its free expression, particularly through the emerging cults of goddess worship. Women in this period had far more personal liberties than ever before, which entailed a lot more freedom of movement. The bourgeois and upper-class women regularly attended concerts, soirees, and parties thrown for them by their suitors, where they freely socialized with other men as they all drank wine and made merry.[170] It was also acceptable and customary for lovers to hold their rendezvous in public places, as in art galleries and gardens. Nor was kissing and cuddling in public frowned upon.[171] Premarital sexual relationships for girls were not categorically forbidden, though the girls could ask their mates to marry them.[172]

It was not only that women had sexual freedom, but there was a validation of their right to its enjoyment. The idea, which in itself was radical, was that a woman was entitled to pleasure from sex as much as any man, and that she was not necessarily a sex toy for men or simply a baby-incubating machine.[173] In the poems of the *Vajjalaggam*, which portray the everyday lives of the people, a mother is shown comforting her daughter, who has been married off to an old man. She tells her daughter not to worry, as she will find plenty of young male lovers in the village, who could meet her in nearby fields or a temple hidden in a tree grove.[174] This forthright acknowledgment of a woman's sexual needs was one reason widows were allowed to remarry, even men below their caste, and they were considered to be reborn if they chose a man with a particularly strong sex drive. They could, however, satisfy their sexual urges even without remarrying, and they were permitted to work as prostitutes to support themselves.[175] However, later in this period, widow remarriage was once again banned.

Men on the other hand, through the study of the kama sutras, were expected to learn the subtleties of foreplay and be more sensitive to a woman's needs so that they would understand how to give her pleasure. The comprehension of female sexuality was extraordinarily progressive. Men were instructed that female orgasms differed from theirs in that it was not driven by ejaculation but by foreplay. It was also pointed out that women were repulsed by men who did not engage in foreplay but attacked them directly for sex, did not stop immediately if the woman was hurting and thought only of their own satisfaction by being totally inconsiderate by ejaculating early in the act. Women, it was explained, also needed prolonged physical contact after intercourse.[176] Men who did not understand all this, it was proclaimed, would never know how to satisfy a woman.[177]

There was much sympathy for women in harems, who were sexually frustrated either because the husband had too many wives or was intellectually and otherwise not stimulating or perhaps was repulsive to their wives because of bad body odour and other personal traits. In such situations, it was expected that women might satisfy their needs through other available means: lesbianism, fruit or vegetable dildos, adultery, liaisons with palace guards or priests sneaked into private chambers, or even with the sons of other queens.[178] Also, if women were sexually and emotionally dissatisfied, they had the moral sanction to leave their husbands.[179]

Like men, young girls, before marriage, studied the kama sutras, which enabled them to ascertain their sexualities, develop their capacity for physical and emotional pleasures, and learn of the intricacies of love-making. Traditionalists who questioned women's ability to learn the techniques of love-making were challenged, and it was asserted that if women could have sex they certainly could learn its theories as well. It was considered ridiculous that a woman should be expected to have sex before she had fully comprehended its processes and studied it to her satisfaction.[180] It was also argued that even after marriage, some women may still need to experiment with different men and sexual styles as married men often did.[181] Disagreeing with the traditional attitudes prevalent through both the Vedic and the Buddhist ages, where women were maligned as being adulterous by nature, a seventh-century philosopher, Varahamihira, argued that women could not be accused of any flaws based on gender bias, even though men thought they were far more virtuous than women.[182] The poet Vidyapati composed more than 500 love songs, and in his poem 'A Bending Lotus' had a radical suggestion to offer—unless a young woman had known 'rapture outside [her] marriage' with at least five other lovers besides her husband, she knew 'nothing of love'.[183] Extramarital affairs for men, however, were justified for other reasons: for gaining wealth, for accessing the political power of another woman's husband, or for an introduction to a friend of the woman he had an affair with.[184]

Where in the Vedic culture women's sexuality was viewed as being frightening and vile, something that had to be contained, restrained and punished, in this era there surfaced a newer and far more liberal attitude. A woman's sexuality was accepted as not merely powerful, but also evocative and inspirational. Symbolically, it was often held on a par with nature and this was specifically so in the literary portrayal of nature as female. Analogous sensual depictions were attributed to both women and nature and both were held to be the ultimate source of power and existence. Thus the change in attitude to the feminine was accompanied by a new vision of the natural world.

Many writings of this period were eulogies of the sensuality and sacred powers of the feminine. A rain-bearing sky was seen as glowing in places like the breasts of a pregnant woman.[185] The night was compared to an adolescent girl, who, as she grew up, struggled to realize her womanhood in endeavouring to free herself; the moon and its phases were the girl's face and expressions, and the clouds were the obstacles that surrounded her.[186] The golden bells on the feet of a girl rang like the passionate cries of lusting geese.[187] Rivers turgid with rainwater rushed to the seas like aroused women ran to make love, felling the trees that came in their way.[188] Young women driven by passion would leave their houses to spend the night in the arms of their lovers,[189] and after a passionate bout of love-making would be so exhausted, their thighs would ache, their lips would be sore, and it would hurt to laugh.[190] The impressions conveyed in these literary works was that a woman's sexuality followed its own course, like nature, and demanded freedom and expression.

This empathetic view of nature and women was contrary to that of the Vedics, who perceived of themselves as dichotomized from and pitted against women and the feminine forces of the natural world that they had to seek the assistance of the gods, through fire ceremonies, to control nature's might.

Women, however, were now encouraged to learn the kama sutras not merely for their personal benefit but also to augment their social status, so that important public figures like kings and ministers would praise them and seek their company, and they could have the choice to marry into the wealthier sections of society. It was also suggested that it would also aid women to be economically independent and earn a living anywhere, even in a foreign country.[191]

Most probably, it was this recognition of a woman's rights to sexual fulfilment and choice that made rape no longer socially permissible, even for kings, as it had been even in the Buddhist period. Rapists were regarded with scorn and mistrust. Men were warned against rape, and historical figures, such as kings and nobles who used it as weapons of power but eventually met with tragic ends, were held up as examples of the calamity that struck rapists.[192] Though marriage by social management or abduction was still recognized as valid, the kama sutras focused on courtship—a relatively new concept. Now if a man was interested in a woman, he had to learn to woo her by understanding her, observing her personality as well as her likes and dislikes and watching for signs of interest and consent on her part.

There was also a revision of certain taboos and associations with regard to feminine sexuality. Earlier, right through the Buddhist period, menstruation was regarded as a filthy, evil and destructive force, and women were completely shunned and socially isolated during their periods. Their husbands avoided not only sex, but even talking to them. However, sex with a menstruating woman was now no longer taboo and the kama sutras even discussed fellatio as a possible alternative to conventional sex for the duration.[193] In fact, in certain cults menstrual blood was revered as powerful and symbolic of life. A cloth stained with menstrual blood would be deified at the altar and worshipped or donned as a symbolic mantle of power by authoritative figures, such as the king of Kashmir. In temples in Kamakhya and Travancore, the goddess's menstrual period would be ritually celebrated.[194]

Other developments in literature and theatre included new portrayals of femininity that to a certain degree challenged the collective male ego. In the play *Raghuvamsham* (Raghu's Dynasty), the dynasty of Raghu met its tragic end with its last king, who was not just a hedonistic, self-serving ruler, but was so pompous that he would extend his foot over the palace balcony so his subjects could pay homage to it. Upon his demise, it was decided that his pregnant queen was the best choice as successor.[195] The idea of having a woman as supreme monarch, as well as breaking ranks with a patriarchal lineage, was radical.

Unmarried women who got pregnant did not have to claim that the sun and wind gods were the fathers of their illegitimate children, as Vedic women did, but instead would demand responsibility from the concerned man, as was done in the play *Abhijnanasakuntalam* (The Recognition of Shakuntala). Shakuntala, a young tribal woman, was seduced by a king who was hunting near her home in the woods. When she discovered she was pregnant, she went to his palace and reminded him of their Gandharva wedding in the forest and laid claim to her rightful place as his wife. The Gandharva wedding was a promise of mutual commitment that two lovers informally made to each other, simply by exchanging garlands with only the gandharvas or heavenly nymphs as witnesses. The king had a convenient memory lapse and refused to acknowledge Shakuntala, accusing her of being cunning. She then confronted him, describing him as shallow as a 'well covered with grass', hypocritical and arrogant in thinking that he alone was the measure of righteousness, when actually he was only pretending to be so. She also rebuffed him, saying that she would not stoop to his level.[196]

In terms of organized religion, however, these neo-feminist philosophies materialized in the form of the powerful Shakta cults. The Shaktas were worshippers of 'Shakti'—the personification of power as feminine, as in a goddess. Displacing the Vedic notion of the formidable masculine pantheon, the central deity now was a goddess. Though there were diverse forms of the goddess, they were all believed to be from a single divine female source.

There is strong evidence that this cult of goddess worship that continues as a strong tradition in India, originated in the pre-Vedic, indigenous cultures.[197] Coins of the Gupta dynasty from the fourth century bear the image of the goddess riding on a tiger,[198] reminiscent of the Indus Valley seals that depict the union of the Divine Mother and Divine Father in the merging of a woman and a tiger.[199] There are other associations: for instance, the headless Chhinnamasta, patron goddess of certain Indian tribes today, can be traced back to a headless goddess relic found in Bhilwalli in Madhya Pradesh and in Inamgaon in Maharashtra from pre-Indus times.[200] Another feature of the Shakta cult, the worship of the vulva as an icon, which continues to the present day at the Kamakhya temple in Assam, is probably from the pre-Indus times. This is evidenced from the discovery of numerous nude goddess figures from about 1200 BC that have their thighs splayed wide apart and the vulva conspicuously displayed. These goddess idols came into vogue again around AD 200 during the emergence of the Shakta cults.[201]

The triangle is yet another symbolic form of the goddess that represents her sexuality and its powers. The deities Bahuchara and Ambika in the present day are worshipped in the form of triangles,[202] but the earliest of such triangular representations was the one found in Madhya Pradesh, which dates to the period between 8000 BC and 10,000 BC.[203]

Although evidence supports the prevalence of a dominant Divine Mother goddess figure in the Indus civilization, goddesses in general were sidelined as consorts and assumed to be secondary to the male gods in the patriarchal Vedic and Buddhist eras. As discussed earlier, the Vedics did acknowledge these goddesses of tribal origins as powerful and formidable. They believed the 'demon' goddesses had the ability to cause them great harm and, therefore, appeased, them with an obsequiousness that they did not show even towards their own goddesses. Nonetheless, these indigenous goddesses were not included in the vanguard of the prominent male gods of the Vedic pantheon, and were evoked only in certain magical ceremonies. In the golden period, however, the tribal goddesses materialized in their full potency in a mainstream movement—that of the Shakta cult—that spread throughout the Indian subcontinent.

The religion of the Mongoloid tribes of the north-east, who were sometimes referred to in the Puranas as Pragjyotisha, was believed to be one of the main arteries of the Shakta movement in this period.[204] The Pala dynasty of AD 12 was instrumental in the spread of the Shakta cult in northern India.The Palas controlled Bengal and Bihar in the east and, as the legend goes, each time a new king was elected to the throne, he would get killed by demons. Finally, the goddess Chandi was approached and she offered her protection to the dynasty. The Palas lived on and expanded their power to Varanasi in the north, never forgetting to honour their patron goddess by ensuring she was worshipped all through their kingdom.[205]

Of immense social significance was the fact that at the very core of the Shakta philosophy lay the seeds of a feminist rebellion. The Shakta goddesses revolutionized the concept of the feminine in India, turning the Vedic male version of it upside down. These goddesses were often immodest, blatantly sexual, unashamedly naked, demanding, sometimes old and decidedly unattractive, and even defiantly dishevelled. They seemed to unequivocally rebuff the bovine placidity of the Vedic goddesses, being invincible warriors who could destroy as adeptly as they could create. Fundamentally, there was a face-off between the earlier dominant male sexuality and the new revolutionized female one.

Female sexuality was not just candidly but often aggressively expressed. It was touted as more than just the power of the feminine to create. The goddess did not even need a male to create a child—the elephant-headed god Ganesha, for instance, was created by his mother, Parvati, simply from the dirt that sloughed off her skin. In another tale, the goddess Ammavaru created the three most powerful male gods from three eggs that she produced.[206] It was now the goddess who granted men their sexual functions. It was not only mortal males that she bestowed with virility, but also the male gods, including the most powerful—Shiva, Vishnu and Brahma. It was said that without her aid they would all be impotent.[207]

It was believed that the goddess was sexuality incarnate. She possessed names like Kamya (desired), Rati (sexual intercourse), Mohini (enchantress) and Kamarupini (the form of sexual desire). It was even said that she was the one who gave the god of love, Kama, his power of awakening desire in humans and that, if she so desired, she could rejuvenate a shrivelled, old impotent man and grant him such sexual prowess that women would drop their girdles and clothes and chase after him.[208] Consequently, the expression of lust, erotic songs and dances and the repeated chanting of words like 'penis' and 'vagina' were regarded as a requisite aspect of goddess worship, as deference to her.[209]

An insatiable lover, the goddess was demanding with the men she opted to be with. However, the issue of her choice was crucial. Often she broke social parameters of caste and clan to be with a lover she desired. The goddess's assertion to her right to choose her sexual partner was not about upholding the traditional framework of society, but about satisfying her individual needs.

According to the sacred legends, both Radha and Sati, in choosing their respective mates, violated revered conventions of caste, class and decorum. Radha, a married woman of a noble clan, fell in love with the dark-skinned, low-caste cowherd god Krishna. This sacred but illicit relationship inspired the creative minds of this period, resulting in a flood of poems that dallied with the secret possibilities that this liaison offered. The *Rasikapriya* explores the various places and ways in which the lovers would meet: in the homes of servants, abandoned houses, the forest, at a festival, using the ploy of an invitation, or an illness so Krishna could be summoned to cure Radha.[210] Bold and wilful, she cared little about the need to hide her affair, and lamented her incompatibility with the man she had actually been married to. She was so adamant about her relationship with Krishna that she declared that love had its own rules, and that for him she would be willing to set fire to her house and leave.[211] In bed with Krishna she often initiated 'a bold offensive', climbing astride him, panting and triumphant in love by the show of her 'manly force' or her dominance over him.[212]

In the story of Sati and Shiva, Sati, a Brahmin girl, fell in love with the god Shiva who was representative of the Chandalas, the lowest and most despised outcastes. With his dark skin, his long, matted hair, his association with dogs and snakes, his rustic lifestyle in the forest and his habit of roaming half-naked on cremation grounds, Shiva was considered most unworthy of Sati's father's noble clan and was rejected by her family. Despite being ostracized by her family, Sati went ahead and married the man she loved.

The concept of the eternal love of this couple in the face of all social barriers was romanticized in the sequel to Sati and Shiva. When Sati died, it was said that she was reborn as Parvati and sought Shiva for a partner once again. This time, Shiva was much too engrossed in his meditation to notice her. Parvati pursued him with a single-minded resolve, matching his willpower with her own—sitting on fire in summer, going naked in winter, subsisting on leaves and air, and balancing on one leg for years. At one point she even recruited the love god Kama to pierce Shiva with one of his passion arrows to awaken his desire for her. Though even that did not work, she managed to attract Shiva and they eventually married. When they set up their home in the Himalayas, the legend goes, they shared an intense sexual chemistry, engaging in sex for such prolonged periods of time that they would cause seismic disturbances in the cosmos, which terrified the gods.[213]

The goddesses also demanded full accountability from philandering husbands despite the fact that some, like Radha for instance, themselves had extramarital affairs. When Lord Vishnu had a relationship with another woman, his wife locked him out of the house and wrecked his transportation, a flying chariot.[214]

The question of a woman's choice, however, was even more important where the age-old custom of rape or marriage by rape was concerned. No longer was a woman a man's privilege to take as and when he willed, as it had been right up to the Buddhist age. The goddess dealt with would-be rapists with a devastating vengeance. So far, muscle power had been solely a male quality and it was what made rape permissible. It was most unsettling for the older male vanguard to witness the goddess flaunting her insurmountable skills as a warrior; she could certainly battle with a vengeful intensity. Even more emasculating to the patriarchal order was the fact that the goddess's battalion consisted entirely of female warriors. More telling though was how all the enemies that she battled and defeated were most perceptibly male. She would lure men who initially had intended to make a sexual conquest of her into battle, laying down her defeat as the precondition to her submission. Her opponents, of course, would regard the outcome of battle with a woman as ridiculously predetermined. But then she would repel their advances, hurling curses at them and vowing to rip them to pieces, which eventually she would do after a bloody battle.[215] She would then decapitate her enemies and wear their heads in a victory garland around her neck.

Recognizing her supremacy as a warrior, armies made her their patron saint, invoking her help before wars by worshipping her in the form of a sword. This practice is followed even today by the Indian military. The goddess had to be appeased with the blood of animals sacrificed to her and, curiously, the sacrificed animals were always male. The manner of the offering implied humility: after beheading the animal, its legs would be pushed into its mouth, its eyes smeared with its stomach fat and a candle lit on its head.[216] This was a symbolic acknowledgment of male submission to the sacred power of the feminine, though some ancient texts also spoke of human sacrifices, and certain temples for the goddess had posts for hanging human heads.[217]

Not only was the female no longer an object of sexual conquest for men but the notion that femininity was to be aesthetically pleasing for men's sexual stimulation was also challenged. The goddess defied earlier notions of femininity by assuming all the characteristics that had been traditionally rejected in women. She did not always have to be fair, young, curvaceous, beautiful and submissive, for she now assumed forms, such as that of the goddess Kali, where she would be old, dark and gaunt, with shrunken, pendulous breasts, claw-like thin hands and wild, dishevelled hair. She would have none of the features—rounded hips and sensual breasts—associated with fecundity. A macabre garland of human heads hung around her neck, blood was smeared on her lips from drinking it and snakes were draped as bracelets on her wrists. When she had sex with her husband Shiva, she preferred to assume the dominant top position.

The idea was that even in her most repulsive and terrifying form, the goddess was sacrosanct. The Shakta movement proclaimed all femininity to be sacred, a strongly feminist statement that was an outright challenge to the Vedic scheme that itemized and appraised women in context of use. In fact, the Shaktas shook up the very foundation of the Vedic perception of social order by challenging even the caste system. The goddess was now worshipped in all human forms that previously had been discarded from society and dissociated from the divine. While the goddess could be enchanting, she could just as well be hideous. She could bestow protection and wealth, but she could also be destructive and become an evil spirit. She could be young and vivacious, but she could also be old and wrinkled. She could be as fair as a million suns and or as dark as a moonless night. She could belong to any caste, even the lowest; she could be a milkmaid and a common cleaning woman. She could be a woman with an insatiable sex drive, demanding to be satisfied.[218]

The goddess's supremacy was incontestable. In fact, she replaced both the mighty Brahma and Shiva as the supreme deity. One particular image that characterized this idea showed the goddess seated on a throne, the legs of which were the main male deities—Brahma, Shiva and Vishnu.[219] She was regarded as so immense that it was said that the male trilogy of gods was only the water contained in a cow's hoof-print, while the goddess was the sea.[220]

She surpassed gods in all the tasks that, traditionally, were done by the three powerful male gods—creation, destruction and sustenance—and did them single-handedly. That is why the goddess was often symbolized in turns by a line, a circle and a triangle. During her creation phase she was a triangle, during preservation, a straight line, and during destruction she assumed the form of a circle.[221]

The most graphic representation of this triple power of the goddess to create, sustain and destroy was illustrated in the goddess Chhinnamasta, one of the ten goddesses known as the Mahavidyas (the Great Revelations). Though she emerged in the Shakta period, she continues to be worshipped by certain tribes and is often depicted in Mithila folk art. In illustrations, Chhinnamasta is shown as having decapitated her own head, which she holds up on a platter with one hand with the weapon in her other hand. From the stump of her neck gush three streams of blood—one stream enters her own mouth in her decapitated head, while the other two streams enter the mouths of two people standing nearby. Below Chhinnamasta's feet are the love god Kama and his consort Rati having sex on a lotus bed, with Rati on top. This entire scenario is placed against the backdrop of a cremation ground.[222]

Here in one graphic image Chhinnamasta encompasses creation, as depicted by the copulating couple she stands on top of; destruction, as depicted in the cremation ground as well as her own beheading; and sustenance, symbolized by the act of feeding her own blood to herself and to others.

This aspect of the goddess signalled an important breakthrough in the collective consciousness. Earlier, creation, destruction and sustenance were perceived as fragmented processes, each assigned to a different male god. The tasks also typified the innate nature of each god: the assumption was that their diverse personalities were suited to different functions. So the creator Brahma, wise and stable, was quite incapable of being destructive, the way the destroyer Shiva, who was vagrant and temperamental, could be; hence Brahma was the creator and Shiva the destroyer. Now the goddess figure was an affirmation of the unity of nature and all its powers, be it creative, sustaining or destructive. This established the premise that the source of all existence is one. The very power that gives birth also nurtures and kills in turn. Shiva himself was believed to have acknowledged the goddess's supremacy in this respect, saying that where Time was the supreme devourer of everything, the goddess could devour Time itself. She was the Ultimate, the one source of all existence and non-existence. For she was neither male nor female. She had form and yet was formless and even as one figure she could appear as many and diverse.[223] It was this recognition that instigated a change in the perception of human society of itself.

Indeed, if the source of all life and its processes was one, it was meaningless to segregate humans along lines of caste and creed, as the Vedic sacred order dictated. The goddess cult was not just a breaking of the gender barrier but the caste and class barriers too. The symbolic assertion of this was in the inter-caste relationships of Radha and Krishna, and Sati and Shiva, and in the affirmation of the goddess being sacrosanct in any human form, irrespective of caste, class and occupation, even that of the lowest and most ostracized, the slave class. No longer segregated from the sacred precept, they too were a manifestation of the divine like the Vedic Brahmins.

It is also likely that matriarchal communities were prevalent in the regions associated with the Shakta cults. The diaries of Chinese travellers, such as Xuanzang, and the Greeks who travelled through India tell of kingdoms that were ruled by women.[224] In the tale of Chitrangada from the Mahabharata, one of the protagonists, Arjuna, a prince from the north, marries the daughter of a tribal king from Manipur in eastern India, a region where women are said to be unconventional and strong. Chitrangada is described as being plain and unfeminine, preferring to wear men's clothing, and a skilled warrior who held a very poor opinion of men's aptitude in warfare. Chitrangada's family raises the couple's child, as she herself stays on in Manipur to help her father rule the kingdom, while Arjuna returns to his home.[225] While there were some queens who were token heads of state, such as Prabhavati Gupta of the Vakataka period in AD 4 and the Chalukya queens, there were others who were powerful monarchs. In tenth-century Kashmir, there were at least two such queens, Didda and Sugandha. And like their male counterparts, they too had to protect their powers by tactically thwarting court intrigue and political rivals.[226]

With the establishment of the Shakta cult, there also emerged a pronounced split along the lines of gender in the collective social psyche. This was apparent in the conflicting versions of myths that tried to ascertain whether the male preceded the female or the female the male in the origin of creation. The Shaiva or Shiva-worshipping cults proclaimed that Parvati emerged from Shiva, after which sexual reproduction became possible, whereas the Shakta cults insisted on just the reverse, that it was Shiva who was given birth by the goddess.[227] The argument of the superior creator is elaborated in a Khond myth. The story goes that when the earth goddess was married to the sun god, her husband wished to create man and vegetation. She forbade him but he took his sweat and threw it on his creations. The goddess responded by inflicting death and diseases on her husband's creations in an attempt to destroy them. The god and goddess then entered into a fierce battle that raged through the earth, sky and waters as they attacked each other with meteors and lightning. In the end the myth is uncertain about who actually won.[228] Temples that were built in honour of male gods were constructed with barriers to obstruct the goddess Kali, who was associated with death and viewed as an evil force, from entering from any side.[229]

It appears that the Shakta cult's aim to establish female dominion possibly had its roots in a subconscious social perception as recorded in numerous legends—the anguish of women caused by the abuse and betrayal of men. In the story of the goddess Ammavaru, the goddess produced three eggs, which hatched into the gods Brahma, Vishnu and Shiva. To sustain creation she then desired to procreate with her three sons, but two of them refused. Shiva agreed on the condition that she would donate her middle eye to him. She did so, only to later realize that she had given away her power to him.[230]

Though the Shakta movement was a necessary psychological counterbalance to the male order, it also represented the chauvinism of the old patriarchal religions. In certain legends, the goddess went so far as to reverse the sexual dominance of men by treating men in the same way women were mistreated during the Vedic age. For the goddess, men were objects she could select and she was entitled to whomever she desired. Incest was her privilege even if her sons were unwilling, just as Aditi, the daughter of the Vedic god Daksha, was repulsed by her father's sexual advances, but had to submit to him in compliance with the sacred laws. In the Ammavaru myth, the goddess, discontented because there was no man to 'satisfy' her lust or 'please' her, propositions each of her three sons. Infuriated when Brahma and Vishnu refuse her, she reduces them to ashes. Like the Vedic gods, the Shakta goddesses too dominated people, using violence and intimidation. The goddess not only has the human race quaking at her powers, but also warns her sons that the power of the 'worlds' was in her 'hands', and that nobody was 'greater' than she was.[231] In the same way as their male predecessors, the Shakta goddesses too demanded absolute power. Between these two furiously opposed camps—one male-dominated and the other female—a torque was set up that essentially tore at the foundation of the collective social psyche.

This split was to be healed through another massive cult movement that emerged in this period, one that had its roots in the Shakta cult. This was the Tantra movement.

TANTRA: UNDOING THE DUALITY

Unlike the Shakta and other tribal cults of this period, Tantrism first emerged as a formal philosophy, as an organized body of research and thought, long before it burgeoned into a popular cult. The evolution of the Tantric theories was complex and accommodated the input of Ayurveda—the science of formal medicine—as well as other fields of study that today might be classified as alchemy, physiology, chemistry, biophysics and kinetic physics.[232]

The Tantric movement is believed to have originated between AD 4 and AD 7. The earliest sects had arisen in the indigenous or artisan communities. In Orissa, for instance, Tantra was known as

Savari vidya (knowledge of the Savara tribals). Kunjika Tantra was said to have originated in the potter community, while Mahesvara Tantra was from the cult of washermen.[233]

Essentially, Tantra articulated in a coherent, cohesive theory what the other cults of this period had been attempting to proclaim through beliefs and customs, namely, that the body was not a source of sin but an aspect of the sacred and could actually serve as a vehicle to salvation.

The basic Tantric theory stated that the mind, or consciousness, was represented as Shiva whereas the body, or matter, was represented as Shakti. The key to salvation was in the perfect union of Shiva and Shakti, or the mind and the body. Tantrism aimed to resolve not only the contentions of the mind–body dichotomy, but also the wide gender split apparent in the philosophies of existent cults. Most Tantric cults regarded Shiva and Shakti as co-creators, and it was said that Shakti as matter, the female principle, was the 'mirror' in which Shiva as consciousness, the male principle, was reflected. Mirror images of each other, the mind reflected matter, and vice versa. From a social and psychological standpoint, this was the first time that a religious theory symbolically regarded the male and female as two absolute equals.

Central to Tantric knowledge was the perception of seven main energy centres in the human body. Called the *chakra*s (wheels), they were often represented by a lotus that lay along the central axis—the spinal cord of the human body—from the top of the head to the coccyx. Each chakra was representative of the cosmos and was of a specific colour, sound and form. Symbolically, this conveyed that the human body was a replica of the universe and all its elements, including the continents, oceans, mountains, planets, stars, the sun, moon, fire, water and ether, and all their processes.[234] This perhaps was better explained by a major school of Kashmiri Tantrism which proposed that the entire existence, including humans, was made of thirty-six elements that have all 'evolved' from a single 'ultimate reality'. This idea is reflected, in a way, in modern science, which postulates that certain fundamental building elements like carbon, sulphur, oxygen, nitrogen and hydrogen are found in all matter.

It has often been suggested that the word 'Tantra', which means 'string' or 'thread', implies the tension in the body that is like a high-strung wire before nirvana is attained. However, more interestingly, the word 'Tantra' also represents the nervous system, and the word 'tantrika' means a nerve.[235] Some studies have observed that the Tantric chakras correspond closely with the major nerve plexuses in the body,[236] each chakra being associated with specific bodily functions. A study in 1985, which used bio-energetics, contended that electric currents could be used to identify the chakras as discernible energy centres in the human body.[237]

In the Tantric theory, six of the seven chakras were said to be located in the body along the spinal alignment and represented Shakti or matter. The seventh chakra was placed in the cranium and was representative of Shiva or the mind, also called pure consciousness. Known as the Sahasrara chakra, it was depicted as a thousand-spoked wheel or a thousand-petalled white lotus.

The energy of Shakti, known as Kundalini or serpent power, was always dormant and in its resting stage lay coiled like a serpent around the chakra at the base of the spine. The Kundalini chakra, also known as the Muladhara chakra, was often illustrated as a four-petalled crimson lotus. When sex was performed according to strict Tantric guidelines, the serpent power was aroused from its dormant state in the coccyx, and travelled up the spine with tremendous energy, forcing open all the other chakras until it finally entered the cranium and united with the seventh and highest chakra. This union of Shiva and Shakti (mind and matter) was experienced as an intense orgasm or sometimes multiple orgasms.

This phenomenal orgasm known as *Maha-Sukha* or *Ananda*, 'supreme bliss', symbolized the attainment of nirvana.[238] It was said that during the experience of supreme bliss, individuals would lose consciousness of their separateness from their partner, as well as the divisions within themselves of their own mind and body. Where in Buddhist sects, nirvana could be attained only after death, this Tantra-induced bliss was the earthly, living experience of nirvana: a powerful state where the individual entered an altered state of reality in which he or she could see through all dualities and contradictions, and recognize that ultimately everything was from one source.[239] As explained by a tenth-century Tantrik guru, Abhinav Gupta, the ultimate aim of Tantra was the awakening of one's own basic nature which is the source of *shuddha vikalpa* (clear perception). It was what allowed the initiate to experience *nirdvanda* or that state which is 'beyond all dualities'.

The argument of Tantra was that a person in search of spiritual salvation could not reject the physical aspects of existence, because there was no division between body and soul. This perceived dichotomy was actually an illusion, which results from a state of ignorance. Similarly, all other dualities or contradictions that we perceive with our minds—as in 'I' versus 'you', sacred versus sinful, high versus low, birth versus death, and mortal versus immortal, among others—were all deceptive and the result of ignorance. In the state of nirvana, ignorance was dispelled by the knowledge or 'clear perception' that, all things considered, contradictory or divided were essentially one and the same. The highest realization was that the self and the ultimate reality, otherwise called the divine, or God, were also indistinguishable.[240]

Tantra's rituals, therefore, were meant to affirm the physical experiences of existence, including sex, in spirituality. One Tantric text called the human body 'the best possible life form' and a 'gift' that is the means to salvation.[241] It pointed out how an individual would not be able to comprehend the purpose of his or her life or even the meaning of salvation without a body. It affirmed that everything a human life conceptualized, even seeking the 'truth', required the body. Therefore, the body had to be revered, nurtured and protected from all diseases and harmful factors. Another Tantric text, confirming the same idea, added that for an 'ignorant person' the body may seem the cause of suffering, but to the wise it was the font of 'infinite delights'. It was because the body brought untold joys through the senses and enabled relationships through human contact that it was possible to endure the sorrows of life.[242]

As much as this may have appeared to be a negation of the Buddhist concept of salvation, in effect it really was an extension of it. Where the Buddha had argued that it was possible to eat without creating a desire for food, the Tantrics extended this argument to all other physical functions, including sex. Their concept was that all sensory functions could simply be a technical aspect of existence as the body itself was, and could be, engaged in the task of salvation without the experience of pleasure or addiction to the sensory. Contrary to Buddhism, however, Tantra regarded the sensory organs as tools and not impediments, which could be used, through stimulation, to achieve that ultimate orgasm which signalled the living experience of nirvana.

In Tantric rituals, therefore, sensory experiences would be heightened through the use of mercury and mica, which were also said to make the body indestructible. It was believed that mercury was Shiva's sperm, and mica, Shakti's eggs, and when the two united, they could convert any metal to gold and make people immortal. Many Tantric practices originated in the Shakta cults, and one of these was the worship of the vulva, which preceded sexual intercourse. It was recommended that nine types of women, between the ages of twelve and sixty, married and single, but post-pubescent, with 'hair-adorned' vulvas could serve as an 'altar'. The adoration of the vulva was like that of most other puja ceremonies where offerings of sandal paste and flowers were made, and it would eventually culminate in actual intercourse.[243]

There were five sensory acts that were integral to this ritualized pathway of sex and were carried out in a thoroughly controlled and procedural manner. This was meant to arouse the devotees gradually, almost like foreplay, to build up to the final orgasm during intercourse. However, it was absolutely essential that the devotee remained completely detached from the process and derived no emotional nor conscious pleasure from it. Known as the *panchamakara*s, the sensory acts included five taboo activities: eating fish, eating meat, consuming alcohol, assuming *mudra*s, or ritual hand gestures, and intercourse. Numerous yoga postures too were incorporated.[244]

Twenty passages for sensory perceptions and information were identified in the human body. These passages were known as *jnana indriya* the 'powers of cognition'. They included those of smell, taste, sight, touch, hearing and speech, as well as the hands, feet, anus and genitals. All the Tantric rituals, including alcohol consumption, meat-eating and sex, were in effect stimulations for the opening of these passages. The sense perceptions, once received by the body, were then used by the 'I' factor of the mind to form 'whole concepts and images'. The 'I' factor was defined as that aspect of the mind that perceived existence on a limited basis as an external objective reality such as 'I am' or 'I have' or 'I see'. However, the higher plane of the mind, called *shuddha vidya* or pure knowledge, in the state of nirvana, was clearly able to recognize that this perceived polarity of 'I', the subject, from the external object, though at one level palpable, was, in fact, a delusion that quintessentially, both subject and object were indeed of a single reality.[245]

The crucial difference between the Buddhist and Tantric concept of nirvana was that the Buddhists believed that worldly existence and the sensory experience of it was an illusion, while Tantrism regarded the dichotomy between the worldly and the sacred, the physical and the spiritual, and existence and non-existence as illusory. In Tantrism, all things that appeared to be in conflict would be eventually recognized as originating from a single source—and it was the knowledge and experience of this state of non-duality that was nirvana.

Since salvation was the state of being mentally and physically free of all dichotomies, Tantra also regarded social divisions of caste, class and gender as illusive and resulting from ignorance. It was similarly dismissive of various religious taboos regarding sex, alcohol and meat-eating. In one Tantric text, Shiva proclaimed that a man from even the lowest, dog-eating caste who possessed the Tantric knowledge of the Shakti goddess was superior to the Brahmin.[246] As such, membership to the Tantric cults was open to all genders, castes and classes.

Tantric ceremonies were usually held in cremation grounds or isolated mountain caves. Practising groups usually involved equal numbers of men and women of a mixture of class and caste. A *yantra* or sacred diagram to invoke the god or goddess who would preside over the ceremony would be drawn on the ground and the devotees would sit in a circle around it. The women would disrobe and place their clothes in a container and each of the men would pick one. That decided the sexual partners for the evening.[247] This random selection of partners was not only meant to dissuade the emotional bonds that form between regular partners or people sexually attracted to each other, but was also a means to emphasize the purely technical aspect of the senses and the ritualistic experience of sex without personal attachments.

To break the illusion of social constructs in some ceremonies, partners would be chosen in a manner that deliberately overrode taboos. For instance, a chosen partner could be a neighbour's spouse, or a member of a forbidden caste. Certain Tantric cults like the Kapalikas (Skull-heads) and Kalamukhas (Black Faces) came to be feared and despised because their practice took this concept of duality to its edge. They would smear their bodies with human ash from cremation grounds, and use a human skull as an eating bowl.[248] Theoretically, this was a drastic manner of challenging the illusive boundaries between life and death, as well as the traditional taboos on handling the dead, a job which was customarily designated as 'impure' and assigned to the outcastes.

The memberships of most Tantric cults, though inclusive of all castes and creeds, still limited the number of members they took in. They tended to be exceedingly secretive, often using a symbolically coded language known only to their members for their ceremonies. It is possible that the cults feared that their new methods of salvation might be too complex for the general public and might get misused. We see this in the strict classification of initiates, for instance. One category of initiates, called the Tamasika (Animal) class, was believed to have an innately unruly nature and had no control over their sexual urges. They were not allowed to participate in actual coition but had to make do with certain substitute acts—at the appropriate moment of the ceremony, a karavira flower, in a phallic form, would be inserted into an aparajita flower, which is shaped like a vulva.[249]

This exclusivity and veil of secrecy that surrounded the Tantric cults could perhaps be one reason Tantric practices became so popular and widespread in the golden period. There must have been something fundamentally sound in these practices that rang true with society, which was still seeking a formal, organized philosophy of salvation that could accommodate an ordinary, earthly lifestyle.

Various former cults such as the Shaivites, Shaktas, Buddhists, Jains and the sun-worshippers branched out into newer sects, some of which adopted Tantric rituals, though sometimes in a manner that deviated from the core Tantric philosophies.[250]

Shakta Tantra, also called 'left-handed' Tantra, was female-dominated and honoured various goddesses depending on the cult. Most members of this cult were artisans. Heavy emphasis was placed on the power of the Shakti goddesses, both in the philosophies and in the rituals, and women played a central role as teachers and initiators, besides participating as consorts in the actual ceremonies.[251]

The cult of the Shaivite Tantra, also called the 'right-handed' Tantra, had a strong patriarchal stance. Directly affiliated with the Vedic system, it idolized prominent male gods, such as Shiva and Vishnu, as the ultimate divine guides. The members pledged to uphold the Vedic order through their rituals and practices.[252]

As for the Vedic sects themselves, many were tremendously resentful of the mounting popularity of the Tantric sects. They were scathing in their condemnation of the Tantriks, reviling them as ignorant, heretical untouchables to be shunned by society.[253] However, many Vedic practitioners adopted certain Tantric customs, hymns and *mandala*s and some softened their attitude towards the lower castes. At temples like the one at Konarak, where the Vedic ritual of sun worship was still practised, all castes were permitted to enter and they worshipped together. Some sects also adopted the Tantric ritualistic use of meats, alcohol and coition in sacred ceremonies. In temples where wine, meat and sex were still not permissible, symbolic substitutes were used, such as ginger instead of meat, coconut water for wine tender and phallic- and vagina-shaped flowers (karavira and aparajita) for coition.[254]

Buddhism too, despite its founder's severe condemnation of the sensory aspect of existence, had certain breakaway sects that espoused Tantric philosophies. Without blatantly subverting the Buddha's teachings, these Tantric Buddhist sects evolved a novel approach to ritualized sensual pleasures. They argued that if sensory experiences endangered the individual and could cause their self-destruction, a controlled application of the sensory experiences could be used as an antidote. This would protect the individual against further 'poisoning' by sensory experiences, just like a controlled amount of snake venom is applied as antivenom as a protection from venom itself.[255] The newly emerging Buddhas were each assigned a female consort called Tara (Saviouress). One of the most famous mystical chants of Tantric Buddhism was '*Om mani padme hum*' (Hail the jewel in the lotus!). The lotus, believed to be symbolic of sexual union between the Buddha and Tara, was said to hold the key to nirvana.[256]

By AD 500, Tantrism had been established as a powerful mainstream religious movement, and its impact was felt all through society. More than fifty-one Tantric centres had been set up throughout the Indian subcontinent.[257] Though practised mostly by the lower castes and tribals, Tantra swiftly caught the fancy of royalty and the upper class, the merchants and nobles. Believed to be in possession of magical powers, Tantric practitioners were patronized by many royal courts and harems and they would often be invited to entertain the courtiers and the queens with magic acts. This in a way also broke social codes of association along class and caste lines as well as countered certain religious taboos regarding women. Certain Tantric ceremonies, for instance, would use the menstrual blood of Chandala women.[258] Not only was menstrual blood a taboo in Vedic ideologies but the Chandalas, being outcastes, were greatly abhorred and barred from all sacred ceremonies. In AD 11, Harsha, the king of Kashmir, had a *dom*, a cremation-ground attendant of the lowest and most despised of untouchables, as his spiritual guide. The dom mixed drinks for the king that were believed to be elixirs, and advised him on his sex life, urging him to take on as many women as possible to prolong his longevity. Some Tantric gurus would be invited to organize giant orgies for the royal harems and for the wives of wealthy merchants. These women would participate in sex with the Tantrics as part of the rituals, and generously donate funds for the building and maintenance of Tantric centres.[259]

Tantra even made its way into the formal arts, such as music and dance. Seven basic notes, akin to the seven Tantric chakras, formed the fundamentals of the body of classical music. The energies of these notes were perceived as emanating from seven different centres of resonance in the human body. As for the very essence of sound, it was said to have originated from the Muladhara chakra. It was believed that through the knowledge of the nature of music and one's own inclination towards God, it was possible to attain nirvana.[260] Classical dance also adopted many mudras or formalized hand gestures used in Tantric ceremonies.

The erotic portrayals in temple sculptures too gained momentum with the spread of Tantrism from AD 500. As Tantrism gained social acknowledgement between AD 900 and 1200, there was a corresponding increase in the intensity and blatancy of the eroticism of the sculptures. Not only were the sculptures more detailed and brazen in the depiction of sexual acts, but where earlier they would be placed on the doorways, pillars and railings of the temples, they were now being carved on the altar adjacent to the deities.[261]

Besides the obvious upsurge of erotic depictions, it is also the nature of the portrayals that indicates a Tantric influence in the temple architecture of this period. Certain mudras as well as positions used in Tantric ceremonies appear in some of these sculptures. One sculpture displays a woman who, while in coition with a man, holds up her right hand in the '*abhaya*' or 'fear not' gesture, an obviously metaphorical representation. Another depicts a woman seated on the left thigh of her male partner the way it would be ritualistically done in Tantric ceremonies.[262] Several of the sexual acts sculpted were far more rigorous and convoluted than even those described in the kama sutras, often with exceptionally precise, almost geometric body alignments, and some showing assistance being offered to ensure accurate positioning. The methodical and complex nature of these positions suggests that these were not customary sexual practices, a plethora of which have been expounded by the kama sutras. Instead, these sculptures were more reminiscent of the strict technical aspect of Tantric rituals, which defined the precise method of coition, step by step, to achieving the supreme orgasm.

Numerous bizarre types of sexual practices portrayed on temple walls are not even mentioned in the kama sutras, but are Tantric practices. Bestiality is one instance—an AD 11 pillar in Rhoda (Gujarat) and another at Ambernath (Maharashtra) show a woman engaging in intercourse with a donkey with the assistance of a man from behind.[263] Other similar representations show horses, dogs and deer.[264] In some sculptures, bestiality is shown as part of a puja or sacred ceremony before the altar of a lingam.[265] It is unclear whether the formal Tantric cults actually subscribed to these practices, or if it was simply one of the numerous local interpretations by the uninitiated people of the Tantric philosophy of non-duality, which assumed that bestiality would dissolve the divide between the human and animal worlds. Bestiality was, in fact, practised in earlier periods as part of sacred ceremonies, as evidenced by the ashvamedha ritual. Similarly, there were sexual depictions of women engaging with trees, with each type of tree getting aroused by different gestures from the women, ranging from a smile, a glance or a kiss to a kick from a foot adorned with a silver anklet.[266]

Also indicative of Tantra are the portrayals of orgies which, again, do not feature in the kama sutras as normal mores, but were an integral feature of Tantra. Some of these orgies depicted the exchanging of partners among couples and others with multiple partners arranged in chain-like formations suggestive of ceremonial procedures.[267] At Motap, an orgy is shown taking place in the presence of Chamunda, the naked goddess, which indicates a religious ceremony.[268] Other scenes that would imply a formalized ritual are those that depict attendants either watching or assisting copulating couples.[269] The Tantric methods were always taught by knowledgeable members to the new initiates so they could be instructed on the precise positions and procedures.

Similarly, the emphasis of certain sculptures on the penis and vulva too are suggestive of Tantric influences. Numerous temples show women flashing their vulvas or men holding up exaggeratedly long and enlarged penises—extending to the heel and sometimes beyond.[270] This may have been a symbolic deification of genitals as the worship of a woman's vulva or a man's penis was a part of the ritual of several Tantric cults.

But, as was initially feared by the founders, with the widespread popularity of Tantrism and the lack of comprehension of its fundamental concepts, Tantric practices were often misconstrued and socially abused. Newfangled sects emerged that experimented with the concept of non-duality by pushing it to the edge of social experimentation. Nothing could be defined as the absolute of good nor evil as all existence was believed to be one entity and thereby validated. Priests and monks in some new Buddhist sects would openly indulge in luxuries and women, claiming that their brand of Buddhism supported these acts. Sometimes it also involved adultery, theft and murder, all conducted as part of a sacred ritual.[271]

EMERGENCE OF THE LINGAM-YONI

At the level of collective social thought, Tantra addressed the conflicts in a worldly existence: male versus female, matter versus spirit, and body versus mind. Humans as conscious subjects perceive their 'reality' through the information they receive from their sensory experiences. This information is received by the 'I' factor or *ahamkar*, which Jung refers to as 'ego'. The ego is limited in its ability to regard information and formulate concepts, and tends to organize its information in a polarized way. The subject, who is the individual, recognizes the object or the world perceived as different from and external to himself or herself. However, the higher mind (shuddha vidya or pure knowledge) that Jung refers to as the collective subconscious is able to clearly see that the object and the subject, the individual and the outside reality, and the polarities of existence, such as darkness and light, death and life, pure and impure, the worldly and the spiritual, matter and mind, man and God, are all indeed contained within a single reality and have a common source.

This profound realization of a unified reality was something that even Jung affirmed in Tantrism. He did not agree with the Buddhist-inspired goals of certain Hindu sects that sought nirdvanda (non-duality) in 'emptiness' through meditation. He said that he, on the contrary, believed that all that life offered was meant to be affirmed, including human companionship. [272] Jung, however, perceived Tantra as different from the other Hindu sects, for at its foundation was a corroboration of the very concept that he had endorsed. Tantra did not attempt to reject or repress human impulses but recognized the sanctity of life as an aspect of the divine, with all its tactile, sensual and living aspects.[273]

Symbolically, the non-dual philosophy was conceived in the image of the *ardhanari* [274] (half-woman god), or *ardhanarishvara* as it was also known, which emerged in this period. The ardhanarishvara cult reached its pinnacle between the tenth and twelfth centuries.[275] The ardhanari idol was an androgynous human figure, half-man and half-woman, personifying Shiva and Parvati, and worshipped as such. A third-century Syrian Christian traveller to India, Bardesanes, provided a fascinating description of a 'twelve-cubit high' statue soaring up on a mountain. He also observed that even though its entire right side was male and the left female, the 'two dissimilar sides coalesced in an indissoluble union'.[276] Each half of the hermaphroditic idol bore the distinguishing and gender-specific features of the two divinities—Shiva's half had his matt locks piled in a knot on his head, half a third eye on the forehead, snakes as bracelets, a tiger skin covering his loins and his rattle-drum in his right hand. Parvati's femininity was emphasized by a conspicuously defined breast, half a dot on her forehead—aligning with Shiva's half third-eye—and her jewellery, a girdle, an anklet and an earring on her left ear. However, the visual impact of the idol was meant to be such that the two sides were completely harmonized so that to the human eye they would appear as a continuum, a single, 'indissoluble' entity that is whole and complete in itself.[277] The non-duality theory was also represented in the lingam–yoni, which has been described as a symbolic representation of the ardhanari or Shiva–Shakti unity.[278] For the first time in this period, the lingam–yoni was conceived of as a single image that fused Shiva's lingam and the goddess's yoni, and many such relic idols can be dated to this period. However, before the golden period, the lingam and the yoni idols appeared separately, with the male-centric cults like the Shaivites (the worshippers of Shiva) worshipping phallic icons, and the Shakta cults of goddess worship venerating images of the vulva.

At a social level, the significance of these non-dual images is realized in a change of attitude towards eunuchs. The Vedic society had a paranoid aversion to eunuchs, who were regarded as effeminate freaks who brought misfortune to people and whose very presence could be emasculating. Therefore, eunuchs were never allowed to be present at the birth of a child, or to be in close proximity to the king. Eunuchs also could not own property, worship or offer food to anybody.[279] However, towards the end of the Vedic period, eunuchs would be hired to tend to the king's chambers, perhaps because they were considered non-virile and less likely than male attendants to assassinate the monarch.

In the golden period, there was radical transformation in the social status of eunuchs, who were now regarded as a human form of the ardhanari. It was believed that the male was exactly equal to the female in a eunuch, and the sexes were indivisible. As such, the eunuch was revered as the incarnation of the divine. Eunuchs, it was said, had the protection of the tribal goddess Bahuchara, whose temples they often lived in, and were believed to be auspicious as they possessed the goddess's powers over human fertility.[280] The kama sutras, in fact, demonstrated a very tolerant approach to eunuchs, devoting an entire chapter to them and describing their different body types and sexual mores in detail.

EMBRACING THE HUMAN EXPRESSION OF NIRVANA

Tantra's notion of totality nonetheless attempted to repress one facet of human existence—the emotional experience of living.

In Tantric practices, the concept of pleasure, as well as all other emotions including envy, love and anger, was negated, and Tantra practitioners were taught to subdue these natural impulses and strive for a state of unemotionality.

However, the evolution of yet another philosophical stream in this period compensated for this shortcoming. These were the arts, which had evolved parallel to the religious movements, but preserved the emotional element of human insight in a more holistic perception of non-duality. The arts, music, poetry, theatre and dance, were regarded as a religious experience, a form of divine illumination. With the overarching influence of the Tantras in society, the formal schools of art too began to conceive of the creative faculty as a religious pathway to nirvana.

The earlier attitude towards the creative arts, as indicated by the second-century BC *Treatise on Dramaturgy* by Bharata, was that the arts were a means for people to earn money and fame, to fulfil their dharma—the caste designated stations in life—and to improve their intellects and learning so that they became more 'pedigreed' and 'cultured'.[281] Contradicting this philosophy, Mammata, a twelfth-century poet and philosopher, said that while the arts could serve as a medium for wealth and fame, their most valuable 'fruit' was in the 'realization of the supreme bliss'. This shift in the perception of the arts came from a change in social outlook. As Mammata himself admitted, the attitude of the earlier generations, especially the Vedics, was pedagogical, while the modern approach to the creative arts was not so much to instruct as to communicate with the audience, like with a 'friend'.[282]

The arts in this period were a tool of philosophical renaissance—they were eclectic and open to debate, which allowed for breakthroughs in new ideas. The prevalent social environment, in which the arts thrived, encouraged vast discussion forums among scholars receptive to avant-garde theories.[283] This progressive attitude is most evident in what Kalidasa, the most prominent playwright of this period, declared: the antiquity of an idea or theory did not mean it was worthy of reverence and, conversely, the modernity of an idea did not mean it had to be summarily dismissed as rubbish. Kalidasa also rebutted the

Buddhist stance towards the arts, which was that they hindered spiritual endeavours.[284]

The arts were distinctly proletarian in this period. Theatre, for instance, was accessible to everyone, including women and the slave class. It also provided a venue to focus on the social conditions, better comprehend and address public concerns, and help people to evolve on an individual basis through the arts.[285] This indicated a considerable maturing of the collective psyche, for it recognized not only the correlation between the state of the individual and that of society, but also realized that many social problems had to be resolved at the individual level.

Though the genesis of most art forms had already taken place in earlier periods, the golden age witnessed their explosive expansion both in creativity and in form, and many formal styles of dance and music that evolved in this period continue to exist today. The organization of theatre guilds was extremely professional, with immaculate attention given to the perfection of make-up, costumes, dialogues and acting methodologies, as well as actual production—acoustics, venues, seating, decoration and ventilation of the halls.[286] Temples were the auditoriums for nearly all artistic performances, with the altar as the stage.[287] The decoration of the stage and halls included sensual forest spirits, the *yakshi*s and *vriksaka*s, as well as wild animals like the tiger, the peacock and snakes that were sacred symbols for various tribal groups.[288]

The art forms of this period, greatly influenced by the prevalent philosophies, absorbed the concepts of sensuality and a climactic union of opposites into their technical form and function. Elemental to the structure of formal music was the representation of opposites, such as night and day, birth and death, and male and female. This was the notion of the ragas, which are standard arrangements of five or six basic notes in Indian classical music that are the creative blocks in compositions. Each raga is identified with a specific mood, emotion or diurnal or seasonal cycle. Raga Bahar, for instance, represents joy, Raga Khamaj, love, and Raga Jogiya, sorrow. Ragas were also classified as male and female; the female arrangements were called *ragini*s. The range and complexity of human moods and emotions explored through music in this period can be appreciated from the fact that the original compilation entailed about 4000 ragas and raginis, which later, during Muslim rule, were whittled down to about 400.[289] The elements of romance and passion were also built into the techniques of music composition with terms like *alap*, a slow and tender introduction, and *jod* or union, as well as in the varying tempos—of conflict and tension, of frenzy, and of a climactic release. In painting, a style called the *ragmala* evolved, depicting the love play between ragas and raginis personified as men and women.[290]

The similitude between terminology in music and love-making is quite apparent. For instance, 'raga' is the term used for passion in the kama sutras.[291] Similarly, *rasa*, meaning 'taste' in the kama sutras, and *bhava* implying 'sensation', are concepts that are also rudimentary to classical Indian music.

Contrary to the Tantras, there was an unreserved acknowledgment of the reality and magnitude of human emotions in the arts. Where Tantra preached emotional detachment during union, the arts proclaimed that human emotions were yet another pathway to union and, therefore, salvation. In the formalized art of love-making, the kamashastras, there was already an ascertainment of the emotional dimension of sexual union so extensively covered in the kama sutras. The other arts too—music, dance, poetry and theatre—utilized emotions as a vehicle to nirvana. Human emotions were soundly researched, and formally classified and applied as a methodology in most artistic disciplines, including music, poetry and theatre.

Eight basic sensory emotions (bhavas), for instance, were considered the essential 'juice' (rasa) of theatre. These were *rati* (lust), *hasa* (humour), *utsaha* (enthusiasm), *krodha* (anger), *bhaya* (fear), *shoka* (grief), *jugupsa* (disgust) and *vismaya* (astonishment).[292] Emotions were also classified as being either innate, such as lust, pathos, fear and daring, or more subtle and transitory, requiring a more insightful comprehension, such as doubt, anxiety, jealousy, longing and despondence.

Part of the goal of this extensive study of human emotionality was to sensitize theatre audiences to the nuances of secondary emotions. Audiences, in turn, were expected to be able to understand, relate to as well as respond to the emotions being communicated on stage, for the emotions contained the very rasa—the sap, the essence, the prime flavour—of the performance. In contrast to earlier dramaturgy, when there was a strong emphasis on technical presentation—in form, appearance and voice—there was now demand for actors to convincingly convey emotions on stage so that the audience felt compelled to empathize with the portrayals.

The same philosophy also marked other art forms. For instance, Indian temple sculptures differed from other formal sculptural styles, such as the Greek and Roman styles, in that while the latter attempted to freeze a moment in time, idealizing it as an isolated image that viewers would behold as supreme, Indian sculptures attempted to create a feeling of movement, continuity and immediacy. Figures depicting elaborate scenes crowded the walls, plastering every inch of the building with receding figures placed in the background and above the central theme, suggesting an extension of space and time.[293] The intention of the portrayals, it seemed, was not to isolate the viewers but to draw them into the display.

Emotions were now understood to be a comprehensive aspect of the human experience of the divine. The idea was that human emotions are universal and are present in all beings, like instincts. So when a spectator watched a play, he would initially relate to the emotion being enacted on stage because it would evoke a personal memory. However, as the storyline developed, the spectator's personal point of reference would become insignificant; he would be drawn into a vortex of emotions that he would experience in their purest essence, as an intense sensation. This was the ultimate goal of theatre, a transcendence to a level that exceeded the mundane and transferred the audience to a plane of superconsciousness where individual emotions became insignificant, and yielded to pure sensations. The boundaries between the artist and the audience then dissolved. At this stage, neither the specific emotion being conveyed nor the artist nor the art form, be it dance, music or theatre, mattered any more. Nothing had a name, or individuality or distinguishing feature, for they were experienced as a single sensation beyond consciousness. This was the plane of 'the supreme bliss'; it represented the essence of the human spirit, its one universal source. To experience it was to get a 'momentary' glimpse of nirvana.[294]

This approach to nirvana was analysed by an eleventh-century monarch, King Bhoja of Malwa, in his books *Sarasvatikanthabharana* (Necklace of Sarasvati) and *Shringaraprakasha* (Illumination of Love). According to him, this state of nirvana attained through a universal emotion was representative of a universal human self that he called 'human ego'. The breakthrough to this stage was the result of the evolution of the social awareness of a collective human identity. Where much of the Tantric and other theories tended to be intangible and numinous, encrypted in mystical cults and their secret rituals, King Bhoja's was perhaps the earliest objective attempt to place the non-duality theory in the real context of human society.

King Bhoja theorized that all human elements that were related to the concept of love—including beauty, aesthetics, emotions, the arts and sex—were manifestations of this universal self's love for itself. Eventually, all these human activities were not about seeking union or connection with another, but were about the human self's desire for itself—it was the search for self-completion. For the human collective identity, this place of self-discovery or wholeness was a 'fire source', an interminable pool of 'energy'. From it were born all the other inspirations and emotions that constituted life. But the process was cyclical: the fire fuelled human emotions and the arts and their continual evolution; the creative forms in turn fed the 'fire source' that sustained them.[295]

The golden age was indeed an explosively creative period in Indian history. Dynasties like the Guptas enthusiastically patronized the development of art, sculpture, music, dance and literature. Voluminous texts of theories and techniques in each field were recorded. And there was exemplary research and innovation in other fields too, including engineering,[296] medicine,[297] astronomy,[298] language and maths.[299]

Not surprisingly, the social environment was conducive to this immense productivity. Fa-hsien, who visited India in the fifth century, took particular notice of the tranquillity of its state of governance. He marvelled at how relaxed the administration was, yet crime rates were low and it was possible for people to travel throughout the country without encountering official bureaucracy about passports, and without the fear of being accosted and robbed—which was a common experience of travellers in many parts of the world at the time.[300] In fact, there was a certain economic equanimity that allowed commoners a degree of contentment in their daily lives. This was probably due to the traditional republican-style governing of the guild states or guild-owned villages. Ownership of agricultural and pastoral land in villages was collective, and fields were partitioned into as many plots as families, with each family getting its own share of produce.[301]

For the first time, individuals of lower castes could own land, as land grants would be sometimes given as payment. Also merchant and artisan guilds received increased official recognition and even had their own laws. Compared to the Buddhist times, when they paid almost 240 per cent in tax to the king, the working class now paid a much lower rate of 20 per cent. Dynasties like the Guptas took a more liberal approach to governance, decentralizing not only resource ownership but also allowing provincial officials more political and administrative leeway.[302]

The state-sponsored hospitals and maternity wards for the public and village physicians were on the government's payroll.[303] Where education during the Vedic period had been the exclusive privilege of the upper caste, it was not so now. The moneyed lower castes could now buy an education, but certain institutions also opened their doors to everyone. For instance, at the university of Nalanda, one of the largest and most renowned universities of the time, any man of any caste who could pass his gruelling entrance exam, was admitted into the university.[304]

There was some social change too no doubt, but one would expect that the philosophy of a universal human consciousness, of non-duality, propounded by this age would have led to radical social progression. The expected development would have been a civic society with a deeper comprehension of humanity and tolerance—one that upheld the equality of women and shattered caste and class hierarchies. Yet, this golden age was unable to fully realize its own potential. It ultimately failed to translate its non-dual theories into a new, wholesome social order, which remained deeply fragmented along lines of gender, caste, class and economics.

PART IV

THE COLONIAL PERIOD

SEX AS SHAME

Despite the wisdom of the Tantras and the rebellious philosophies of cults like that of the Shaktas, the golden age failed to generate a universal social order that would realize the equal human worth of all members of society. Perhaps the greatest obstacle to the progress of a people's collective thinking towards a true democracy was a massive psychological block consequent upon numerous centuries of patriarchal rule as well as the irrational entrenchment of a caste and class hierarchy that regarded humans as intrinsically unequal.

There were other impeding factors as well. For one, many guild-based villages, some of which operated as republic-style communities, might have experienced increased internal dissensions due to enhanced trade possibilities and more lucrative opportunities for private business. The cohesiveness of these guilds, after all, depended on the cooperation and support of its members, but this began to abate over time.[1] Social fragmentation also resulted from the occupation-specific nature of these guilds, such as potters or farmers or cattle herders, each with a sub-caste identity—which led to inter-caste conflicts. Another significant contributing barrier was related to culture—although there was tremendous creativity and innovation in various fields in the golden age, the formal establishment of each field embedded them in rigid laws and procedures, all believed to be of divine revelation. This was so as much for art, literature, music and philosophy as for mathematics and even medicine. Their inflexibility and the association with the incontrovertible divine set a barricade on the creative thinking that had inspired the evolution of these fields in the first place. *Vastu Shastra*, the formal treatise that elucidates the laws of architecture, was ascribed to the celestial craftsman Vishvakarma, said to have constructed both heaven and earth, and to the demigod Maya. The architecture treatise was hence sacrosanct and it provided directions—not to be disobeyed—on the minutest details of temple-building from the direction the temple should face to the location of windows, roof beams and towers. The head architect had to memorize these instructions as if they were religious injunctions and ensure his workers followed them devotedly.[2] The shilpashastras specified every aspect of the sculpting of images—the body proportions, postures, gestures, expressions, clothing and decoration—and warned that if a deity was not constructed in accordance with those guidelines, the image could not even be assumed to be beautiful.[3] Nevertheless, this smothered the space, the autonomy and the stimulation required for the evolution of these fields.

A regression in social order was noticeable in terms of customs and mores. The complex philosophy of Tantra became a shallow statement of fashion and provided the justification for a wildly hedonistic lifestyle, especially for the upper classes. The record of items such as wine, dates, pearls, gold, silver, topaz, glass, frankincense, slaves and even women imported into India during this period gives an idea of the pleasure-seeking culture of that time. There was, in fact, an objectification of women that went so far as to use them as a trading commodity. Indian kingdoms would trade their women with those of other countries as items for the harem.[4] And husbands would act as pimps and prostitute their wives. In one poem, a married woman complains that her husband, who had been tempted by a certain Venugopala's offer of a house and jewellery in exchange for sex with her, compelled her to prostitute herself since, in his opinion, 'whoring is no sin'.

And when she resisted he mocked her, called her a 'super-caste'.[5] The few liberties that women had in the golden age were also revoked. Widows once again could not remarry and there was a wild resurgence in the practice of sati.[6] Around AD 1200, 'hero stones' were erected all over Gujarat and Rajasthan in the west, to commemorate the death of men in battle, and along with these, 'sati stones' were raised as memorials to the war widows who had committed sati. The sati stones were marked by the symbolic right arm, laden with bangles, to signify the deified status of the women who had died in this way.[7] Scholars have suggested that there might even have been a violent ideological confrontation between matriarchal and patriarchal systems, resulting in the subjugation of matriarchies by an unprecedented increase in the practices of hypergamy, girl child marriages and sati.[8] However, in regions such as Kashmir where the Shakta and Tantric cults had been prevalent, the practice of sati was greatly discouraged,[9] showing an ideological conflict between the goddess- and god-worshipping cults.

As the temples accumulated more wealth, the priests became increasingly powerful and corrupt, and would often demand supplies of new devadasis from patrons. The whole philosophy behind the devadasi system was disregarded, as these women were exploited and became a cheap source of sexual entertainment for priests and the upper class. The devadasis were known to confide in each other about the depravity of the abuse and that priests were having sex with them not out of a religious sense, but unabashed lechery. This hankering for sex, it appears, became more of an addictive obsession than an ideological one, and it was also said that the incompetence of several kings in protecting their territories from warring invaders was because of their preoccupation with sex. Even while their kingdoms were being attacked, some kings would continue revelling in sexual pastimes in their harems, or with courtesans on the battlefield.[10] Legend has it that the armies of the king of Vijayanagar took along 20,000 courtesans to war. The defeat in battle of certain Hindu kings like Prithviraj Chauhan to invading Muslim armies was attributed to overexertion from sex, which supposedly left them too tired and drowsy to fight.[11] And some kings like Hariraja of Ajmer would spend huge portions of their revenues on parties and dancing women, such that their treasuries would be drained of the funds they needed for their armies and defence.[12]

There was greater inequity of wealth, and an associated increase in communalism and infighting. Rulers attempting to protect their self-interest and curb insurgent movement would alienate themselves from their neighbours possibly to minimize foreign intervention in their internal affairs. As mistrust increased, there was also less sharing of information, as well as fewer discussions and debates that had fuelled the philosophical growth in the golden era. Not surprisingly, the resulting insularity caused a stagnation in the cultural, economic and ideological growth that the period was once associated with. This recessive period between AD 800 and 1200 is sometimes referred to as the Dark Age. The associated recession in social order and administrative cohesiveness made individual kingdoms all the more vulnerable to foreign attacks.[13]

The viciousness of upper-caste repression during this time was strengthened by wealth. The Brahmins and upper castes—many of whom were lower-caste members who had upgraded their castes through wealth—once more tightened the observance of caste rules. The economically deprived slave or the servant caste's social status was the worst ever, with even their shadows regarded as polluting. Others of the lowest castes, the commoners who provided labour, including artisans and peasants, were demeaned, their jobs disdained, and the system of guilds and knowledge accumulation that had empowered them was eroded. All this stemmed from the Brahmins' fear that it was this system of cohesive bonding and information that had given the lowest caste its power.[14] Unfortunately, even though the wealth of the golden period had provided an opportunity for the lower castes to promote their social identity by purchasing their way into the upper-caste strata, the intention was not so much to seek equality as to gain a position of privilege from which they could inflict on others the degradation they had once suffered.

Many commoners who had received inheritable land grants became feudal lords and took on self-exalting, grandiose titles like raja (king), *samanta* (feudal prince) and *thakur* (god). Now with both the king and the feudal lords siphoning off revenues from the land, the condition of the commoners deteriorated. As the food and manufacturing surplus ultimately benefited only the ruling classes, the peasants and artisans tended to keep their production levels at a minimum. This, of course, affected the overall economic yield of the kingdom and hampered trade. Revenues from the royal treasury were usually diverted towards the king's hedonistic excesses instead of being invested in the development of the state and its infrastructure.[15]

The elaborate and ostentatious temples which formed the most distinguishing feature of the golden period became the focus of political power and the centre for the display of the gluttonous wealth of the privileged. There are accounts of how kings who desired a little extra revenue would raid the temples of a neighbouring kingdom. Legends of these temples being wealth-mountains travelled to distant countries over trade routes, and drew invaders from various parts of the world, who colonized the Indian subcontinent in disparate fractions.[16] Turkish and Arab raiders periodically attacked northern India and after looting the temples they would raze many of them to the ground, apparently as a symbolic destruction of idolatry. One of these temples was said to have had five gold icons, each four and a half metres high, and 200 silver icons. At Somnath, another demolished temple, the altar was said to have had fifty-six jewel-studded pillars.[17]

India, with its wealth of natural resources like spices, cottons, silks and sandalwood and other rare and exotic items, had also become an enticing 'honey jar' for Arab and European adventurers, who for long had tried to seek out accessible sea routes to the country.[18]

From the fag end of the golden period, for more than a millennium, almost until the mid 1900s, the Indian subcontinent was repeatedly invaded and occupied by foreign armies—of lone opportunists as well as those of imperial crowns—seeking control of land, resources, markets and cheap labour. These included the

Turks, Afghans, Arabs, Mongolians and the British, as some of the major players, and in smaller measure, the French, the Dutch, the Danish and the Portuguese.

The impact of the colonial powers was radical—both on the existent philosophies of native religions and on the collective social and moral outlook of their Indian subjects. The concepts of universal humanity, such as love, beauty, aesthetics, desire and pleasure, leisurely nurtured and explored in the golden age, and raised to the highest level of the human awareness of the divine, would now be deemed shameful and undesirable. One of the most conspicuous changes was the almost complete halt in the building of erotic temples. This custom, which had lasted more than a millennium during the golden period, could not have been sustained that long, simply as a newfangled architectural trend. Fashions that are only the product of a social whim are invariably ephemeral and it is only the momentum and power of organized religion that allowed for these erotic sculptures to embellish sacred walls century after century. And indeed, it was the power of yet other organized religions, Islam and Christianity, that ensured the demise of these erotic temples and with them a wholesome philosophy. Once more, sexuality was dichotomized from religion and from God and pushed under the veil away from social inspection and introspection.

The colonial era ushered in one of the most sexually repressive periods in the history of India. It introduced a moral outlook which in the aftermath of the golden period was tantamount to ideological regression. Yet, this apparent setback actually propelled the momentum of the non-duality ideology, forcing its confrontation at a conscious and social level for Indians.

THE ARRIVAL OF ISLAM

The Muslim invaders who now arrived in India were not the first foreigners to colonize the Indian subcontinent. In earlier periods there had been the Vedics of course, as also the Greeks, the Scythians, the Kushans and certain Central Asian invaders who periodically occupied small chunks of the land. However, the Muslim invaders were among the first to successfully consolidate a large portion of the Indian subcontinent, consisting of independent warring kingdoms, under a single administrative power. The last time this had been done was under the Buddhist emperor Ashoka in the third century BC.

Unlike Ashoka, who implemented official policies of secularism and tolerance for all religions, the Greeks, who delighted in familiarizing themselves with the land and its native customs and often joined local religious sects, and the Vedics, who jealously guarded their religion, ensuring the natives could not access it, the Muslim rulers intended to replace the existing religions with Islam. They attempted to impose, often ruthlessly, their theological beliefs on the pre-existing social and religious environment without any comprehension of it and with unmitigated conviction.

However, India's initial contact with Islam, which began around AD 800, had been peaceful, when Arab and Persian traders settled down in eastern coastal towns like Konkan, Malabar and Calicut. They married Indian women, built large mosques and continued to practise their faith unobtrusively. Other Muslim settlers came around AD 1000 to preach, and they too continued to exist harmoniously with the locals.[19]

Around AD 1000, commencing with the Turks, certain Muslim principalities began to periodically conduct violent raids on Indian kingdoms, usually looking to usurp money, wealth as in gold and jewels which the temples abounded in, and women. As they galloped back to their countries laden with their booties, they would destroy towns, villages and temples in a jubilant celebration of their victory as well as in fulfilling their Islamic obligation as iconoclasts.[20]

In time came occupation, particularly by vagabond Muslim invaders, many of them exiles, who had no significant place or position at home to return to and thought it best to establish something more permanent on the Indian subcontinent.[21] Many of these early conquests were ferocious. Emperor Babur, in his memoirs in the 1500s, wrote of his intent to 'subdue' India, a land he had already raided five times before finally establishing occupation. It was with much pride that he recalled the subjugation of Bajaur—the 'infidels' or non-believers of Bajaur, as Babur saw them, had their heads chopped off and then arranged into a victory pyramid.[22] Yet when his troops entered Agra, and the terrified inhabitants fled, Babur complained that his troops could find no food for themselves and their animals. He also believed that other locals, out of 'spite', were accosting and robbing his men on the roads.[23]

The first significant Muslim occupation of India was by the Turks circa 1200. By the mid 1200s they had established the city of Delhi in the north as their base and continued to consolidate large portions of India into their empire for the next two hundred years. They were followed by the Afghans, and later the Mughals, who were of mixed Turkish and Mongolian descent.

The Muslim rulers capitalized heavily on the infighting among various kingdoms on the Indian subcontinent. Hindu rulers would often be willing to align themselves with the Muslim invaders to overthrow a neighbouring Hindu king. The Muslims would sometimes also take advantage of the festering anger of the lower castes in a kingdom to instigate insurgencies. They recruited large numbers of soldiers from the lower, economically struggling castes whom they would remunerate with modest salaries and small land grants, inducting them into Islam in the process.[24] Indian kings who converted were made allies and spared brutal, obliterating attacks.

A majority of those who converted to Islam voluntarily were from the lower castes, attracted to a religion that preached the equality and brotherhood of all men.[25] The conversion provided long-awaited relief from the inhumanely oppressive caste system. It was the first time since the Buddhist period that the caste hierarchy, based on the belief of an inherent worth or worthlessness of human beings, was being not only challenged, but also deemed as the mark of an inferior religion. The incentive to convert was economic for some inhabitants, as the Muslim rulers had imposed on the colonies a faith-based tax called the *jizyah* (poll tax) and *kharaj* (a land and property tax) to be levied on so-called 'infidels', the non-Muslims. Furthermore, conversion could lend protection from attack. Muslim army commanders were actually encouraged to attack the property and temples of the infidels with the incentive that they could keep one-fifth of the captured booty for themselves, while handing the rest over to the Muslim ruler.[26] However, many Muslim converts retained their Hindu traditions and customs, and even maintained their caste, especially if they were from the upper castes.

Upper-caste communities, once the master class, were now diminished in their social standing, and were despised and ridiculed as inferior pagans by the Muslim rulers. Laws were imposed to undermine and weaken their positions in society. They were not allowed to build any new temples in territories under Muslim rule, nor rebuild old temples destroyed by the Muslim armies. They were not to ride horses or possess any weapons, which essentially squashed their potential for rebellion. They were to dress the way they normally did, that is, only partially covered, which the Muslims regarded as barbaric, and not try to emulate the Muslim way of clothing. They were not to live in Muslim neighbourhoods, introduce their customs to other Muslims, hire Muslim servants, or prevent people from converting to Islam. However, they were to allow Muslim travellers to stay in their houses and temples.[27]

An important historical function of Islamic rule in India was a fundamental restructuring of the social power hierarchy. Not only were upper-caste Hindus—once the master class—forced into subservience, but their position too was deemed even lower than that of the low-caste Hindus who had converted to Islam. This role reversal must have seemed a godsend to the long-suffering slave classes, who now not only had an economic edge over the upper caste in not having to pay the infidel taxes, but also had much greater freedom of social movement than ever before.

However, in reality, life did not get that easy for the lower-caste converts. Even though theoretically, under Islamic law, all Muslims were regarded as equals, this basic dignity perhaps being the main incentive for many lower-caste Hindus to convert, a distinct social hierarchy existed, based on race, colour and national origin. The Muslim rulers, bound by their racial prejudices, were unable to honour the fundamental call of Islam, which affirms universal brotherhood and equality for all. The people of Turkish, Arab or Persian origin, called the *ashraf*, were regarded as superior to the Indian Muslims, who were known as *ajlaf*. At the helm of this Islamic racial hierarchy were the ulemas. The ulema, the Islamic theologian, now replaced the Hindu priest in his covetousness for supremacy and political influence. Using the Sharia, the laws of Islam, the ulema became a powerful authority in the Muslim rulers' courts, directing most administrative decisions.[28] Education was denied to the lower-class Muslims for fear that they would aspire to the more important positions in society—in governance or revenue collection, and as officers and rulers. This was not simply a matter of prejudice but an officially implemented policy. In one fatwa, the Islamic teachers were given strict instructions not to feed 'precious stones' to the 'dogs' or adorn the necks of the 'pigs' with gold collars. They were to teach the 'worthless', 'low-born' nothing more than the perfunctory customs of prayer, fasting, alms-giving, the pilgrimage to Mecca and a few mild doctrines.[29]

Ironically, Islamic rule ultimately subjected the Indian Muslims to the same sort of socio-economic marginalization and abuse that had been the lot of low-born castes in the Hindu system. This oppression compelled many Indian Muslims to get false genealogical charts constructed to establish a superior bloodline of Turkish or Afghan origin.[30]

The disparaging attitude of the Muslims towards their Indian subjects is revealed in the diaries of the first Mughal emperor, Babur. For him India was a land of 'few pleasures' and uncultured societies. Nothing about the people—their mannerisms, food, arts, crafts, knowledge, design or architecture—seemed to impress him. He also found the people extremely unattractive.[31]

THE BIRTH OF HINDUISM AND A NEW MORAL INCENTIVE

Perhaps one of the most momentous events of Muslim rule in the Indian subcontinent was the birth of modern Hinduism. The unification of the Indian subcontinent was more a political and administrative strategy and would happen eventually. But first the colonizers found it necessary to assign a common identity to the disparate communities of mind-boggling diversity who inhabited India's vast land mass. It was not until the Muslim occupation that the inhabitants of the Indian subcontinent assumed a common religious identity. The older literatures acknowledged Tantrism, Buddhism, Vedism, Shaktism and so on as different and diverse religions,[32] and the various kingdoms as separate countries. An acknowledgement of diversity would have been a validation, almost an unspoken acceptance, of the other, which to the Muslim rulers was unthinkable. As far as they were concerned, the alien people were all the same—a challenge to the supremacy of Islam. The pagan subjects were, therefore, considered a single definitive category termed as Hindus, followers of a pagan religion and residents of the land where the river Indoo or Indus flowed. India itself was perceived as a unified entity and was henceforth known as Hindustan, a Persian term denoting 'the land of the Hindus'.

Accompanying this dogmatic refusal on the part of the Muslim rulers to accept India's multiplicity of faiths was a blind prejudice, akin to that of the invading Vedics, and a certain want of logical refinement and curiosity that had actually been shown by at least some of the earlier colonizers.The Greeks, for instance, explored and recorded with immense zeal the new and unfamiliar nuances of India—its people, clothing, customs, the religions, as well as flora and fauna, some even adopting local religions as Buddhism. There were of course a few Muslim intellectuals, like Al-Biruni, who were exceptional in their observations and comprehensive study of every aspect of India, but these were few and far between. Al-Biruni, a Persian scholar believed to be a reluctant detainee at the court of an eleventh-century Muslim ruler, wrote a book, *Kitabu'l Hind* (The Book on India), which is an unprejudiced, meticulously detailed and reliable source of information about India in that period.[33] One Muslim ruler who was an exception to the general apathy that the others bore towards the Hindus was the Mughal emperor Akbar.

Initially, Akbar began like most other Muslim rulers, conquering the domains of the Hindu kings ruthlessly. He consolidated much of India under his reign, an accomplishment matched only by the Buddhist emperor Ashoka, who had similarly begun with a campaign of bloody military conquests. Akbar even broke the resolve of the grand Rajput kingdoms that till then had been legendary for fending off Muslim attacks.[34] Initially, he resorted to forcefully converting people to Islam,[35] but later saw the acrimony it created among natives and realized that, for Islam to survive in India, the Muslim rulers needed to be more tolerant and flexible. Greatly influenced by the philosopher Ibn-al-'Arabi, Akbar, quite like Ashoka, underwent a radical change when he experienced a spiritual upheaval and renounced governance through both violence and orthodox Islam.[36] Subsequently, his outlook on religion and governance was nothing short of radical. His vision for India was that of progressive reform and unity amid diversity. He wanted to launch a spiritual and cultural renaissance in his empire, and argued that if traditionalism was indeed the only way life was meant to be, then prophets would have no new messages to bring and new ideas would wither as each emerging ideology signified change. In an environment as conservative as Akbar's, it was daring to assert that traditions could suffocate reason and innovation.[37] He did not enforce the Islamic laws of the Sharia and instead fostered an eclectic atmosphere in his empire. He married Hindu princesses, ordered the translation of Hindu scriptures into Arabic, prohibited the killing of cows, which Hindus held sacred, and personally engaged in discourse with the preachers of other minority religions such as the Christianity and Zoroastrianism.[38]

However, his unorthodox approach was not appreciated by many in the conservative Muslim sections of society, including his own courtiers, who grudged him for deviating from the Sharia in his governance. Upon his death, Muslim clerics celebrated the news as good tidings.[39] Not only did the Muslim rulers regard themselves culturally and racially superior to the Hindus, but they were also convinced of a moral superiority bestowed on them by their religion and its laws of conduct.

Idol worship by the Hindus was disparaged and the lingam condemned. Amir Khusru, in 1311, expressed his wish for vengeance against Hinduism, saying that when the superior Hindu gods received 'the kick of the horse of Islam', they would land in Sri Lanka across the ocean, and the lingam too would flee as if it had legs.[40] Some clerics lamented that Muslim rulers, in their greed for land revenue and the infidels' taxes, were permitting the Hindus to practise idol worship and build lavish temples. One writer observed that this would never enable Islam to overthrow the infidels. Instead, he suggested that the Hindus be slaughtered until the entire country succumbed to Islam.[41] However, even though the population as a whole could not be brought to its knees, the Sharia was imposed and began to govern every aspect of life in India.

Alcohol, gambling, music and dance were banned, and wine sellers and musicians imprisoned and fined. The Italian traveller Niccolao Manucci noted that Emperor Aurangzeb was so sternly against the use of alcohol that he expelled all Christians—assumed to be habitual drinkers—from the city. The homes and shops of all citizens—Hindus and Muslims—were searched, and those in possession of alcohol would lose one hand and a foot. They were then dragged to a dung heap and left there to die.[42] The *hijra* community, eunuchs who cross-dressed or engaged in sodomy, were banished and sometimes given corporal punishments. Brothels were illegalized and, as a public reprimand, the brothels of the more popular courtesans were ordered to be demolished 'brick by brick'.[43] The Muslims were particularly revolted by the near-naked style of Hindu dressing. Until then, Hindu men and women had dressed more or less alike, in a delicately spun, translucent loin cloth, and were usually bare-breasted, with copious amounts of jewellery adorning every part of the body. It was the Muslims who introduced stitched clothing in India, and the paintings of this period reflect the new Hindu attire that consisted of a short, tight bodice for women, a long, flowing skirt and a veil draped over the shoulders and head. The Muslim rulers were also repulsed by the candid expression of sexuality among the Indians. The ruler Nasir-ud-Din Haidar, after witnessing a man flirting with a woman on the streets and caressing her breasts, had the man's hands and the woman's breasts cut off.[44] Essentially all the key elements—sex, sensuality, aesthetics, prostitution, eunuchs and alcohol—that had played an important role in the religious and social ceremonies of the golden period were now deemed immoral under Islamic laws, and rigorously outlawed.

Hindu society adapted swiftly to the moral governance of its new masters. This perhaps was one reason Hinduism outlived Buddhism to a much fuller measure in India and endured 500 years of Muslim rule. Also, unlike Buddhism, Hinduism was not a centralized religion nor a congregational one. It did not require temples and monasteries for its cohesiveness or continuity. With the influence of the bhakti movement of the golden period, priests and their complicated ceremonies had been made expendable. A Hindu could build an altar at home, however small and modest, and still continue his or her tradition of worship without a priest, a congregation, sermons or even the scriptures. But for Buddhism to survive, the functioning of monasteries and the orders was fundamental. The concentration of monks in the Buddhist orders in monasteries, and their uniform saffron robes and shaven heads, made them easy targets for the invading Muslim armies, who slaughtered them en masse, demolished their monasteries and burnt their libraries, often mistaking them for Hindu priests.[45]

Among the Hindu sects, especially the Tantrists, many went underground. Among the bhakti sects, the most fluid and adaptable of all, unbound by rigid institutional rules and formalities, thrived the best. Many bhakti cults operated at the grassroots level and did not require wealthy patrons, grandiose temples or elaborate rituals to survive. The members could meet in the open air, under a tree, or by a river, and sing hymns together, inspired simply by a shared moment of a sacred, common destiny. Anyone could initiate a cult anywhere, gathering a few believers to give validity to their sect. And just as the bhakti sects had evolved as collusions of various often-conflicting faiths, like the Vedic and tribal religions, they now also incorporated elements from the Islamic religion as they continued to evolve all through the Muslim period. One the most prominent was the sect of the saint Kabir. Born into a low-caste weaver community, Kabir combined the ideologies of Hinduism and Islam in his teachings. He called his god Rama, a Hindu deity. However, like the Muslims, he rejected idol worship and was a theist. He also criticized the caste system, and used numerous words and expressions from Persian and Arabic in his sermons. Above all, he remained true to the core of the bhakti philosophy, choosing his object of devotion as his sole focus. However, his altar was not dedicated to a god, but to a vision of a common humanity devoid of caste, creed and gender. He also believed that to honour the individual was to honour the divine.[46]

However, the new Hindu morality that emerged under Muslim rule was almost an antithesis to the philosophies of the golden period. Sensuality was decried as a way of living, and its expression even in the arts and literature was condemned. Tulsidas, a prominent Hindu poet of the late 1500s, boasted of how his poem 'Lake of Rama's Deeds' was clean and free of sensuality. He proclaimed quite virtuously that it was not something that would feed the lust of people who like 'crows'—the filthy creatures they are supposed to be—seek their gratification from literature.[47]

The impact of the Muslim period on women was particularly devastating. The Muslim attitude towards women was most telling during the reign of Razia Sultana who, even though a brilliant, capable and just ruler, was not regarded as a suitable monarch because she was a woman. This sexist outlook was even reflected in styles of poetry. Among the styles of formal poetry narration was the *rekta*, which was a traditionally male form, performed only by men. As much as it emphasized structure, its recitation was also regarded as a measure of male sexuality, for it was said that a man's 'sexual powers' could be gauged by his performance. Conversely, for these very reasons, the female form of poetry, *rekti*, was not allowed public recitation as it was deemed immoral and obscene—and in time it perished.[48] The male opposition to rekti was that it made frequent references to *chapti* or lesbian love, where women were shown as preferring women lovers, not just as sexual partners, but also emotionally.[49] This sexist attitude resounded in the Hindu quarters. The Hindu poet Tulsidas spoke of women as talkative 'drums', like illiterate lower-caste people and cattle, who need to be tamed by beatings.[50]

The devadasi tradition gradually faded out during Muslim rule. The zenana, or the women's segragated quarters, became a standard architectural feature of most homes. Earlier, it was only the palaces of Hindu kings that had separate quarters for the queens, actually detached palaces probably built to give the king some space away from bickering wives, and to protect him from being poisoned by an ambitious wife desiring the throne for her son. However, the zenanas of the Muslim period were built with the idea of cloistering women. The zenana could be accessed only through the men's quarters in order to thwart any visits from strange men.[51]

The doorways to the zenanas were always guarded by eunuchs who, though unpopular with the early Muslim rulers, later became the most trusted of servants. There was a steady supply of harem-keepers as young men would be regularly castrated for the purpose. In some regions, the poor would castrate their sons and sell them to the Mughal courts as eunuch servants. Many eunuchs selected for the courts were young and good-looking, for they not only guarded harems, but were also meant to entertain the men of the palace, and were subjected to sodomy and sexual abuse.[52]

As harem-keepers, the eunuchs always meticulously checked people entering the zenana, to make sure the veiled visitor was not a man in disguise. They were also instructed to prevent the smuggling of wine and opium to the bored and frustrated queens inside, and also possible dildos in the form of vegetables like radish and cucumbers.[53] Hindu women also adopted the purdah, the customary Islamic veil, in many regions, often simply out of compulsion.[54] When a Hindu man was unable to pay up his infidel taxes to the emperor, his wife would be taken away and imprisoned. Sometimes these women would be raped, and would face condemnation when they were released, with their in-laws disowning them. A woman who was raped was regarded as sullied and a figure of shame for the family. This was, again, another facet of the new Hindu morality. Earlier, in the Vedic society, even though rape was almost a privilege for high-caste men, the raped women were not stigmatized. Men were also known to marry young, unmarried pregnant women, who may have been raped. In the golden age, rape was regarded as a socially unacceptable act for men, even kings, to inflict on women, and it was believed that rapists met with heinous ends.

A sixteenth-century poet, Chandrabati, in her poem 'Sundari Malva', wrote of the anguish that Hindu women, particularly of the peasant communities, faced under Muslim rule. The poem laments the plight of a young woman who, after her release from a lock-up, was driven out of the house by her father-in-law. He told her that she had drawn the misfortune to herself and faulted her for being too beautiful. He said that in their times even the women of privilege from the Hindu royal households were not safe. But while Muslim women wore the veil, the Hindu peasant women who worked in the fields remained unveiled as they had to continue working.[55] One also observes here an ironical shift in the attitude towards the concept of beauty and aesthetics since the golden age. Where these traits were once regarded as auspicious and divinely inspiring, and meant to be flaunted, they were now a cause for misfortune and shame, and, therefore, to be concealed.

Another custom that flourished under Muslim rule was that of harems. The practice of polygamy prevalent during the Vedic times was a social acknowledgement of a man and his wives, and the Vedic texts frequently referred to the complications in personal relationships that multiple spouses created. In fact, during the Buddhist and the golden eras, there was an emergent belief that urged men to practise monogamy. According to the moral commandments for the lay Buddhist, husbands were specifically ordered not to commit adultery and to respect their wives.[56] In contrast, the harem culture that emerged during Muslim rule provided a social leeway for men to build an impersonal playground of female sex toys, and was freely adopted by Hindu kings as well. Harems could be expanded to grotesque sizes[57] and were so removed from the concept of domestic life that sometimes it was hard to tell which of the king's sons belonged to which of the women in the harem.[58] The Muslim emperors had the privilege of choosing from the daughters of their courtiers and subjects. To collect women in the hundreds, and to maintain them in splendid palaces, was not an uncommon pastime.[59] Some of the women were war trophies that symbolized in an overt way the sexual victory of the Muslim ruler over a Hindu one. The wives of the Hindu kings defeated in battle would be forced into the victor's harem, and sometimes Muslim kings, as obeisance from a Hindu king, would demand the gift of a woman of his clan, a dishonour that some Hindu kings would try to avenge with bloodshed.[60] Women were also used as objects of trade. Despite the Sharia's injunctions forbidding suicide, most Muslim rulers showed little objection to Hindus practising sati, which increased during this period.[61]

There was a strong taboo on the open association of men and women in public. The shifting gender dynamics is also well reflected in the Hindu arts of this era. There was a noticeable boost in the depictions of men going to war and hunting. Others displayed men as heroic and resplendent, together with submissive women in tight bodices with their heads veiled. Still others proclaimed men's victories over the much dreaded female tree spirits of the indigenous religions. One portrayal of a hunt illustrates the defeat of a tree spirit who is strung upside down from a tree. Her blouse is left on, but her lower garments are stripped off, exposing her vulva between her naked legs in a pose that depicts both rape and humiliation. Where these tree spirits were once regarded as invincible and feared by men, this showed the figurative stripping of their powers, and the subjugation of their sexuality. This increasing aggressiveness in the social definition of male sexuality can also be seen in the changing portrayals of Radha's relationship with Krishna. Contrary to

Krishna's earlier personality where he was often shown as a gentle and playful lover, paintings, such as of the *pratishthana* genre of this period, depicted him as being forceful and violent. He did not employ his flute to serenade women any longer, but used kama's bow and arrows to pierce objects of feminine symbolism, such as the trunks of trees (which embodied the female spirit) and the pots of milkmaids, imageries representative of aggressive sexual conquest.[62] Radha, in numerous instances, was projected as sexually gratuitous and painted as a selfish, vindictive personality. Her relationship with Krishna was declared illicit, but she was given redemption by an assumed marriage, where she was referred to as his 'wife'.[63]

Southern India, however, presented a different story. There was much fiercer resistance to Muslim occupation here, and independent Hindu kings continued to maintain their stronghold, which is why the cultural impact of the golden period lasted for a longer time. The Vijayanagar dynasty, one of the last powerful Hindu dynasties that held out till 1646, was viewed as the ultimate barricade against Muslim hegemony. The Vijayanagar king maintained a military with 60,000 salaried soldiers and 24,000 horses, a hefty garrison for those times.[64] Another custom of the golden period that seems to have prevailed in the Vijayanagar kingdom is the administrative attempt to foster the growth and tolerance of all religions. In 1368, the monarch Bukka Raya attempted to stem the persecution of Jain practitioners by the Vaishnava sects and issued an order that 'each [was] to pursue their own religious practices with equal freedom'.[65] Moreover, despite their resistance to Muslim occupation, the rulers of Vijayanagar accepted Islam, integrated its practices in their polytheist approach to religion, along with Vedic and tribal customs, and even wore Muslim attire on occasion.[66] However, unlike their northern counterparts, women in southern India did not adopt the Islamic veil, and still do not use it today. These regions, which remained relatively free of Muslim rule for a longer period, also witnessed the building of some of the last erotic temples in India. The fourteenth-century temple of Hampi, for instance, which is still fairly well preserved, was constructed under the patronage of the Vijayanagar dynasty.[67] The devadasi tradition, too, which along with the erotic temples had died out in the north, continued to persist in the south as well as in parts of eastern India, where Muslim rule had not yet extended. Puri, Assam, Rajarajeshwar in Thanjavur, Arcot, Tirunelveli and Guntur were among those places where the devadasi tradition still thrived.[68] Also, not surprisingly, many of the women saints who emerged after the golden period and initiated their own cults—the Kannada saints Akkamahadevi and Sule Sankavya of the thirteenth century, the fourteenth-century Maratha saint Janabai, the sixteenth-century Rajput saint Mirabai and the Andhra saint Atukuri Molla of the early seventeenth century—were all from regions that were not under strong Muslim control.[69] Sensuality, too, was still an integral feature of the literature and the arts in the south. The saint Akkamahadevi spoke of God with the familiarity of a lover: God, she said, was drawn to her because of her 'billowing breasts' and 'brimming youth'. And Sule Sankavya, who was also a courtesan besides being a saint, would confide in Lord Shiva about the hazards and problems of her trade.[70]

Chinese travellers to the fifteenth-century independent kingdom state of Calicut, ruled by a Hindu king, Samudri Raja, were struck by the general contentment of the people and the strictly defined ethics of trading and business that the city's merchants abided by.[71] A Turkish visitor, Abdul Razzaq, who represented the Muslim prince of Herat, observed that Calicut also had a substantially large Muslim community that had built numerous mosques. The city's most prominent merchants also were Muslims, as was one of the judges.[72] The kingdom also nurtured tolerance for religious and cultural differences, a quality it shared with the golden-age dynasties.

HYPOCRISY OF THE NEW MASTER CLASS

Despite their puritanical decrees, and their religious fervency, most Muslim rulers, and the Mughals in particular, maintained a highly decadent lifestyle. It was the Mughal nobility that introduced sports like horse polo and horse racing to India. Animal contests, earlier unknown to India, were another favourite pastime of the nobility, when tigers, cheetahs, leopards, elephants and rhinoceroses would be pitted against each other. The royals and their guests would watch from a safe distance, from across the river, sitting on the palace terrace in the shade of elegant marquees that were stitched with gold and silver thread. On the other side of the river, about a hundred men with red-hot-iron-tipped spears would goad rutting animals to battle each other.[73] Another much loved recreation was the *mushaira* or poetry recital. These were organized in opulent settings, where guests and renowned poets would sprawl out comfortably on handmade Persian rugs, amidst perfumed satin cushions, and display their poetic prowess under the soft glow of exquisite crystal chandeliers. During these revelries, gourmet food and alcohol would be served in silver platters and goblets, and people would drink to shed inhibitions, smoke opium and flirt through poetic repartee.[74]

Certain Mughal emperors were so addicted to alcohol and drugs such as opium and hashish that drinking and snorting binges would intermittently punctuate all their daily activities. For instance, Emperor Babur's diary is replete with such references: seeing an enchanting vista he drinks to it; he visits a tomb and needs a drink; a drinking party follows the noon prayers; while gifts are being presented in court, he sucks on a hashish lozenge; he takes a boat ride and drinks all the way; and he enjoys the music concerts he attends only when they are accompanied by copious amounts of liquor.[75]

Although the devadasi tradition died out mainly because the temples that sustained this practice lost their wealthy Hindu patrons, the courtesan tradition, which had evolved independently of the temples, still thrived under the Muslims. The Mughals were enthusiastic patrons of the arts and the courtesans were sought after for their beauty as well as their superior skills in music and dance. Many prominent courtesans served as court entertainers for the Muslim nobility and some became their mistresses, travelling with them wherever they went. Muslim towns like Faizabad became renowned as homes to some of the most famous courtesans.[76] However, even though these women were highly appreciated and patronized for their skills in classical music and dance, they lost the respectability they were once awarded in society.[77] The 1899 novel *Umrao Jaan Ada*,[78] made into a movie in 1981, was supposed to be an autobiographical account of a famous nineteenth-century courtesan of the same name.[79] The story goes that Umrao Jaan, who was much coveted by the nobility as one of the most beautiful and talented courtesans, fell in love with a nawab, a Muslim nobleman. However, despite the intensity of their attraction, both on a physical and on an intellectual level, the nobleman's family refused to accept Umrao, as she was a courtesan, and therefore a disreputable woman. Eventually, there was a tragic end to the relationship when the nobleman was compelled by his mother to marry someone else.

Despite their high-handed religiosity, many Muslim rulers were notorious for their sexual excesses. For instance, Wajid Ali Shah, who governed Lucknow, would help himself freely to any of the hundreds of women who worked in the palace—the palanquin-bearers, servants as well as the courtesans. He would then put his sexual escapades into poetry and brag about them by reading them aloud in public.[80]

Notwithstanding the Sharia's condemnation of homosexuality, and its ruling of the death penalty, often by brutal means—like stoning and burning alive—for homosexuals, the Muslim royalty in India inculcated a culture of homosexual practice. The trend of using 'bazaar boys' evolved, particularly in the urban marketplaces, where men across all classes and races, from musicians, judges, doctors and flower sellers, would mingle to find companionship and sexual pleasure. There was much indulgence in homo-erotic poetry that dwelt on the beauty of the lover and the sensuality of the relationships. There were also different preferences. *Amrad parast*, for instance, was a term used for men who preferred boys. Many rulers would become involved with fine-looking eunuchs in their courts, and some had their own favourites.[81]

The Muslim rulers were art enthusiasts and generously patronized artists as well as the arts. Under their benefaction, elegant new genres in various art forms emerged, which introduced the subtle elegance of Persian influences into colourful and ornate Indian styles, and embellished Islamic artefacts with Hindu motifs. This confluence of two antagonistic civilizations and religions emerged with an inspirational harmony in unique and spectacular art forms that would live on long past the Muslim rule in India. These included the Kathak dance form, ghazals (stylized lyrical songs based on poetry), the miniature-style paintings and murals that were painstakingly detailed, and an exotic nouvelle cuisine known as 'Mughlai', which blended Indian spices with the cream, nuts and dried fruits more typical of Persian cooking and introduced oven-baked foods like the kebabs and naans to the Indian palate. Not least of these art forms was the magnificent Mughal architecture that fused Turkish and Persian elements—domes, minarets and arches—with Hindu leitmotifs. The Taj Mahal, though perhaps not the most brilliant example, is still the best-known exhibit of the architecture of this period. However, the arts too had lost much of the overt sensuality of the golden age and were also no longer an expression of the sacred.

Yet, Islam was not to remain unaffected by the depreciated yet still alive sensuality of Hinduism. Regardless of the demise of the ancient temples and the near disappearance of the Tantric cults and their organized philosophies, the daily rituals of Hindu worship contained the unmistakable affirmation of the sacredness of sexuality and sexual union. The persistence of the lingam–yoni all through this period, in the form of small idols in people's homes, was perhaps the most apparent indicator. But even more remarkably, this ancient sensuality of the sacred was affirmed through one of the most popular Islamic cults that spread through India, a cult that, unlike mainstream Islam, spread not by force or compulsion, but of people's own volition and need. This was the Sufi cult. The Sufis were bohemians, wandering minstrels who revolted against the politicized and conservative Islamic structures that bound the Indian administration of that period. Much like the bhakti cults, and much against the basic tenets of Islam, the Sufis used music, dance—where they whirled into a frenzy—and alcohol to mediate with God. They freely adapted Hindu myths, local Indian languages and terms into their sermons, which made them much more accessible to the locals.[82] They held great appeal for the lower-caste people, and their devotional songs, called *chakka-namas* (literally, the songs of the wheel), usually used metaphors from the various jobs of the labour class. Women were also drawn to the Sufi saints in large numbers, one reason being the superstition that the Sufi mystics and their ceremonies had the power to grant fertility to women who wanted children. But unlike conventional Muslim sects, the Sufis permitted women to attend their meeting and sermons together with men.[83] Also, like the Hindu religions of the golden period, the Sufis celebrated the love of the sacred as an erotic experience and communion as a sexual union with the divine. *Ishq-I majazi*, romantic love,[84] they believed, was the fastest and most direct route to perfection (*kamal*) and union with God (*wisal*).[85] In fact, like the early bhakti practitioners, there were deviants among the Sufis too who took this union with God rather literally and translated it to mean copulation with idols.[86]

Other Hindu practices were also incorporated into Islamic ceremonies. For instance, the elaborate Shia ceremony of 'marrying' twelve beautiful virgins, referred to as the 'undefiled', to twelve imams or Muslim clerics, complete with a mock birthing in a delivery room, was a distinctly Hindu influence.[87] This trend, of course, infuriated the Muslim clerics. An early seventeenth-century treatise, the *Hujjat ul-Hind* (The Indian Proof), lambasted the Hindu beliefs 'creeping' into Islamic practices.[88]

All the while, the lot of the commoners worsened under the increasing burden of taxes levied to fund the Mughal empire's decadence. Despite the immense amounts they spent on themselves, the Muslim rulers did very little by means of erecting public facilities and infrastructure such as bridges, highways and canals. Much of the wealth from the treasury was exhausted on the urban centres, a handful of scattered towns and cities that housed the rulers and other nobility, and was used for building grand forts and palaces. Official records show the massive hoarding of wealth by the Muslim nobility. Emperor Akbar, for instance, had seventy million rupees in cash, while at least two of his nobles had amassed six million and ten million in cash alone.[89]

Francisco Pelsaert, who worked for the Dutch East India Company in the early 1600s, observed with shock the 'avarice' of the Mughal nobility, and the 'vanity' which prompted 'injustice, excessive pomp, [and] chicanery', when 'hundreds and thousands' in the country were so poor. He observed the 'autocratic' method of governance that was driven primarily by greed of wealth. In the case of capital crimes, as theft and murder, the poor were dragged to their execution, while the wealthy, simply by relinquishing their property, went scot-free. In the case of the death of a man who had previously been granted land by a ruler, the king's officials would waste no time in reclaiming everything he owned, including the clothes and jewellery of the widow, rarely ever leaving the family enough to subsist on.[90]

Much of India under the Muslim rule was still rural, with the inhabitants living in mud houses and struggling to pay their land and infidels' taxes.[91] The personal memoirs of many emperors—Babur, Jahangir and Shah Jahan, for instance—refer to the use of punitive measures to extract land revenue from villagers. If villages were defiant about paying their dues, the emperors would order severe punishment, such as slaughter, rape, arson and enslavement. Villages would be burnt down to the ground while soldiers collected a massive booty for themselves and enslaved women and children. Sometimes the villagers would flee to the forests and ravines to hide or to seek protection in a Hindu king's state, but the Mughal emperors would send their armies out to forcefully reinstate the absconders to their villages.[92]

Enslavement through the raiding of villages became a profitable practice for the Muslim emperors. When Qutbuddin Aibak, the first sultan of the Slave dynasty, invaded Gujarat in 1195, he captured 20,000 slaves and seven years later, at Kalinjar, he got another 50,000. Certain fourteenth-century texts like the *Khairu'l Majalis* even described methods to squash rebellions so as to use them as a source of acquiring slaves. There was such an abundant supply of slaves that in the slave markets in Delhi, they sold for less than a low-grade horse. Even the poorer Muslims could own slaves. Nur Turk, an impoverished mystic in Delhi, lived off the earnings of his male slave, who worked as a cotton carder. Those who had female slaves would put them to work in the spinning business. Most slaves could not escape and had to do whatever was expected of them. Much of the magnificent architecture from the Mughal period still existent today were indeed the creation of this form of slave labour.[93] Centuries of Muslim hegemony over India was eventually usurped by another invading colonial power—the British.

THE BRITISH PRELUDE

The British arrived in India almost a thousand years after the earliest Muslims. Their pattern of conquest, however, was quite similar to that of the Muslims—both arrived peacefully, initially as traders lured by the country's wealth in gems, textiles and spices, before they turned to a violent occupation of the land. Both believed their conquest of India to be indicative of the superiority of their race and religion.

The first formal trading company from Britain to operate in India was the East India Company. It began by exporting cotton, textiles, silk, indigo, spices, sugar and saltpeter to Europe. Its beginnings in the 1600s were modest, as also its capital which then was only one-tenth that of a Dutch company trading in India at that time. The European traders also had to answer to the Mughals, who still were governing India and had their capital in Delhi. Gradually, the East India Company was able to set up fortified trading posts in all the major cities, including Delhi, Calcutta and Bombay. In 1757, after defeating the Muslim ruler Siraj-ud-Daulah, the East India Company took over his territory in Bengal and came in possession of his treasury, which then held half a million sterlings. With a puppet ruler on the throne, the British could run Bengal like feudal lords, feeding off its land revenue. The wealth they accumulated provided incentive for them to do the same with the rest of India, which they proceeded to conquer in parts.[94]

Unlike the Muslim rulers though, there were individuals in the British administration who were greatly fascinated by Indian culture and civilization, which they regarded as superior to many others, and engaged in prolonged scholarly studies of its various fields.[95] There was also much appreciation for the skills of Indian surgeons and veterinary scientists; the British in fact borrowed knowledge in these two fields.[96] There was also a tremendous curiosity about the complex philosophies and practices of Hinduism.

The British, in defending their colonial policies, often claimed to be better masters than the Muslims. Britain's policy on the colonization of India was far more sophisticated and organized than that of the Muslim invaders and based on careful observations. They recognized a major flaw in the Muslim administration of India and took this into strategic consideration. They believed that the despotic zeal of the Muslim rulers tended to alienate the Indians. So for their part, the British chose a more sanctimonious approach. They preached that they were there for the rescue of the nation in darkness and were implementing a system to benefit the people. As one British administrator stated, the Indians would submit to them much more readily if they could be convinced that the British were actually more 'just' than the Muslims, more 'humane' and 'anxious' to improve the native's lot.[97]

SAFEGUARDING THE CHASTE

At the time the British Crown had established its governance of a substantial portion of India in the early nineteenth century, the Church of England was the most powerful factor shaping the English morality and outlook. It was an outlook that was exceedingly parochial, puritanical and intolerant of differences. Except for the cohort of intellectuals who took an unprecedented interest in Indian culture and religion, the British typically regarded Hinduism with contempt as a pagan religion, and

Indians as sexually and morally degenerate as well as racially inferior. They reasoned that the only redeeming hope for the natives lay in Christianity.[98]

Kipling in his famous poem 'Kim' spoke of the fear he felt before the Hindu altar with its imagery of 'dead' lamps and coiled grey snakes, with the eastern gods making threatening faces at him.[99] The feeling expressed is that of vulnerability and discomfort. Similarly, the writer E.M. Forster described the goddess Chamunda as 'a barbaric vermilion object'.[100]

The lingam was particularly shocking to Western sensibilities. Many called it 'obscene', as did the eighteenth-century French missionary Abbé Dubois, who thought it 'incredible' that something which in 'civilized nations' was unspeakable would be worshipped in India.[101] One Italian explorer spoke of how 'decency' prevented him from even naming it.[102] Christian missionaries would forcefully remove the lingam pendant from around the necks of Indians who wore them to church for the Sunday sermons.[103] A Scotsman, Alexander Hamilton, reporting on his travels in India in the early 1700s, spoke with disgust of how some women bowed their 'silly heads' reverentially before a naked priest, who wore a gold ring on his penis. The women, according to Hamilton, took the organ between their hands and kissed it as the sage chanted his 'filthy' prayers.[104] The British believed that Hinduism had distorted the Indian psyche, making lustful behaviour like that of Krishna's acceptable, and that the blood and gore associated with goddess worship increased the Indians' propensity for violence. Hindu concepts such as *maya* or illusion, and rebirth according to karma, were seen as rendering Indians fatalistic and indolent.[105] It was not only Hindu religion and philosophy that were believed to have impaired the natives, but their arts and customs as well. In 1920, F.E. Keay, an English writer, observed that much of the Indian literature from the bhakti period was 'erotic' and 'of a very unhealthy type'. Trying to explain what he regarded as an Indian obsession with sex, he concluded that it was because of customs like child marriage, seclusion of women and arranged marriages (therefore, a lack of courtship rituals), that personal love and romance were not given as much importance in gender relationships by Indians as sex was.[106]

Love and romance, however, were integral to the study of the kama sutras, and considered an important prelude to sex in the golden age. However, possibly with the arrival of Islam and its emphasis on gender segregation through the veiled confinement of women to the zenanas, there was little scope for romance, and marriages became predominantly social contracts arranged by the families.

Another institution—that had barely survived the Muslim era—which the British too found particularly shocking was the devadasi institution. Their attitude is odd, for the custom of temple prostitution had been prevalent in parts of Europe in the pre-Christian era, for instance, at the temple of Delphi. Alexander Hamilton in the early 1700s spoke of the devadasi institution as a 'seminary of female lewdness' where young girls were coached for the 'destruction of unwary youths'.[107] John Stuart Mill observed how Hindu laws allowed for 'every unlawful species of sexual indulgence', and that this 'depraved state' was not 'unnatural' to a primitive or 'rude people'.[108] Equally appalling to them was the blithe disregard Indians seemed to have for nudity. A certain Mrs Colin Mackenzie wrote in 1847 of how shocked she was by the apparent lack of a 'sense of decency' among the natives. She observed with horror that even on the streets of India people wore little or no clothing. She found it inconceivable that people did not seem bothered about their state of nakedness in public, and both men and women could be seen going about their business 'bare down to the hips'.[109] Missionaries, in fact, often enforced clothing on tribal converts, sometimes in European styles, with long-sleeved shirts, khaki shorts and coats.[110]

Back in Britain, it was feared that the reprehensible Indian morality would be imported into the country by returning Englishmen and would corrupt the English society at large. A comedy called *The Nabob*, performed at Dublin's Royal Theatre in November 1773, had as one of its characters a certain Sir Matthew Mite, who upon his return from India wanted to set up his own harem in England with women of different races.[111]

Horace Walpole lamented how it mattered little if England had become a 'sink of Indian wealth' if in the process the cost was to be a loss of its 'principles, genius and character'.[112]

Not surprisingly, a radically libertine faction that arose in Britain in the nineteenth century showed great enthusiasm for the hedonistic aspects of Hinduism, adopting them as revolutionary concepts. It was an attempt to mock the hypocrisies of the church and the Crown which also had their own sexual promiscuities and criminal transactions.[113]

For the British, the subjugation of the Indian subcontinent was an inherent proof of their superiority over the conquered people. For many colonizers, this was also indicative of divine intervention, the proof of which, to them, seemed ample. For instance, between 1824 and 1860, the British administration in India had introduced steamships, the telegraph and railways in the country. These amenities not only facilitated a smoother and more cohesive management of the country, but also helped augment trade, making it much more profitable for the British Crown. Many in the administration regarded these technological advancements as part of a chosen godly destiny, where the Almighty, through the means of science, assisted the British in their task of imperial conquest.[114] George Otto Trevelyan, a civil administrator, spoke of the railways in India as symbolizing 'the mightiest and most fruitful conquest of science' of a savage land.[115] In a parliamentary paper he presented, he declared that the railways would also be the 'greatest missionary of all', facilitating the demise of Hinduism and establishing the supremacy of the Christian faith.[116] He asserted that even though the Indians, 'wily' and 'tortuous' as they were, regarded the British as 'oppressive' and 'contemptible', they eventually had to 'acknowledge' their 'vast superiority' over them, in that it was the English who had conquered them. After all, in his perception, the supremacy of their 'imperial race' showed even in the manner that white people walked—'with freedom and easy insolence'.[117]

It was extremely important for the British to maintain this sense of superiority both by preserving the purity of their race and by asserting the irrefutability of the Christian faith. In the 1800s, when Britain adopted 'God Save the King' as the national anthem, Britain's imperialistic ambitions were being steered by its monarchy and the Church of England, which had become firmly linked. Britain, some demanded, should rule its colonies as a 'church state', and a viscount complained how Calcutta had no conspicuous churches, which he felt was unseemly for a city that was the 'head of a mighty Christian Empire'.[118] The British battles fought for supremacy, it was said, were 'under the direction of God' and their imperial preponderance in the world was the will of the divine. Reviling the French as 'Anti-Christ', in the aftermath of the French Revolution, Lord Auckland, the Governor General of India in 1835, expressed grave concern about the 'French disease' spreading among the British, influencing them to abandon their religion. He warned that doing so would mean that Britain would lose its 'prosperity and opulence' as it would fall in the grace of God.[119]

It also seemed extremely important to the British to maintain a clear physical boundary between the white and the brown races, and between the rulers and the subjects. This manifested, over a period of time, as a system of apartheid which prohibited Indians from entering or using facilities reserved exclusively for whites, such as clubs, schools, cinemas and shopping centres. Noticeboards would openly declare: 'Indians and dogs not allowed'. Cities had colour-segregated residential areas: the posh and wealthy quarters for the whites, and the filthy, congested and squalid ones for blacks. As Trevelyan noted with a certain aplomb, the whites even managed to keep the Indians out of first-class train carriages and, similarly (though Indian royalty were permitted), the children of the Indian merchant classes were selectively excluded from British schools like Eton and Harrow.[120] By the mid 1800s, the term 'nigger' was being freely and disdainfully used to refer to Indians in general,[121] and one British officer in a letter home noted how, unlike the Portuguese colonizers, the English never intermarried with Indians nor mixed with them in everyday affairs on an equal footing.[122]

But since contact with the natives was inevitable, one of the immediate concerns of the British administration in India was to take measures to immunize its officers from what they considered the depraved morality of the natives as well as outlaw any form of racial mixing. To the British, the Indians as a race were physically unappealing with coarse and revolting social manners.[123] The racial inferiority complex the Indians had already borne since Vedic times made it relatively simple for the British to establish white skin as superior to the brown. Aldous Huxley had correctly noted that in India 'superiority' was simply a matter of the 'epidermis',[124] while Robert Byron commented on how white skin was shown the 'homage of a divine attribute'.[125]

As moral safeguard, in the earlier years, the British men who arrived in India as officers of the East India Company had to concede to a strictly enforced puritanical code of living. The young officers, called writers, had to live in dormitory-style housing within the factory complex. They were obliged to dine together and attend regular mass in a chapel. They also had to observe various rules and take oaths, swearing that they would not get drunk, use profane language or neglect prayers, and they had to sign an oath of allegiance to always uphold the honour of God and their country. They also had to swear not to engage in 'sinful practices', a euphemism for prostitution.[126] They were to maintain racial segregation and not visit the 'black towns', the segregated districts meant for Indians. All these rules caused sexual frustration and loneliness among these young men who did not even have the choice to get married. The East India Company believed that a bachelor would be more productive than a married man because he was less likely to be distracted by domestic concerns, and it prohibited marriage for all its young employees.[127] A heavy duty was imposed on those who violated the marriage injunction.[128]

However, as far as interracial relations went, marriage or no marriage, these were unequivocally labelled as immoral and thus a social taboo. British laws even prohibited any reference to sexual liaisons between the British and Indians in fiction writing.[129]

Reginald Herber, an evangelical bishop in Calcutta, despaired at what he regarded as unholy unions with heathens.[130] The idea of cross-breeding was seen as so preposterous that it would often be treated with acerbic humour. During a Masonic-style initiation of a European Club, a certain Captain Campbell, 'a grave and respectable' man, confessed to the 'sin' of fathering three 'black babies'. The other members found the news so strange and implausible that they thought it would be hilarious if they let it slip to Mrs Campbell.[131]

There was a notion that no Britisher of class and good breeding would marry an Indian. And those who did were generally the white trash, the 'tommies' and 'riff-raffs', who also ended up with the low-class Indian women.[132]

When British women married into aristocratic Indian families,[133] it was not only scandalous, but it was also argued that moneyed Indians could afford to purchase 'culture', that is, emulate the British upper-class style of living and manners. Yet, it was insisted that despite the 'polished and veneered' exterior an Indian was still 'racially unfit' for marriage to a white person.[134] A British woman writing about the marriage of a Jane Digby to an Indian, Medjuel-el-Mezrab, spoke of the shock and revulsion she felt at the news. Her observation was that even if he was 'a very intelligent, charming man', the thought of 'contact with that black skin' was unbearable.[135]

THE INDISPENSABLE SIN

The indignant response to the sensual element in Hinduism was perhaps more surprising coming from the British than the Muslims, since Christianity in Europe in its early years had incorporated many pre-Christian practices, and was not alien to the expression of sexuality. Medieval churches in Europe depicted nude goddesses (with the vulvas emphasized), 'Sheila-na-gig', probably of a fertility cult, in key positions and places, including sacred edifices.[136] In fact, till as late as the nineteenth century, Christians in Europe were using amulets in the phallus shape, probably symbolic of the pre-Christian phallic god Priapus, as protective charms.[137]

Indeed, the social climate in Britain at the time of contact with India and till the late 1800s was quite steeped in eroticism though perhaps not as unconstrained as India was. With the advent of the Victorian age and the institutionalization of Puritanism, in a moral battle won by the Evangelical clergy and public school masters, Britain would become far more sexually repressed after 1880.[138]

However, in 1850, an official census recorded about 50,000 prostitutes in Britain, and at least 1000 brothels in London alone, which included speciality joints such as sado-masochistic parlours.[139] London acquired the reputation of being 'the whoreshop of the world' and a white slave trade ensued, where prostitutes were taken off the streets of London and exported to other parts of the world.[140] Around this time, there was also substantial indulgence in erotica in British literature, and one bookshop, when raided, was found to be stocked with about 2000 erotic prints and eighty-one sex-related books.[141]

India became an amusing playground for the lonely officers of the empire, notwithstanding the increasing squeamishness of the Victorian age. Indulgence in paedophilia, homosexuality, harems and native sexual remedies were all a part of this amusement. Edward Sellon, as a sixteen-year-old cadet, in 1834, recounted how upon his arrival in India he embarked on 'a regular course of fucking' local women,[142] a customary experience of most young British initiates. There are, in fact, numerous memoirs with accounts of such adventures. Another account of a bisexual officer includes titillating details of a three-week orgy in a brothel in Bombay.[143]

The devadasi and courtesan establishments, though not officially endorsed, were discreetly used by many officers. Though declared immoral by the government, these establishments were never actually dismantled. The colonial administration, with its grand business sense, decided to merely tax them instead.[144] In their rush for immediate sexual gratification, young British soldiers never quite grasped the complex and refined philosophies of the kamashastras, the art of love-making, which the courtesan traditions were based on, nor could they appreciate the associated culture of classical music and dance that went with it. For them, the women were simply cheap entertainment, and there are repeated references to them in British journals as 'wenches'.[145] Many officers would secretly visit them at night for a quick encounter, and the courtesans apparently did not think much of them either, often dismissing them as uncultured louts. However, without the patronage of the Indian nobility, the courtesan culture more or less petered out; in the eye of a Victorian ethos the courtesans, the elegant artists of the past, were no better than street-level prostitutes. Degraded and humiliated, these courtesans would be preyed upon by local police and other Indian authorities, who, earlier on, would not have had the privilege of accessing these women.[146]

Some of the British men, however, found the courtesans delightful and they regarded them as upper-class prostitutes. Though they considered them as being expensive, they also saw them women as being 'very different' from European prostitutes, in that they were clean, were not given to alcoholism, lived in splendour, dressed tastefully in lavish clothes and expensive jewellery, and were well educated and talented in music and dance. Besides their unique skills in love-making, the officers also appreciated the varied and contortioned body postures these accomplished women could assume.[147] One aspect of Indian prostitution that held special appeal to British men was that the women waxed their pubic hair. Wealthy men in Britain had to spend extravagantly to acquire pre-pubescent girls,[148] but, as Edward Sellon noted, men with Indian prostitutes could just 'fancy' that they had an 'unfledged girl', unless they noted the breasts.[149] Some of the prostitutes who serviced the British officers were actually as young as twelve years, as was reported by Private Frank Richards in his memoirs in as late as, 1936.[150]

The British also turned to native remedies for sexual rejuvenation, which were openly advertised in magazines that would offer products and 'confidential' guidance in 'sexual science'. This was a service used by both British men and women.

One satisfied customer in a September 1947 issue of the *Liberator* spoke of how effective the products had proved for her as her husband now found her to be as 'good as a virgin of sixteen'. Remedies for virility were also sought and popular among British women were products that were believed to be the 'secrets' of Eastern femininity. Some may have been sold by wily Englishmen doing a bit of business on the side—a depilatory, for instance, was sold as the 'closely guarded secret of the Hindus', imparted by an Indian soldier in gratitude to a Britisher who had saved his life.[151]

Another source of sexual entertainment that was different and unique to India were the eunuch brothels. Sent to clandestinely investigate the presence of British officers in these brothels, Richard Burton reported that even senior army officers were clients there.[152] The practice may have been viewed as a subversive form of homosexuality, which was illegal in Britain. Till 1861, homosexuality in Britain was a capital crime, and from 1800 to 1835, about fifty men had been hanged for sodomy. The general public would respond with a moralistic rage to reports of homosexuality, and mobs would chase and stone rumoured homosexuals.[153] In India, however, there were numerous accounts of the indulgence of British men in homosexual encounters. Lieutenant Kenneth Seabright of the Queen's Own Regiment, wrote poetry about his erotic adventures with a wide variety of men from across the country from Bengal in the east to Peshawar in the west.[154] There were also incidents reported where British commanding officers practised this sexual behaviour on Indian soldiers, something treated as a joke among other officers. But from some reports of Indian soldiers who attempted to murder their officers, there are indications that some of these cases may have involved rape.[155]

The Hindu erotic temples were a popular sightseeing spot for British officers, where they indulged in a bit of voyeurism in the open display of various sexual acts, many of which were legally prohibited in England.[156] Other men delighted in the practice of harems—Sir David Ochterlony, originally from Boston, who came to India in 1777, had a harem of thirteen women.[157]

Prostitution, however, proved to be a far greater problem for the British than simply a question of morality. The massive spread of venereal diseases among the British officers was an excessive drain on the Crown's pocket, and had to be dealt with urgently. In the late 1800s, up to a third of the British troops were infected with syphilis each year, and each soldier could spend up to fifty days in quarantine, undergoing treatment.[158] It was then that Act XXII of 1864 was passed, making it compulsory for all prostitutes in towns and ports where the British lived to be registered and to undergo routine medical examinations.[159]

Organized prostitution was acceeded to as a clinical remedy, perhaps morally wrong, but still a necessary step. Being the master class of this period, the British had the luxury to twist their own moral boundaries to best suit their purpose. Like monitored hospital wards, the British set up prostitution camps for the restricted use of British officers. The camps were set up near army cantonments and prostitutes would be hired to serve only military clientele, each being assigned an individual cabin on a designated street. Three times a week, the prostitutes would be examined by army doctors, who would put them into quarantine if they detected any infections. The military police regularly patrolled the camp, and used the baton on any Indian male who dared even initiate conversation with these exclusively reserved prostitutes.[160] Implicit here is a parallel with the British norm of reserving public spaces, clubs, cinemas and malls for 'whites only'.

The British also moved from tight-lipped disapproval of officers desiring to marry to actually encouraging them to get married. This too was seen as another solution to the venereal calamity. It was hoped that with an increase in marriage rates, the officers would not need to resort to prostitutes.[161] In fact, one administrative suggestion was that married men should be hired instead of single ones as marriage created a 'barrier to immorality'.[162] Initially, British officers were specifically instructed to marry only European women, not Indians. The selection of marriage permits followed a lottery system, where officers had to put in applications for marriage. In 1870, only twelve out of every hundred men were allowed marriage licences.[163]

However, dissuaded by tales of a rough, hot and humid climate, diseases, a constant fear of death, and a long, uncomfortable sea voyage fraught with the hazard of being kidnapped by pirates, not many European women initially ventured into India. Besides, early on, the British East India scribes were so poorly paid, at about ten pounds a year,[164] that they were not regarded as good husband material. The extraordinary luck that colonialists like Robert Clive and Warren Hastings, among others, struck by garnering almost two million pounds between them evaded most of the young, hopeful fortune hunters, who came to India and endured heat, discomfort, diseases, loneliness and death, but still remained economically hard up. Their lifestyle was not very appealing either. Initially, there was no social life of the sort that the British were accustomed to back in England—no libraries, race courses, esplanades, hotels or theatres.[165] Life for a young British woman in India would have seemed extremely drab and confined. The death rate was so high that living in India was akin to gambling with one's life. In Calcutta in one year, of the 1200 Britishers settled there, 460 died just between August and January.[166]

In the absence of available British women, till about the end of the eighteenth century, British men would marry Portuguese women from Goa, which then was a Portuguese colony in India. Taking their cue from the Portuguese, who lured young, eligible women in Portugal to travel to India by providing them with generous dowries, the British initiated a similar scheme to bring in British women. However, instead of dowries, they provided board and lodging for a year in India, during which the women were permitted to socialize in the British circles and find a suitable match. But if they did not marry within that year, the displeased East India Company would label them as hussies and send them back to England. Another problem was that many of the British women who arrived in India did not fit the class prerequisites of good breeding (for that was necessary for the British to maintain their distinction from the Indian natives) and needed to be groomed to fit into the appropriate mould, that is, taught 'good English' and the right manners before they could be considered suitable as brides.[167] Many of these women, due to economic hardships they faced in England, chose to stay on in India and work as prostitutes. The Cursetji Sukhlaji Street in Bombay, where many British women set up shop, became infamous among the British who regarded it with much anger and shame. A Bishop of Calcutta called them 'moral lepers', and missionaries would patrol the streets to dissuade customers, at the risk of water and fecal matter being dumped on them by the indignant prostitutes.[168]

The attempt to import decent brides for officers in India did not prove to be very successful at first. In 1765 the East India Company could account for only thirty-nine British women in the city of Bombay, of whom thirty-three were married. The single women on banquet invitations would be pointedly referred to as, for instance, 'Winnifred Davies, unmarried woman'.[169] Extramarital affairs within these constricted circles were commonplace and often ignored.[170] The wife of the governor of Bombay wrote of the furore that 'a cargo of young damsels from England' created upon their arrival one winter, such that the only topic of discussion in the British circles for the next weeks was a detailed analysis—height, beauty, age, manners and background—of the new arrivals.[171] In fact, such was the urgency for brides, who by administrative stipulation had to be British, that men would often propose to widows of fellow officers even before the mourning period was over. One sergeant who proposed to a widow on the very day she had buried her husband thought he had been a bit too hasty when she broke into tears. However, it appears she was just upset that she had accepted the proposal made to her by another officer, on her way out of the cemetery and did not think he was half as good as the second one.[172]

Eventually, the ban on racial segregation for marriage had to be lifted to ease the frustration of the company's officers in finding brides, and they were permitted to marry Indian women. However, this did not represent a diminishment in prejudice as it was just another administrative solution to the problem of prostitution, venereal diseases and rampant alcoholism among the soldiers. It was now officially decided that marriage with any race was acceptable, so long as it helped to stabilize the men. There were official conditions set by the East India Company regarding mixed marriages. First of all, it was assumed that Indian women had far fewer needs than European women and, therefore, they were allowed only half the allowance that European women were given to run their homes. Secondly, when the husbands returned to England their Indian wives and half-breed children would not be permitted to accompany them, though some of the men made monetary provisions for the families they were leaving behind.[173] Many British soldiers married Indian women only to tide over their sexual and domestic needs during their stay in India and would ultimately abandon their 'black wives' when they returned to England.[174]

The term 'Anglo-Indian', generally used for mixed-race children, came to take on a derogatory connotation. The British could never fully accept that these children were at least as Anglo-Saxon as they were Indian and preferred to think of them as the 'borderland area' where there was only one 'drop of white blood' in an ocean of black.[175] The Anglo-Indians were rejected by both the Indian and the British societies. Though British soldiers could marry Indian women, their manuals specifically warned them not to get involved with Anglo-Indian girls because they could find themselves socially isolated.[176] However, there was also a very grimly utilitarian aspect to the vast number of Eurasian children that were produced from mixed marriages. There are indications that a breeding programme might have ensued as part of an administrative strategy. Where the British regarded the Indians with absolute contempt as being lazy, lawless and undisciplined, they believed that 'one drop' of white in the Anglo-Indian would make him a much better junior administrator than the Indians.[177] Hence, the breeding of Eurasians seems to have been encouraged in the strategic interest of the empire.

The paucity of British brides, however, had to be dealt with more systematically. It was remedied by organizing a much more comfortable and attractive lifestyle for the British in India to lure women from working-class backgrounds desiring a more glamorous life overseas than was possible for them in Britain. As a result, by the 1800s, more European women began arriving in India looking for husbands and the custom of keeping native mistresses began to die out.[178] Their numbers swelled, and many young women either came to India on their own volition or were sent by their families with the sole purpose of finding a suitable husband. These women were dubbed the 'fishing fleet'.[179]

The new lifestyle created for the families of British officers was meant to be a statement in itself—one that spelt romance, gaiety and extravagance. It included private secretaries, a retinue of servants, splendid bungalows and a very active social life that was almost a non-stop party. Banquets and receptions with music and dance events were held almost every evening at the club, occasions that were also an opportunity for some light-hearted flirtation. It was said that the lifestyle of the British in India was so addictive that wives who later had to return to Britain longed for the leisure and glamour that their time in India had allowed them.[180]

A light work routine was adopted to make life more comfortable for the British civil servant. Take, for instance, a workday in the life of a John Beams, who was a magistrate in a court in Cuttack in 1873. He arrived at his courthouse at 11 a.m. and left at 4 p.m. In that space of five hours, he would spend about four and a half on work, leaving enough time for a leisurely lunch break in a room with a view of rivers and 'blue hills'. The rest of the day, after he returned home, would be spent riding, inspecting his rose garden, entertaining friends and visiting the club in the evening to socialize.[181]

Officers lived in sprawling houses, called bungalows, located on half-acre plots or five to ten acres, depending on seniority, that had well-maintained gardens and a full staff. The townships, called cantonments, where the British officers lived were designed to be self-sufficient in all respects. They had markets, utility stores, clubs, sports facilites, bars, ballrooms, libraries, canteens and churches.[182] A retinue of servants that tended to almost every conceivable household task became an indispensable aspect of this lifestyle even for the officers on more modest salaries. So there was the *khidmatgar*, the butler, *bhisti* or water-carrier, *sircar* or cashier, *durwan* or doorkeeper, *dhobi* or laundry-man, cooks, sweepers, nursemaids, *doreah* or dog-keeper and even a *hookah burdar*—a servant who prepared pipes for smoking.[183]

SEX IN THE POWER EQUATION

While in time it had become acceptable, to a certain degree, for British men to marry Indian women, the converse was not so. When British women did marry Indian men, it was assumed that these women were naive and under the misapprehension that all Indian men were princes. When some women did marry into Indian royal families, they were dismissed as low-class women—'manicurists' and 'nightclub entertainers'—women of 'doubtful' backgrounds. Though extramarital affairs were frequent among the expatriate British, the affairs that British wives had with Indian men caused a greater furore. In one divorce case, the irate husband explained that what he found particularly objectionable was that his wife would be 'so low' as to cheat on him with 'a native'. Even when some British women took to prostitution, the idea that they would be servicing brown men was particularly revolting to the British clergy in India. To the British, a coloured man with a white woman was an intolerable subversion of their racial superiority, a snub to their collective male ego. In the novel *Anglo-Indians*, the male protagonist felt a 'repulsion' for an Indian's prince's love for the heroine, a repulsion which he felt was normal since nature intended women to 'breed upwards, not downwards'.[184] The sexual access of British men to Indian women was, therefore, regarded as both a privilege of the superior race and an assertion of their conquest of India.[185]

In 1903 two British soldiers beat their cook to death when he failed to procure a woman as they had ordered him to. The case was eventually dismissed, with the ruling that 'the evidence was entirely native'. There were only four witnesses to the murder, all of them Indian. In fact, there were numerous incidents where native servants would get beaten to death by their British masters for trivial offences. When an attempt was made to introduce the Ilbert Bill, which would have permitted some of these cases to be tried by qualified Indian barristers who were district magistrates and session judges, it caused an uproar among the British expatriates in India. They declared that this bill would put British women at jeopardy, the assumption being that it would then enable Indian men to molest them and get away with it scot-free if an Indian judge presided over that case.[186]

The very subjugation of India was visualized as a metaphor of sexual conquest, where India was feminized as a sensuous, dangerous and alluring creature that needed to be tamed. As Kipling had once put it, the ruler and the ruled were like a couple: the former a firm, mature groom and the latter a wilful, young wife.[187] He also suggested that India was like an 'insatiable' woman with 'many lovers' whose behaviour seemed beyond 'reform'.[188] This kind of thinking created a seductive image of imperialism and the very process of colonization was romanticized in British minds.

A strongly masculine image was also built up of the British men who came to live and work for the empire in India. These were the brave, young men who dared to conquer and tame a vast and savage land, and place it like a valuable, hard-won prize at Britain's feet. This romantic image was a source of such national pride that it was constantly evoked in all aspects of living in Britain—in plays, musicals, editorials, school books and even in advertisements. Lipton brought tea directly 'from the tea gardens [in India] to the tea pot [in England]'. An exhibition held at Wembley in 1924, titled 'The Empire Exhibition', highlighted the valour and victories of British men who had subdued such a vast expanse of the world for Britain—the adage being the sun never sets on the British empire—and conquered new markets for their domestic products. The imperial army and navy became the focus of interest for boys who wanted to grow up and join them.[189] It was said that the trials they underwent in India—the heat, diseases, natives and wild animals—shaped the British boys who went to India into men of 'proven sterling metal', and 'the best' that 'England bred'.[190]

It was also the glamorous lifestyle in India—which included plenty of hunting—that enhanced this masculine romantic image. Hunting was viewed as a character-building exercise for men, and India with its vast wildlife provided ample opportunities for it. Expeditions were regularly organized and involved the killing of dangerous, 'exotic' animals like tigers and cheetahs. After a hunt, a trophy photo was a must, the hunter posing with rifle in hand and his foot on the carcass of the dead beast. The heads and skins of the animals were proudly displayed as wall-mounts and rugs in British homes, where impressive hunting stories were recounted to entertain guests at dinner parties. In the novel *A Romance of Central India*, set in the colonial era, a British woman spoke of how she would like her husband to be manly enough to hunt tigers and not behave like an 'old woman'.[191] Indeed, virility and conquest were regarded as crucial aspects of the development of a boy into a man. Aristocratic families in Britain, sometimes concerned about their young son's lack of development in this respect, and the morbid fear of homosexuality, would send him to live in the country for a while and bed every woman he could find in the village from the household servants to the milkmaids.[192]

British men also regarded themselves as more refined and civilized lovers than Indian men. Consequently, women became objects of conquest and ownership in the battle of male egos for dominance. When the Indian soldiers' mutiny in Vellore in July 1806 was investigated, it was found that the soldiers had the surreptitious backing of Indian officers who were disgruntled with the shoddy treatment they received from their British colleagues. But what seemed to irk them most was that, because the white officers were better paid than they, they had access to the more beautiful women. According to one complaint, the Indian officers were too embarrassed to meet the 'fine women' and dared not even hope to court the 'slave' of the most sought-after woman in town.[193]

The British believed that this difference in preference was because the Indians 'degraded' their women, while in more 'civilized' societies like theirs, women were 'exalted'. They expressed disdain for the manner in which Indian men treated women, which they felt was 'base' and contemptuous, disregarded women in matters of education and law, allowed them few personal rights, and did not even permit a wife to eat alongside her husband.[194] Many spoke of Indian men as being sexually perverse. When Katherine Mayo's book *Mother India*, describing the plight of child brides in India, was published in 1927, the revelations in the book horrified the West. It became a best-seller in England. There was also much distaste for the practice of dowry and the violent abuse of Indian women.[195] Sati, in particular, was perceived by the British as a repulsively barbaric practice. Between 1813 and 1825, it was recorded that 7941 women had been burnt alive on their husband's pyres in the state of Bengal alone.[196] There were numerous horrific first-hand accounts of the practice of sati as witnessed by British men. Thomas Twining in his memoirs described the gruesome details of a ceremony where the widow was a very young woman. Appalled by the prospects of her imminent death as the priest prepared her for the ceremony, Twining tried to dissuade the young woman, promising her a pension. However, he said that the woman looked helpless and seemed resigned to her fate. He spoke in excruciating detail of how two men hauled her on to the pyre and tied her down to her husband's corpse, pinning her down with fuelwood till she was buried beneath. When the pyre had been burning for a while there was a loud explosion, followed by another. These were greeted with sounds of 'satisfaction' by the crowds, as signs that both skulls had burst in the furnace.

In another reported incident on 27 September 1823, a widow managed to escape from the burning pyre twice. Her legs were burnt the first time, then three men grabbed her and forced her back on the pyre, where they covered her with logs. The second time, her whole body was in flames, but she ran towards the river and jumped into it. However, her attempt was futile as the men dived in after her and held her underwater till she drowned.[197]

British men also regarded themselves as the gallant protectors of white women. The conviction was that Indian men, because they were not accustomed to female company, having always cloistered their women, would be aroused by the mere sight of British women who lived far more 'free and unrestrained' lives as they rode in public, drove in open carriages, dined, conversed and even danced with other men. This, it was believed, stimulated vile thoughts in the heads of Indian men, which was why British men were reluctant to take their wives and daughters to parties that were also attended by Indian men. Indian men were alleged to have such gauche manners that it was considered inappropriate for a British lady to even travel in the same railway compartment as them. A Britisher observed they were, therefore, obliged to keep Indian men out of first-class train compartments. He also commented on how his countrymen, because of their 'chivalry', submitted to a queen as monarch and regarded their women as 'goddesses'. He said that this behaviour apparently puzzled Indian servants, who treated their Indian mistresses with contempt, or as 'playthings' as they had seen their Indian masters do.[198]

This battle for sexual power was not limited to symbolism, but played itself out in a graphic and morbid manner in the rape, sexual mutilation and kidnapping of women. In battles with certain tribesmen, the Baluchis and Afghanis, for instance, British soldiers who were caught were killed and disfigured. A British couple straggling behind their camp was found murdered, with the man's chopped-off penis placed in his wife's mouth, and her excised breasts placed in his mouth as a symbolic humiliation. As the Duke of Wellington observed, when tribesmen murdered British officers and molested their wives, it undermined the power and control of the British Empire.[199]

Newspapers in Britain often carried gruesome accounts of the rape, torture and murder of British women by Indian men, particularly during mutinies. There were stories of women being hacked to pieces, a certain captain's wife boiled alive in ghee, and of forty-eight Englishwomen marched through the streets of Delhi, before being publicly raped and killed.[200] The popular *London News* reported on how a Miss Wheeler in Kanpur shot herself with a pistol so that she did not have to surrender to lecherous Indian soldiers. In another account, which became memorialized in the public's mind through a Christina Rossetti poem, a certain

Alexander Skene shot his wife and then himself at their home before the Indian soldiers got to them.

The diaries of Englishwomen who survived the 1857 mutiny contain some harrowing accounts. Many of them witnessed their husbands' execution, while they themselves were held prisoners by gangs of drunken soldiers who leered at them and kept them at their mercy.[201] It is hard to determine exactly what these women may have endured, for given the squeamishness about rape even in Victorian society, it is highly unlikely that the survivors would have admitted to being raped. Though many of these reports went unconfirmed and some were later refuted, the idea of the modesty of British women being sullied by Indian men caused an outrage in England and evoked the chivalry of men, who felt compelled to protect their honour. This sentiment was expressed in poems and paintings. In Joseph Paton's painting *In Memoriam*, exhibited at the Royal Academy in 1858, a group of frightened Englishwomen huddle together as they are attacked by evil-looking Indian soldiers. A child's severed head lies nearby, while one woman clasps an infant to her breast and another clutches a Bible.[202] The image conveyed the idea of a vulnerable and sanctified womanhood—of the mother and wife that nurtured Britain's future—being in mortal danger, beseeching her men to come and rescue her. Such outrages so infuriated the writer Charles Dickens that he declared that they should do their best to 'exterminate the race' that had inflicted that 'stain' on them.[203]

REDEFINING WOMEN

The British believed that, ultimately, the only hope for the moral redemption of Indian society lay with its women. Treating this as another imperialistic goal, they began by defining what they saw as a fit model of the ideal Indian womanhood. They delineated a new emerging middle class, where women upheld the requisite values of approved gentility. Any expression of sexuality was not only 'crude' and 'licentious', but also branded as the 'behaviour of lower-class women'. As sexuality had been such an integral aspect of the formal arts—music, dance, theatre and the courtesan culture—all through the golden age, women artists were now considered as belonging to the lower classes and looked down upon with contempt. Many of these artists, who were once patronized by the nobility and the upper class, found themselves socially ostracized and destitute. Courtesans, who even during the Mughal period had continued to flourish as artists and retained their glamour, were now regarded as common prostitutes. Ultimately, for many other female artists too the only option left was to eke out a living from street prostitution.[204]

Through a rigorous campaign by means of the radio and popular magazines, Indian women were informed of the domestic and moral roles that they were expected to play in their homes and in society. The target audiences were the middle- and upper-class urban women. Home science was popularized as an excellent subject for women to study in school and college, and was made compulsory. One home science teacher described it as a sort of 'town planning' to better the lives of the 'poorer' Indian sisters. Declared by the Women's Indian Association as being a progressive and enlightening step forward for Indian women, home science, it was said, distinguished the lady of high bearing, both culturally and morally, from the other women.[205]

The Englishwoman was held as the paragon of Christian virtue for the new image the Indian woman was urged to adopt. The grooming of an Englishwoman to mould her into the perfect idea of womanhood principally involved her knowing how to keep a clean and efficiently running household where the needs of the husband and children were fully taken care of. In India, British housewives were also required to undertake what was considered the proper supervision of the domestic staff. In *The Complete Indian Housekeeper and Cook*, the author, Flora Annie Steel, instructed English housewives in India in the techniques of handling their domestic retinue. The 'first duty' of the housewife was to know how to give 'intelligent orders' to the servants. The 'next duty' was to enforce the tasks, and should the servants not listen, Steel recommended punishments such as administering a spoon of castor oil, as with a disobedient child.[206]

There was also a customized personality for the ideal woman. Young English women on the lookout for eligible husbands in India had certain stipulated rules of decorum. They were to be 'properly dressed', to speak in low tones, never to have more than two glasses of wine at a meal, and to always close the day with psalms and prayers.[207] Women were expected to be plain, selfless and modest. To indulge their sense of aesthetics or dwell on thoughts of beauty was deplored as vanity, and they were to take no pleasure in their appearance. The book *Pleasant Quippes for Upstart Newfangled Gentle Women* suggested that the more women 'look in their glass' the less likely they were to 'look to their house'.[208] Though the early fashions of the Victorian era allowed for a generous display of cleavage, by the late 1800s, Englishwomen had to button up to the neck and keep all parts of their bodies, except the face, concealed. They wore ankle boots, layers of petticoats and long, lace-cuffed sleeves that covered them up to the wrists.[209]

Nor were women to nurture any desire for sex or the enjoyment of it—they were expected to assume a childlike naive unawareness of it and to reveal no understanding 'of the pleasures of the flesh'.[210] However, a wife was still expected to engage in it as a duty towards her husband and a means to bear him children. Women also had no control over their sexual cycles as birth control was frowned upon, and as a result, due to frequent childbirths, death during labour was not uncommon; many Englishwomen also suffered from distorted pelvises.[211] Moreover, they were to accept that sex was a man's requirement—when Marquess Wellesley wrote to his wife, Hyacinth, in England, asking for her consent for him to keep a mistress in India, she was extremely obliging. She replied that she hoped he would meet his sexual needs with the 'honour, prudence and tenderness' he had shown her.[212] For a man, sexual urges were said to be 'spontaneous' and not of his own will, but a sex drive in a woman was considered unnatural. It was believed that the primary and natural feeling in women was not that of lust but love.[213] The medical opinion of a British physician in 1914 was that nine in ten women were 'indifferent' to sex or detested it, but that a woman who liked it would inevitably be a 'harlot'.[214] This was also the prescribed model for Indian women—a far cry from the sexual liberalism of the golden age, when the sex drive in women was affirmed as natural and women were encouraged and taught how to explore and take pleasure in their sexual needs.

Women in Victorian England who had pregnancies out of wedlock were regarded as sexually promiscuous and depraved. Unwed mothers were socially ostracized and one factory even made their unwed pregnant workers wear yellow clothing to mark them as 'disorderly and profligate'. These women did not even have the option of giving the babies up for adoption, as a baby would be accepted for adoption only if the mother could prove that she was raped.[215]

The social choices that accompanied these tightly restricted boundaries in sexual and personal matters for women were just as limited. In Britain, women still had no right to vote, and no legal protection against domestic violence. Ironically, even when a queen was in power, they had to be content with being second-class guests at her birthday celebration. At Queen Victoria's golden jubilee gala in 1887, women were served food only after the men were done and while they only had cake and sandwiches, the men feasted on roast beef, mutton, potatoes, plum pudding and beer.[216] Women were expected to bear these slights in virtuous silence, and still strive to serve as icons of morality by inconspicuously caring for their homes and performing social service. Their place in society was clearly demarcated. They were to restrict their activities to their own houses, keep to their cooking and needlework obediently, and leave the goverance of society and all its functions to men—otherwise as Lord Tennyson's 1847 poem 'The Princess' declared, there would be 'all . . . confusion'. It was believed that a woman's weak intellect and physique made her incapable of innovation, discovery, defence and command, and that she should simply keep to 'sweet ordering'.[217] Indeed, even the woman in command of the empire, who contrary to all stereotypes of feminine abilities occupied Britian's throne, was at the forefront of the social resistance to any show of strength and initiative in women. A certain Mrs Duberly, the wife of a British officer, had, against all conventions, accompanied her husband to the war front during the Crimean War. When she published her journal describing her experiences, Queen Victoria was so offended by her forwardness that she refused to shake her hand at a royal reception.[218]

To prevent this new, prescribed image for Indian women from appearing too Christian and thus too alien, the British aligned their model with the patriarchal Vedic one, and declared the ancient Vedic value system to be the best role model for Indian women on how to be virtuous. A 1925 publication, *Women in Ancient India*, written by an Englishwoman, extolled the selflessness of the Vedic women, their service to their family, and their extreme devotion to their husbands, such that they would even commit sati for them. The loss of these Vedic values in Indian society was blamed on the rise of indigenous cults.[219] Obviously, the author of this book had not investigated the sexual lives of Vedic women very scrupulously—their open expressions of lust, or the liberties they took with multiple lovers, causing Vedic men much resentment and mistrust about what they regarded as women's 'innate' tendency to commit adultery. Often the Indian translators, whom the British depended on for accessing the Vedas, would in consideration of Victorian squeamishness repackage the scriptures and omit references to sex.

This was not surprising, given that much like the Vedic men, British men too viewed sex as a primarily male arena where women simply played the role of a detached womb. Besides the medical verdict that declared the sex drive as being unnatural to women, the English sentiment in general regarded female sexuality with much unease, suspicion and resentment.

Some of the beliefs that underlay the Victorian discomfort with female sexuality were astonishingly similar to Vedic notions. For instance, the concept that women interested in sex were so treacherous that they could actually suck the brain tissues out of a man, down the spine and through the penis, threatening his sanity and health,[220] paralleled the Vedic fear that women would rob men of their semen and cost them their lives. Menstruation too caused much angst in both communities. Till the late nineteenth century, the pious communities of England believed that menstruating women had destructive powers: their mere touch could wither the crops in the fields, kill honeybees in their hives and rust iron and steel.[221] English vicars would refuse communion to menstruating women or those who had had sex the night before.[222]

Indeed, the British were exceedingly uncomfortable with the remnants of the sexual liberalism of Indian women that had carried over from the golden period and were vehemently opposed to it. James Mills commented on how, despite the much proclaimed gentle beauty of Indian women, they actually lacked 'refinement', in that they were able to listen to the 'indelicate expressions' in some of the religious texts like the *Hitopadesa* 'without a blush'.[223]

Members of certain Indian cults like the Vaishnavas were singled out as being particularly licentious and were persecuted. The 1891 British census of India noted that such grassroots cults were accessible to all people, including women, irrespective of caste, class and breeding. In fact, the travelling Vaishnava groups provided a safe haven for some of the most persecuted members of society, such as outcasts and widows.[224] This classlessness was most disconcerting to British administrators who were banking on the creation of class boundaries to build the moral paradigm of the ideal Indian woman. Besides the class mixing, the British were also most disapproving of how single women as well as married ones would sometimes abandon their families to join these bohemian groups, and freely travel with them all over the country. The British felt that these 'unbridled' cults that encouraged the 'licentiousness' of women were a dangerous social influence and had to be curbed.[225]

Perhaps most scandalous to the British was the sexual liberalism of the Vaishnava culture. Love was the basis of the Vaishnava philosophy, which included physical and sexual love. Vaishnavas lived in communes called *akhras*, and women were free to get involved with any men they were attracted to and change partners as they desired. Worse still was the fact that the Vaishnavas advocated adultery. They believed that if people deeply desired to experience the divine, they could do so only through adulterous relationships. It was said that marriages, constricted by social conventions and laws, became suffocating and mundane for both partners. It was only when a person fell in love with someone who was married to somebody else that one could experience the passion, the intensity, the longing and the mysterious pleasure of divine love. The Vaishnavas held Lord Krishna's affair with Radha, a married woman, as the ultimate example of how this form of divine love worked.[226]

Many Vaishnava women were also singers and performers. While sensuality was an inextricable aspect of their music, their songs were most likely some of the earliest vocalized expressions of women's desire for freedom. The Vaishnavas often sang of the life and issues that concerned women, their domesticity and their place in society. Perhaps what irked the British was that the Vaishnava women would perform these songs for the entertainment of upper-class housewives, who, because of their cloistered existence, enjoyed these at-home concerts. Sometimes upper-class homes would even allow Vaishnava women—many of whom were literate—to tutor their children for a small fee, which was additional income for them. The British administration pushed for the social isolation of Vaishnava women by setting up class boundaries and redefining respectability. It was no longer permissible for genteel middle- or upper-class women to associate with Vaishnava women, considered of a low social bearing. In the process, Vaishnava women also lost their already meagre incomes from performing and teaching and were often compelled to turn to prostitution.[227]

A similar fate befell various other female artists: musicians, actors and dancers, the *tarja* and *jhumur* troupes, who depended upon upper-class patronage to survive. In the eighteenth and nineteenth centuries, women artists and folk singers would form their own bands and tour the country unencumbered, performing impromptu for villagers and the upper class alike. They sang songs about women's emotions, their anger and desperation, their loves and their love-making, the songs striking a chord with their mostly female audience who identified with the lyrics. Often the compositions were witty and humorous, and were not shy of being sexually explicit either. One nineteenth-century song in Bengal, for instance, was about a married woman whose numerous lovers were always knocking at her door, much to the shock of older women neighbours. The song goes on to ridicule the tedium of a 'boring' husband whom the woman had to 'suffer for an hour' daily, indicating the wife's sexual dissatisfaction and hence her need for other lovers. These undoubtedly shocked the British for they labelled the women as bawdy, with no virtue, and would send in the police to disband their shows.[228]

Along with the artists, the Indian arts too began to languish. It was no longer considered respectable for the middle and upper classes to allow their daughters to learn music, or dance or stage-acting, as most of the arts had evolved into formal disciplines in the golden period and contained strong elements of the sensual and sexual. In 1891, according to one government census, there were 17,023 female artists. By 1901 there were only 3527.[229]

Another Indian tradition that was unappealing to the British was that of matrilineal communities. The few matrilineal lineages and their customs that survived in India were attacked. Women in these families not only were the bearers of the clan name as well as inheritors of family properties, but they also had plenty of sexual freedom and choice. In certain communities in present-day Kerala which had been matrilineal for many centuries, the British imperial law intervened—the practice was denounced as aberrant and the adoption of the more 'natural', patriarchal forms of social structures was urged.[230] As a result of these new laws, the social and economic position of women in these societies was considerably undermined.

The moral reshaping of the Indian woman also involved either the sanitization or total ban of all literature, modern and ancient, that the British regarded as profligate. One of the books banned and put out of circulation was a translation of *Radhika Santvanan* (Appeasing Radhika) by an eighteenth-century Telugu poet, Muddupalani, who was also a courtesan in the court of the king of Thanjavur. Descendant of a matrilineal clan, which she often boasted of, Muddupalani was not only well educated and versatile in the arts—music, dance and literature—but she also owned property through inheritance, was wealthy, socially respected and had the freedom to travel where she willed. In her work, she drew on her professional expertise on sexuality and human psychology and, in the form of instructions to Lord Krishna on how to pleasure Radha, she essentially talked about what women wanted during sex. She provided a series of candid dos and don'ts—for example, Radha's nipples were to be held gently with the fingertips, but not squeezed too hard so that it did not cause discomfort and pain. Sometimes, Muddupalani depicted Radha as sexually assertive, 'stabbing' Krishna with her firm breasts, as well as instructing her young niece on the art of sex, urging her to freely explore her desires.[231]

Though this book stayed in circulation through the British period, the editions were often sanitized versions of the original. In 1910 Nagaratnamma, herself a well-known courtesan and musician, decided to restore the book to its original form through a fresh translation. The British, however, found the newly released version morally corrupting and capable of ruining the Indian mind. They seized all copies of the book and charged Nagaratnamma with obscenity under Section 292 of the Indian Penal Code. Numerous other books from the classical age, which like Muddupalani's had been regarded as literary masterpieces in the past, were also taken off the shelf. More interesting was the response from some Indian writers at that time, for it was an indicator of the enormous changes that had occurred in the Indian mindset about sexuality under the influence of a colonial Victorian regime. What at one time was appreciated as art was now regarded with contempt. The writer Kandukuri Veereshalingam, for instance, vehemently denounced Muddupalani's works, calling her an 'adulteress' and a prostitute who had no sense of shame,[232] an accusation which two hundred years after the writing of the book made little sense.

These new Victorian sensibilities of Indians were perceptibly radical, considering that even in the mid 1800s wealthy merchants of Calcutta who organized elaborate celebrations of the Durga Puja festival at their residences would include a nautch show (provocative dance performances) as part of the nine-day ritual worship of the goddess Durga. An invitation card from 1817, from a merchant, Prankrishna Haldar, to all the British families of Calcutta, 'respectfully solicited' their company for a 'Grand Nautch', with dinner and wine.[233] This new moral squeamishness of the Indian middle class was reflected in the emerging designs of Indian clothing, which now closely mimicked the British dress sense—a dress sense that was highly unsuited to India's hot, tropical climate.[234] Yet the British had continued to wear wigs, bonnets, high-collared uniform coats, cravats, hoops, farthingales, petticoats, tight pantaloons and top hats, as they did in England, and consequently, there were frequent bouts of illness from heat strokes and spells of fainting among the women.

Despite the absurdity of this attire the Indian bourgeoisie, both men and women, eagerly adopted various features of Victorian dressing as well as its stuffy sense of propriety, which focused on keeping much of the body concealed. The clothing of Indian women, even among the upper class, initially did not include blouses or petticoats—just a five-yard, translucent sari, which was draped around the body. Not only was the torso left bare, but the cotton was so diaphanous that it was almost see-through.[235] One Indian writer commented that the women seemed virtually 'naked'.[236] It was believed that the traditional clothing worn by Indian women inside the zenana was inappropriate for more public occasions. Thus it was with quite a bit of zeal and improvisation that the 'reformed dress' for Hindu women finally materialized.[237] They now adopted the Victorian-style long-sleeved blouses with high collars, sometimes with lace ruffles at the neck and the wrist. Where earlier they went barefoot, women now wore shoes and socks under their saris. The volume of the cloth worn around the legs was draped with manifold layers of pleats in the sari, now worn over petticoats. These bales of cloth, most probably totalling nine or more yards, would be modestly held in place with ornate broaches of Victorian designs, a piece of jewellery so far unknown to India, despite the extensive styles of jewellery created for almost every part of the body since the golden ages. But then again, we see a shift in the function of clothing and jewellery from the golden period, when these were utilized not so much to conceal the body as to enhance the natural beauty and sensuality of the naked human form.

The practice of using cloth to cover the body, an object of shame, had already been adopted during the Muslim period, when stitched clothing was introduced in India. During the Muslim era Indian women wore short blouses—some, strangely enough, so short that they barely covered the nipples—veils, and long skirts, with a wide expanse of the midriff still exposed. Interestingly, this was the first time skirt-like clothing was worn in India. The translucent loin cloth worn during the golden age, which was pulled up between the legs, had allowed women a certain freedom of leg movement, which the skirt physically constricted. Also, in keeping with the Muslim style of the purdah, a billowing head-to-foot tent-like covering for the female body, the sari evolved as adapted clothing for Hindu women. However, there was still a certain consideration given to comfort, and upper-class Indian women secluded in their homes kept their torsos naked despite the volume of the sari. Women of the lower working classes continued to move through society unselfconsciously bare-chested. The Muslim rulers saw this as an aspect of the uncivilized manners of the pagan people, marking them as non-Muslims. However, the British felt morally obligated to civilize the Indians, which resulted in the blouse and petticoats being worn under the sari.

It cannot be denied, however, that the British had a certain historically significant and constructive impact on the social bearing of Indian women. Numerous laws pertaining to women's rights in India followed in the footsteps of similar laws initiated by the women's suffrage movement in England. In terms of political consciousness and gender balance, many of the new laws were the equivalent of an earthquake in Indian society, ridding it of some centuries-old plagues, abhorrent practices like sati. For the first time ever in Indian history, the individual and collective rights of women were addressed at a legal and administrative level. These laws, in effect, set the base for tackling human rights issues for Indian women, and actually affirmed their rights to dignity and, to a certain degree, to choice in their own lives. Where earlier girls were not permitted into formal educational institutions, in 1823 the first girls' school was inaugurated. Within five years, thirty more such schools, mostly run by missionary organizations, had been established. Oddly enough, upper-caste Hindu families initially refused to allow their daughters—whom they kept cloistered at home—to attend these schools; so most of the students were from the poorer, lower-caste families or were the daughters of prostitutes.[238] However, over time, wealthy, upper-class families, particularly those of the Brahmo sect, started surreptitiously educating their daughters. The Brahmo Samaj was a reformist Hindu sect that was highly influenced by Christianity and westernized thinking. It rejected various fundamental Hindu beliefs and practices, such as the caste system, idol worship and the Vedic doctrines, and borrowed certain Christian ideologies like the belief in a single creator, and the need for social enlightenment. In the 1901 census it was found that 55.6 per cent Brahmo women were literate and almost 31 per cent were fluent in English, compared to a 5.6 per cent literacy rate for Hindu Brahmin women, of whom only 0.1 per cent were fluent in English.[239] The other section of Indian society in which women had a high propensity for education was the upper-caste converted Christians.[240] By 1875 women in India were joining universities and the Hunter Commission in 1882 further emphasized the importance of the education of women. Several acts both before and after this sought to improve the condition of women. In 1859 the Hindu Widow's Remarriage Act legalized a widow's right to remarry, and the Indian Succession Act of 1925 gave her the right to her dead husband's property. Women also won the right to independent earnings through the 1874 Married Women's Property Act, where a woman could independently own property and wealth that she earned through her own talents, without her husband automatically claiming ownership of her assets. One of the most momentous legislatures was of course the Bengal Sati Regulation Act of 1829 which banned the practice of sati outright. In 1860 rape, abduction marriages and bigamy were made illegal, and in 1929 the Child Marriage Act set a minimum age of fourteen for the marriage of girls.[241]

However, as eager as the British were to redefine Indian femininity, the Indian men were just as adamant about retaining their patriarchal licence to power. For example, in 1890, a girl less than ten years was married off to a much older man; she died from haemorrhaging after he had sex with her on the night of their wedding. Consequently, the government decided to introduce an age of consent law, raising the minimum age by only two years (from what it was then) to twelve. The law garnered the support of only a small group while it caused tremendous agitation among the majority of Indian men, who organized huge protest rallies. It even became a heated topic of debate at the annual meeting of the Indian National Congress, the political party at the helm of India's social and political movement for democracy. It was stipulated that Hindu scriptures entitled adult men to pre-pubescent girls—for instance, a man of thirty could marry a twelve-year-old girl, and a twenty-four-year-old man could have a girl of eight[242]—and that the custom should be allowed to continue. Muslim clerics argued that Muhammad himself had slept with his wife Ayesha when she was barely nine.[243] Eventually, the Indian National Congress decided to vote in favour of upholding Indian men's rights to child brides. The British response was that it was not an unexpected conclusion for a barbaric people who habitually 'degraded' their women. Though the minimum age law still held sway, the British dared not implement it or examine it again for fear of reviving social unrest till almost thirty years later.[244]

Similarly, the issue of a widow's right to remarry and her right to her husband's inheritance ran into trouble with the public. This law was akin to a disruption of certain patriarchal privileges that so far had been zealously guarded by men. A widow who inherited her husband's property and then married a man outside her husband's family could cause the husband's lineage to lose some of its property and wealth. Secondly, there was the issue of shame. It was scandalous for a family to have a daughter-in-law, even if she was widowed, in an intimate relationship with a man outside the family.[245]

As much as the British advocated the emancipation of the repressed Indian woman, it was still more of a humanitarian gesture than an invitation to power-sharing in the legal, political and administrative arena. Where women in Britain—after a long and embittered battle—had finally won the right to vote in 1918, the colonial British government was not prepared to make the same accession to Indian women. In 1919 the Southborough Committee rejected a resolution passed by Indian national parties, under pressure from women's lobby groups, asserting their right to vote. The committee rather opportunely surmised that women's suffrage was 'out of harmony' with most Indian customs and practices.[246] Other British policies, such as those concerning artisans or matrilineal property laws, also had a tremendously negative impact on the economic powers and status of women in society. Furthermore, the British sabotage of India's indigenous textile industries affected the livelihoods of village women in the worst possible way, destroying the economic sustenance for many. These women now, instead of working from home and being in control of their own trade and finances, had to work as labourers in factories, which, oddly, was seen as a liberation by many. These women would work as hired labour for almost twelve-hour days for a meagre wage of ten rupees a month—insufficient to even feed a family of four or five—so they were constantly in debt.[247]

A peculiar feature of the women's liberation movement in India was that the most vocal Indian advocates for numerous issues concerning women's rights seemed to be men and not women. Astonishing as that may seem, there was a rationale for this. Many of the prominent male activists had been educated in Europe, and were highly influenced by Western concepts of democracy and human rights. They desired for India the same degree of social and economic advancement and freedom as they had witnessed in Europe. They realized that issues like dowry, sati, illiteracy and child marriage held back Indian society, and that it was imperative that Indians consciously and proactively addressed them. Raja Rammohan Roy, one of the most vocal reformers, observed with shame that Indian women were often treated with less regard than 'inferior animals' and were considered as nothing more than household slaves.[248] Ishwarchandra Vidyasagar, who led the fight for widow remarriage, faced staunch social opposition. He prevailed, but eventually conceded that the Widows Act was really a lip service, as the 'conventional hostility' towards widows was too deeply embedded in society for a simple Act to change it.[249] Numerous male writers also attempted to revolutionize Indian thinking through the medium of female protagonists in their novels. In the novel *Gora* by Rabindranath Tagore, a woman attends her son's wedding to an out-of-caste girl, much against the wishes of her family. Also in Tagore's *Aparichita* (The Stranger), a girl's father asks the groom's family to leave after they blackmail him with dowry demands on the eve of the wedding. The father was also shown to love and cherish his daughter as he would his son, conversing with her on various topics, and seeking her views and opinions. In Bankim Chatterjee's *Bishabriksha* (The Poison Tree), when a man brings home a second wife, his first wife refuses to accept his bigamy and leaves him. In *Streer Patra* (The Wife's Letter) by Tagore, a wife confronts her husband's chauvinism, telling him that while he delights in her beauty, her intelligence makes him uncomfortable. And in Sarat Chandra Chattopadhyay's *Sheshprashna* (The Last Question), the character Kamal is shown to be unimpressed by the Taj Mahal. She challenges people's idealization of it as the epitome of love saying that even if the emperor built it as testimony to his eternal love for his wife Mumtaz, it could not be held as proof of his single-minded devotion to one woman—since besides Mumtaz he had a whole harem of women.[250]

While the exposure to Western thinking was a source of intellectual stimulation for a vast section of Indians, there was also a substantially large portion of middle-class Indian men who greatly desired to emulate the lifestyle of the British for no reason other than their sycophantic awe of the ruling classes. Socially ridiculed by both Indians and the British, and derogatorily referred to as *babus*, these men thought it fashionable to have their Indian wives adopt Western customs, and, perhaps even be a little educated. The babus perceived an educated wife as vital to the domestic environment of the refined Englishman, as she made a far 'better housewife' than their own uneducated wives.[251] The British wife could not only run the house more efficiently and create a comfortable and aesthetic home environment, but could also do so in a marvellously effortless manner. She also looked pretty and composed at an occasion like a dinner party, sitting down to eat alongside her husband, unlike Indian wives who served their husbands first and often discreetly ate later in the kitchens. The British housewife also had enough awareness of issues outside her housework to be able to engage her guests in conversation and keep them entertained. The babu's wife on the other hand was cloistered and uneducated, and could not even manage the household accounts or the house without help from her husband. She was much too inhibited to entertain guests she was unfamiliar with—nor could she provide good companionship to her husband.[252] The novelist Sarat Chandra Chattopadhyay said that Indian men were 'depriving themselves of something' that is extremely 'valuable' by not educating their women.[253] True to its male-centric roots, the change in gender roles in Indian society was, to a degree, still motivated by the view of women as commodity.

Later, when large sections of Indian men began to feel their patriarchal position and social dominance challenged by educated women, who had begun to demand equality and participation in all aspects of public life, they protested and called for a halt of women's education. As the manifesto in one newspaper declared—men were not against the education of women, but believed that its sole purpose should be to make women 'better wives and better mothers'.[254] In their view, women were weak and fickle and forgot their traditional values and lost their femininity when they concerned themselves with issues outside the domestic realm. Apparently, in the process, they also neglected their homes and families. John Elliot Drinkwater Bethune, who established the first girls' school for upper-caste Hindus in 1849, and later the first women's college in 1879, was accused of causing Indian women to lose their traditional virtues. It was argued, therefore, that Indian women ought not to be educated since they had to be shielded from the ill effects of Western values.[255]

Even some of the most influential leaders of this time, for instance Gandhi, at some level, resisted the notion of the total empowerment of women. Giant literary male figures, such as Tagore and Sarat Chandra Chattopadhyay were uncomfortable with the idea of women's economic independence. Salaried jobs, it was presumed, was only for the lower-class women who worked as maids and vendors, especially as fish and vegetable sellers.[256] Some of the earliest Indian women doctors in the late nineteenth century faced immense public hostility from men, who felt discomfited by the high earning abilities of these women and subjected them to intense campaigns of slander.[257] Oddly enough, while many of the literary works by men on one hand rallied for women's rights, they also concurred with the Victorian notion that a woman was to be domesticated and contained in her house. Sarat Chandra Chattopadhyay, who showed much sympathy for women who had to endure the constrictive lifestyles that were enforced on them, in his book *Pather Dabi* (Bid for the Pathway) was not so sympathetic towards women who sought independent identities outside their homes and in politics. Tagore, a champion for widows, failed to appreciate the show of willpower and self-assertion by women in politics. In his novel *Char Adhyay* (Four Chapters), the protagonist Ela, a revolutionary leader, concedes defeat in the end and is advised that the powerful woman is the one who reigns at home over meals and her family and that, ultimately, it is 'unnatural' for women to fight in the political arena.[258]

THE INDIAN WOMAN AWAKENS

Despite the camaraderie that European and Indian women were expected to share in their common goal of achieving the idealized femininity, socially, the two had little in common and did not associate extensively. With a few exceptions, British wives in India preferred to stay within the confines of their expatriate society and rarely ventured out to explore or understand the alien Indian culture. Their insularity bred insecurities and deep prejudices and it was even suggested that they managed to divorce the British officer from his Indian troops, as well as Britain from India.[259] There have been similar observations, even from Indian quarters, that early during the colonial period British officers who had Indian mistresses were far more open to mingling with the Indian soldiers in their regiments and to experiencing local customs than the British officers who came later and were married to their own kind,[260] though the reasons for this change are debatable.

However, the British women's attitude towards Indian women in general is comparable to that of a wife towards the mistress. There were undercurrents of a mute hostility that British women appeared to feel towards their Indian counterparts, an anxiety that regarded the Indian woman as an exotic, mysterious and sensual being, who was a threat to the stability of British marriages. Indeed, the Indian woman's beauty was often a topic of contemplation for male British writers. Godfrey Charles Mundy in his *Pen and Pencil Sketches*, while observing women washing and fetching water at the river bank, commented on how 'graceful' and 'elegant' the Indian woman appeared even in labour. He marvelled at how she 'floats past unencumbered', even though her 'slender neck' seemed almost too delicate for the heavy pots she carried on her head. Mundy also remarked that where British men were fascinated by the beauty of Indian women and appreciated the hard labour they had to do, Indian men seemed to take them for granted.[261] Not only was there much eagerness among British women to discover the feminine secrets of seduction in Indian harems, but it was also said that a European woman's sensuality would miraculously emerge when she wore Indian clothes and jewellery.[262] British women would also exchange contemptuous gossip about their Indian counterparts, while some would simply be condescending. Annette Beveridge in her diary noted that the wife of Keshub Chandra, a prominent Indian intellectual, appeared to her like an 'uncultivated' peasant in her red sari, without any shoes or stockings, and even 'sat like a savage' with no grace or decorum.[263]

Yet, undoubtedly, the women's suffrage movement in England was a catalyst for changes not only in the legal standing but also in the social consciousness of women in India. Between 1880 and 1930, several women's organizations were established, with national and local chapters. These included the Women's Indian Association, Sakhi Samiti (Association of Women Friends), Bharat Stri Mahamandal (Great Circle of Indian Women) and the All India Muslim Ladies Conference, all of which campaigned for women's rights.[264] Despite the occasional female monarchs in Indian history, the average Indian woman's role in society till then had been limited to the domestic realm—her only concern was her immediate family and the cohesiveness of her clan. For the first time, women were asserting their right to a public role. They wanted equal participation in the decision-making processes of the society they lived in, which included the legal, administrative and organizational aspects. Women broke the taboos of the purdah, threw off their veils and jumped wholeheartedly into India's freedom movement. Thousands participated in the swadeshi movement, boycotting British goods that flooded the Indian market and crushed Indian businesses as well as people's livelihoods. Many women, under Gandhi's tutelage, took to spinning their own khadi cloth, while others would serve their families uncooked meals—generally fruit and milk, thus boycotting food products used for cooking, most of which were processed in Britain. Scores of women also participated in non-violent protests under scorching skies, and endured appalling police brutality, from bashing in of their skulls with batons[265] to intimidation and humiliation by rape, often gang rape.[266] Women also joined the underground movements that employed more radical means of protests like capturing the British armouries, sabotaging rail and telecommunications, and launching open attacks with guns and bombs. They stoically submitted to months of imprisonment in jail cells that were effectively cages with bars. Open on all sides, including the roof, they faced the public road on one side. The women prisoners had no privacy to change their clothes, or relieve themselves, for the toilet was an open drain inside the cage. There were also no beds or separate bathing facilities. A canvas over the bars served as an inadequate cover during the monsoons, leaving the women soaked.[267] And despite the British government's strenuous resistance, there was also forceful and massive lobbying by women all over India for the right to vote. They demanded it as their 'right' as equal citizens of the country and not a charity bestowed on them 'out of grace'.[268] They eventually attained this right, along with a representation of eighty legislative seats in 1937,[269] at least ten years before India's independence.

Formal education was perhaps one of the most critical tools of empowerment for Indian women during British rule. Earlier, formal education was a privilege afforded to very few Indian girls, largely from the upper castes and the courtesan communities, but they too would be educated at home since girls were not permitted to join educational institutions. By the early 1800s, Christian missionaries had opened some of the earliest Hindu girls' schools in India and soon other schools followed for the lower castes and Muslim girls.[270] Maintaining the caste and religious divisions in this manner actually gave Indian families an incentive to send their daughters to school, which they otherwise would not have done if the schools accommodated students across all communities. In less than thirty years, from 1863 to 1890, the number of girl students, in just one state—Bengal—grew from 2500 to 80,000.[271]

One of the most dynamic outcomes of this rapid increase in female education was observed in the field of literature. Though there had been some women writers in earlier periods, writing mainly poetry, which was often devotional, Indian women now began to write with more intensity than ever before. Their writings were an effective medium not only to address the social issues that concerned them, but also to define their individualities, independent of their traditional identities as wives, mothers and daughters.

Between the late eighteenth and early nineteenth centuries, an unprecedented number of Indian women wrote their autobiographies,[272] and published other books. They also began to contribute profusely to newspapers and regional language journals, many of which were published by women for women—*Sundari Subodh* (in Gujarati), *Zenana* (in Telugu), *Khatoon* (in Urdu), and *Bamabodhini Patrika* (in Bengali)—so they had a venue to express their views, opinions, hopes and protests. Most importantly, some of these women, though the products of the British system's initiative to uplift Indian women, saw themselves as independent voices and not as the British Empire's mouthpiece. Pandita Ramabai, for instance, a Brahmin who had converted to Christianity, was criticized by her Christian peers for so unabashedly expressing dissent in certain political matters. She retorted that she had fought hard enough to rid the Hindu priest's 'yoke' from around her neck, and she was not going to submit to any other one.[273]

These writings revealed an eagerness among Indian women to access new avenues outside their homes, indicating a deep need for change—one that would be more progressive and supportive of women's choices. Besides the fact that it symbolized a powerful emergence of the woman's voice in the Indian social arena, this vociferous penmanship of women was significant for yet another reason. Throughout Indian history, there is a conspicuous absence of diaries, journals and autobiographies by Indians that provide descriptive, objective and analytical observations on the existing society. Where such historical records are available, they are usually by individuals who were conquerors, travellers or visitors to India. The writings of Indians (almost all men) tended to be either discursive or instructional, often assuming an omniscient air of divine revelation, but always failing to provide an individual and critical viewpoint that placed the observer outside the context of the culture he lived within. This ability to objectively analyse and discuss social issues is extremely essential to the collective psychological growth and evolution of a society as it is indicative of its ability to self-reflect, and its absence in Indian history is particularly disturbing. The emergence of the objectivity and critique in the writings of the women in this period, therefore, is especially momentous not just for the women's movement in India, but for the field of Indian philosophy as a whole.

As Rasasundari Devi's 1876 autobiography, *Amar Jiban* (My Life), reveals, there was an irrefutable air of expectation that it was time for some positive changes for women in Indian society. Raised in a small village in Bengal, Rasasundari Devi, after her marriage, secretly taught herself how to read and write by practising on the sooty walls of the kitchen where she often felt like a prisoner. She was indignant that the idea of an educated woman should be a social stigma even if it was no 'crime' as such, and believed that the superstition of an educated woman being unlucky was entirely generated by men. Yet, she observed with a certain amount of glee that times seemed to be changing for women, that more women were taking on jobs that only men could do earlier, and there was even a woman on the throne—Queen Victoria. She also eagerly contemplated, out of a sense of her own leanings, that as more opportunities opened up, there might even be scholarly gatherings of women, organized intellectual debates and book discussions. Rasasundari Devi then concluded triumphantly that in time women would be able to make men seem worthless—'good-for-nothing' in her words.[274]

For the first time, Indian women were taking an unprecedented lead in defining their own collective identity and challenging the one created for them by men, with far-reaching social implications. Both the purdah and the zenana were rigorously denounced as forms of social confinement for women that meant not just their psychological but also their physical imprisonment. Women, even child brides as young as seven years, had to keep their heads and faces covered with a long veil, and not address anyone, not even their mothers-in-law or husbands.[275] The writer Nirad Chaudhuri wrote in his autobiography of how his mother in 1887 had not spoken to her own mother-in-law or even shown her face to her for five whole years after her marriage, even though both women lived under the same roof. The only communication was through the nodding of the head, indicating a 'yes' or a 'no'.[276] On the rare occasions that these women stepped out of the house, they not only were obliged to be properly veiled but they were carried out on the shoulders of bearers in closed box-like palanquins. When these women needed to take their ritualistic holy dip in the river Ganga, the bearers would immerse the entire palanquin into the river, with the women sitting inside.[277] In one narrative about the upper-class Indian compulsion with the purdah, a heavily veiled Muslim woman waiting to board a train slipped and fell on to the tracks. The maid accompanying her was unable to get her back on to the platform, but she refused to allow the porters standing by to lend a hand, as that would be a violation of the purdah. Eventually, it seems, the train ran over the woman on the tracks.[278]

Rokeya Sakhawat Hossain in her play *Sultana's Dream* ridiculed the practice of cloistering women in the zenana. She hypothesized an equivalent impounding for men which she called the *murdana*, a place where she suggested men would be kept in isolation, with no exposure to the outside world or understanding of it.[279] Other women too had been extremely critical of this enforced isolation of women. Pandita Ramabai had said the women in zenanas were virtually 'prisoners' and this 'shameful' treatment of them was a terrible 'cruelty'.[280] Many women likened their experience of the zenana to that of a 'cage', where they were kept like 'animals'.[281] In her journal, a woman from Rajshahi railed at how it was a means to curb women's 'freedom of choice' and 'freedom of action',[282] while Krishnabhabini, in her writings, spoke of how it was like being 'blind' even though she had eyes, and how 'crazy' she would be with longing to see and experience the world outside, eagerly probing the men allowed to visit the zenana for information. She questioned why, if women, like men, are 'human beings', they should also not be permitted to freely travel and learn about the world in the same way. Later, when Krishnabhabini was able to realize her dream of travelling to Europe, she wrote with incredulity about an immense joyful sense of freedom and of how she could finally 'breathe' in the 'open air'. Life she declared was 'so different' for her that it had caused a 'significant change' in her 'attitudes and values'.[283] Others like Krupabai Satthianadhan condemned the manner in which Hindus devalued their daughters, ignoring them as individuals, denying them education and raising them as 'inferior' beings. Krupabai spoke of how she longed to prove that women were 'in no way inferior' to men.[284] But perhaps the most critical female voices to be heard in this period were those of the widows. Though sati had somewhat abated as a practice, the treatment of widows in society was still abominable. Several men like Ishwarchandra Vidyasagar had championed the cause of the dignity of widows, and politically campaigned for their rights. Numerous women now felt compelled to draw social attention to the inhumanity of this practice, by sharing through their writings excruciating first-hand accounts of their own plight as widows. What emerged was a very confrontational presentation of their suffering and humiliation, one that demanded a radical change in the social attitude towards widows.

One widow recanted how her social status fell instantaneously, almost to the minute, upon her husband's death. No one would touch her as she was considered evil and a carrier of bad luck. Three low-caste barber women were immediately summoned to rip the clothes and ornaments off her. Ornaments and colourful clothing were meant to enhance a woman's beauty and therefore her sexuality, but a widow was no longer entitled to hers. The barbers stripped her violently, injuring her as they tore the ornaments off her ears and nose, and crushed the bangles still on her hands with stones. She was then made to follow her husband's funeral procession at a distance, behind everybody else, so that even her maligned shadow would not fall on people. All through the journey she was treated with anger and contempt, as if she had committed a crime. The funeral procession took periodic breaks to drink water, because of the heat, but she was not allowed any, for it was believed she did not deserve to have her thirst quenched. On the banks of the river where the body was to be cremated, she was forced into the cold water and had to remain there for the entire length of the long ceremony, even though she was freezing. And later, when she fell ill, she was not tended to nor provided with any medicines. Living as a widow in her in-laws' house, she was allowed only one meal a day and repeatedly reminded that she had nothing to live for any more. If she wept, she was called a snake that had killed her husband and shamelessly wanted another. She was treated like a slave and was often beaten up. If she tried to flee from the house, she was called a whore. It was because of this social stigma that numerous widows in similar situations had committed suicide. Mocking the government's ban on sati, she questioned what good it had ultimately done for widows, because the life they were compelled to lead was like a slow, agonizing death. Perhaps sati, she declared in despair, was preferable.[285]

Rasasundari Devi in her autobiography too spoke of the humiliation she had to endure when she was forced to shave her head after her husband died. Hair, another conventional symbol of female sexuality,[286] was no longer a widow's entitlement. With much bitterness, Rasasundari Devi wrote of how she had given all her life to working for the house and caring for her family, and yet it seemed to her that her whole life could not compensate for the misfortune she was accused of bringing on her husband. She spoke of how she felt as if her entire existence had been dismissed by society in that one miserable moment of her husband's death.[287]

Despite the 1937 Hindu Women's Property Act passed by the British government, which entitled widows to their husband's property or at least his share of it if the property was joint,[288] widows would often be swindled out of their inheritance by conniving relatives of her husband. Many widows would be sexually abused by male relatives, who took advantage of their social and economic vulnerability. Terrified, several of these women, if they were not already driven to suicide, would run away from home. Many found solace in the Vaishnava cults, which not only gave them social acceptability but an environment where widows could revive their lives and their sexuality—grow their hair, take pleasure once more in jewellery and clothes, and find new partners.[289] However, with the British government's persecution of the Vaishnava cults, and curbing of their earnings through a ban on their music and entertainment, many of these widows, like other women in the cult, were driven to prostitution to survive.

For several literary writers of this period, both male and female, the treatment of widows was unconscionable, and became a major theme for many of their works. Male writers like Tagore, Sarat Chandra Chattopadhyay, Premchand and Nagarjun wrote novels with widows as central characters and by exploring their lives tried to appeal for public sympathy. Among the women writers were Ramabai Saraswati, Ramabai Ranade, Paravibai Athawale and Lakshmibai Tilak. Yet there was a noticeable difference in the approach of male and female writers to the widows' cause. The outlook of male writers can perhaps at best be termed as patronizing as they tried to portray the widow either as a saint deserving of male sympathy or a beautiful seducer craving attention. Women writers, on the other hand, were extremely frank about the social conditions of widows and spoke of it openly with sharp insights. Their writings were contemptuous of certain men who married widows as if it was an act of charity, or those who had fallen in love with widowed women, but were too cowardly to defy conventions to be with them. The attempt was to highlight the strength and resourcefulness of women, some of whom were widowed very young, and had learnt to survive despite the impossibility of a normal existence. And, as many of the women writers saw it, the solution for widows lay not simply in remarriage, but in the restitution of their lives and their dignity through access to education, jobs, inheritance rights and economic independence, as well as encouragement through women's support groups.[290]

Other women protested against the heinous dehumanization of widows in more demonstrative ways. Tarigonda Venkamamba, born to a Brahmin family in Andhra Pradesh, refused to shave her head as she was expected to do when she was widowed, and instead declared herself married to God and, therefore, an eternal bride. She always dressed up as a bride would, adorning herself with flowers and jewellery, tending to her make-up and ignoring public ridicule that labelled her as brazen and a lunatic.[291]

Indian women activists were also realizing the necessity to ensure the education of all women for their gender's empowerment. Tarabai Shinde, a Marathi writer, attributed the common social perception of educated women as being westernized and therefore depraved to male insecurity. She emphasized the absolute need for women's education so that women could fight their own oppression with logic and insight. Pandita Ramabai Saraswati, who opened a home for widows, was a highly educated woman and worked relentlessly to promote the education of girls and women. Despite being a converted Christian, she insisted that her school would remain 'wholly secular'. She strongly emphasized the need for women to understand their right to choice on every matter that impacted their lives: in choosing a husband, their right to refuse marriage when they were not ready, their right to education and their right to demand a female physician if they were not comfortable with a male doctor. Another enterprising woman, Swarnakumari Devi, published a Bengali journal, *Bharati*, for thirty years. Its editorial policy was to prioritize articles on new scientific discoveries and information. The idea was to give this knowledge to all women, especially housewives and those who could not read and write English, the language in which most scientific journals were published then. Swarnakumari even coined some of the technical terms in Bengali.[292]

Yet there was a certain cynicism about the degree to which education would help women revolutionize their social status. The writer Mokshodayani Mukhopadhyay had observed wryly that it was not just women's lives that were in need of reform but men's minds as well.[293] Many women felt that the reformist men were treating women like passive recipients of benefits that men bestowed upon them; it was not a recognition of women's inherent rights to the same social opportunities as men. Women writers like Geeta Sane, Vibhavari Shirurkar, Kusumavati Deshpande and Indira Sahasrabuddhe also spoke of the ambivalence of the role of education in women's lives. They pointed out how, despite their education, the individuality and potential of women were systematically suppressed, their desire for self-expression stifled and their lives still unfulfilled.[294] Where the British intended education to be a medium for civilizing the Indian women in terms of what they considered feminine, graceful qualities, and to make them better housewives, the Indian woman wanted substantially more than that.

There was clear resentment expressed by women about the system that compelled them to be what Tarabai Shinde called 'powerless dull prisoners' in their houses, one that constricted their existence and suffocated their individual identities. Rasasundari Devi wrote of the tedium and exhaustion of her job as a housewife. Her husband's immense, extended family, which the couple lived with, as was the norm, had eight maids, but due to caste restrictions the maids were not permitted to work inside the house; so most of the household chores had to be done by Rasasundari. Between cooking for the entire family, serving their meals, tending to her own children and husband, there were days when she would not have time to sit down or even eat a single meal herself. Moreover, she resented how the household consumed her and left her with no identity of her own. In her frustration she mocked God, asking if that was his idea of 'kindness' to her, reminding him that she prayed to him only because her mother taught her to.[295]

However, many women felt it necessary to push for their individualism despite the social resistance they faced. Binodini Dasi, who descended from a family of artisans and prostitutes, was herself a legendary stage actor. She funded and set-up the Star Theatre in Calcutta, despite intense opposition and public hostility from locals who, in their Victorian squeamishness, did not want an establishment in their city that was run by a 'prostitute'. But she persisted—and succeeded, surviving one near-fatal attack on her life.[296]

But one of the most radical demands by women, now that they could voice their individualities, was their push for sexual expression and freedom. When Vibhavari Shirurkar's novel *Kalyanche Nishwas* (The Sigh of Buds) was published in 1933, it caused a furore. For in it, she openly asserted women's natural sexual desires. She said her intention was to counter the general assumption that women were impassive beings with no sexual feelings, inclinations and desires. She also declared that in her opinion it was men's egos that had sexually repressed women. She even introduced the possibility of lesbianism for women as a means to explore their sexuality. She was branded as an obscene and indecent woman, and her life was threatened numerous times.[297] Geeta Sane went a step ahead and in her novel *Nikalele Hivakani* (The Dislodged Diamond) condemned marital rape, which she defined as the sexual imposition of men on their wives. The protagonist in this novel found her husband physically repulsive and greatly resented her pregnancy. She regarded sex with her husband as 'sinful', because it was agonizing, unjust and not based on love. But when she finally found the courage to leave her husband, society was not willing to accept her choice and wrote her off as a 'bad woman', persecuting her so harshly that she lost her mental equilibrium and eventually died.[298] Yet, in a society where 'love marriages' were now frowned upon and girls forced into alliances of their family's choosing, many writers spoke of a woman's right to the choice of partners, as well as her freedom to experience and express her emotions, including romantic love. In her 1914 novel, *Kahake* (To Whom), Swarnakumari Devi explored a young woman's curiosity about love, her experience of it and the wonder at her own growth in the process. The heroine of the novel mused on how she was always falling in love with one man or another, and yet she was mystified by how sometimes she could love with no intention of marrying the man.[299]

However, there was also an unmistakable fury in the writings of many women—an anger that was clearly directed towards men for their role in the subjugation of Indian women. It was an anger that demanded answers, an admission of guilt and responsibility on the part of men, and was contemptuous of the fragile male ego that felt the need to subdue women to build its own sense of self-esteem. Swarnakumari Devi in *Kahake* equated this anger to a dangerous sea that could unsettle men.[300] Tarabai Shinde spoke frankly about the inability of men to come to terms with their own shortcomings, which explained their compulsion to use women as scapegoats to vent their violent and domineering ways on.[301] Vibhavari Shirurkar too expressed a similar sentiment, implying that it was the male ego that was responsible for the destruction of many women's lives.[302] The writer Kailasbasini Debi asserted that it was men's intention to keep women in 'perpetual slavery' by denying them education[303] because they feared competition from educated women, while Madhumati Ganguli fumed that even though God had given women the 'same organs, feelings and faculties of mind' as men, Indian women could not progress because men caged them in zenanas like 'animals'. She alleged that 'only men' were to be 'blamed for the deplorable condition of women'.[304]

Kalyanamma, a playwright, in one of her productions, *Suryasthamana* (Sunset), questioned the historical role of men in dehumanizing women and treating them like objects of trade. In the play, the Rajput king Mansingh, who formed an alliance with the Mughal emperor Akbar by marrying off his sister to him, is confronted by his sister. She demands to know how he could barter his own sister as part of a pact with his enemy.[305] Here there is a clear implication of a sense of collective betrayal of women by men, one that strangely echoes the sentiments of the Shakta movement in the golden period. However, now the issue was more strongly and directly worded, and was posed not simply as an emotional matter, but as a social one as well.

Rokeya Sakhawat Hossain in 1905 wrote *Sultana's Dream*, a work which her husband, one of her staunchest supporters, termed as a 'terrible revenge' on men. In it, she presented a hypothetical utopian world in which gender roles were reversed—women governed the country while men were confined to the murdana, male quarters, where they were forced into seclusion and not permitted contact with the outside world. Hossain then goes on to show that with women in command of government, war and crime became alien concepts, and the society was orderly, productive and safe. She also portrayed cooking as a pleasurable art form instead of domestic drudgery, and science as a humble servant of society, working to resolve problems, instead of being used as a tool of power and control.[306]

However, this collective, emerging wrath of modern Indian women was not directed simply at Indian men, but British men as well, even though, ironically enough, the British had been champions of the emancipation of Indian women from inhumane oppression.[307] Shinde accused Indian men of colluding with the British to drive women, particularly female artists, to despair and poverty.[308] Muktabai lambasted the priests for attempting to use the Vedas, under British dictates to reconstruct society, to repress women further.[309] Ramabai Saraswati, too, held the British responsible for the demeaning of women's positions and for restricting their choices in society. Furthermore, the British government's reluctance to permit women to join the legislative sphere outraged many women's groups. *Stri Dharma*, a leading women's journal,[310] in 1928 challenged the earnestness of the British government's goal to socially elevate Indian women, for it argued that reform was impossible unless women were strengthened through political and legislative positions, and could themselves implement change.[311]

GANDHI: THE MORAL ARCHITECT OF MODERN INDIA

However, the struggle for power that eventually became the highlight of the colonial period was not that of the women's movement, but that of a colonized people battling for their freedom.

The British may have claimed to be better masters than the Mughals but, economically, they crippled India in a manner that even the Mughals could not. The Muslim rulers were freely operating warlords on the lookout for a personal fortune. For many, India was the only home as they had nowhere else to go. For the British, however, India was a primary resource for the British Crown's treasury and its exploitation was meant to benefit all of Britain. Perhaps the British propensity for discipline and organization made their system of exploitation all the more efficient. They astutely figured out how best to benefit by making India's economy work against itself, using India like a mine of raw materials and manpower for the manufacture of British goods. The finished products would be processed in British factories and sold to expanding markets in Europe, America and, ironically, back in India as well. This did not just milk India dry but also strangled its domestic industries and forced its population on to the edge of starvation.[312]

The British had realized that the tax system of the Muslim rulers had zamindars or feudal lords as the middlemen who with their significant, often independent powers, could take away a substantial part of the projected revenues. So the British ensured that all middlemen—feudal lords and local rulers—were brought under the strict control of the centralized British administration and would not be able to retain a larger share than they were permitted.[313] As a result, the feudal lords came down on the peasants with a heavier fist than ever before, extracting from them takings over and above what they were expected to pay up to the British government. While under the Mughals a farmer paid 40 to 50 per cent of his produce, under the British he could be made to give up 65 to 80 per cent.[314] The system of taxation was both relentless and unconscionable. Sometimes, peasants would sell their produce just to be able to fulfil the tax demand and some were even compelled to sell their seeds, cattle, clothes and utensils.[315] Others would borrow the money at interest rates as high as 25 per cent, which permanently put them at the mercy of insidious moneylenders.[316] From 1880 to 1884, around 45,000 people were arrested for debts, in the state of Punjab alone.[317] In 1819, a peasant's forum from Malabar presented a petition to the governor in which they gave accounts of how men and women in their region were dying of hunger by the roadside because of the inhumane tax burden.[318]

James Forbes, a British official, had noted in 1813 that the 'despotism' of the government was creating situations of 'artificial' famines in India. The situation was so dire that parents were selling their children for a bag of rice. Forbes spoke of how he had been able to purchase an Indian boy and a girl, about eight years of age, for less than the price of a pair of pigs in England. Though he handed them over as household help to an English woman, he figured that children likewise were also being sold into prostitution or bonded labour.[319] Christina Sinclair Bremmer, a 'blue stocking' who had campaigned for women's rights in Britain, was extremely critical of Britain's supposed free trade policies in India. She said that India did not have 'free' but 'compulsory' trade, all of which was organized by Britain to suit its own convenience. Where India should have been growing food, it was instead compelled to grow cash crops like cotton, jute and tea for export. And while millions died of famine in India, 'shiploads' of foodgrain were being sent out of the country.[320] Yet another English woman, Fanny Parker, whose Indian journals are an extraordinary source of information about the daily life in India during British colonial rule, provided a heart-wrenching eyewitness account of the suffering inflicted by the famine. At one marketplace, she saw men, women and children who had become 'living skeletons', begging for food. There were those who had already died and people were so desperate that they had stolen the clothes off one of the dead bodies. As Fanny Parker observed, 'these people . . . [were] not beggars but the tillers of the soil'.[321]

India, a nation that for centuries had been invaded by foreign powers, and had always remained disunited and embroiled in its internal conflicts, never succeeding to fend for itself, was now pushed so hard against the wall that for the first time in its history, it felt a compulsion to unite across caste and cultural barriers and fight for its freedom. And the man that India chose as leader for this fight was Mahatma Gandhi.

As a people's leader, Gandhi assumed a role that was unique, for he was not only India's political mentor but the nation's spiritual guide as well. It was in fact his religious outlook on all aspects of nation building that earned him both his stewardship position and the title of 'Mahatma' or 'The Great Soul', a title commonly bestowed on saints and spiritual teachers. By forcing the union of religion and power politics, Gandhi became for India 'a new kind of religious prophet'.[322]

The war that Gandhi led against the British in India was in essence a sacred war. For Gandhi not only derived his inspiration from Hindu scriptures, but he also viewed India's fight for independence as an outright moral battle, the outcome of which, he believed, would ultimately determine the fate of the human race. Where the British had colonized India on the presumption of their own superior morality, Gandhi retaliated with a deft reversal of roles. His conviction was that the moral superiority was in fact theirs—the colonized people's. He set up this moral fight in the very language he used to describe the two camps. He announced that the British government was 'evil' and that he was 'born to destroy' it.[323] His forecast was that once the 'satanic' imperial rulers and their 'vassals', those Indians who wanted to negotiate with the British, had been defeated and India became free and self-governing, the 'rulers' who of course would then be all Indians would be 'virtuous automatically'.[324] Gandhi proclaimed that the Western countries were lands of 'bhoga' or sensuality and physical pleasures, while India was a nation of 'karma', implying that it was pious and spiritually motivated.Hence he declared that India was meant for the 'religious supremacy of the world'.[325] He thus bestowed on India an inherent moral superiority in an interesting take on Nietzsche's master–slave hypothesis. What the colonial master class defined as superior according to its own bearing and desire for power, the slave class rebutted with a whole different system of morality, redefining superiority according to its own needs for freedom and dignity.

Gandhi's moral stance, with its strongly religious undertone, was his most powerful weapon in directing the Indian masses. He wielded it in the application of his strategic non-violence and non-cooperation ideologies, insisting that where the British had used violence to restrain India, non-violent resistance was a morally superior retaliation.

However, freedom, democracy and non-violence were not the only basis of Gandhi's assertion of moral pre-eminence. For him, it was necessary to establish that the very culture and customs that the British had reckoned as barbaric, the religion they had ridiculed and the people they regarded as perverse, had in fact the moral upper hand.

Where for the British, upon initial contact, the minimal clothing habits of ordinary Indians seemed indecent and outrageous, Gandhi resorted to going around near-naked, his torso bare, with a short cotton loin cloth wrapped around his hips. He responded to Winston Churchill's barb about him being India's 'naked fakir' with a letter, ten years after the comment was made, informing Churchill that he had with much effort finally become India's naked fakir, a job he regarded as 'sacred' and took pride in.[326] Along with his austere lifestyle and emphasis on simplicity, Gandhi became a touted symbol of the ascetic, non-materialistic wisdom of an ancient Eastern civilization, supreme in its stand against the greed of a wealthy, hedonistic, vice-ridden Britain.

Gandhi, however, extended the moral superiority argument indiscriminately and with a blind religious fervour to almost every aspect of political and social life in India. He identified all the distinguishing features of colonial power as 'evil' and pitted his battles against them. He vehemently opposed industry and technology. He would earnestly speak of how 'the gods' would not live in places that were inhabited by technology and engines.[327] In 1929 he attacked the printing press, opposing the access of rural Indians to newspapers, saying it did them no good other than exposing them to the 'dirty' aspects of the world, such as motion pictures, murders, gambling and the stock exchange,[328] even though he depended on the press and media to get his messages across to the people of India. He believed that the railways, which he used frequently to travel and preach around India, were evil for they contributed to the spread of diseases and they fuelled communal violence by increasing awareness among people of cultural differences.[329,330]

Another of Gandhi's favoured ideologies, one that he not only practised himself, but also propounded with much zeal as an integral aspect of his social and political preaching, was that of celibacy.

Interestingly, as averse as Gandhi was to Western influences, his thinking on the issues of sex and sexuality had strong nuances of Victorian morality. As a young student in England, he often met and conversed with Christian clergymen and had become an enthusiastic member of the Esoteric Christian Union.[331] His own religious background was that of Vaishnava, a cult that the British had initially regarded with much hostility because of the erotic and sensual nature of songs sung by wandering Vaishnava groups. These cults themselves evolved over time to better suit Victorian sensibilities, and some became extremely conservative. However, in Gujarat, where Gandhi grew up, it was the Jain religion that strongly prevailed. With philosophies akin to Buddhism, Jainism preaches non-violence and celibacy as its fundamental tenets, which had a significant influence on Gandhi's thinking.

Gandhi firmly believed celibacy to be a prerequisite for spiritual salvation. He was convinced that it was only the sexually abstinent who were 'pure' enough to be able to receive God 'face to face', that is, without shame.[332]

However, in terms of ordinary living as well, Gandhi regarded sex as an 'impure' practice for all people, including married couples. The time when this 'rule' could be an exception, he believed, was when sex was conducted specifically with the purpose of conception.[333] When Gandhi spoke of this as a 'rule', he actually meant it as an injunction—one that all members of his ashram were expected to abide by. He advised married couples to resolve that they would have no physical contact, and avoid sharing not just a bed but also a room, unless they intended to have a child.[334] However, Gandhi was furious when his son Harilal married Gulab, his sweetheart, and had children with her, for it implied they were having sex despite his insistence on their celibacy.[335] To punish Harilal, Gandhi forced him to be the first in the family to court arrest for India's self-rule movement in 1908.[336] Being a lawyer, Gandhi represented Harilal in court and urged the judge to award him the maximum sentence. Harilal was in jail for a year, and all the while he fretted for Gulab, who was in poor health.

Gandhi's preoccupation with sex invariably took precedence over all other social and political issues that he was confronting. Despite his denouncement of the practice of untouchability and the mistreatment of tribal communities, he rarely placed Adivasis or tribals in responsible positions in his ashram. This was because he disapproved of their sexually liberal traditions and their custom of men and women dancing while holding each other.[337]

Gandhi also correlated his celibacy doctrine with his political philosophy of non-violence, preaching that non-violence meant 'universal love'. A person who exhausted love on a personal relationship as, for example, on a husband or wife, could never achieve the 'height of universal love'. He asserted that in order to truly obey the 'law of ahimsa' or non-violence, one could not marry or indulge in any type of sexual gratification.[338] His advice to all his followers was not to marry. For those couples who were already married, but who wanted to master non-violence as a weapon for political ends, he suggested they regard each other as 'brother and sister', so that they could devote themselves wholly to 'universal service'.[339]

On a personal level, Gandhi was deeply convinced that the political effectiveness of his non-violence strategy was somehow linked to the potency of his own celibacy. He measured each political setback in the light of his personal failure to harness his libido at some unconscious level. During periods of major crises in the country, when there were religious tensions or political dissensions, he would reassess his inner conflicts with his sexuality.[340]

The year 1947 was a political nightmare for India, one that no one, not even Gandhi, had envisioned. It was the year India attained independence, but was also the time when the country was partitioned on the basis of religious hatred and mistrust. Hindus and Muslims drifted across the subcontinent en masse, the populace permanently splitting into two along lines of religion. The process, however, was unimaginably macabre—the citizens of the two newly formed nations engulfed each other in uncontainable waves of violence, arson, rape and mass murder. Bodies were strewn everywhere and people walked past them on the streets with an anesthetized indifference. As India writhed in this bloodbath, Gandhi in his despair turned to his abstinence philosophy for an explanation of what was happening. This was the ultimate failure of his vision of non-violence for India. While journalists and writers numbly tried to make sense of an incomprehensible situation, flooding newspapers with intensely political analysis, Gandhi chose instead to write five articles—all on celibacy. This of course puzzled people, but they seem to have dismissed it as an eccentricity.[341] However, in Gandhi's mind, the connection was abundantly clear—the unspeakable violence was the result of unabated libido.

The association between sex and violence has been the subject of numerous studies, and to a certain degree, Gandhi did have a point. But his perception of sex itself was biased. He could only categorize it as an independent evil entity, not a human activity that individuals chose to participate in when they wished. He could not reconcile to the fact that any human activity can be constructive or destructive, depending on the intention of the doer, as well as the vision of the perceiver. Gandhi fumbled with the same mental block in his prejudices towards all other things he deemed evil—including technology and educational institutions.

Gandhi's vision for celibacy was that some day it would be embraced universally, along with the doctrine of non-violence. Both concepts for him were inextricably linked and he even proclaimed that the 'world's honour' hinged on celibacy. He was convinced that even if the 'whole world' could not achieve this goal of celibacy during his lifetime, the goal was 'attainable', even if it took 'thousands of years'.[342]

Gandhi's wrangling with his libido played out in a lifelong ordeal, as he obsessively experimented with all sorts of strategies and weapons with which to subdue 'the insidious enemy'.[343] Even late in his life, he would often speak of how difficult it continued to be for him to exercise self-control.[344] He tried to achieve control through food, exhaustively categorizing various food items into those that fed the libido and those that killed it. For example, onions and milk were banned from his diet. He also believed that in order to minimize the sensually stimulating impact of food on the body, one had to eat it like 'medicine', that is, without actually tasting it, and only in the quantity needed for the body to survive.[345] Fasting, he asserted, was another mode of subduing the palate and reining in the senses.[346] This was a method he used often, particularly when he was rallying for an important social or political cause, and needed his celibate power to be at its peak.

Perhaps the most striking irony of Gandhi's life is that while he had so ardently preached non-violence and peace to humankind, his own life had been a horrific, angst-ridden battle against himself. This internal conflict is often couched in his writings in war terminology. He admitted to being a person of intense 'sexual passion' as well as 'greedy of palate'.[347] Yet he rejected this aspect of his being, choosing instead to alienate it within him as another dichotomized entity he called 'the insidious enemy'. He often spoke of needing constant 'courage' and 'vigilance' in his 'war' against this 'enemy', and described his battles in metaphors of victory and defeat.[348]

Interestingly, as explained by Jung's theory, this 'enemy' of Gandhi—his libido—constituted his 'shadow self', that aspect of a person's being that is repressed by pushing it into the personal unconscious because he or she is unable to consciously come to terms with it. According to the shadow theory, rejecting the shadow only forces it to take on a more powerful and, sometimes, insidious role in the person's life, often instigating unhealthy situations which may result in neurotic behaviour. Rejection of the lover shadow, according to Jung, was often expressed either in sexually perverse behaviour or even puritanism, both of which Gandhi exhibited amply. His experiments in sleeping with naked young women to test the resolve of his celibacy were indeed risqué—one of these girls was his own great-niece. The fact that he called them 'experiments' meant that he was open to the possibility that the outcome could go either way. Since these women were young and gullible, some still in their late teens, Gandhi's behaviour was extremely irresponsible, but he insisted that his motives were harmless because he acted as 'God's eunuch'.[349] When he was told that his experiments were injudicious because, as Freud would say, he may have been unconsciously pursuing the very urges he was trying to repress, Gandhi responded that he knew nothing about Freud.[350] His repression of sexual desire may have been replaced by an eccentric obsession with all other bodily functions—for example, he proposed that human excrement, or 'black gold' as he liked to call it, should be put to effective social use, such as in agriculture. He also showed an intrusive curiosity in the processes of other people's bodies, often greeting people with an inquiry about their bowel movement that morning. He was always eager to offer remedies to the women around him on their problems with constipation and vaginal discharges, and often personally administered saline enemas to his acquaintances since he believed enemas were the panacea for all ills.[351]

Yet, Gandhi seemed to understand that, at a certain level, that very libido he treated as an external agent and attempted to defeat was an aspect of his own self. He spoke of how he could 'suppress' the 'enemy' even if he could not 'expel' it, but also declared that he could destroy it with the 'power of truth'.[352] Paradoxically, in the light of Jung's hypothesis, facing the truth would mean accepting the shadow as an integral aspect of a personality, causing it to lose its dichotomy from the inner self, and its power over the person through inner conflict. For Gandhi, the 'truth', of course, was not an individualized realization but a universal principle, external to his being and inextricably linked to his dogmatic adherence to celibacy.

This bitter conflict between Gandhi and his shadow self was manifested in his habits and outlook. Even though he was fastidious about shunning food he believed might evoke lust in him, he did not apply a similar principle as a precaution to other choices, specifically women. He was constantly surrounded by young women who tended to his personal needs and comforts, including full body massages, and participated in his experiments of sleeping naked with him. He also used women as props for the support of his body as he walked, draping his arms around their shoulders, when a walking cane, or a couple of young men would have served just as well. Moreover, as fixated as he was on eliminating the possibility of sensory stimulation through food, he did not apply this to other sense organs—he continued to enjoy his body massages by young women, the smell of flowers and incense and music.

He also contradicted himself in other ways. Despite his staunch opposition to wealth earned by industrialization, he accepted large donations from rich industrialist families like the Birlas, the Sarabhais and the Bajajs.[353] Nor was Gandhi very consistent in his non-violent philosophy. He believed that children of unwed mothers were like vermin who deserved to die, which was one of the reasons he avoided contact with orphanages.[354] He was also supportive of honour killings, when fathers murdered daughters who had been raped, so that the family name was not sullied. According to Gandhi, these were the 'purest form[s] of ahimsa',[355] or non-violence. In 1919, in Amritsar, when unarmed protestors gathered in a park to peacefully protest against British rule, a British general, Reginald Dyer, commanded his troops to surround and shoot the unarmed, trapped crowd. More than a thousand innocent civilians, who desperately tried to find escape routes, were massacred. While this unwarranted brutality caused tremendous agitation in the rest of India, Gandhi refused to acknowledge the civilians as 'heroic martyrs'. He asserted that if they were heroes they would either have pulled out their swords to retaliate or would have 'bared their breasts' and died like heroes—but they would not have tried to flee as they did.[356] At other times, Gandhi's response to bloodshed seems almost macabre. During the non-violent protests, hundreds of unarmed, non-resisting women participating in these marches would be kicked, beaten, sexually taunted and gang-raped in police custody. Gandhi's response to one woman's trauma seems perversely blithe. He spoke of how he would have 'smiled with pleasure' to see her sari 'made beautiful' with bloodstains, of how 'excited' he was at the news, which he said did not distress him in the least.[357]

One of Gandhi's arguments for the non-violent route to freedom was that Indians did not have the 'necessary strength to stand the consequences' of warfare with the British. He proclaimed that even India's traditional warrior clans, like the Rajputs, had 'reduced themselves into Banias', the merchant class, and were better in money-dealing than in weaponry.[358] More so, Gandhi's idea of non-violence was not necessarily dissociated from bloodshed. Non-violent shedding of blood—which occurred when row after row of non-violent protestors had police units batter them with *lathis*—took greater courage, self-control and an implicit fearlessness than violent retaliation, which Gandhi regarded as an act motivated by a cowardly, uncontainable fear. Indeed, Gandhi believed that only the celibate had the capacity for non-violent action, saying that men who had sex were bereft of 'stamina' and were 'emasculated and cowardly'.[359]

Gandhi's puritanism may well have been a result of his upbringing and the colonial sensibilities that prevailed in India at that time. However, his background reveals that his inner conflict in matters of sex was in all likelihood a reaction to his personal childhood experiences. Gandhi's family had promised him in marriage to Kasturba when both children were about seven years of age, and they were formally married when they turned thirteen. The teenaged husband and wife, both at the advent of puberty, experienced what was most natural for their age—an extreme curiosity about their newly found sexuality. They explored it with gusto, engaging in sex at every available opportunity.

Gandhi was still an adolescent when his father, aged and ailing, took to his deathbed. Gandhi took turns with other family members to care for his father, massaging his legs and tending to his needs. However, in his adult years, he recollected with much shame of how, even while he tended his father, his mind would be eagerly anticipating sex with his wife, and he would rush to her room as soon as he was relieved from his duty. It was during one such frantic love-making session that his father died. The incident left a deep impression on young Gandhi, casting an inerasable shadow of guilt over his life, one that led to his lifelong siege against sex.

Even as an adult, Gandhi could not reconcile with the natural instincts of his adolescence, and would rue his 'lust' for causing him to fail in his duty to his father. He would regard the death of the child born to his wife a few months after his father's demise as a punishment for his sins.[360]

Today, most psychoanalysts would regard the trauma of the father's death and the guilt association with sex as an understandable response of young Gandhi, as children often tend to assume guilt for traumatic experiences that they cannot control, such as death and divorce in the family. What perhaps makes Gandhi's psychological distress even more of a classic case of misappropriated guilt was Gandhi's own view of his father's sexuality. Gandhi's mother was his father's fourth wife, and when they were married, she was barely eighteen, while he was in his forties. The age difference somehow bothered Gandhi, for he believed his father to be 'oversexed' and, all his life, regarded the union of an older person with someone very young as 'debauchery'.[361] Perhaps Gandhi's own sexual experience at the time of his father's death seemed a horrific reflection in him of the sexuality that he rejected in his own father.

That Gandhi thought it fit to integrate this personal conflict-ridden reflection on sex into his social and political manoeuvres meant that it also had an impact on his devoted followers, particularly those in his ashram. Sexual curiosity among the adolescent boys in his communes, who were otherwise prohibited to court girls, that sometimes led to flirtations and sex play among themselves would displease Gandhi.[362] Young women in his commune would attempt to win his approval by impressing him with the resolution of their celibacy, boasting of how no man could tempt them.[363] As a teacher, Gandhi believed that his students were in a way obliged to submit their sexuality to his spiritual mentorship. He was known to sometimes ask women to take on a lifelong vow of celibacy as a *dakshina* (an obligatory student fee) paid to him.[364] And not surprisingly, these women also mirrored the paradoxes of Gandhi's own thinking on sexuality. While some of them actually volunteered to sleep naked next to him, it is difficult to even apprehend their psychological state, given their youth. It was well known that women in his entourage constantly vied for physical proximity to him, competing like star-struck adolescents for their idol's touch and jealousy was common, especially when Gandhi singled out a woman too often to serve as his crutch.[365] Women who shared his bed or his close confidence were known to get 'hysterical', exhibiting rejection anxiety, if he turned them away.[366] The confusion and upheaval in the minds of some of these women is revealed in the dream recollections of Prema Kantak, one of Gandhi's disciples. Prema, like many other women attracted to Gandhi,[367] was already carrying a psychological load when she sought solace in his mentorship. From the age of sixteen, Prema had developed a revulsion to sex, regarded her parents with 'disgust' for conceiving her, and thought of her own body as 'dirty'. In one particular dream narrative, she was a small girl in Gandhi's lap, drinking milk that spurted from his breast into her mouth. She recalls the intense alarm she felt in the dream when the milk did not stop streaming out, even when she was satiated and her clothes and her body were drenched, while Gandhi kept coaxing her to drink more.[368] Even though Gandhi brightly assured her that it meant she felt safe with him, the symbolism of semen as milk, and the pent-up sexual content of their relationship are unmistakable elements here of Prema's psyche.

The impact of Gandhi's internally conflicted vision of sex and sexuality had a much wider implication than that of a personal crisis. As Gandhi's rejected shadow—the repressed and vilified libido—cast itself, long and mysterious, over the Indian psyche, it became the dictum for modern India's uneasy and confounded outlook on sex. The ultimate sway that Gandhi had over millions of people in India was not necessarily a people's validation of his political savoir faire. Nehru, as a close associate of Gandhi's, had observed that perhaps what appealed to the masses was Gandhi's emphasis on 'piety' more than on ideas, and Nehru often worried about the future implications of this approach for India once the country had to govern itself.[369] The complexities of Gandhi's non-violence theories, or for that matter even novel concepts like democracy and constitutions, would have had little impact on the largely illiterate and uneducated masses struggling to fill their bellies every day. Theirs was an instinctive reaction, a mob response, a mesmerized, almost a trance-like massive cult following of a saintly figure. While middle-class Indians ascribed a certain godliness to Gandhi, to the rest he was God himself. Indeed, the illiterate masses of India truly believed Gandhi to be an incarnation, an avatar, of the god Vishnu.[370] It was this near-divine status of Gandhi that the majority of Indians could relate to. For them, it was only religion that gave purpose and meaning to their impoverished lives. Gandhi's much proclaimed celibacy, no doubt, was an integral aspect of the saint-like status that had been conferred on him, for the sacred powers of celibates had long been accepted through asceticism in the Hindu religion. Add to this his naked, lean appearance, his stark lifestyle, and his renunciation of all that was worldly, and Gandhi perfectly exemplified the chaste, wise and powerful ascetic—a god-man who could be blindly trusted. Gandhi's role in India was, in this respect, crucial for it was the only factor that could bind this massive nation.

Some of Gandhi's own proclamations of divine intercession reinforced his devout persona. He spoke of how God had intervened on his behalf and 'saved' him, keeping him 'pure' whenever he was tempted by lust. The first time was when he visited a brothel while still very young,[371] while later on, when he decided to be celibate, God helped him when he was constantly surrounded by young women who aroused his 'sexual desire'.[372]

Although Gandhi was certainly not single-handedly responsible for the repressive, squeamish and bafflingly conflicted attitude towards sex in post-independence India, he most probably was one of the most prominent and revered confirmations of it. There were also two other specific sex-related ideologies endorsed by Gandhi that would eventually have a serious repercussion on the social environment of India in the twentieth and twenty-first centuries. One relates to reproduction, the other to female sexuality.

Gandhi had declared that the only circumstance under which sex was permissible was when the aim was reproduction. He vehemently opposed all forms of contraception for he argued that birth control measures only perpetuated sexual pleasure and averted pregnancies, which in his opinion was perverse.[373]

This conviction, however, has become the nemesis of India in the twenty-first century. Having already crossed the one billion population mark, India is now poised to outdo China as the most populous nation in the world, and more so it is unable to adequately feed, clothe, house or educate close to half its people.

Gandhi's view of female sexuality was not very different from the firmly entrenched centuries-old patriarchal view. He believed that menstruation was a manifestation of the distortion of a woman's soul by her sexuality. Therefore, when a woman was a true celibate, that is, with a pure soul, her menses would stop completely.[374] The argument in itself is fundamentally unsound for it would imply that all women in their natural reproductive years are impure, whereas all post-menopausal women must be celibate. However, the most conflicting aspect of Gandhi's view on women was a further ratification of the long-established tradition of ambiguity towards female sexuality in Indian culture. While, according to him, menstruating women were impure, he held mothers in high esteem. He cherished a supremely idealized vision of motherhood, equating it with the sacred cow that gave birth and suckled children, caring for and nourishing them too.[375] He spoke of envying women and said that he would sometimes imagine himself as one.[376] Whether he made a conscious connection between the reviled menstruation and exalted motherhood is hard to say. He belittled women who used contraception as prostitutes,[377] and accused them of sexually tempting men into immoral behaviour.[378] As for prostitutes, he held them in such contempt that he refused to admit them into the Congress party.[379] He also believed that women had to bear the wrath of God for the sins of their fathers and husbands.[380] In one incident at his ashram, where some men were caught sexually harassing women, he felt that an appropriate preventive measure was for the women to cut off their hair.[381] Not only were these poor women being made to 'pay' for the men's crimes, but were also accused of tempting the men. Gandhi furthermore believed that women who were raped should consider suicide since they had lost all their worth.[382] In effect, his basic attitude towards women was very much the essence of the Indian patriarchy and his virtuous preaching of not treating women as 'inferior'[383] was at best patronizing.

At its core, this kind of thinking reduced women to commodities, useful only for reproduction, but otherwise reviled and treated as disposable. This was adequately demonstrated by the inhumane treatment meted out to women during the period of India's change to a free, democratic state. In the riots that erupted at this time from the partitioning of India and Pakistan, thousands of women were raped, abducted and murdered. No official record was even kept of the number of women who may have been abused, or were displaced or missing during this period. In fact, there was a deliberate attempt to avoid official investigations and records.[384] The majority of these women were regarded as shameful burdens on their families and those who were raped were often abandoned, driven out from their homes, their names erased from the family's memory who preferred to think of them as dead. Under India's staunchly patriarchal social outlook, this attitude resulted in one of the most ghastly crises facing the nation in the twenty-first century: that of female genocide.

PART V

THE DEMOCRATIC PERIOD
A SEXUAL PARADOX

The question of the sexual ethos of present-day India is not just one of interest but one of an inescapable urgency, as the three most catastrophic issues that India faces in the twenty-first century are all sex related. These are population explosion, the AIDS epidemic and female genocide.

India may be prissy about sex, but its people are no doubt having plenty of it. The nation's population is ballooning even faster than what the UN had earlier predicted. Previously, it had been estimated that India will overcome China as the world's most populous nation by 2050. But chances are that this is likely to happen even before 2030, when India's population is expected to touch 1.49 billion. As one UN official put it, it seems to be—ominously—getting 'earlier and earlier'. Even more alarming is the fact that at least 50 per cent of India's population is under the age of twenty-two,[1] a prime reproductive age. In rural India, where child marriage is still widely practised, the number of sexually active and reproducing individuals under eighteen runs into the millions.[2] In the meantime, India's capacity to provide for its people has lagged far behind. As the UN noted, India has failed to provide even the basics of human necessity, adequate shelter, food and health care for a majority of its population.[3]

In the face of such impending human disaster, one would expect the nation to be geared into a population emergency plan: a blitzkrieg of birth control alerts popping out of billboards, television advertisements, newspapers and public announcements, educational workshops, and birth control provisions and incentives. It would be the obsessive number one national priority. However, the issue hardly ever surfaces in the country's agenda of urgent matters.

The problem of AIDS in India shares a common glitch with that of population control, in how the country deals (or has failed to) with these two issues. The feasible solution for both of course is the condom. However, the condom implies sex for individual pleasure and not for having children. Conventionally, sex was the unspoken assumption of marital life that inevitably resulted in children. An unavoidable aspect of the AIDS discussion is acknowledging people do have sex for recreational purposes whether or not they are married and that they need to understand how to fulfil that need while protecting themselves. How does one introduce the function and technical use of the condom when the mere mention of sex in public causes such unease and alienation?

And while India chooses to remain in denial or agitation over increasing rates of premarital sex, one 2001 survey in Delhi revealed that one in three of the unmarried youth and teenage respondents admitted to having engaged in sex. More alarmingly, almost 50 per cent of them did not use condoms.[4]

AIDS for India is not an impending crisis: with 2.5 million HIV-infected persons[5] the country will soon replace South Africa as the world's largest casualty of AIDS. Yet India remains mulishly cavalier towards this catastrophe and instead directs colossal funds towards its nuclear warfare programme and military fighter aircraft. The government lacks the sense of urgency and aggressiveness that is required of the AIDS crisis. In a recent national television poll, viewers were asked whether the problem of the AIDS epidemic in India was overblown. Forty-nine per cent of the viewers—all assumedly educated and of the middle class, as this was an English-language channel—thought it was overblown.[6]

However, of the three looming sex-related crises facing India, the one that as of now receives the least attention on the part of the government is female genocide. It is the culmination of a long history of patriarchal traditions in India that has unremittingly reduced women to the status of a sexual commodity, to be utilized to procure male heirs and discarded at will. Female infanticide dates back to the Vedic times. There are hymns that speak of 'rejecting' female children when they are born.[7] A 1901 census report on India showed that there were 3.4 million women that the country could not account for. The report took special note of the practice of female infanticide as an accounting factor.[8] However, with the legalization of abortions since the 1970s, it is now estimated that India has systematically eliminated almost fifty million of its women.[9]

TWO WORLDS, ONE NATION

The sexual sensibilities of twenty-first-century Indians are so polarized that they appear to occupy two separate worlds altogether, one ultraconservative and the other neo-liberal. For about 90 per cent of Indians, still crouching in the shadows of a Victorian morality, sex remains a distasteful topic. Anything that suggests sex and sexuality is customarily frowned upon. Even the utterance of the word 'sex' is blasphemy.

Society is ordered to keep the sexes apart at a modest distance from each other to minimize the hazards of sexual attraction. In classrooms, boys and girls sit in separate gender-designated rows. They usually play, study and converse exclusively with members of their own sex. The rules get sterner as they cross into adolescence, and then adulthood, when the dangers posed by their sexual drives become more imminent. Talking to a member of the opposite sex who is not a relative is cause for rumours and immediate investigation. Even for the millions of marriages that are arranged in India each year, where the families analyse the compatibilities of the proposed pair from every angle—economics, height, weight, colour, physique, religion and caste—the idea of inquiring into sexual attraction would be repugnant. The closest that one comes to confirming sexual chemistry is through the remote medium of horoscopes. A priest is hired to compare the horoscopes of the prospective couple to verify their compatibility, and check for what is called *yoni poruthamv*. Based on the positions of the planets in the charts and information from ancient texts like the kamasutras, the prospective couple's sexual organs are classified into types, based on size and depth of organs. For example, a woman could have an elephant- or deer-type vagina, and a man a hare-, a bull- or a lion-type penis. The elephant vagina and the lion penis, for instance, are assumed to be incompatible.[10] Accordingly, based not on physiological verification but the information provided by the horoscopes, a couple's sexual prospects are examined.

Young lovers who belong to different communities often face overwhelming resistance from their families and communities. These couples are often forced apart and coerced into marriage with people that their parents have chosen for them. Periodically, in an inconsequential corner of a newspaper, is a report about a father who, with the assistance of other villagers, has murdered his own daughter and her lover.

Essentially, intercourse as a free act of lust and individual choice, outside rigidly defined social boundaries, is regarded as unclean. At best, sex is an unspeakable, functional act, permitted only to asexually matched, married couples for the purpose of reproduction, and if in the process it fills physical needs, this is not talked about. Even for the married, sex is supposed to be simply a mundane chore to be dealt with.

But then there is a whole different realm of sexual logic in India. This is India's liberal block. Sex in these circles is fast acquiring acceptability as a normal facet of relationships between dating couples, who may or may not be in love. Though these sexually unconventional pockets do not amount to more than 8 to 10 per cent of Indian citizens, they still add up to a hefty eighty million people or so, a large enough number that constitutes a sizeable world of ideas and lifestyles existing alongside, yet isolated, from the conventional majority.

Certain English-language newspapers and magazines that circulate in this small world openly feature sex advice columns with some very candid responses to queries and issues that readers raise. Noticeably, these columns do not regard sex solely as a means for childbearing but rather as a form of personal fulfilment and partnership building. Young urban men and women, as well as teenagers, in these circles date openly and speak freely of their relationships. Some are not squeamish about publicly affirming the necessity of sexual compatibility.

In the upper-class urban environment, there appears to be an increasing acceptance of variations in sexual lifestyles and choice of sexuality. Some of the celebrity hairstylists, fashion gurus, dress designers and artists in the major cities are openly gay. A prominent fashion designer who has created lines of clothing that fuses the gender gap believes that India is prepared for designs that are 'truly androgynous' and that a certain strata of society is quite comfortable with the idea of 'cross-dressing'.[11] Similarly, theatre and private productions, like *Pandora's Box* and *Vagina Monologues*, that explore concepts of womanhood and sexuality have played to full house in some cities.

Where even ten to fifteen years ago it was socially deplorable for girls from 'respectable' families to participate in beauty pageants or work in films or as models, jobs that often require a flaunting of one's sensuality, today middle-class India regards its Miss World beauty queens as icons of national prestige. Exposing skin for jobs that pay does not seem vulgar any more, and increasingly upper-class urban women are more comfortable and unselfconscious about their bodies and clothing. Grooming schools for models and beauty queen aspirants too have become remarkably popular in urban India.

This small liberal corner of India is not too shy when it comes to publicly conversing about sex. In 2004, a mobile phone video footage of two high-school students having sex was circulated in public. It prompted a series of programmes broadcast on the English-medium channels on television, where people voiced their indignation. While many protested against the incident and the precedent it set for other teenagers, there were some on the panels who called for a more open-minded and progressive approach to shifting social trends. This was, in fact, a tremendous statement of change, as the public discussion of sex even a few years earlier would have been quite unthinkable.

Some of these social changes are reflected in the system of laws and judicial injunctions. When a lesbian couple in Punjab got married in a civil ceremony and was taken into police custody upon the families' appeal, the courts decided that there was no justification for their arrest as the women were adults and free to choose their own lifestyle.[12] This stand was taken despite India's antiquated laws that ban homosexuality.

However, as optimistic as these social changes may seem, the fact remains that they are isolated, and often limited to a small section of the elite, wealthy and educated urban circles, and are not indicative of any significant change in India's conventional thinking on the issues of sex and sexuality.

Besides their outlook on sex and sexuality, the other defining factors that can loosely be used to identify these two moral sections in India, the conservative and the liberal, are wealth and education. The conservative section is largely made up of the rural population, constituting about 80 per cent of the nation's poor, as well as the urban slum-dwelling people. These communities are either illiterate or barely educated. Most do not have running water or electricity—and many are lucky if they get three square meals a day.

However, a rapidly increasing section of this conservative section is now formed by a notable section of India's expanding middle class, India's nouveau riche. Unlike their impoverished counterparts, these communities enjoy the benefits of copious wealth accumulation and a luxurious, upper-class lifestyle that

India's feudal economy makes generous allowances for. Their children are educated, and often in professional and other well-paying executive jobs, as well as in influential government and administrative positions.

The undersized liberal section, conversely, is much more uniform in its composition, comprising primarily people who form the middle- or upper-income strata in cities and large towns. They are on the average quite well educated, English-speaking, and westernized in their dress, food and lifestyle.

Perhaps the only other factor, besides polarized moralities, that identifies as well as sets apart these two moral sections is religiosity. Religion is an inseparable aspect of the conservative group's outlook on life, whether the people in this section are rural or city-dwelling, rich or poor, educated or illiterate, professionals or farmers. Life in these sectors revolves around sacred ideals and traditions. No ritual of living—birth, death, marriage and jobs—is acceptable unless it has been subject to priests, prayers and a divinity's guidance. Religious festivals, taboos and customs are adhered to fiercely, for their violation would be tantamount to a negation of life. Religion is both the sword and the shield of this group, used to enforce on society its practices and beliefs, as well to defend them.

The members of the liberal section on the other hand regard religion as an inherited piece of antiquity, something they might periodically acknowledge. Some might even have a rare image of the god Ganesha, for instance, on their mantlepiece, not because it intensifies the sacred aura of their homes for them, but because they think it blends well with the aesthetics of their fashionable living room. They may participate in festivals like Diwali or Holi, but treat them as occasions for feasting and merrymaking rather than as reverential offerings to the god worshipped in that particular festival. The liberal sector makes its choices, such as selection of a spouse, like most people in the Western world would—based on what they desire and on the information and the options available to them, without ritually inviting the intervention of the divine on their behalf.

WHO WILL BE MASTER OF THE DEMOCRATIC WORLD?

The million-dollar question is: will the liberal sector or the conservative one set the moral precedence for the outlook on sex and sexuality in India of the twenty-first century? The hypothesis for this book is that the prerogative will belong to the dominant bloc, the 'master class' that will steer the power machinery of the system. This is the section that will define the social, communal and political impulses of the masses and pilot the 'herd instinct' of society. It will embody the social milieu in its visions, outlook and sensibilities—and it will most certainly be the pre-eminent barometer for India's moral pulse.

The inclination of scholars and social scientists so far, when analysing India's chaotic, corrupt and poverty-laden state of affairs, has been to bring India's affluent, educated and westernized elite—the group that also includes the liberal bloc—to book. Much has been said about India's 'exclusionary growth', an economic prototype also seen in Brazil and Mexico, where a small section of the society becomes exceedingly, in fact obscenely, wealthy while the bulk of the population continues to languish in wretched and sub-human conditions.[13] In the global market, India's appalling poverty and the compulsion of its majority to work at exploitatively low wages make the country an attractive sweatshop for foreign companies. The nation's elite terms this feature as a national asset, a temptation for foreign investors.

It has been generally assumed that it is this elite class that is the power bloc, India's post-independence master class. The scholarly conception is that this elite class, because of its educational privileges and wealth, has selfishly exploited the Indian system for its own gains, driving the country's illiterate and helpless majority into the black hole of poverty. If that is so, if India's current liberal bloc is to be the dominant faction, according to our morality hypothesis, we can envisage a future for India where sexual sensibilities would not differ much from that of Western countries. However, as India's economy grows, India's reviled middle- and upper-class affluence will absorb an increasingly larger number of people from India's conservative bloc, people who at one time were part of the struggling, poorly educated, lower-middle-income classes. This upwardly mobile group has firmly established a robust stewardship role for itself, in opposition to the liberal section, in the nation's political destiny as well as its economic exploitation. However, where they clash with their rivals, it is in their formulation of India's moral prospects.

As confusing as this scenario is, it still must be kept in mind that post-colonial India has traversed only about sixty years. In terms of historical time periods, that is only a start. There really is no telling how the power structure of this democratic era will unfold as it moves into its own.

Nonetheless, one of the supreme measures of the operative power in a democratic society is in the clout of the vote. And in India, that power, as has been repeatedly demonstrated, lies almost entirely with India's impoverished majority. The wealthy people in the cities are generally reluctant to endure the tedious voting process, which entails bureaucratic procedures, avoidable paper work and endless waiting in queues, sometimes under inclement weather conditions. Indeed, if the vote is a method of effecting change, the urban wealthy of India have no incentive to want that change. On the other hand, on more than one occasion, against all expectations of the poll pundits, the impoverished electorate has decided to revamp India's administration by ousting parties in power. In 1977, when Indira Gandhi, one of the most popular leaders for her 'abolish poverty' campaigns, was unceremoniously ousted by a landslide public mandate in her renewed bid for the prime minister's seat, it was an expression of public outrage at the fanatical 'family planning' projects implemented during her term in office.

Besides their unyielding hand in deciding the political fate of the nation, India's impoverished masses are also the critical moral meter of the politics of the nation. Consequently, Indian politics compulsively plays up to the moral impulses of the underprivileged. Politicians, whatever their personal preferences may be, are compelled to assume a social and moral persona that is acceptable to India's conservative majority. They robotically assume an orthodox stance because the social conditioning of the majority of voters is largely patriarchal and their approach to the subject of sex and sexuality is very conservative.

This is reflected in dress too. A woman campaigner may wear jeans in her personal circle but her political image demands that she is clad in a traditional sari or salwar-kameez whenever she makes a public appearance. Similarly, male politicians favour the Indian kurta-pajama even though a majority of urban Indian men wear Western clothes. Religious ceremonies and processions are image-boosting factors of the campaign trail, and are patiently endured by politicians who may be agnostic in their outlook. Being accompanied by a boyfriend or girlfriend to a campaign or political function would be inconceivable, though a wife in the retinue greatly boosts the conventional image. A husband in a female politician's entourage though might not have the same effect. Some politicians have even felt the need to righteously declare themselves celibate.

Every time celebrity figures have, intentionally or inadvertently, resisted the status quo of the time-honoured conservative model, they have faced overwhelming public resistance. When an Indian film star dared to openly state that it was ridiculous for men to expect women to be virgins at their wedding in this age, she had twenty-five defamation law suits filed against her and was forced to apologize publicly for her statement.[14] Another film actress, who was swept off her feet and given a friendly peck on the cheek at a public meeting, by an exuberant Richard Gere, also had law suits filed against her. When the director Deepa Mehta attempted to make the film *Water*, in which she examined the social situation that has led to thousands of widows driven out of their homes to beg on the streets of Vrindavan and Varanasi, or forced into prostitution, it caused such a public uproar that the courts forced Mehta to stop filming.[15]

The politicians' reticence to foster effective action on issues of population control, AIDS awareness and female genocide is also largely in conformity to the conservativeness of the rural public and the traditionalist urban middle-class. The impoverished conservative bloc is often answerable neither to the law nor to the Indian Constitution in its sanctimonious and sometimes violent effort to secure its moral territories. In 2005, a supervisor of the Child and Welfare Department who was working to prevent child marriages in rural central India had her hands chopped off by one irate man. Just a few hours after the incident, more than 50,000 child marriages took place to mark the auspicious day of Akshaya Tritiya. The chief minister of the state responded somewhat dismissively, emphasizing a community's need to preserve its culture and traditions.[16]

The political disregard of and sometimes allowance for sectarian violence among the poorest communities—violence that in its scale and propensity is often anarchical—is indefensible. This has resulted in violent attacks on women, with men venting their aggression on each other's communities by gang-raping, and murdering, women.

However, the greatest irony is this: in the larger moral prognosis of India's conservative majority, it is the diminutive liberal sector that is sexually deviant, degenerate and 'westernized'; they are believed to be the doom of India's moral culture.

Even if this westernized section adopts a non-traditional lifestyle within the cloistered boundaries of its posh homes and clubs, it is extremely important that it is not allowed to 'pollute' the general social milieu with its loose moral values. In fact this 'degeneracy' is regarded as such a threat that there is an urgent demand for social moral policing to salvage the culture's sanctity. National censor boards, axe in hand, zealously stand guard over the silver screen—only the suggestion of sex can be conveyed, such as images of two flowers touching each other, or in the frenzied pelvic thrust of buttocks in a dance sequence. However, a simple mouth-to-mouth kiss is too obscene for general viewing. Even the hazy phone video clipping of an actress apparently kissing her boyfriend at a discotheque was cause for a public uproar. Regarded not as the couple's personal business, but as news, the incident was splashed all over national newspapers and the couple was accused of exhibitionism.

While men urinate openly in public, the sight of lovers holding hands or kissing is considered much too obscene and revolting. In Bangalore, India's trendiest city, with umpteen bars and discotheques, the police feel morally obliged to keep the park benches clear of couples trying to find a quiet spot for a tête-à-tête. In India's capital, Delhi, men often pelt lovers strolling in the parks with stones, while in Chandigarh, men of the moral patrol have been known to demand sexual favours of the girl if the lovers caught by them wish to keep their 'immoral' acts from getting known.[17]

The moral baton of the conservative sector comes down particularly heavy on women. Premarital sex for women is the ultimate sin. A high premium is placed on a woman's virginity at the time of marriage, and in some villages it is customarily heralded by the public display of blood-stained sheets after the couple's first night together. Even though a married woman is expected to fulfil her duty of providing sex to her husband and bearing his children, sex is too vulgar a topic for her to demonstrate prior knowledge of or explore on her own. The idea of a young unmarried woman deriving pleasure in her sexuality immediately places her in the category of whores. Girls are repeatedly warned against showing any curiosity about sexual processes or any interest in the opposite sex. Consequently, most Indian women have learned to dissociate themselves from their own sexuality, and even after marriage live in complete oblivion to the idea of sex as a personal need.

The social and psychological evaluation of the modern Indian women's sexual history reveals that they often leave their genitals nameless. A vagina, even in a doctor's office, is vaguely referred to as 'that place' or 'down there'. Some women never discover that urine and babies do not emerge from the same opening. During sex, many just grit their teeth and pretend they are urinals for their husbands to conduct their 'business' in. And they do so fully clothed, for their nakedness, even during sex, would render them lewd and shameless.[18]

Even a film like *Fire*,[19] which gently explores the idea of two unhappily married women, both prisoners of social and familial milieus, seeking physical and emotional reprieve in each other, was considered too obscene a subject for public viewing. It evoked violent protests across India, as hoards of men rampaged through movie halls tearing down posters and vandalizing buildings.[20]

Women are not only expected to be impassive about sex, but they must also be restrained in their appearance—as in dress, manners and demeanour—taking care to rein in all independent expressions of sexuality. A woman's sexuality is not her own to assert her individuality with and she must accept the fact that it is for the exclusive use of men, even if they are rapists. In the aftermath of a campus rape in Mumbai, a dress code for women was considered an appropriate preventive measure as opposed to community awareness, rape counselling, social re-education or self-defence seminars. Other campuses and communities all over the country soon followed suit. Most of the clothing targeted were in the Western style, considered 'lewd' and 'provocative', thus reinforcing the notion that rapists are normal, decent men who otherwise would not rape were it not for the invitation that a woman sends them by her attire and appearance. There are even different degrees of modesty assigned to different Indian clothing. Some school students in Calcutta have agitated against their teachers wearing the salwar-kameez, clothing considered less modest than the sari.[21] Oddly enough, according to one city survey, over 95 per cent of rape victims are from the lowest income strata[22]—women who wear the salwar-kameez and sari, the most conventional of attires.

In 2005, in Maharashtra,1500 licensed dance bars were forced to shut down abruptly, rendering over 20,000 women who worked as dancers in these bar jobless and practically destitute. At a meeting of the state Legislative Assembly, the male members rejoiced in their successful 'moral policing', and suggested that it was preferable for these women to commit suicide because of unemployment than be dancers at a bar.[23]

WOMEN AS SEX OBJECTS FOR THE PATRIARCHY

Yet the paradox is this: notwithstanding its demagogical puritanical front, it is India's conservative section that indulges in an uncontested sexual permissiveness. It is an indulgence that is woven into antiquated traditions, customs and beliefs, and that continues to persist in society. More importantly, this privilege of perversion is afforded exclusively to the male order. The role of women is also a paradox, for the patriarchy that on one hand patronizes them as incarnates of a goddess also regards them as sex toys.

Indeed, the current structure of India's social and legal systems is such that it obligingly accommodates both the conservative patriarchy's need for sexual autonomy and its sexual objectification of women, stripping them of will, choice and individuality. In marital norms, for instance, the law in general advocates monogamy, but makes munificent leeway for religious and regional customs, some of these under the shield of so-called personal laws. Muslim men in India, for example, are permitted to practise polygamy and can have up to four wives. However, this law also conveniently serves non-Muslim men, even among the wealthy and famous, who by a token conversion to Islam can also take second wives. Muslim women, however, do not have a reciprocal privilege.

Fraternal polyandry is another example of the tolerance of male sexual licence through the social corridors of marriage. In certain hill communities, such as in Kinnaur, Lahaul and Spiti in Himachal Pradesh where fraternal polyandry is practised, it is customary for a family of brothers, however many there may be, to have a common wife. The woman then not only serves as a domestic serf to the brothers but also a sexual one. The brothers, if they so desire, can marry more than one woman, but each wife must be married to all the men, that is, be prepared to have sex with all of them.[24]

Though the Hindu Marriage Act of 1955 illegalized bigamy in India, it is widely practised, particularly among the lower economic sections. According to the 2001 census data, almost ten million women in India are married to bigamous men.[25] Rural men often migrate to the towns or cities for work, and some may occasionally send home a portion of their income. It is customary for many of these men to take on new wives in the cities with whom they start a family—they may occasionally visit the family in the village or abandon them. These marriages usually are in unofficial Hindu ceremonies instead of court marriages, and the process of 'divorce' involves the man simply leaving his first wife and setting up a home with another.

Women who want to bring bigamy charges against their husbands face almost unsurmountable legal hurdles because the conditions set by the Indian judiciary for proving bigamy are extremely perplexing. To begin with, given the wide variance in regional marriage customs among Hindus, the Indian courts do not clarify the parameters of what constitutes a legalized Hindu marriage.[26] Even a registration certificate of the second marriage is not regarded as adequate proof of bigamy nor is a verbal admission by the husband.[27] Women also face social disapproval because most communities tend to be very contemptuous of women who attempt to legally prosecute their husbands.

Among the worst impacts that India's marriage laws have on women are those that pertain to child marriage. In 1986, the health ministry in the state of Uttar Pradesh established that there were certain villages in their state where every girl above the age of eight was already married.[28] The Government of India stipulates eighteen as the legal age of marriage for girls, but child marriage is widely practised in India. A 2003 estimate by the United Nations Fund for Population Actvities (UNFPA) projects that within a decade more than a 100 million girls under the age of eighteen will be married in India.[29] As far as the courts are concerned, even if these girls are below the stipulated legal age, the marriages are still held as valid. Besides, according to the Indian courts, the child's parents and relations who organized the marriage or the priests who conducted the ceremony cannot be prosecuted or charged with 'abetment'.[30]

Not only do women have no control over their marital state, but they have no jurisdiction over their own reproductive systems either. The patriarchy expects women to provide men with sex and also bear children, particularly sons. The number of children a woman eventually has is entirely her husband's choice. Women, chiefly among the poorer classes, who seek tubal ligation or birth control measures on their own often have to endure abuse from their husbands.[31] About 65 per cent of girls in India get married under the legal age of eighteen,[32] and then compelled to endure multiple pregnancies, which wreak havoc on their health and on their lives.

In 1975, the Government of India's Department of Social Welfare released a report[33] on the status of Indian women. The report was harshly critical of the general treatment of Indian women and contemptuous of their social standing as 'expendable assets'. Factors that were identified as contributors to the breakdown in women's health were child marriages, multiple pregnancies and lack of medical aid and facilities.[34] It was also observed that the younger a woman was, particularly if she was below eighteen years of age, the more likely she was to endure pregnancy-related complications. More than thirty years since, there has been a negligible change in that status.

To ensure that only male children are born, many women are compelled by their husbands' families to undergo ultrasound examinations and selective abortions. In 2000, UNICEF and the World Health Organization report stated that annually almost 136,000[35] women die in India (that is one pregnant woman dies every five minutes[36]) due to childbirth, unsafe abortions and other pregnancy-related causes, one the highest maternal mortality rates in the world.[37] Women who are found to be carrying female foetuses face additional violence, both psychological and physical from their spouses and in-laws. In one incident, a man shot his wife dead when he discovered she was pregnant with his third daughter, while another man chopped off his pregnant wife's nose.[38]

However, one of the most treacherous impacts of the cultural institution of marriage in India on women is that of AIDS. In 1998, in response to the Supreme Court case 8 SCC 296, scores of people had campaigned for the rights of AIDS-afflicted men to marry without having to reveal their infection. However, the Supreme Court had ruled that it was obligatory for the infected person, as well as anyone with knowledge of the infected person, such as doctors, to give the information, and that this would not be tantamount to breach of confidentiality as with other medical conditions. There have been numerous cases in which the parents of an AIDS-infected man have arranged their son's marriage, without revealing his condition to the girl's family. In India, where a majority of marriages are arranged by the families, sex and reproduction are an assumed part of the contract, which essentially make marriage to an infected man a death sentence. As of now, there are no laws compelling HIV-positive men or their families to reveal the man's condition to prospective brides.[39]

Almost 50 per cent of Indian women with AIDS are unsuspecting wives infected by their husbands who had contracted the disease from outside sources. A majority of these women have faced abuse from their in-laws, who have accused them of causing the illness and death of their sons. Once the man dies, his wife is generally evicted from the house by her in-laws. In numerous such cases, women thus infected, pregnant, and impoverished, suddenly find themselves on the streets with no social refuge. Some are even compelled to give birth on the streets.[40]

The military is another hazardous factor in the AIDS impact on women in India. The joint UN programme on HIV-AIDS (UNAIDS) has warned that armies are among the highest-risk segments of society and are exceedingly susceptible to acquiring and transmitting the virus. It reports that the military exposes women to infection either through prostitution, a service commonly used by soldiers, or rape.[41] India has a colossal army, one of the largest in the world. Soldiers posted in different parts of the country often have to live in separation from their families for extended periods of time and are known to resort to prostitutes for their recreational needs. The Indian military has finally acknowledged the problem, admitting to the increasing HIV infection rates among its soldiers.[42] However, with the armed forces posted in the politically disturbed regions of the country, where there often is fear of political insurgencies, the rape of local women by soldiers has long been a contentious public issue. In situations of military occupation like these, rape is often used as a weapon for establishing authority by some military personnel, or as a form of retribution against politically dissident locals. Most appallingly, the issue has long been ignored by India's Central government.

Rape is one of the worst violations of a woman's most intimate and individual right to choose—to refuse sex. Yet, some of India's archaic laws and its treatment of rape victims are a virtual validation of the objectification of women as sexual commodities, assumed to be devoid of choice.

It begins with the legal definition of rape, which is categorically defined as penetration with genital injury, and proved by the presence of semen. Should a rapist be unable to finish the act he intended due to his inability to attain a full erection or penetrate, the incident is not recognized as rape, and is treated as a lesser crime, regardless of the psychological trauma to the victim. This compulsive focus on penetration and ejaculation is consistent with the male concept of the female as a sexual apparatus, a receptacle for semen and babies. An unmarried virgin's worth hinges on an unbroken hymen, while a sexually active married woman, once raped, is viewed as 'contaminated' with another's seed, bringing shame to the patriarchy she is married into.

In 2003 a thirteen-year-old girl in a Chhatisgarh village was raped and when she was found pregnant she was forced to marry her rapist, as according to local belief she had no 'marriage value' left. In another case the same year, a nurse in a city hospital who was brutally raped and had her eye gouged out by a ward boy in the same hospital was made a brazen offer of marriage by the rapist. The offer, curiously, was regarded by some of the victim's supporters as a 'well-meaning' gesture on the part of the rapist to reinstate her honour, and some even advised her to accept it. The rapist's insolence did not seem to infuriate the presiding judge either. He did not perceive it as a mockery of the victim and the judicial system, and instead conveyed the proposal to the prosecution for consideration.[43] It is little wonder then that most rape victims in India never file a police complaint or report the matter to anyone in authority.

Perhaps the most crucial validation of a woman's worth as simply a sexual commodity comes from India's laws on marital rape. Indian courts currently do not openly acknowledge marital rape. In fact, standard rulings of the court in certain cases are almost akin to facilitating marital rape.

In situations where a couple is separated and the wife files for maintenance, the husband can, as a matter of routine, claim restitution of conjugal rights (RCR). This essentially is the legal blackmailing of women, who may have no home or personal assets of their own. If they also have children, it traps them in a desperately tight corner, often compelling them to return to their husbands against their wishes, or taking a chance with destitution.[44]

The perception of the Indian courts, which continue to grant RCR, on the idea or even the question of a woman's individual rights is that it has no place in the home, as it challenges the sanctity of the marriage. Furthermore, it is affirmed that RCR serves a social purpose, that of 'the prevention of break-up of marriages'.[45]

The travesty of India's treatment of rape is that where women have literally been stripped of all power and dignity in public and domestic spheres, even the space of their own bodies is not theirs to control. In 2005, in a highly publicized rape case, a woman called Imrana was raped by her father-in-law. The village council, in accordance with its own interpretations of Islamic laws, decided that Imrana was too contaminated even for her husband to cohabit with, and, therefore, she had to marry the father-in-law and regard her husband like her son. What should have been treated as a self-evident criminal act subject to severe and immediate police action became a media event that provided fodder for a vigorous public debate. The debate was about the validity of Muslim personal laws in India, not the violation of a woman's human rights. At a time when even the UN has declared rape to be a gross human rights violation, it was incomprehensible that India would see it a fit topic to use for a public religious duel, instead of abiding first and foremost by the inalienable human rights of the rape victim as any civilized nation would.

Muslim personal laws in India, which bestow various privileges on Muslim men, have often been reinforced by Hindu politicians,[46] a typical case of a dominant patriarchy permitting privileges to a hierarchically lower patriarchy in order to ensure its political alliance. But as proved in Imrana's case, this extends the patriarchy's capacity for the sexual abuse of women to a sphere beyond that of the house, instituting a much larger social and political conspiracy.

In India, rape has been repeatedly used as a political weapon in testosterone wars between feuding castes and religious communities. Though this occurs regularly in small villages, where personal vendettas between families, clans and castes are avenged through the rape of women of one another's communities, one of the recent and most horrific incidents of mass-scale rape was witnessed in Gujarat in 2002. To avenge the death of Hindu passengers in a train rumoured to have been set ablaze by some Muslims, violent Hindu mobs in Gujarat took anarchical control of the state. Muslim homes and shops were looted and razed to the ground, and women gang-raped and killed in the most sadistic manner. This scene was a repeat of what the Sikh community had to endure in Delhi, at the hands of Hindu mobs in 1984. A majority of the victims of the gang-rapes and murders in the Delhi and Gujarat riots still await justice.

Ultimately, the sexual objectification of women in India is intrinsic to the power structure of the patriarchy. It is power that is backed by two millenia of religious sanctions, and is defined by the control of women as dehumanized, commoditized resources. As a non-entity, the idea of a woman's choice—her choice of life, love and dignity—cannot be entertained. Choice is the patriarchy's prerogative, its tool of supremacy, and a woman's very existence hinges on the wielding of that choice by men.

In an alarming increase of such incidents, male suitors in India, who are spurned by the woman they desire disfigure the woman by throwing acid on her face.[47] In 2003, in just nine months, and in only one district in Uttar Pradesh, there were thirteen cases where young people who had dared to fall in love were murdered by their fathers and male relatives.[48] In each of these cases, there is an imminent and distressing threat to the collective male sense of power and 'ownership' over female sexuality. If lovers started pairing up by choice, and women start taking the initiative of deciding who they wanted to have sex with, and whether with or without marriage, it would put the patriarchy's very existence into jeopardy. That is why love marriages are frowned upon in India, even prompting murder. In one case, a girl's father, who along with other villagers had tortured and killed his daughter and her lover, expressed his intense 'hatred' for the concept of love.[49]

For the Indian patriarchy, the woman is a sexual resource, a compilation of a womb, breasts and a vagina for its use; she is a negotiable, marketable commodity. The unfortunate reality is that she is not assessed much differently by her own parents. From the moment of her birth, a daughter is viewed as a financial liability. Being of little use to her parents, she is raised for the consumption of others, namely, the sexual and reproductive needs of the patriarchal lineage in which her marriage will be arranged. Her parents are willing to dole out gargantuan amounts for her dowry, sometimes even procuring loans to do so. But they would not consider investing that money instead in her education, qualifications and economic independence. Nor do these parents recognize their daughter's rights and privileges as an individual: her right to safety, dignity and respect. The girl is brought up insensible to the idea of sex and in strict isolation from possible love entanglements; if she gets sexually tainted it would be quite impossible to marry her off because 'used goods' have little worth. Also, she must be married within the prime of her reproductive age, by her early twenties, or even before her first period, as is the custom in many rural areas. In the village where all the girls above eight years of age were married, the reason given was that the dowry demand increased exponentially after the age of eight.[50] By the time a girl is in her early twenties, parents eager to 'give her away' are willing to pay exorbitant amounts in dowry. The prospective grooms' families, mindful of the parents' desperation, see it as the business opportunity of a lifetime. Parents often coerce their daughters into the beds of complete strangers, an act that seems horrifically inhuman and that many would interpret as facilitating rape, but it is seen as the closing of a financial deal.

The daughter is a liability discharged—a disinvestment—for the parents.

Undeniably, particularly in the case of India, the worst outcome of this severe social objectification of women is that it makes them as disposable as any other object. Indeed, the routine elimination of women from the population is perhaps one the most depraved secrets that India conceals in its folds of democracy and traditionalism. Reports based on census studies[51] estimate that at least fifty million females have been removed from India's population.[52] There are villages in north India where the gender ratio has been reported to be as low as thirty-one women to a hundred men.[53] Government records also show that there are villages in Rajasthan where there have been no reports of the birth of girls for decades.[54] The methods of elimination include female feticide, female infanticide, dowry murders and the death of pre-adolescent girls through wilful neglect of nutrition and medical care.

Women all over India, often within the first few years of marriage, are slaughtered, literally on an hourly basis,[55] by their husbands and in-laws, incidentally for not fulfilling their dowry demands. This is a form of murder, which without a firm government crackdown has gone out of control and there is a consistent increase in the number of such cases reported each year. For instance, there were 2209 cases reported in 1988, 4835 cases in 1990, and 5157 cases in 1991.[56] In 2004 Amnesty International estimated that there were close to 15,000 dowry murders committed every year,[57] while independent surveys report as many as 25,000 women killed in dowry-related cases in India each year.[58]

The abnormally high mortality rates for pre-adolescent girls compared to that for boys,[59] which has been documented to be due to the deliberate deprivation of nourishment and health care of young girls, would in enlightened legal systems be tantamount to homicide by negligence. A 2007 CRY report on Indian children revealed that of the total number of girls born in India each year, 1 in 4 would not live past the age of fifteen, and about 33 per cent would die before the age of one.[60] Also in 2007, the UNICEF report on the State of the World's Children said: 'A girl in India is more than 40 per cent more likely than a boy to die between ages of one and five'.[61] Studies reveal that in some regions, girls aged five or even younger had an almost 50 per cent higher mortality rate than boys of the same age.[62] In one of India's wealthiest states, Punjab, a study estimated that of the children who died below the age of three, 85 per cent were girls.[63] In many instances, parents would rather let their ailing daughters die than spend money on their treatment, especially if they already had another daughter.[64]

Infanticide is yet another method of female homicide in India that has been practised for many centuries. Appalled by its pervasiveness and social acceptability, the colonial British administration had in fact outlawed it. Once infanticide had been strictly banned by the British under the Infanticide Act in 1870, and the law imposed with the threat of punitive action, it forced the practice underground.[65] Today, female infanticide is prevalent more in the rural areas where ultrasound and abortion facilities are not always easily available or affordable. In a horrifying attestation of the widespread practice of infanticide in Bihar in 1995, midwives who were interviewed confessed that they were paid by families to discreetly dispose of almost 50 per cent of the baby girls they delivered. Methods used included strangulation, poisoning or burying the baby alive in a pot.[66] Baby girls are abandoned in garbage dumps, where occasionally they have been known to be killed and eaten by stray dogs.[67] In Kerala, incidentally one of India's more progressive states with the highest literacy role in the country, it is reported that annually at least 25,000 infant girls are murdered soon after birth.[68]

In cities where ultrasound facilities are available, expectant parents in India are able to eliminate their would-be daughters while still in the womb. Especially with the legalization of abortion in India, since the early 1970s, the targeted elimination of unwanted daughters has taken a particularly vicious turn.[69] Earlier on, billboards in parts of India openly advertised competitive prices for the detection and abortion of female fetuses.[70] A UNICEF-sponsored study of abortion patterns, conducted as early as in 1984 in six clinics in Mumbai, showed that of the 8000 abortions performed by these clinics 7999 were of female fetuses.[71] Other studies not only revealed similar trends of weeding out females, but also confirmed that parents preferred to keep the fetus if it was male, even if the ultrasound indicated genetic abnormalities.[72] In the 1990s, it was estimated that close to half a million female fetuses were being aborted in India each year, and the number is estimated at more than a million a year now.[73]

The investigative journalist Gita Aravamudan, who in her book *Disappearing Daughters* presents her observations from ten years of field study of female feticide and infanticide in India, compares this systematic and targeted extermination of women to a 'serial killing'. She says that in this 'holocaust', 'a whole gender is getting exterminated . . . [in] a silent and smoothly executed crime which leaves no waves in its wake . . . In some parts of . . . [India] almost two generations of women have been exterminated'.[74]

And a holocaust it is, not just metaphorically speaking, but as a ground reality, which meets at least four of the five definitions for genocide as set by the United Nations. The charter for the UN Convention on Genocide in 1948 had established that genocide comprised killing, gravely harming through physical or mental violence, subjecting the group to living conditions that causes its devastation, or preventing life continuity by controlling the birth and normal existence of a group.[75] Going by this definition, as well as the rapid decline in the ratio of the female population in response to a targeted and systematic elimination,[76] it goes without saying that India accounts for one of the largest, and silently ongoing, genocides in human history.

To hold India accountable for the genocide of its women means that it is not the crime of a small section of society, but includes the complicity of an entire nation of people. Dowry, illiteracy and poverty are often heralded as the prime motivations for female extermination in India. The general belief is that poverty-ridden parents who cannot afford the monstrous sums of money they are expected to pay for dowries consider the birth of a girl a lifelong debt, which is why the girl is killed at birth or aborted as a fetus.

However, female genocide in India is not an inadvertent by-product of ignorance and monetarily compelled choices. Some of the highest rates of female foeticide are recorded in the affluent areas of south Delhi, among some of the wealthiest and educated communities in India.[77] The wife of a senior executive of a multinational company, herself a school teacher, underwent nine pregnancies and eight abortions to purge female fetuses. The ninth she carried to full term because it was a boy, but two days after she delivered the child, she died.[78] That this mentality is born of a cultural value system which is profoundly misogynist, and is independent of economic and educational factors, is also confirmed by the fact that the immigrant Indian populations in the UK, Canada and the United States are also now showing abnormally skewed gender ratios.[79] Newspapers like *India Abroad* run enticing advertisements to tap into the market, with announcements like 'Desire a Son?' and 'Choosing the Sex of your Baby: A New Scientific Reality'.[80] In December 2006 in a United Nations' General Assembly speech, it was announced that the gender ratios at birth recorded for the Asian American population was 'biologically impossible'.[81]

Dr Robert Lifton,[82] a psychologist who through interviews has attempted to understand the psychology of people, their thought processes and motivations in having participated in the horrendous genocide of the Jews during the holocaust in Europe, has observed that ultimately all classes of people, wealthy or poor, uneducated or professional, participate directly or implicitly in a system that is genocidal.[83] Essentially, for a genocidal tendency to thrive in a culture or community, there has to be a tacit compliance and participation of that community at large.

Often, in the case of dowry murders in India, the eventual murder is a cooperative team effort involving the husband and members of his family. Usually, a member of the family will restrain the woman physically while others proceed to kill her, be it by dousing her with kerosene and then setting her alight or hanging her from the ceiling or forcing acid down her throat. But even later, if at all there are police inquiries, the family members close ranks and shield each other.

Scores of women who survive vicious attacks—including second- and third-degree burns—are coerced by their in-laws and even their own parents to refrain from registering a police complaint or taking the matter to trial for attempted murder. Parents of the woman, too, are often hopeful of reconciliation, even after the horrific abuse, torture and hospitalization of their daughter. A divorced daughter is regarded as not just a financial burden by her parents, especially if she also has children, but as a stigma which brings shame to her family. Parents often protect their own self-interest at the cost of the lives and safety of their daughters.

However, it is not just the extended family but often even the larger social and legal system that is complicit, either through apathy or sometimes participation, in creating a prison of torture for these violently abused women. Most dowry cases go uninvestigated or else are written off as suicides or accidents. Wealthy families that kill their daughters-in-law can afford to bribe the police. In areas where hospitals keep records to track the progress of new-born girls, the police have been known to use the lists to extort money from families who have killed their infant girls.[84]

People who may not agree with or practise female genocide, but believe they would be betraying Indian culture by denouncing it, can be said to be complicit, just as the Germans who refused to oppose the Nazi regime.[85] Modern, educated Indians will go to great lengths to either rationalize or to defy the revolting images of Indian culture that emerge from the nation's past and present. A well-known author, in one of his recent books, vociferously supports age-old Hindu traditions like sati, lauding it as a plan of ancient wisdom devised to immortalize the love of the husband and wife.[86]

Lifton also observed that ultimately all who participate in genocide not only serve as the driving force behind it, but also derive some benefit from their complicity.[87] In India, almost all sections of society that participate one way or another in female genocide actually derive personal benefit from doing so. This is perhaps the primary reason why the Indian system is said to have 'actively facilitated' and 'condoned the genocide of women'.[88] It is well known that despite the ban on the revelation of gender through ultrasound it is all too easy to locate a doctor in India willing to illegally conduct the ultrasound as well as the abortion.[89] Dr Puneet Bedi, a senior gynaecologist at the Apollo Hospital in Delhi, told the BBC in an interview that 'most' Indian gynaecologists are 'directly involved' in what is now a 'business' of female fetal abortions in India because there is much 'money for the doctors to be made'.[90] He sees it an 'an organised industry, an organised mafia among doctors'.[91]

What that also means is that the moral world view of India's conservative bloc that regards women as sexual objects that serve the needs of the patriarchy and that can be disposed of at whim is the dominant moral system in democratic India. These are values that dictate to the social 'herd instinct' that Nietzsche spoke of because they serve the need of the social system.

In some villages in northern India, there are so few women left to marry that marriage brokers kidnap brides from other states or even buy them off their parents. To economize or because they cannot afford to purchase additional brides, the bride 'bought' for the oldest brother is sometimes made to sexually service all the other brothers in the family, as well as the father if he is a widower, while she is also made to keep house for them all. This form of polyandry is in fact catching on in quite a few regions in India now, specifically where the gender ratios are excessively skewed.[92]

The trafficking of kidnapped women as 'brides' across state boundaries is creating a thriving flesh market.[93] In one known instance, a woman sold as a bride was then resold to another man, who along with his son utilized the woman as a sex slave. They further capitalized on their purchase by forcing the woman to work as a brick-kiln labourer during the day to fetch them some extra money.[94]

Female genocide ultimately is a symptom of a deep and systematic process of the complete dehumanization and commoditization of women, a process that is rooted in the conservative patriarchal foundation of India's cultures and traditions. The Merriam-Webster Dictionary gives the broader definition of 'patriarchy' as a society where men 'control . . . a disproportionately large share of power'.[95] Others elaborate that it is the 'systematic domination of women by men'[96] with the control and subordination being 'sturdier' than other kinds of segregation, 'more rigorous', 'more uniform' and 'more enduring'.[97] Studies also reveal that levels of patriarchy in a society are a direct measure not only of the ill health of women in that society, but also their lowered access to positions of decision making.[98] But the most relevant research data indicate that female homicide rates also increase proportionately to the levels of patriarchy in a community.[99] That is, the stronger the patriarchal identity of a community, the higher the levels of female homicide associated with it.

The forensic psychiatrist Robert Simon has observed that extreme aggression, which verges on psychopathy, as genocide does, is often an exceptionally vindictive manifestation of narcissism. To the psychopathic narcissist, the world is at his disposal to exploit as he wishes and dispose of as he pleases.[100] India's conservative patriarchy, which adulates its own masculinity in a narcissistic obsession, and deems women as sexual objects to use and dispose of as it pleases, undoubtedly harbours this psychopathic element.

KILLING THE 'OTHER'

The millions of people who participate in the female genocide in India are not regarded as deranged psychopaths; they are in fact ordinary, integrated members of society. They could be any of the so-called average people one sees in the fields, on the streets, in the markets, movie halls and shopping malls in India. The distressing question, therefore, is: what could possibly enable individuals to strangle, poison, or drown newborns, or routinely have a potentially healthy daughter medically terminated, or participate in cold blood in the murder of a wife and a daughter-in-law, and carry on living with an incomprehensible air of normality? Also, how does a nation permit itself to witness this bloodbath, and continue existing, unalarmed, as if genocide was an integral aspect of its social function?

A very peculiar aspect of female genocide in India is that it is never called 'genocide' in plain terms. It tends to be presented as a gender ratio predicament, like an arithmetic problem gone awry. The accepted wisdom is, if one boy does not equal one girl in the final sum total of gender demography, the equation will upset quite a few other social parameters: there could be increased incidents of rape, prostitution and promiscuity, decline in family lineages, social dissent and—heaven forbid—brutal male competition. It is this cold, numerical, almost clinical treatment of what is fundamentally a national crisis, a mammoth breakdown in India's moral and legal system, that is the clue to its cause.

Robert Simon has observed that psychopathic aggression is often characterized by an eerie absence of empathy, of compassion, guilt and remorse for other people,[101] values and emotions that are critical to creating human bonds. However, in genocidal societies, it is through the cultivated absence of these bonding emotions that the victimized segment of a community is alienated and excised from the very society they are rooted in. Alienation is in fact as obligatory to the act of genocide as fuel is to building a fire. Alienation occurs as a gradual process and builds up to a point where it can foster genocide.

The process of dissociating daughters is enmeshed in the very logic of Indian culture. As one Indian proverb says, raising a daughter is like watering a plant in your neighbour's yard. After marriage, the girl becomes a stranger, *parayi* to her own parents. They have successfully got rid of her—she now belongs to her in-laws. The in-laws on their part are not able to reconcile to having another individual in the family. As far as they are concerned, the bride is always an 'outsider', whose sole use is to propagate their lineage.

It is this process of alienation of one human community by another that often causes people to lose perspective of their own humanity and become perpetrators of genocide. Similarly, in the saga of dowry murders, women are reduced to a mode of cash transaction—a disinvestment for the parents and a source of revenue for the in-laws. In a BBC programme, the family of a dead bride was actually shown haggling with the groom's family for the reimbursement of the dowry payment, with the police arbitrating the debate. The murdered woman herself seemed an insignificant factor, her presence or absence inconsequential.[102] In fact, it has been seen that in 90 per cent of dowry murders, the victim's family, the prime witness to the crime, turns hostile in court. This happens if a financial settlement with the murderers of their daughter is reached, after which the victim's family does not wish to pursue the case any further.[103]

While researching female feticide in India, the journalist Asha Krishnamurti reports overhearing one conversation in an abortion clinic where a pregnant woman and her mother-in-law were having a heated argument on when to kill the unborn female fetus, whether they should abort it or wait till it was born.[104] There are reports on how parents are now trying to avoid charges of infanticide by carefully plotting the newborn's murder. The child is fed alcohol or wrapped in a wet blanket and then taken to the doctor who writes out a diagnosis of diarrhoea or pneumonia depending on the case. The parents then return home and find the right opportunity to kill the child. They then have the doctors' diagnosis to show to the police in case they check, knowing fully well that they would not thoroughly investigate the death anyway.[105]

The processes of alienation which engender emotional numbness and detachment in human relationships are essential to the objectification and the eventual annihilation of victims in genocidal communities. The victims are culturally characterized as 'the other', the alien group, the one that the dominant faction deems itself as separate from and superior to.

Female genocide in India is essentially the attempt of the collective male ego to establish its absolute supremacy by the negation of women, by regarding them as the dichotomized 'other'—to be reviled and mistrusted. Needless to say, this polarized vision of gender and system of oppression and control of women has an extended history in Indian society.

However, the wisdom of the Tantric ages had at its core a revelation that was contrary to the Vedic vision of life that dichotomized gender. The Tantriks believed that salvation was represented by the state of non-duality, a unification of perceived opposites: man and woman, Shiva and Shakti, spirit and body, high and low, good and evil, life and death and the impure and the sacred. The lingam (penis) and yoni (vagina)—which until this period had been worshipped as separate entities, the male-centric cults glorifying Shiva as a lingam and the female-centric cults exulting in the power of Shakti as a yoni—in the Tantric period evolved as a unified structural whole. The lingam–yoni, an erect penis conjoined at the base to a vulva, represented the undivided state of the male and female, which was believed to be the embodiment of the divine. The *ardhanari* idol, which also evolved in the Tantric period, was the anthropomorphic version of the lingam–yoni, and depicted the divine as a human figure that is half man or Shiva and half woman or Shakti.

In this image was the message of the Tantriks who spoke of the illusion of opposites. Even though the divine is said to be comprised of opposites—the Shiva and the Shakti—that perception too is really an illusion. It is only the soul that has attained transcendence, or moksha, which is able to recognize that dualities are not intrinsically conflicted elements, but are two exactly equal, indivisible and complementary halves of a single whole. This theory of transcendence further emphasizes that this knowledge of non-duality is always known to the human unconscious, which is a part of the divine universal soul. It is only the human mind—with its shallow perception—that creates dichotomized categories through its conscious thoughts. However, according to Tantric philosophy, when the individual's conscious mind welcomes the wisdom of the unconscious and overcomes its illusion of dichotomies, it attains its freedom from the endless cycles of rebirth.

Ironically, this notion of human dichotomies being nothing more than the mind's delusion is well illustrated by the phenomenon of female genocide in India. One of the most grotesque aspects of this genocide is that it is being committed not by one race, religion or community on another, but by a person's own family. Where the family represents the idea of 'belonging', safety and comfort, India's women are being annihilated by their own parents, grandparents, husbands and in-laws. The genocide in India challenges the basic social construct of 'otherness'. Where 'otherness' has always been a convenient platform to explain genocide in human communities, the lesson from India is that 'otherness' is in fact a relative concept with shifting boundaries, which are conveniently demarcated to suit the violator's goals. The daughter raised by her parents is said to belong to the 'other' family that she is or will be married into. But in the 'other' family as well the woman always remains an 'outsider'.

THE PUZZLE OF THE LINGAM-YONI

The Tantras, however, seem to hold the answer to modern India's other issues of sexual malfunctioning too. Besides gender, the Tantric ideology also embraced the union of flesh and spirituality. Unlike the preceding age, which under Buddhist influence regarded sex as a base aspect of human existence at odds with the higher realm of spirituality, the Tantriks saw no dichotomy between the two. Indeed Tantrism advocated sex as a glorious path to achieving oneness with the divine. That is why ritualistic sex was adopted as a part of religious rituals by the Tantrics.

Interestingly, the idea of sex as a sacred part of the divine experience is found even in some popular Hindu myths—including the one on the death of Kama, the god of love. The legend goes that the goddess Parvati, after numerous attempts to woo a deeply meditating Shiva, remained unsuccessful in getting his attention. She appointed Kama to help her in her goal. At a critical moment, when Parvati stood before Shiva, Kama shot one of his fiery love arrows at Shiva, with the intention of forcing him out of his trance. If he could do that, Shiva would fall in love with Parvati as soon as he laid his eyes on her. Shiva, however, was outraged by this insolence and burned Kama to ashes. The spirit of Kama then roamed the earth for many eons, while his own love, Rati (sexual pleasure), mourned for him. Finally, when Shiva and Parvati were united, Kama's body too was resurrected and he was able to find his communion with Rati. The legend thus relates carnal desires to divine love and regards them as eternally linked.

The lingam–yoni, which continues to be worshipped by millions in India even today, is perhaps one of the most blatant sexual allusions in Hinduism. It is not just the terminology, the actual use of the words 'penis' (lingam) and 'vagina' (yoni), but it is the representation as well, the idol being a faithful likeness of the respective anatomies fused at the base—and an unambiguous portrayal of sexual intercourse.

Yet, surprisingly, most Indians will vehemently deny any sexual imagery that might strike others in the lingam–yoni, insisting that it has no implications other than that of the divine. For practitioners of most other major religions of course, it would be inconceivable to have a similarly shaped structure at their holy altars for them to worship, however symbolic it may be of God.

The Indian state of denial is akin to someone staring at light, calling it 'light', but refusing to accept it as such. What is it that makes a sexually squeamish people adulate an icon like the lingam–yoni and still repulse its sexual connotation?

Freud's theory holds a certain justification here. Freud's argument in this case would have been that the Hindu idols, myths and customs with a sexual connotation most probably pertain to a time when sex was a very acceptable aspect of the social and religious customs. These symbols continued to exist, even though sex itself as a concept came to be forcefully repressed over time, as something shameful. In the colonial period, with the arrival of first the Muslims and later the British, sex in the collective social thinking of Hindu society came to represent a 'dirty' act, a 'sin', one that sullied the individual and was ideologically dichotomized from all things sacred and divine. Freud's theory in a way throws light not just on the psychological conflict that

Indians have with their perception of the lingam–yoni, but also elucidates the seeming contradictions of how a society with a smothering conservative front could also harbour subcultures of sexual deviance.

Freud's inference that the repression of the unconscious underpinning of this conflict could result in massive social turmoil could be of grave consequence, particularly in the light of modern India's face-off with sex-related catastropes—population explosion, the AIDS epidemic and female genocide.

Yet, Jung's hypothesis in the context of the lingam–yoni and its social significance does explain India's recoil from its Tantric past. Jung's hypothesis about religious symbols was that each represented an unconsciously perceived concept in the culture where it is revered, a concept that the society, even as it worshipped the associated symbol, might not yet be prepared to consciously accept. However, the concept itself, according to Jung, would be universally profound, existing in the collective unconscious of all humanity, and could be applicable to any human being's conscious perception of his or her larger existence. These concepts that seem fundamental and innate to the processes of the human mind are what Jung called archetypes. Comparable to very ancient, pre-rational modules that all humans inherit, archetypes contain the basic patterns of human thought on which, under conditions of appropriate nurturance, more sophisticated thinking processes are built. Jung identified a number of universal archetypes, and the lingam–yoni perhaps best corresponds to the 'Self archetype'.[106] According to Jung, the archetype of the Self was in the unity of being or in what has also been called the *coniunctio oppositorum* (the union of opposites). In the Self archetype, opposites (such as light and dark, good and evil, matter and spirit, man and woman, high and low) are recognized as an integral, balanced part of a continuum and not a process of internal conflict.

The universality of the Self archetype is self-evident. Even though the idea of the reconciliation of perceived opposites as the path to inner peace may seem like common sense, what is it that makes it an ideal held exclusively by the human species? All other animal species live by the instinct of the survival of the fittest, of winning or acceding, of being dominant or submissive, of eating or being eaten. Yet, human cultures all over the world have shown an innate tendency to search for equality and empathy as the essence of human worth. This perception of existence in human consciousness often overrides its animal instincts by its emphasis on overcoming differences, dissolving barriers, reaching out and embracing 'the other'. The process of resolution involves a tremendous struggle of the human spirit, and yet remains one of the highest human ideals.

Yet Jung, like Freud, also served a warning with regard to religious icons and the archetypes they typified. He believed that if the culture that revered the symbol also resisted the conscious acceptance of its veiled concept, that is, if that peoples' social reality was unable to accommodate the need of the archetype to express itself, the resulting internal conflict could cause mass-scale psychological disturbances in the community.

Female genocide in India is the psychopathic fallout of the socialized dichotomy of men and women and sex and the sacred, and the inability of Indian society to overcome this schizophrenic vision. Still entrenched in Vedic dogmas that regarded women as non-human, sexual objects for the use of men, and clinging to a colonial prudery that debased sex as profane, the Indian patriarchy has chosen to disregard the wisdom of the Tantric ages as embodied in the lingam–yoni, which ironically, it still continues to adulate. In the Tantric path to salvation, the male and female were regarded as absolute equals. But even more significant was the recognition of the fact that not only were men and women indisputably the same, but each was also contained within the other—such that each man had a female element within and each female a male. Thus salvation, nirvana, was not just in the physical union with 'the other', but also in the recognition and union of the male and the female elements within one's self. This concept—that what is perceived as 'the other' is ultimately contained within us—is repeated in numerous Indian myths, legends and traditions.

When Maitreyi, the wife of sage Yajnavalkya, was eager to be acquainted with the knowledge that could attain her immortality, he told her that when a woman loved a man, or a man a woman, they actually were seeking that aspect of themselves which they saw in the other.[107]

Along this same line of thought, it has also been suggested that misogyny—which leads to situations like violence on women and female genocide—may be an expression of men's bewilderment at or fear of their own feminine aspects. The bio-neurological rationale offered for this is that until the sixth week of life, all male and female fetuses are structurally similar, and this common 'primordial' form is essentially female. It is only after the sixth week that testosterone impels the development of the masculine characteristics in fetuses with an X and a Y chromosome.[108] In later development, despite the raucous assumption of masculinity that is engineered through cultural and psychological conditioning, men tend to remain nervous about the 'abiding femaleness' that is an innate aspect of their ontogenic history, and that they fear might overpower or negate the fragile social 'veneer' of their assumed masculine identity. Thus the hostility or violence that men either individually or as a social group exhibit towards women, 'the other', is a 'psychopathological somatization of this sense of inner-defilement'—in other words, a form of self-hatred.[109]

Moreover, even though mainstream Tantric philosophy identifies the gender dichotomy within each person in terms of Shakti, the female element, as 'matter' and Shiva, the male element, as 'mind', the fundamental idea relates more to the perception of the 'other' within oneself and not necessarily to the gender categorization of mind or matter. In some Buddhist Tantric cults, matter was represented as male (upaya) and mind as female (prajna).[110] Nor does this concept exclude sexuality. While there is the ardhanari, the androgynous statue representing the union of Shiva and Shakti as a single, unified human figure that is half man, half woman, there is also the idol that represents the same idea in the union of the male gods Shiva and Vishnu, called Harihara. Each half of the male image is represented by the respective weapons and accessories of the gods.[111] In Vaishnava traditions, male devotees would assume the role of females so they could attain a union with a male deity. In other Vaishnava cults, a deep and intimate relationship would ensue between two male devotees, one who identified with the goddess Radha and the other with the lord Krishna.[112] In some Tantric sects, male–male intercourse was believed to augment the creative and spiritual potential of the participants.[113] Undoubtedly, myths, icons and practices of the Hindu traditions render the concepts of gender and sexuality as transient, mutable and nebulous. The character Ila, for instance, the offspring of Manu, Hinduism's Adam, besides sporting a transgender name, underwent fluid transitions of gender and sexuality and went from being a man to a woman and back to a man again in a continuous cycle. In the process, while he was in his female forms, Ila also bore children.[114]

Some Jungian analysts, who argue that archetypes are in essence androgynous, internally polarized and multifaceted, have also presented this idea of the fluidity of the formulation of sex and sexuality. When gender, or for that matter sexuality, are pigeonholed into absolute concepts, it is essentially a manifestation of a society's perception of reality at variance with the androgynous nature of the archetype in their collective unconscious. To resolve this inconsistency, the collective unconscious attempts resolution, not confrontation. It does this by creating an 'image' of the 'other' sex or sexuality, and assigning to it all the characteristics that were not included in the first.[115] It has often been argued, even from a sociological standpoint in modern times, that both gender and sexuality, the idea of man versus woman or homosexual versus heterosexual, are in fact social constructs, artificial categories defined by social markers like clothing, labour, mannerisms, behaviour and goals, just as they are directed on how to behave within a social context.[116] What is more, not only does science testify to the presence of male and female hormones in both men and women, it also supports the theory that sexuality cannot be categorized in black-and-white terms.[117] Freud had further theorized that all human beings are innately bisexual at birth, and it is the social, cultural and personal experiences that shape their sexual preferences in later life.[118]

The Tantric concept of salvation overrides both sex and sexuality, which seem equally irrelevant to its fundamental precept: the idea that the salvation of an individual is in the knowledge, the wisdom, that everything he or she perceives as 'the other' in all of existence is contained within himself or herself. Ultimately the division, the separation, the strangeness of 'the other' is only an illusion of the mind. A story in the Hindu epic Mahabharata illustrates this. When the wise King Janaka, said to have acquired the ultimate knowledge of non-duality, was approached by the female mendicant Sulabha, he refused to entertain the idea of a woman's ability to attain salvation through yogic union. He declared that women were much too distracted by lust to achieve this goal. Sulabha then challenged his supposedly non-dual vision, for she pointed out that if indeed he was supremely enlightened as he claimed he was he would be able to identify her in himself, as he would all other living entities.[119]

INDIA AT A CROSSROADS: WHICH WAY WILL IT GO?

The clash between sex and the sacred is a ceaseless battle for modern India. Notwithstanding India's escalating AIDS epidemic, its exploding population and its practice of female genocide, the Indian thought process keeps circling this seeming contradiction, trying to reconcile with it through its films. The Indian film industry, which churns out more movies than even Hollywood does every year, has for decades been incessantly obsessed with a singular theme: that of unfeasible love. Lovers parted by social milieus—class, culture, caste, and even sexuality—resist family and community coercion for a socially coordinated asexual match, holding their mutual attraction and passion as the ultimate truth, sometimes tragically seeking it at the cost of life.

Vital to the process of overcoming this paradox is the need to adopt a progressive and candid social attitude towards sex and sexuality. It would require a massive revamping of the concepts of morality as it relates to sex in the current milieu. It necessitates an environment that fosters information, learning and dialogue in these matters.

What is really needed is for sex to be liberated from its shackles of shame and irreverence. It must be released from its insidious utilitarian status as a patriarchal tool for sexual fulfilment, self-propagation, lineage building and social control. Sex has to be recognized as a biological need, the rightful choice and the personal expression of each individual; its outcome, be it offspring or AIDS, is then the responsibility of the individual.

But is the Indian society of the twenty-first century prepared to finally make room for the veiled wisdom of the lingam–yoni? Can it allow the synonymy of sexuality and spirituality to materialize in its social reality?

India's current mindset, especially on the issue of sex, is a far cry from what is needed by it to evolve as a healthy and progressive nation. The country's overwhelming majority, at least about 80 per cent, still regard sex as a taboo subject, to be veiled from the public sphere, and impounded in the institution of marriage. Though a section of this conservative majority is from the urban areas constituted primarily of the poor living in shanties and slums, as well as the reasonably educated but exceedingly parochial middle class, the predominant bulk of India's conservatism is sustained by the inhabitants of its rural hinterland.

To understand the rural people's tenacious adherence to a prudish value system, an overview of the world they inhabit is essential. India's rural community constitutes about 80 per cent of the nation's poor. Moreover, even though the government has more than fifty million tonnes of food grain in its stock, only about 27 per cent of the poor in India actually receive subsidized food grain through the public distribution system.[120] As for the other basic amenity of life, water, 36 per cent of rural Indians still do not have access to clean and safe drinking water.[121] If the nation's basic needs for food and clean water are not met, there is even lesser hope in other fundamental areas of governance. About 80 per cent of rural Indians and 50 per cent of the urban poor have no electricity.[122] In 1981 an estimated, 86 per cent of Indian villages had no medical facilities, not even a basic dispensary with a medical professional in attendance. By 1998 the conditions had not improved much, with only 926 hospital beds available for every million people.[123]

But illiteracy is the principal warden of this prison of poverty. Close to 70 per cent of rural Indians and about 50 per cent of Indians across the board, including the urban poor, are illiterate.[124] Provisions for thumb prints in lieu of signatures on legal and government forms, such as those used in banks, job applications, legal documents, hospital formalities and post offices, are still needed in India. It is little wonder then that the daily newspaper is in demand in only 4 per cent of rural households.[125] In the twenty-first century, when people do not have the security of the very basic things that give dignity to human existence—food, water, electricity, education and health care—what could their job prospects be? About 95 per cent of Indians, mostly from this illiterate, impoverished mass, depend for their survival on the informal sector.[126] A majority of this sector consists of subsistence farmers or farm labourers, barely eking a livelihood, existing hand to mouth. The rest who migrate to urban slums are either self-employed as vendors or work in daily-wage jobs, such as in construction sites and in factories as load carriers, as porters and taxi drivers. These jobs offer no securities or guarantees, not even that of everyday earnings. There are no health benefits nor life insurance, not even if a person lost his life or a limb at work, and there certainly is no scope for betterment.

The much touted economic miracle of modern India has done little to help those desperately in need. If anything, it has amplified the gap between the nation's minority haves and the majority have-nots. Despite the massive numbers of highly qualified professionals India churns out every year—in science, medicine and technology, many of whom migrate to other countries—the overall educational scenario is dreary and pathetic. It is estimated that if the total years of schooling of all Indians was to be averaged, the 'mean years of schooling' for adults over the age of twenty-five would be only 2.4 years,[127] which would be at the kindergarten level. How far can a nation of kindergarteners go? How can it be capable of complex thinking? Does it have the ability to even comprehend the conflict between sex and the sacred in its own collective thinking, leave alone the capacity to examine it?

Human society over the last 5000 years has been a virtual creation of the printed word and the human ability to use it to communicate, register, research, archive, network and implement ideas. The modern world—built entirely on abstract concepts (like democracy, due process, globalism and free trade) and conceptual institutions (such as judiciaries, universities, parliaments and multinationals)—is a complex function of this evolved capacity of the human brain. What this means is that millions of people in India are living an existence comparable to that in the stone age, not being able to comprehend the language, leave alone the technology, that speaks in terms of photons, nanometers, retroviruses and so on. It is precisely to this bleakness that religious fervour appeals. Tradition is the cornerstone, the unchanging factor that provides a person with absolute certainty about life and is the only source of reassurance. These millions of Indians are, consequently, focused on the basics of existence—food, marriage, procreation and death—activities that all their rituals and religious beliefs converge on. Traditions that survive only through oral communication are followed obsessively, as if the people's very survival depended on it.

For people struggling with a wretchedly impoverished and a seemingly hopeless reality, sexual conservatism is a form of self-esteem. They may be poor, but the advantage—as they see it—that they have over the wealthy is that they know how to uphold their conventional value system. The wealthy, on the other hand, are seen as imprisoned in their inaccessible, privileged societies, and depraved in their morals and lifestyle.

The patriarchal order of rural and poverty-stricken India, still rooted in a minute, primeval, pre-alphabetic moment in human consciousness, finds itself pitted against a world that is many centuries ahead of its comprehension. Unexposed and colossally underdeveloped, it seems incapable of exploration or growth, because it lacks the tools to grapple with the very logic of the modern technocratic, globally oriented India that encloses yet excludes them. They can borrow bits and scraps from it—fizzy drinks, chocolates, mobile phones, televisions or refrigerators—but cannot hope to be integrated into the space-age vortex that produces these gadgets. In environments like this, the conditions for an overhaul in the ideas and moral attitudes of the traditional patriarchy seem bleak.

Economic insecurity and social instability compel the conservative patriarchy to adhere to its existing identity by enforcing with a greater ferocity its traditions of sexual perversity and female oppression. Besides, it is the permissiveness of the conservative bloc's severely patriarchal traditions that enables—primarily in rural communities and in the migratory urban poor—the boisterous flaunting of laws and continuation of practices such as bigamy, caste wars, killing of new-born girls, lethal neglect of adolescent girls, kidnapping and selling of brides across state boundaries, honour killings of young lovers, rape as a form of community justice, economic and reproductive subjugation of women, the practice of dowry and dowry murders. The police force that is meant to implement laws regarding feticide, female infanticide and dowry murders is recruited from these sections of society, and has no deep moral incentive to do so. Even the section of the conservative bloc that has managed to haul itself out of the poverty trap, India's nouveau riche, harbours deep insecurity that money and formal education cannot overcome, which is why the old traditional values and antiquated systems of morality provide the reassurance they seek.

It appears that India thus saddled with an outmoded patriarchy could easily plunge into a social, political and economic cataclysm ensuing from overpopulation, AIDS, female genocide, nuclear wars or insurgency movements like those of the Dalits and the Naxalites, India's rapidly expanding Maoist movement that recruits from among India's poorest.

If India's oblivious continuation on its current path seems self-destructive, the message of its collective unconscious from yet another ancient Hindu myth, that of the Kaliyuga (age of annihilation), does not give much consolation. According to the myth, humanity currently inhabits the epoch that had been predicted as the Kaliyuga, an age dominated by technology, and characterized by greed, decadence and the dissolution of the human vision of the divine. Hinduism's apocalyptic vision prophesied that this state of the world would signal the end of existence. But given Indian's present state, it could in fact actualize this imminent doom—and become a self-fulfilled prophecy of destruction.

Interestingly, the Kaliyuga was the divination of the Veda-based patriarchal vision. It spoke of Kaliyuga as a period when the common people would disregard the Vedas. One folk song elucidates the patriarchy's fears of losing control over women's sexuality, and the power of its own masculine one. As the song goes—during Kaliyuga, women in 'sheer clothing' will roam around 'half-naked' in public with no sense of 'shame', while men will become emasculated. The song predicts that women will start engaging in 'manly' activities like smoking cigarettes, and men will go out of their way to indulge these women.[128] The scriptures also predicted that eventually God in the guise of Kalki, a Brahmin, will descend on earth and destroy all the non-Vedic religions—the Muslims and Christians, and the lowest castes, to restore the earth to its former glory.[129] Thus an alternative interpretation of the Kaliyuga could be that it is the patriarchy's foreboding of the loss of its social dominion, leading to its own demise. In this sense, Kaliyuga need not necessarily indicate the extinction of all life, but perhaps an end to existence as it has been known: that is, a radical change in the preconceived hierarchical social order that was once foisted by the Vedic culture, and the evolution of a more equitable society. In another sense, the Kaliyuga could also be interpreted as the patriarchy's unconscious fear of the collective feminine, for the element of destruction is associated with the goddess Kali: the feminine personification of power.

However, Kali, in the Shakta traditions was also representative of other communities besides women—as the lower castes and outcasts—that have been marginalized and repressed within India's patriarchal system.

So it seems India's need for the moment is really an even more comprehensive visualization of the lingam–yoni. The underlying philosophy of the lingam–yoni as elaborated in the Tantras addresses more than just the recognition of the complete parity of the sexes. It also urges a conscious move towards the resolution of *all* social dichotomies. Jung had a valid point when, in a rebuttal to Freud, he contended that ultimately a cultural symbol or archetype was not just about (sexual) repression, for it offered the possibilities of individuation—that is, the evolution and growth of human consciousness towards a far more comprehensive and integrated sense of reality.[130]

Jung held that an individual's concept of self could evolve all through his or her entire life. He did not think that this process was directed entirely by sexual urges (as Freud would have argued), but that the motivation was self-completion, a deep, innate impulse to seek a sense of personal harmony and wholeness—what he called 'Individuation'. The process of individuation also manifests in how a community or for that matter a nation evolves as a whole. Jung observed that the fundamental philosophy of the Tantras provided an independent and analogous corroboration of the process of individuation.[131]

The Tantras had indeed propagated the idea of self-completion as the ultimate aim, where sex or the physicality was only an aspect, but still an integral one, a first step to the process of completion.

Jung too emphasized that this meant a need to affirm all 'biological impulses' as well.[132] Sex as a biological drive and as a biological identity is clearly the beginning of self-perception, an understanding of the self relative to the 'other' or the larger environment one inhabits, which is why its wholesome acknowledgement is critical.

As a biological identity, it also underlies other variants such as race, colour, class and caste.

Perhaps one of the finest inspirations for the processes of 'Individuation' comes from Hinduism itself. About 3500 years of age, Hinduism is perhaps the oldest living faith in the world today—and a prominent one, accounting for almost one-fifth of humanity. More impressively, its icons, rituals, practices, beliefs and even hymns, which can be traced right back to its beginnings, are a powerful testimony to a firm and unbroken chain of continuity. Yet the true miracle of Hinduism is this: while every other religion that incubated in the wombs of the world's ancient civilizations—in the Americas, Africa, Europe, Middle East and China—had to succumb to the ferocious onslaught of Christianity, Islam and communism, Hinduism alone managed to survive them all, and not merely in a small measure, but as an unremitting, vigorous and gargantuan faith.

Yet, the secret of this religion's survival lies not so much in the strength of its traditions as it does in its flexibility—in its amazingly creative adaptability to changing environments and its ability to absorb the very elements, often alien and hostile, that would destroy it. History reveals, time after time, that Hinduism was not only tolerant of divergent views and rebellious new philosophies, but that it also developed the art of accommodating the contradictions smoothly into a single continuum. It is this secret that renders modern Hinduism as a polytheist, multi-sected religion of impenetrable complexity.

Perhaps it is this holy grail that has mesmerized the spiritual seekers of the world. Over the centuries, they have come here in quest of the enigmatic resolution to a ceaselessly conflicted existence—the answer that India often seems to hold the key to. Conceivably, the mysticism of India, the secret it guards is this: it epitomizes in its absolute being—in its long, tumultuous history, in its bountiful religions and in the racial and cultural multiplicity of its people—the very journey of the human soul. There is no aspect of existence, from the most inspiring to the absolute macabre, that India cannot find within itself. India is a repository of the evidence of human growth, amalgamation and change over time, as well as the eternal seed of future evolution. Change therefore is predestined; the question is, in which direction will India go?

The guide for this journey, however, is not Hinduism. Jung had warned that the answer to a community's salvation was not offered in the proclamations of the '-isms' of its time.[133] If a people's religion—the myths, symbols and legends—is the warehouse of that culture's collective unconscious, its customs and beliefs are in effect how the community *instinctively* deals with the contents of its collective unconscious. The word 'instinctive' is key here and stands opposed to rationale. This is why religious approaches vary and are often in conflict, and social orders and moral systems undergo periodic upheavals, as they swing terrifyingly from one extreme to another compelled by uncontainable gargantuan forces. This is why Jung had insisted that the solution to salvation, even at the collective level, lay in the individual. Individual self-reflection, he advised, was the sure start to finding the 'cure'.[134] Where Freud saw a community's neurosis as a conflict between a people's biological instincts and cultural impositions, Jung interpreted it as an inner conflict within each individual: a conflict between the person's basic instincts and his spirit, that is, his or her capacity to develop as a human being. What Freud labelled as repressive behaviour, Jung extolled as the possibility of spiritual and human evolution.[135] Thus what Jung prescribed was a social environment that allowed for the individuation of all its members. While this was an affirmation of human individuality, it was still not an emphasis on individualism. The distinction that Jung made between individuation and individualism was that the latter is focused on the alienated Self and its own self-contained 'peculiarities'. Individuation, however, is a far more 'complete realization' of Self, and the full potential of our human capacity. It takes the 'collective' into consideration and is able to define, differentitate and intergrate itself into a much larger and more diverse existence.[136] For a society to be healthy, it is imperative that its members are whole. Jung observed that eventually the process of individuation or wholeness is not directed by the outcomes of the battle between conflicting powers, but is actually guided by the calm and intentional shaping of systems through the resolution of contradictions and the communication of conscious intent with subconscious wisdom. This does not mean the annihilation of one or the other, nor does it mean the dissolution of dissimilarities. It simply involves an intelligent acknowledgement and embracing of 'the other' as a valid entity in a shared world.[137]

India now stands at the crossroads of a new era—a democratic one. Will this be the era that for the first time ever in its history will be shaped not by the uncontrollable outcome of a power conflict, but by the conscientious resolution of it? That is a question that hopefully India's millions will ask as they contemplate the lingam–yoni in a meditative prayer every day.

NOTES

INTRODUCTION

1. Bhutesvara temple, Mathura, AD 2 (Indian Museum, Kolkata).
2. Bhutesvara temple, Mathura, AD 2 (Indian Museum, Kolkata).
3. Lingaraja temple, Bhubaneshwar, AD 11.
4. Kandariya Mahadeyo temple, Khajuraho, AD 11.
5. Kandariya Mahadeyo temple, Khajuraho, AD 11.
6. Pampapati temple, Hampi, AD 14.
7. R.P. Conner et al., 1997, p. 18.
8. Subhadra Sen Gupta, 2001, p. 78.
9. P. Mitter, 2001, p. 79.
10. P. Poddar and P. Poddar, 1995.
11. In December 2003, Italy adopted some of the most restrictive reproductive laws in Europe, denying technology-assisted parenthood to single parents and gay couples.
12. In Poland, where abortion was outlawed in 1993, a doctor fought desperately for the docking of a ship that carried RU-86, the abortion pill, so Polish women could receive help on-board, thirty-two kilometres offshore on international waters, where they could not be prosecuted. In Nicaragua, a nine-year-old girl, impregnated by a rapist, was refused permission for an abortion. For the sake of their already traumatized child, the parents braved excommunication from the church and society to get her the medical help she urgently needed. Abortion doctors in the US are compelled to live and work like wanted criminals, in secrecy and

under the constant threat of the gun, many of their colleagues having already been murdered.

13. In October 2003, in its rather convoluted position on sex, the Vatican launched a global siege on contraception. It announced that condoms do not protect against AIDS. It recommended abstinence as a universal panacea, as though the human species is prepared to do away with sex altogether when, evidently, judging from the number of paedophilic priests on trial, many who have even taken the chastity vow are not prepared to give up sex. But for a great number of Catholics, particularly in the poorer nations of Asia, Africa and Latin America where the word of the Pope is taken as the word of God, this sanctimonious boycott of the condom could prove to be a death warrant. Africa today has the highest rate of conversions to Christianity; it also has the highest percentage of HIV+ people in the world. In Botswana, almost 40 per cent of the adult population is HIV positive. In the Philippines, a primarily Catholic nation, families living in utter squalor in slums persist in having large families because the Pope will not sanction the condom. Manila has also declared its Christian mentorship by shutting down all projects related to AIDS, contraception, abortion and sex education.

14. G. Bell, 1982, cited in M. Ridley, 2003.

15. Scientific theories concerning the evolution of the sexes, however, propose that the female gender preceded the male.

16. A. Cockburn, 1991, pp. 191–229.

17. John Maynard Smith was one of the first biologists to pose this question. (M. Ridley, 2003, p. 2.)

18. Gandhi was a staunch advocate of celibacy.

19. Jared Diamond, 2002, pp. 62–65.

20. Jared Diamond, 2002, p. 65.

21. R.F. Murphy, 1986, p. 173. Bronislaw Malinowski had said that religion was the mechanism that human societies evolved to cope with anxiety and fear.

22. Karl Marx, 1963, Critique of Hegel's Philosophy of Right, T. Bottomore (trans.), New York: McGraw-Hill, cited in Robert C. Solomon, 1997, p. 347.

23. In an experiment on the conditioning of fear in humans, it was seen that after a period of punishing responses to a certain behaviour or desire, the fear of punishment prevented the subject from reaching for that desire, even turning him away from it (J.B. Watson and R. Rayner, 1920, pp. 1–14). The fear and rejection of the desired object remained even when the punishments had stopped. It was further observed in other

experiments that through periodic reinforcement, either with punishments or rewards (as public approval would be), these kinds of fearful responses could become a part of an automatic behaviour pattern or social habit (B.F. Skinner, 1979), as often happens with taboos in a society.

24. E. Abravel and H. Gingold, 1985, pp. 614–23.

25. Friedrich Nietzsche, 1964a.

26. I. L. Janis, 1982.

27. L. Man, et al., 1982.

28. F. Nietzsche, 1964a.

29. P. Festy, 2000, p. 5. In other countries like Finland, France and Norway, also believed to be similarly disinclined, at least 70 per cent of people are still choosing to get married. Moreover, the fact that far more children are born of married couples in western Europe than out of wedlock, even though there are no legal stipulations that would compel this trend, is an indication that the traditional concept of the family unit still holds validity.

30. Nietzsche, 1964a.

31. Nietzsche, 1964b.

32. Nietzsche, 1964b.

33. Nietzsche, 1964b, cited in R.C. Solomon, 2003, p. 583.

34. R.C. Solomon, 2003, p. 111.

35. Nietzsche, 1969, p. 122.

36. Geoff Waite, 1996, p. 234

37. J.H. Van Der Hoop, 1999, p. 118.

38. Sigmund Freud, 1955, cited in R.F. Murphy, 1986, p. 175; D. Pick and L. Roper, 2004, pp. 39–40.

39. S. Freud, 2001, pp. 36–37.

40. Michael Palmer, 1997, pp. 12–14.

41. Freud's suggestions, however, would not fit the characteristics of what Jung considered a symbol and in Jungian psychology would be just indicative of a sign of repression (Carl Jung, 1976a). Jung was making an obvious point about whether a cultural icon should be regarded as a sign or a symbol. Others too have made this distinction: while a sign, for instance a woman's stick-figure image on the door of a public toilet, gives specific information on an object or situation, and entails a precise response which is reinforced through social conditioning, the scope of interpreting a symbol is much more expansive (Donis A. Dondis, 1981).

42. Donis A. Dondis, 1981.

43. Jung's hypothesis of the collective unconscious and its assortment

of inherited archetypes is also somewhat analogous to Noam Chomsky's theory of an inborn universal blueprint for grammar in human speech (Nancy Parrott Hickerson, 1980). Jung's theory, like Chomsky's, assumes two factors: firstly, these concepts contained in the archetypes, like the blueprint for language, are not taught to humans through external conditioning but are inborn. Secondly, again like the blueprint for language, the archetypes too represent a framework of concepts that simply indicates an inherited capacity for further development of thinking. Just as language has to be developed through proper conditioning of the external cultural environment, so does this framework of archetypal concepts. The archetypes do not deliver whole sentences, ideas or complex philosophies: they simply support the potential for the evolution of complex thought (A. Samuels, 1985, pp. 23–45).

44. C.G. Jung, 1976a.

45. Spencer A. Rathus, 1990, pp. 324–26.

46. Other evidence supporting the notion of inborn, inherited concepts comes from controlled laboratory studies on theories of learning. Experiments in psychology show that not all concepts are learnt through environmental conditioning or mechanical response to an external stimulus. When exposed to a difficult situation, subjects are often able to creatively invoke new methods of conceptualization to deal with the situation, methods that they have never been taught, that seem to be intrinsic to them but were previously unconscious and unexpressed. Technically termed as 'insight', the concept is said to materialize suddenly, in the manner of what is described as a 'flash', and once it has registered in the subject's consciousness, the subject is able to apply it innovatively to other situations (Spencer A. Rathus, 1990, p. 272). More evidence in support of the human inheritance of common archetypes comes from numerous comparative studies that reveal the similarities and even repeat of these archetypes in myths and icons, across ethnicities, religions and cultures that are widely disparate and have evolved in geographical and social isolation. Furthermore, the plausibility of the idea that concepts that define primordial consciousness of self are inborn is bolstered by the now general acceptance that concepts that form the basis of human emotionality—anger, joy, jealousy, puzzlement, mine, yours, known and unknown—are intrinsic to all human beings.

47. C.G. Jung, 1976b.

48. A. Samuels, 1985, pp. 23–45.

49. In these respects Jung's theory of inherited archetypes also parallels the biological theory of inherited genes. The archetype or

primordial concept behaves quite like the gene: so one may inherit a gene for a particular disease like diabetes or a condition like schizophrenia, but the gene is expressed only when exposed to a specific conditioning or environment, and the degree to which it impacts on the individual is determined by the individual's own experiences and activities.

50. However, many have questioned whether concepts can be acquired before the development of speech and communication. Some cognitive psychologists, notably Jean Piaget, have reasoned that certain basic concepts must and do precede language (J. Piaget, 1976). That is to say, a concept has to be first conceived internally in the brain before it can be labelled by sound or language. It would seem that the role of sound-based language as far as human consciousness goes is not so much that it is a gateway to consciousness as much as it is the form which consciousness uses to express itself, sometimes in widely varying ways (Ferrucio Rossi-Landi and Massimo Pesaresi, 1981, pp. 21–38). However, many agree that even though the primordial stages of language development are steered by certain elemental, inborn concepts in the brain, later the language becomes a tool for generating further complex concepts (C.G. Jung, 1976b).

51. The question is that, if language is an external form that the primordial concepts assume, in what form did they exist as archetypes in the unconscious recesses of the brain before language development? Jason Brown in *Mind, Brain and Consciousness* explains that initially, all concepts, whether object specific or abstract, exist only as hallucinogenic 'images' in the brain's unconscious region. When the environment is conducive, these concepts are conceived in the preconsciouness where everything, even the self, is perceived as an object that cannot be verbally expressed. Finally, when the concept is distanced from perception, it is externalized in the form of language (F. Rossi-Landi and M. Pesaresi, 1981, p. 33).

52. C.G. Jung, 1976a.

53. C.D. Smith, 1990, p. 53; and S. Salman, 1997.

54. Spencer A. Rathus, 1990, p. 17.

55. S. Rowland, 2000, p. 246.

THE VEDIC PERIOD

1. R.S. Sharma, 1996, p. 1.

2. A. Eraly, 2002, p. 66.

3. R. Thapar, 1990, p. 41.
4. A. Eraly, 2002, p. 66.
5. A. Eraly, 2002, p. 59.
6. R. Thapar, 2002a, p. 27.
7. *Encylopaedia Britannica*, 1981, *Macropaedia*, vol. 9, 15th ed., p. 336; R. Thapar, 2002a, p. 51.
8. A. Eraly, 2002, p. 21.
9. A. Eraly, 2002, p. 26.
10. *Encyclopaedia Britannica*, 1981, *Macropaedia*, vol. 9, 15th ed., pp. 339–40.
11. A. Eraly, 2002, p. 27.
12. D. Pool, 1993, p. 31.
13. *Encyclopaedia Britannica*, 1981, *Macropaedia*, vol. 9, 15th ed., p. 342.
14. A. Eraly, 2002, p. 39.
15. A. Eraly, 2002, p. 39; A.L. Basham, 2004, p. 19.
16. A.L. Basham, 2004, p. 19.
17. *Encyclopaedia Britannica*, 1981, *Macropaedia*, vol. 9, 15th ed., pp. 342–43.
18. *Encyclopaedia Britannica*, 1981, *Macropaedia*, vol. 9, 15th ed., p. 343.
19. Pupul Jayakar, 1989, p. 67.
20. A. Eraly, 2002, p. 60.
21. A. Eraly, 2002, p. 35.
22. S.R. Weart, 1988, Ch. 1 (accessed on www.nytimes.com/books/first/w/wear-war.html).
23. See S. Mukerji, 1969.
24. A.L. Basham, 2004. p. 19.
25. S.C. Dube, 1992, pp. 2, 3.
26. A. Eraly, 2002, p. 51.
27. W.T. De Bary, 1958, p. 1.
28. W.T. De Bary, 1958, p. 1; T. Hopkins, 1971, pp. 6, 7.
29. *Encyclopaedia Britannica*, 1981, *Macropaedia*, vol. 9, 15th ed., p. 343; T. Hopkins, 1971, p. 7.
30. Ralph T.H. Griffith (trans.), *Hymns of the Atharva Veda* 11.2.5. INK 'http://www.sacred-texts.com/hin/av/index.htm' www.sacred-texts com/hin/av/index.htm, cited in P. Jayakar, 1989, p. 69.
31. P. Jayakar, 1989, p. 67.
32. Madho Sarup Vats, *Excavations at Harappa*, plate CIII, p. 304, cited in P. Jayakar, 1989, p. 67.

33. Sir John Marshall, 1931, pp. 61–63, cited in Joseph Campbell, 2000, p. 170.

34. P. Jayakar, 1989, pp. 70, 74.

35. A. Eraly, 2002, p. 46.

36. This form is seen not just in Mohenjodaro (in Madho Sarup Vats, *Excavations at Harappa*, plate XCVI) but also in Kalibangan (Kalibangan Seal, Indian Archaeology 1962–63, *A Review*, plates XXIIIB and LXIIC), cited in P. Jayakar, 1989, pp. 72–73.

37. P. Jayakar, 1989, p 74.

38. P. Jayakar, 1989, pp. 137, 138.

39. A. Eraly, 2002, p. 45.

40. *Rig Veda* hymn 10.121 (O'Flaherty, 2000, p. 27).

41. W.T. De Bary, 1958, p. 6; *The Rig Veda* hymn 10.129 (O'Flaherty, 2000, pp. 25–26).

42. A. Coomaraswamy, 1938, cited in D. Desai, 1985, p. 102.

43. *Aitareya Brahamana* X, 3.2–4, cited in D. Desai 1985, p. 102.

44. *Rig Veda* hymn 10.101 (O'Flaherty, 2000, p. 67).

45. *Rig Veda* hymn 9.112 (O'Flaherty, 2000, p. 235).

46. *Rig Veda* hymn 10.101 (O'Flaherty, 2000, p. 66).

47. *Rig Veda* hymn 10.90 (O'Flaherty, 2000, pp. 30–31).

48. *Rig Veda* hymn 10.129 (O'Flaherty, 2000, p. 25).

49. O'Flaherty, 2000, p. 79.

50. *Rig Veda* hymn 10.129 (O'Flaherty, 2000, p. 25).

51. T. Hopkins, 1971, p. 32.

52. *Rig Veda* hymn 8.48 (O'Flaherty, 2000, p. 134).

53. *Rig Veda* hymn 8.30 (O'Flaherty, 2000, p. 22).

54. *Rig Veda* hymn 1.26 (O'Flaherty, 2000, p. 26).

55. A. Eraly, 2002, p. 159.

56. *Rig Veda* hymn 8.48 (O'Flaherty, 2000, p. 134).

57. *Rig Veda* hymn 4.5 (O'Flaherty, 2000, p. 113).

58. P. Conner et al., 1997, p. 44.

59. P. Conner et al., 1997, p. 44.

60. *Rig Veda* hymn 2.35 (O'Flaherty, 2000, p. 106).

61. O'Flaherty, 2000, p. 116.

62. *Rig Veda* hymns 8.79, 8.48, 4.18, 9.74 (O'Flaherty, 2000, pp. 121, 134, 142, 123).

63. J. Dowson, 2004, pp. 124–25.

64. *Rig Veda* hymns 1.32, 10.28, 4.18 (O'Flaherty, 2000, pp. 142, 147, 149).

65. *Rig Veda* hymn 10.119 (O'Flaherty, 2000, p. 131–32).

66. A. Eraly, 2002, pp. 163–64.
67. *Rig Veda* hymn 6.70 (O'Flaherty, 2000, p. 206).
68. *Rig Veda* hymn 6.70 (O'Flaherty, 2000, pp. 94, 206).
69. A. Eraly, 2002, pp. 58, 108.
70. A. Eraly, 2002, pp. 129.
71. *Rig Veda* hymn 1.32 (O'Flaherty, 2000, pp. 149–50).
72. *Rig Veda* hymn 6.70 (O'Flaherty, 2000, p. 206–07).
73. R. Conner et al., 1997, p. 44 (reference from *Saura Purana*).
74. A. Eraly, 2002, p. 176.
75. *Atharva Veda* III.25, cited in Pavan K. Varma and S. Mulchandani, 2004, pp. 29–30.
76. P. Varma and S. Mulchandani, 2004, p. 53.
77. P.V.J. Ayyar, 2002, p. 4.
78. A. Eraly, 2002, p. 105.
79. *Rig Veda* hymn 6.70, cited in W.T. De Bary, 1958, p. 8.
80. O'Flaherty, 2000, p. 79.
81. *Rig Veda* hymn 9.74 (O'Flaherty, 2000, p. 123).
82. *Rig Veda* hymn 10.94 (O'Flaherty, 2000, pp. 124–25).
83. *Rig Veda* hymns 7.103, 9.112 (O'Flaherty, 2000, pp. 235, 234).
84. *Rig Veda* hymn 5.83 (O'Flaherty, 2000, pp. 172, 173).
85. David Kinsley, 1997, pp. 7–13.
86. *Rig Veda* hymn 1.164 (O'Flaherty, 2000, p. 81).
87. *Rig Veda* hymn 2.35 (O'Flaherty, 2000, pp. 105, 106).
88. *Rig Veda* hymns 1.162, 1.163 (O'Flaherty, 2000, pp. 87–92); A. Eraly, 2002, pp. 105–65.
89. O'Flaherty, 2000, pp. 126, 127.
90. *Rig Veda* hymn 1.179 (O'Flaherty, 2000, pp. 250–51).
91. *Brihadaranyaka Upanishad* 6.4.3, cited in G. Feuerstein, 1998, p. 17; D. Goodall, 2001, pp. 106–07.
92. *Rig Veda* X.95.15; VIII.33.17, cited in P. Mukherjee, 1999, p. 11; A. Eraly, 2002, p. 136.
93. P. Varma and S. Mulchandani, 2004, p. 26 (*Rig Veda* X.95).
94. *Rig Veda* hymn 10.95 (O'Flaherty, 2000, pp. 253–55).
95. *Satapatha Brahmana* 2.1.2.1–14, cited in W.T. De Bary, 1958, p. 21.
96. A. Pike, 1992, p. 526.
97. *Rig Veda* hymn 5.83 (O'Flaherty, 2000, p. 174).
98. *Rig Veda* hymn 10.85 (O'Flaherty, 2000, pp. 267–71).
99. *Rig Veda* hymn 4.18 (O'Flaherty, 2000, p. 142).

100. *Rig Veda* hymn 5.2 (O'Flaherty, 2000, p. 103).
101. *Rig Veda* hymn 10.5 (O'Flaherty, 2000, p. 117).
102. *Rig Veda* hymn 4.5 (O'Flaherty, 2000, pp. 114, 115).
103. *Satapatha Brahmana* 2.1.1.1–14, cited in W.T. De Bary, 1958, p. 21.
104. *Rig Veda* hymn 4.5 (O'Flaherty, 2000, p. 114).
105. *Rig Veda* hymn 10.5 (O'Flaherty, 2000, p. 117).
106. *Rig Veda* hymn 1.116 (O'Flaherty, 2000, pp. 183, 185).
107. *Rig Veda* hymn 6.55 (O'Flaherty, 2000, pp. 194–95).
108. *Rig Veda* hymn 10.10 (O'Flaherty, 2000, pp. 247–49).
109. *Rig Veda* hymn 10.162.5 (O'Flaherty, 2000, p. 292).
110. Daksha was the son of the Creator god Brahma.
111. *Rig Veda* hymn 1.164 (O'Flaherty, 2000, p. 76).
112. *Laws of Manu* 9.127–135, 9.22 (W. Doniger, 1992).
113. *Rig Veda* hymn 8.91 (O'Flaherty p. 257).
114. *Laws of Manu* 9.10–18, 30, 32, 33, 41, 42 (W. Doniger, 1992, pp. 198–202).
115. *Rig Veda* hymns 1.92, 10.86 (O'Flaherty, pp. 180, 259–61).
116. *Rig Veda* hymn 1.126 (O'Flaherty).
117. *Laws of Manu* 5.154, cited in Rajul Sogani, 2002, p. 5.
118. *Rig Veda* 10.86 (O'Flaherty, 2000, 259–61).
119. *Laws of Manu* IX.13, cited in P. Mukherjee, 1999, p. 11.
120. *Laws of Manu* IX.17, IX.14–15, II.213–214; *Rig Veda* X.95.15, VIII.33.17; *Satapatha Brahmana* III.2.4.6, cited in P. Mukherjee, 1999, p. 11.
121. *Satapatha Brahmana* (in A. Eraly, 2002, p. 131).
122. *Laws of Manu* 5.164 (W. Doniger, 1992, p. 116).
123. *Laws of Manu* II.1.578, IX.14–15, II.213–14, cited in P. Mukherjee, 1999, p. 11.
124. *Laws of Manu* 9.10–18, 30, 32, 33, 41, 42 (W. Doniger, 1992, pp. 198–202).
125. *Rig Veda* (in A. Eraly, 2002, p. 129).
126. *Aitareya Brahmana* XXIII.1–2, cited in R.S. Sharma, 1996, p. 66.
127. *Rig Veda* hymn 7.104, 10.97 (O'Flaherty, 2000, pp. 292–95, 285–6); R. Svoboda, 1993, p. 16. (Texts also describe the soma plant as smelling like butter, producing a milk-like substance, looking like golden reeds. D. Wujastyk, 1998, pp. 171–72, 77).
128. *Rig Veda* hymn 4.58 (O'Flaherty, 2000, pp. 126–27).
129. A. Eraly, 2002, p. 172.

130. J. Dowson, 2004, p. 296.
131. A. Eraly, 2002, p. 172.
132. A. Eraly, 2002, p. 178.
133. *Atharva Veda* 9.2.25, cited in P. Jayakar, 1989, pp. 59–60.
134. P. Jayakar, 1989, p. 60.
135. D. Kinsley, 1987, p. 13.
136. *Atharva Veda Samhita* 5.7.8 cited in P. Jayakar, 1989, p. 62.
137. P. Jayakar, 1989, p. 161.
138. *Jaiminiya Brahamana* I.161–63, cited in P. Varma and S. Mulchandani, 2004, p. 48.
139. *Rig Veda* hymn 10.59 (Kinsley, 1987, p. 13).
140. *Rig Veda* hymn 10.146 (O'Flaherty, 2000, p. 242).
141. *Atharva Veda Samhita* 8.10, cited in P. Jayakar, 1989, p. 62.
142. *Rig Veda* 7.104 (O'Flaherty, 2000, p. 295.
143. *Atharva Veda Samhita* 10.8.31, cited in P. Jayakar, 1989, pp. 58, 164.
144. *Atharva Veda Samhita* 4.20.5, cited in P. Jayakar, 1989, p. 59.
145. *Atharva Veda Samhita* 8.10, cited in P. Jayakar, 1989, p. 62.
146. P. Jayakar, 1989, p. 40.
147. P. Jayakar, 1989, p. 60.
148. *Atharva Veda Samhita* 15.1–18.1, cited in P. Jayakar, 1989, pp. 62–63.
149. *Rig Veda* hymn 7.104 (O'Flaherty, 2000, p. 294).
150. The indigenous people the Vedics called Dasas or Dasyus were darker-skinned with Afroid features, while those they called the Panis are believed to have been of Semitic origin and perhaps lighter complexioned. The Panis were known to be traders and it is possible that they were absorbed into the colour-coded caste hierarchy at the level of the merchant class, higher than the Sudra or slave caste, which most probably included the black-skinned Dasas.
151. The word for the colour red, 'lal' in Hindi, often substitutes for brown, as 'lal ghora' or a 'brown horse'.
152. D. A. Mackenzie, 1993, p.xxv. (Also see pp. xxii–xliv, for a discussion on the composition of the various races that occupied early India.)
153. *Rig Veda* hymns 7.103, 9.112, 10.101 (O'Flaherty, 2000, p. 61.
154. J.J. Meyer, 1989, pp. 169–70, cited in *Laws of Manu*, W. Doniger, 1992, pp. ix, 59.

155. T. Burrow, 2001, pp. 380–86, cited in R. Thapar 2002a, p. 51.

156. T. Burrow, 2001, pp. 380–86, cited in R. Thapar 2002a, p. 51.

157. R. Thapar, 2002a, p. 23.

158. A.A. Macdonnell, 1989, *A History of Sanskrit Literature*, cited in R. Thapar 2002a, p. 72.

159. *Brihadaranyaka Upanishad*, cited in P. Varma and S. Mulchandani, 2004, pp. 54–55.

160. *Brihadaranyaka Upanishad*, cited in P. Varma and S. Mulchandani, 2004, p. 55.

161. A. Eraly, 2002, pp. 114–15.

THE BUDDHIST PERIOD

1. *Laws of Manu* 7.37–7.42, 7.85–88, 7.133–136 (W. Doniger, 1992).

2. *Aitareya Brahmana* 2.33, 3.19, cited in W. Doniger, 1992, p. xxix.

3. *Laws of Manu* 7.3, 7.5, 7.8–7.15 (W. Doniger, 1992, pp. 128–51).

4. *Laws of Manu* 4.248–51 (W. Doniger, 1992, p. 97).

5. *Laws of Manu* 4.229–37 (W. Doniger, 1992, pp. 95–96).

6. *Arthashastra* 2.1.24 by Kautilya (Ed. and Trans. L.N. Rangarajan, 1992).

7. *Laws of Manu* 7.129 (W. Doniger, 1992, p. 141).

8. *Arthashastra* 5.2.39–45 by Kautilya (Ed. and Trans. L.N. Rangarajan, 1992, pp. 272–73).

9. *Arthashastra* 5.2.46–68 by Kautilya (Ed. and Trans. L.N. Rangarajan, 1992, p. 273).

10. *Laws of Manu* 7.128–32 (W. Doniger, 1992, p. 141).

11. *Arthashastra* 1.3.8, 3.8.26, 3.8.27, 8.1.41–43, 3.15.17, 3.15.18, 3.13.3, 3.13.20, 3.20.17 by Kautilya (Ed. and Trans. L.N. Rangarajan, 1992, pp. 48, 52, 57).

12. *Laws of Manu* 8.120–42 (W. Doniger, 1992).

13. *Laws of Manu* 8.287 (W. Doniger, 1992).

14. *Arthashastra* 2.27.1, 2.27.28, 2.27.12 by Kautilya (Ed. and Trans. L.N. Rangarajan, 1992, pp. 63–65).

15. *Arthashastra* 1.3.8, 3.8.26, 3.8.27, 8.1.41–43, 3.15.17, 3.15.18, 3.13.3, 3.13.20, 3.20.17 by Kautilya (Ed. and Trans. L.N. Rangarajan, 1992, pp. 48, 52, 57).

16. *Arthashastra* 3.5.30–32 by Kautilya (Ed. and Trans. L.N. Rangarajan, 1992).

17. *Arthashastra* 3.5.10–15, 3.6.1–12 by Kautilya (Ed. and Trans. L.N. Rangarajan, 1992).

18. *Arthashastra* 7.17.16 by Kautilya (Ed. and Trans. L.N. Rangarajan, 1992, p. 48).

19. *Arthashastra* 3.1.12, 3.16.32, 3.3.20–24 by Kautilya (Ed. and Trans. L.N. Rangarajan, 1992).

20. *Arthashastra* 3.2.42, 3.2.38–40 by Kautilya (Ed. and Trans. L.N. Rangarajan, 1992).

21. *Arthashastra* 4.12.15–19 by Kautilya (Ed. and Trans. L.N. Rangarajan, 1992, p. 67).

22. *Arthashastra* 3.4.36 by Kautilya (Ed. and Trans. L.N. Rangarajan, 1992).

23. *Arthashastra* 3.2.20, 3.5.10–12, 3.5.28, 3.2.23 by Kautilya (Ed. and Trans. L.N. Rangarajan, 1992).

24. R. Thapar, 1990, p. 44.

25. *Arthashastra* 4.12.36–40 by Kautilya (Ed. and Trans. L.N. Rangarajan, 1992).

26. R. Thapar, 2000, p. 50.

27. *Arthashastra* 1.18.1, 1.18.12 by Kautilya (Ed. and Trans. L.N. Rangarajan, 1992, pp. 169–70).

28. *Arthashastra* 1.20.15–17 by Kautilya (Ed. and Trans. L.N. Rangarajan, 1992).

29. A.L. Basham, 2004, p. 122.

30. *Arthashastra* 1.20.1–3, 1.21.9–11, 1.20.14–21, 1.17.22–27, 1.17.30–33 by Kautilya (Ed. and Trans. L.N. Rangarajan, 1992, pp. 150–55).

31. R. Thapar, 1990, p. 57.

32. *Arthashastra* 1.21 1 by Kautilya (Ed. and Trans. L.N. Rangarajan, 1992, p. 152).

33. A. Eraly, 2002, p 149.

34. *Arthashastra* 4.3.13–16 by Kautilya (Ed. and Trans. L.N. Rangarajan, 1992).

35. *Laws of Manu* 2.201 (W. Doniger, 1992, p. 37).

36. *Brihadaranyaka Upanishad* II, iii, cited in D. Goodall, 2001, pp. 62–63.

37. W.T. De Bary, 1958, pp. 26–29; A. Eraly, 2002, p. 189.

38. *Laws of Manu*, 6.36–38, 97 (W. Doniger, 1992).

39. *Laws of Manu*, 6.26–6.34, 42–60 (W. Doniger, 1992); and *Mundaka Upanishad* 1.2.1–13, *Taittiriya Upanishad* 2.1–6, cited in W.T. De Bary, 1958, pp. 26–29.

40. *Laws of Manu* 9.334–35 (W. Doniger, 1992).

41. A. Eraly, 2002, p. 240.

42. See S. Mukerji, 1969.

43. R. Thapar, 1990, pp. 50–53.

44. *The Gospel of Buddha* XVI.6–7 (P. Carus, 1995, p. 30).

45. *The Gospel of Buddha* IX.18 (P. Carus, 1995, p. 33).

46. *The Gospel of Buddha* IX.5 (P. Carus, 1995, p. 30).

47. *The Gospel of Buddha*, II.20 (P. Carus, 1995, p. 4).

48. *Laws of Manu* 10.44, 10.43, cited in R. Thapar, 2000, p. 34; S.C. Dube, 1992, pp. 7–8.

49. T.W. Rhys Davids, 1903, p. 298.

50. D.A. Mackenzie, 1993, p. 133.

51. *Laws of Manu* 12.94–97, 8.310.

52. *Laws of Manu* 10.50.

53. *Laws of Manu* 10.20–23, 2.40 (W. Doniger, 1992, pp. 21, 237).

54. R. Thapar, 1990, pp. 58–59.

55. *Majjhima Nikaya* 2.147, cited in W.T. De Bary, 1958, pp. 140–42.

56. *The Gospel of Buddha* LXXV.3–5, LXXIX (P. Carus, 1995).

57. R. Thapar, 1990, p. 63.

58. *Digha Nikaya* 3.180, 3.58, cited in W.T. De Bary, 1958, pp. 123, 124, 136.

59. S. Mukerji, 1969, p. 8.

60. S. Mukerji, 1969, p. 31–33, 14–15, 78, 81–83, 181–83.

61. R. Thapar, 2000a, p. 28.

62. *Laws of Manu* 4.165–69 (W. Doniger, 1992, pp. 89–90).

63. *Arthashastra* 4.10.13, 4.10.13, 4.12.21 by Kautilya (Ed. and Trans. L.N. Rangarajan, 1992); *Laws of Manu* 8.267, 8.284 (W. Doniger, 1992, pp. 181–83).

64. *Laws of Manu* 3.360; 8.352–8.353 (W. Doniger, 1992).

65. *Laws of Manu* 10.31, 10.50–56 (W. Doniger, 1992).

66. *Arthashastra* 4.13.34, 4.13.35 by Kautilya (Ed. and Trans. L.N. Rangarajan, 1992).

67. *Laws of Manu* 11.49, 11.105 (W. Doniger, 1992).

68. *Laws of Manu* 9.85–9.86 (W. Doniger, 1992).

69. *Laws of Manu* 9.149–54 (W. Doniger, 1992).
70. De Bary, 1958, p. 94.
71. *The Gospel of Buddha* XVI.13, XLV.2 (P. Carus, 1995).
72. *The Gospel of Buddha* LI.17–18, XVI.8, XVI.6 (P. Carus, 1995).
73. *Digha Nikaya* 1.4 ff, cited in De Bary, 1958, pp. 114–15; Richard H. Robinson and Willard L. Johnson, 1982, p. 49.
74. *Laws of Manu* 6.76–81 (W. Doniger, 1992).
75. *Laws of Manu* 12.38–40 (W. Doniger, 1992).
76. *Laws of Manu* 4.220 (W. Doniger, 1992, p. 94).
77. *Laws of Manu* 6.62, 5.63, (W. Doniger, 1992, p. 105).
78. *Laws of Manu* 5.9, 5.19 (W. Doniger, 1992, pp. 100, 101).
79. *Laws of Manu* 2.108, 2.52 (W. Doniger, 1992, pp. 29, 69).
80. *Laws of Manu* 7.44, 7.47, 7.48, 7.221, 7.225 (W. Doniger, 1992).
81. *Bhagavad Gita* 1.45 (B.S. Miller, 1986, p. 26).
82. T.W. Rhys Davids, 1903, pp. 292, 284 (Book of the Great Decease, iii, 33).
83. T.W. Rhys Davids, 1903, p. 297 (edict no. 3).
84. R.E. Svoboda, 1993, p. 11.
85. T.W. Rhys Davids, 1903, pp. 296–97.
86. 'Asoka'. *Encyclopaedia Britannica* Online. Accessed on 22 November 2005 <http://search.eb.com/eb/article-9009884>.
87. Smith, Vincent A., 2002, pp. 136, 140–42.
88. A.L. Basham, 2004, pp. 67, 70.
89. A. Eraly, 2002, pp. 319–20.
90. A. Eraly, 2002, p. 323.
91. R. Gross, 1992, p. 332.
92. A. Eraly, 2002, p. 315.
93. *The Gospel of Buddha* XXXIII.9, XXXIII.16, XCII.3 (P. Carus 1995, pp. 93–94, 228).
94. D.D. Gilmore, 2001, p. 176.
95. R.H. Robinson and W.L. Johnson, 1982, p. 57; A. Eraly, 2002, p. 315–16.
96. R. Gross, 1992, p. 37.
97. R. Gross, 1992, p. 10.
98. H. Okano, 1995, p. 17.
99. R. Gross, 1992, pp. 10–11.
100. R. Gross, 1992, p. 33.
101. J.W. Coleman, 2002, p. 142.
102. D. Gilmore, 2001, pp. 81–82.

103. *The Gospel of Buddha* LXXX (P. Carus, 1995, pp. 200–02).
104. *The Gospel of Buddha* LXVI (P. Carus 1995, p. 183).
105. R. Gross, 1992, p. 83.
106. R. Gross, 1992, p. 83.
107. R. Gross, 1992, p. 32.
108. H. Okano, 1995, p. 17.
109. J.W. Coleman, 2002, p. 141.
110. R. Gross, 1992, pp. 83–84.
111. R. Gross, 1992, pp. 84–85.
112. R. Gross, 1992, p. 58.
113. A. Eraly, 2002, pp. 247–48.
114. *The Gospel of Buddha* IV.2–3 (P. Carus, 1995, pp. 7–8).
115. P. Jayakar, 1989 (pp. 161–62).
116. *Digha Nikaya* of the Pali Canon iii, 181ff, cited in A.L. Basham, 2004, p. 288.
117. Even though Strabo had not travelled to India his geographical records of India are said be the records of the first-hand experiences of men who accompanied Alexander the Great in his campaigns in India. One of these was Nearchus, a soldier in Alexander's army. Many of Strabo's accounts of India are believed to be credible as they have been corroborated with modern evidence (Q. Gaufurd, 1817, vol. 2, p. 253).
118. A. Eraly, 2002, p. 526.
119. *Laws of Manu* 6.37 (W. Doniger, 1992, p. 121).
120. *Laws of Manu* 9.18 (W. Doniger, 1992).
121. *Astadhyayi* of Panini, III.3.21, IV.1.49, VI.2.86, cited in P. Mukherjee, 1999, pp. 87–88.
122. *Laws of Manu* 4.205–6, 11.36–7 (W. Doniger, 1992 pp. 93, 254).
123. *Laws of Manu* 9.1–4, 9.7–17 (W. Doniger, 1992).
124. P. Mukherjee, 1999, pp. 66–67.
125. *Laws of Manu* 3.362, 8.362 (W. Doniger, 1992).
126. H. Raychaudhuri, 2000, pp. 144–45. The four wives bore the titles: Mahishi (the chief queen), Privrikti (the neglected queen), Vavata (the favorite queen) and Palagali (daughter of the last court official).
127. *Kusa Jataka* no. 531 cited in H. Raychaudhuri, 2000, p. 145.
128. *Dasaratha Jataka* no. 461 cited in H. Raychaudhuri, 2000, p. 145.
129. *Laws of Manu* 9.80–81 (W. Doniger, 1992).
130. A. Eraly, 2002, p. 527.

131. *Laws of Manu* 8.572 (W. Doniger, 1992).
132. *Laws of Manu* 5.147–54, 5.160–66 (W. Doniger, 1992).
133. *Laws of Manu* 4.207–18 (W. Doniger, 1992, pp. 93–94).
134. *Arthashastra* 4.7.14 by Kautilya (Ed. and Trans. L.N. Rangarajan, 1992).
135. A. Eraly, 2002, pp. 531–2.
136. R. Sogani, 2002, p. 10.
137. A. Eraly, 2002, p. 265.
138. A. Eraly, 2002, p. 261.
139. 'Buddha'. *Encyclopaedia Britannica* Online. Accessed on 9 December 2005. <http://search.eb.com/eb/article–230773>.
140. A. Eraly, 2002, p. 323 (from the *Digha Nikaya*).
141. S. Kramrisch, 1933, plate IX, no.36 (The Gudimallam linga, 100 BC), cited in D. Eck, 1985, p. 36.
142. See A.K. Tripathy.
143. *Vamana Purana*.
144. R. Conner et al., 1997, pp. 197–98.
145. H. Okano, 1995, pp. 17.
146. A. Eraly, 2002, p. 193 (from *Svetasvatara Upanishad*).

THE GOLDEN PERIOD

1. R. Thapar 1990, p. 71.
2. *Kamagita Gathas*. 'The Legend of the Song of Love', cited in P. Jayakar, 1989, p. 86.
3. H. Mukhia, 2004, p. 170. The *Ain-i-Akbari* noted that Holi was primarily a festival of the lower castes, an indication of the tribal origins of the festival.
4. *Bhagavat Purana* cited in P. Varma and S. Mulchandani, 2004, pp. 77–79.
5. S.C. Dube, 1992, p. 17.
6. S.C. Dube, 1992, p. 15.
7. A. Eraly, 2002, p. 173.
8. D. Eck, 1985, p. 52.
9. S.C. Dube, 1992, p. 8.
10. R. Thapar, 1990, p. 215–16.
11. Rhys Davids, T.W., 1903, pp. 88–96.
12. S. Mukerji, 1969, pp. 23–24,114.
13. A.L. Basham, 2004, pp. 219–20.

14. R. Thapar, 1990, pp. 109–13.
15. R. Thapar, 1990, p. 111.
16. R. Thapar, 2002a, p. 42.
17. R. Thapar, 2002a, p. 42.
18. R. Thapar, 2002a, p. 32–33.
19. G.W. Spencer, 1970, 'Royal Initiative under Rajaraja I: The Auditing of Temple Accounts', *Indian Economic and Social History Review* 7, cited in R. Thapar 2002a, p. 43.
20. R. Thapar, 1990, p. 154.
21. R. Thapar, 2002a, p. 33.
22. Gautama, xii.4–6, cited in T.W. Rhys Davids, 1903, p. 118.
23. H. Raychaudhuri, 2000, p. 489.
24. H. Raychaudhuri, 2000, p. 143.
25. R. Thapar, 2000, p. 32–39.
26. A.L. Basham, 2004, p. 70.
27. A.L. Basham, 2004, p. 105.
28. H. Raychaudhuri, 2000, pp. 485–86, 512.
29. *Aitareya Brahmana* VIII, 17; *Satapatha Brahmana* 9.3.1, cited in H. Raychaudhuri, 2000, pp. 155–57.
30. S.C. Dube, 1992, pp. 12, 13.
31. D. Desai, 1985, p. 151.
32. R. Thapar, 1990, pp. 122, 174.
33. Kapila's *Bhagavat Purana* 11.27.7–51, cited in W.T. De Bary, 1958, pp. 334–37.
34. D. Desai, 1985, p. 37.
35. W.T. De Bary, 1958, p. 208.
36. S.C. Dube, 1992, p. 119.
37. R. Thapar, 1990, p. 214.
38. F.E. Keay, 2003, p. 27.
39. Narada's *Bhakti Sutra* (Aphorisms on Devotion), 1–22, 25–70, 72–84, cited in W.T. De Bary, 1958, pp. 327–30.
40. *Bhagavat Purana* 7.9.10, cited in W.T. De Bary, 1958, p. 341.
41. S.C. Dube, 1992, p. 119.
42. Narada's *Bhakti Sutra* 1–22, 25–70, 72–84, cited in W.T. De Bary, 1958, p. 327–30.
43. *Purana of the Lord*, Book 11, cited in W.T. De Bary, 1958, pp. 333–36.
44. Kautilya's *Arthashastra* 4.13.41 (Ed. and Trans. L.N. Rangarajan, 1992, p. 485).
45. P. Jayakar, 1989, pp. 86–87.

46. The Oxford Hindi–English Dictionary, 2001, (9th reprint), New Delhi: Oxford University Press, p. 1082.

47. W.T. De Bary, 1958, p. 254.

48. Manikkavachakar in 'Sacred Utterances' and Nammalvar in *Tiruvaymoli* 2.4.1, cited in W.T. De Bary, 1958, pp. 349, 351.

49. F.E. Keay, 2003, pp. 37–38.

50. M. Eliade, *Yoga: Immortality and Freedom*, Bollingen Series, 56, Pantheon Books, 1958, pp. 305–06, cited in D. Desai, 1985, p. 91.

51. Kakolee Chakraborthy, 2000, pp. 18, 29, 31; Abbé J.A. Dubois, 1924, *Hindu Manners, Customs and Ceremonies* (Trans. and Ed. Henry K. Beauchamp), London: Oxford University Press, p. 585, cited in K. Chakraborthy, 2000, p. 16; W. Crook, 1918, 'Prostitution', in *Encyclopaedia of Religion and Ethics*, vol. 10, 3rd reprint, 1952, p. 407, cited in D. Desai, 1985, p. 108; and D. Desai, 1985, pp. 162–64.

52. P. Jayakar, 1989, p. 36.

53. A. Getty, 1920, *The Gods of Northern Buddhism*, Oxford: Clarendon Press, p. 118, cited in D. Desai, 1985, p. 92.

54. R.L. Mitra, 1880, *The Antiquities of Orissa*, vol. 2, Kolkata: Moti Chandra, pp. 81, 131, cited in D. Desai, 1985, p. 91.

55. A. Daniélou, 1994, p. 18.

56. A. Daniélou, 1994, p. 18.

57. A. Hitebeitel, 1991, p. 387.

58. P. Jayakar, 1989, p. 42.

59. *Kama Sutra* 1.4.27 (A. Daniélou, 1994, pp. 69–70).

60. H.C. Chakladar, 1992, *Social Life in Ancient India:Studies in Vatsayana's Kamasutra*, p. 192, cited in D. Desai, 1985, pp. 177–78.

61. *The Kama Sutra of Vatsyayana* (R. Burton, 1993, pp. 74–75).

62. D. Desai, 1985, pp. 177–78.

63. D. Desai, 1985, pp. 179–81.

64. C. Sivaramamurti, 2002, pp. 9–12.

65. D. Desai, 1985, p. 178.

66. *Kama Sutra* 2.4.26, 2.5.41–42 (A. Daniélou, 1994, pp. 131–41).

67. D. Desai, 1985, pp. 186–87.

68. D. Desai, 1985, p. 186.

69. *Shringarashataka* verse 19, cited in D. Desai, 1985, p. 187.

70. C. Sivaramamurti, 2002, p. 11.

71. *Kama Sutra* 2.6.49, 2.7.1–35 (A. Daniélou, 1994, pp. 156–57, 159–69).

72. *Epigraphia Indica*, vol. 35, pp. 97, 98; vol. 33, p. 272; and A.S. Altekar, 1934, *The Rashtrakutas and Their Times*, Poona, p. 295, all cited in D. Desai, 1985, p. 163.

73. R. Sewell, *A Forgotten Empire*, New Delhi: Publication Division, Government of India, reprint 1961, p. 234, cited in D. Desai, 1985, p. 108.

74. *Ubhayabhisarika* in *Shringarahata*, pp. 122–23, cited in D. Desai, 1985, p. 162.

75. A.S. Altekar, 1934, *The Rashtrakutas and Their Times*, Poona, p. 295; and *Indian Antiquary*, vol. 11, p. 125 (in D. Desai, 1985, pp. 162, 170).

76. *Kama Sutra* 6.1.1. (A. Daniélou, 1994, p. 392).

77. *Kama Sutra* 1.3.16–22 (A. Daniélou, 1994, p. 56).

78. *Kama Sutra* 6.3.46 (A. Daniélou 1994, p. 434–36).

79. *Kama Sutra* 6.5.5, 6.1.1–33, 6.5.1–39 (A. Daniélou 1994, pp. 391–404, 452–68).

80. *Kama Sutra* 6.3.46 (A. Daniélou 1994, pp. 434–35).

81. *Kama Sutra* 6.1.1–6.1.17 (A. Daniélou 1994, pp. 391–97).

82. A.L. Basham, 2004, p. 185.

83. R. Thapar, 1990, p. 211.

84. A. Daniélou, 1994, p. 9.

85. *Kama Sutra* 6.1.22–27 (A. Daniélou 1994, pp. 398–99).

86. D. Desai, 1985, p. 166.

87. B.J. Sandesara, *Itihasa ane Sahitya* (in Gujarati), p. 105, cited in D. Desai, 1985, p. 167.

88. A. Daniélou, 1994, pp. 3–4.

89. *Kama Sutra* 1.4.1 (A. Daniélou, 1994, p. 57).

90. *Kama Sutra* 1.5.24 (A. Daniélou, 1994, 1.5. 24, pp. 81–82).

91. *The Kama Sutra of Vatsyayana* (R. Burton, 1993).

92. *Kama Sutra* 1.4.31 (A. Daniélou, 1994, p. 71).

93. *The Kama Sutra of Vatsyayana* 2.1.1 (R. Burton, 1993).

94. *Kama Sutra* 2.2.1 (A. Daniélou, 1994, p. 106).

95. *Kama Sutra* 2.2.29 (A. Daniélou, 1994, p. 106).

96. *Kama Sutra* 2.2.31 (A. Daniélou, 1994, pp. 111–13).

97. *Kama Sutra* 2.3.1–32 (A. Daniélou, 1994, pp. 119–31).

98. *Kama Sutra* 2.5.34–35, 2.6.52, 2.3.6, 2.5.20 (A. Daniélou, 1994, pp. 143, 121).

99. *Kama Sutra* 7.2.1–59 (A. Daniélou, 1994).

100. *Kama Sutra* 7.1.36–37 (A. Daniélou, 1994).

101. *Kama Sutra* 7.1.10 (A. Daniélou, 1994).

102. *The Kama Sutra of Vatsyayana* 2.1.1 (R. Burton, 1993).

103. The Oxford Hindi–English Dictionary, 2001 (9th reprint), New Delhi: Oxford University Press, p. 954.

104. J. Gonda, 1939–40, 'Abharan', *New Indian Antiquary*, vol. 2, p. 72, cited in D. Desai, 1985, p. 110.

105. D. Desai, 1985, p. 189.

106. A.L. Basham, 2004, pp. 212–14.

107. R. Alkazi, 2003, pp. 13–20, 106–128.

108. R. Alkazi, 2003, p. 8.

109. D. Desai, 1985, p. 103.

110. D. Desai, 1985, p. 110.

111. *Rig Veda* I.33.8, cited in D. Desai, 1985, p. 110.

112. D. Desai, 1985, pp. 110–11.

113. *Kama Sutra* 1.4.4 (A. Daniélou, 1994, p. 58); D. Desai, 1985, p. 23.

114. *Kama Sutra* 1.4.5–6 (A. Daniélou, 1994, p. 59).

115. *Kama Sutra* 1.4.10–12, 1.4.4 (A. Daniélou, 1994, pp. 63, 65).

116. *Kama Sutra* 7.2.39 (A. Daniélou, 1994, p. 517).

117. A.L. Basham, 2004, p. 215.

118. *Kama Sutra* 7.1.3–6, 7.2.39 (A. Daniélou, 1994, pp. 490, 517).

119. C. Sivaramamurti, 2002, pp. 13–14.

120. P. Varma and S. Mulchandani, 2004, p. 14; P. Jayakar, 1989, p. 89

121. *The Gitagovinda of Jayadeva*, II.14–15 (B.S. Miller, 1984, p. 80).

122. S.K. De, 1947, *A History of Sanskrit Literature*, Kolkata: University of Calcutta Press, p. 384, cited in D. Desai, 1985, p. 188.

123. Bilhana's *Caurapancasika*, cited in P. Varma and S. Mulchandani, 2004, pp. 208–13.

124. *Cephalandra indica*, also known as red bitter melon, is a climbing shrub with edible fruits.

125. *Padma Purana* 5.74.171, cited in R. Vanita and S. Kidwai, 2001, p. 91.

126. Kalidasa's *Rtusamharam* (Gathering of the Seasons) I.4 (Chandra Rajan, 1989, p. 105).

127. S.K. De, 1947, *A History of Sanskrit Literature*, Kolkata: University of Calcutta Press, p. 62, cited in D. Desai, 1985, p. 188.

128. D. Desai, 1985, pp. 188–95.

129. D. Desai, 1985, pp. 3, 7.

130. D. Desai, 1985, p. 10.

131. D.H. Gordon, 1958, *The Prehistoric Background of Indian Culture*, Mumbai: Bhulabhai Publications, Bombay, 1958, pp. 115–16, cited in D. Desai, 1985, p. 10.

132. D. Desai, 1985, pp. 11, 12, 14, 15.

133. R.S. Sharma, 1996, p. 69.

134. U. Singh, 2002, pp. 23, 35, 91.

135. U. Singh, 2002, p. 52.

136. Moti Chandra, 1951, 'Architectural Data in Jain Canonical Literature', *JBBRAS* 26: 180–81, cited in D. Desai, 1985, p. 23.

137. J. Burgess, 1964, 'Report on Buddhist Cave Temples and Their Inscriptions', p. 91, *Archaeological Survey of Western India*, vol. 4 (reprinted), Varanasi: Indological Book House, cited in D. Desai, 1985, p. 25.

138. Moti Chandra, *BPWM* 6: 21, cited in D. Desai, 1985, pp. 17, 20.

139. P. Mitter, 2001, p. 24.

140. 'Archaeological Remains, Monuments and Museums', 2 parts, *Archaelogical Survey of India*, New Delhi, 1964, p. 60, cited in D. Desai, 1985, p. 17.

141. T. Hopkins, 1971, p. 61.

142. P. Mitter, 2001, p. 25.

143. G.N. Banerjee, 1981, pp. 66, 73.

144. P. Mitter, 2001, p. 20.

145. R. Thapar, 1990, p. 152.

146. D. Desai, 1985, p. 80.

147. D. Desai, 1985, p109.

148. *Kama Sutra* 1.1.5 (A. Daniélou, 1994, p. 18).

149. *Kama Sutra* 1.2.12 (A. Daniélou, 1994, p. 29).

150. *Kama Sutra* 1.2.12 (A. Daniélou, 1994, pp. 29–30).

151. *Kama Sutra*.1.2.17 (A. Daniélou, 1994, p. 33).

152. *Kama Sutra* 1.2.11 (A. Daniélou, 1994, pp. 28–29).

153. A. Daniélou, 1994, p. 18.

154. P. Varma and S. Mulchandani, 2004, p. 14.

155. Kama Sutra 1.3.15 (A. Daniélou, 1994, pp. 51–55).

156. D. Desai, 1985, p. 186.

157. *Kama Sutra* 2.9.33–34, 2.5.34–35, 2.6.52 (A. Daniélou, 1994, pp. 121, 190–91).

158. A. Daniélou, 1994, p. 8.

159. *Kama Sutra* 3.5.28 (A. Daniélou, 1994, p. 269).

160. *Kama Sutra* 3.5.29–30 (A. Daniélou, 1994, pp. 269–70).

161. *Kama Sutra* (A. Daniélou, 1994, pp. 271–72).

162. *Kama Sutra* 3.1.23 (A. Daniélou, 1994, p. 224).

163. *Kama Sutra* 5.2.1–23 (A. Daniélou, 1994).

164. *Kama Sutra* 3.4.7–9 (A. Daniélou, 1994, p. 252).

165. *Kama Sutra* 3.2.28–29 (A. Daniélou, 1994, p. 236).

166. 'A Loveless Marriage As a Cause for Adultery' in *Kuttanimatam*, cited in P. Varma and S. Mulchandani, 2004, p. 155.

167. Kakolee Chakraborthy, 2000, p. 7.

168. Susie Tharu and K. Lalita, 1997, pp. 56, 70.

169. Kakolee Chakraborthy, 2000, p. 6.

170. *Kama Sutra* 1.4.4, 1.4.10–12 (A. Daniélou, 1994, p. 63).

171. *Kama Sutra* 1.2.18 (A. Daniélou, 1994, pp. 33–35); *The Kama Sutra of Vatsyayana* (R. Burton, 1993, pp. 77–79); and C. Sivaramamurti, 2002, p. 12.

172. *Kama Sutra* 1.5.3 (A. Daniélou, 1994, pp. 75–76).

173. *Kama Sutra* 1.2.12 (A. Daniélou, 1994, pp. 29–30).

174. P. Varma and S. Mulchandani, 2004, p. 132.

175. A. Daniélou, 1994, p. 8, p. 75 (1.5.2), pp. 294 (4.2.31), 295.

176. *Kama Sutra* 2.1.11, 14, 15, 17, 19, 27, 34; 2.3.4 (A. Daniélou, 1994, pp. 94–96, 99, 101, 121).

177. *Kama Sutra* 1.2.17–18 (A. Daniélou, 1994, pp. 33–34).

178. *Kama Sutra* 5.1.54, 5.6.3, 6, 28, 30, 32, 34 (A. Daniélou, 1994, pp. 321–22, 377–83).

179. *Kama Sutra* 4.2.31–32 (A. Daniélou, 1994, pp. 294–95).

180. *Kama Sutra* 1.3.1–12 (A. Daniélou, 1994, pp. 49–51).

181. *Kama Sutra* 4.2.34, 5.1.54 (A. Daniélou, 1994, p. 295).

182. Varahamihira's *Brhasamhita*, ch. 74, cited in P. Mukherjee, 1999, p. 11.

183. P. Varma and S. Mulchandani, 2004, pp. 263–64.

184. *Kama Sutra* 1.5.8–18 (A. Daniélou, 1994, pp. 78–80).

185. Kalidasa's *Rtusamharam* (Gathering of the Seasons) II.2 (Chandra Rajan, 1989, p. 110).

186. Kalidasa's *Rtusamharam* (Gathering of the Seasons) III.7 (Chandra Rajan, 1989, p. 117).

187. Kalidasa's *Rtusamharam* (Gathering of the Seasons) III.1, III.24 (Chandra Rajan, 1989, pp. 116, 120).

188. Kalidasa's *Rtusamharam* (Gathering of the Seasons) II.7 (Chandra Rajan, 1989, p. 111).

189. Kalidasa's *Rtusamharam* (Gathering of the Seasons) II.10 (Chandra Rajan, 1989, p. 105).

190. Kalidasa's *Rtusamharam* (Gathering of the Seasons) IV.6 (Chandra Rajan, 1989, p. 123).

191. *Kama Sutra* 1.3.16–1.3.22 (A. Daniélou, 1994, p. 56).

192. *Kama Sutra* 1.2.33–36 (A. Daniélou, 1994, p. 42).

193. *Kama Sutra* 2.9.34 (A. Daniélou, 1994, pp. 190–91).

194. D. Chattopadhyaya, 1959, p. 306, *Lokayata: A Study in Ancient Indian Materialism*, New Delhi: People's Publishing House, cited in D. Desai, 1985, pp. 119, 175; and N,N. Bhattacharya, pp. 11–12, 'Indian Puberty Rites', in *Indian Studies Past and Present*, cited in D. Desai, 1985, pp. 119, 175.

195. Kalidasa (Chandra Rajan, 1989, p. 37).

196. Kalidasa Chandra Rajan, 1989, p. 239).

197. David Kinsley, 1998, pp. 96, 99.

198. H. Raychaudhuri, 2000, p. 486.

199. *The Kalibangan Seal, Indian Archaeology 1962–63, A Review*, plates XXIIIB and LXIIC, cited in P. Jayakar, 1989, pp. 72–73.

200. P. Jayakar, 1989, p. 33.

201. H.D. Sankalia, 'Central India 3000 Years Ago', *Illustrated London News*, August 1971, p. 42, cited in D. Desai, 1985, p. 12.

202. P. Jayakar, 1989, p. 82.

203. P. Jayakar, 1989, p. 40.

204. S.C. Dube, 1992, pp. 8–9.

205. R. Thapar 1990, p. 222.

206. D. Kinsley, 1998, pp. 44, 201.

207. *Devi Bhagavata Purana* 3.5.4; 7.33.13; 12.8.77; 7.29.26–30; 7.29.7 (D. Kinsley, 1998, p. 137).

208. *The Saundaryalahiri* 6, 13 (The Flood of Beauty), W. Norman Brown (trans.), Cambridge, Massachusetts : Harvard University Press, 1958, p. 52, cited in D. Kinsley, 1998, p. 142.

209. P. Jayakar, 1989, p. 42.

210. Keshavadas's *Rasikapriya*, cited in P. Varma and S. Mulchandani, 2004, pp. 264–68.

211. Edward C. Kimock, Jr., and Denise Levertov (trans.), 1967, *In Praise of Krishna: Songs from the Bengali*, p. 51, Garden City, New York: Doubleday; *Vidyapati Love Songs*, Deben Bhattacharya (trans.), 1963, London: George Allen and Unwin , p. 65; and *Love Songs of Candidas*, Deben Bhattacharya (trans.), 1967, London: George Allen and Unwin, p. 135 (all cited in Kinsley, 1998, p. 86).

212. *The Gitagovinda of Jayadeva*, II.14–15 (B.S. Miller, 1984, p. 123).

213. *Shiva Purana, Rudra Samhita* 3.32, 4.1.44–46 (D. Kinsley, 1998, p. 43).

214. K.S. Behera, 1970, 'Laksmi in Orissan Literature and Art', pp. 100–02, in D.C. Sircar (ed.), *Foreigners in Ancient India and Laksmi and Sarasvati in Art and Literature*, pp. 91–105, Kolkata: University of Calcutta Press, cited in D. Kinsley, 1998, pp. 34, 88.

215. *Devi Bhagavata Purana* 5.2–20, 3.30.2–26, 5.12.14–30, 5.16.46–65; *Devi Mahatmya* 5.56–65 (D. Kinsley, 1998, pp. 97–99, 109).

216. D. Kinsley, 1998, p. 202.

217. N.N. Bhattacharyya, 1971, 'Indian Mother Goddess', p. 54, in *Indian Studies Past and Present*; T.V. Mahalingam, 1967, 'The Cult of Sakti in Tamilnad', p. 28, in D.C. Sircar (ed.), *The Sakti Cult and Tara*, Kolkata: University of Calcutta Press, both cited in D. Kinsley, 1998, p. 145.

218. P. Jayakar, 1989, pp. 38, 83–84.

219. *Devi Bhagavata Purana* 3.5.4, 7.33.13, 12.8.77, 7.29.26–30, 7.29.7 (D. Kinsley, 1998, p. 137).

220. D. Kinsley, 1998, p. 122.

221. P. Jayakar, 1989, p. 39.

222. D. Kinsley, 1998, pp. 161–162, 173, 174, 177.

223. *Mahanirvana Tantra* 4.30–34, 5.140–41, 6.68–76, 10.102 (D. Kinsley, 1998, p. 123).

224. N.N. Bhattacharya, 2005, p. 118.

225. O. Ghosh, 2001, pp. 145–52.

226. R. Thapar, 2002b, p. 416.

227. D. Kinsley, 1998, pp. 50, 133.

228. P. Jayakar, 1989, p. 160.

229. *Epigraphia India*, vol. 13, p. 56, cited in D. Desai, 1985, p. 108.

230. D. Kinsley, 1998, p. 201.

231. Maleya Madesvara (a Kannada folk purana), P. Varma and S. Mulchandani, 2004, p. 327–31.

232. Vasant G. Rele, 1950, *The Mysterious Kundalini: The Physical Basis of the 'Kundalini (Hatha Yoga)'*, in *Terms of Western Anatomy and Physiology*, foreword by Sir John Woodroffe, 1927, 7th ed., Mumbai: Taraporevala Sons; Hiroshi Motoyama, 1985, 'Function of Ki and Psi Energy', *Research for Religion and Parapsychology* 15: 1–83; and Arthur Avalon, 1978 (1st edition 1918, 6th ed. reprint), *Shakti and Shakta*, New York: Dover Publications, pp. 78–79, all cited in G. Feuerstein 1998, pp.xi, 148–49, 174.

233. P. Jayakar, 1989, pp. 41–42.

234. *Yoga and Shiva–Samhita* 2.1–5, cited in G. Feuerstein, 1998, p. 61 .

235. The Oxford Hindi–English Dictionary, 2001 (9th reprint), New Delhi: Oxford University Press, p. 431.

236. Vasant G. Rele, 1950, *The Mysterious Kundalini: The Physical Basis of the 'Kundalini (Hatha Yoga)'*, in *Terms of Western Anatomy and Physiology*, foreword by Sir John Woodroffe, 1927, 7th ed., Mumbai: Taraporevala Sons, cited in G. Feuerstein, 1998, p. 148.

237. Hiroshi Motoyama, 1985, 'Function of Ki and Psi Energy', *Research for Religion and Parapsychology* 15: 1–83, cited in G. Feuerstein, 1998, p. 149. Also see H. Motoyama, 2001.

238. P. Jayakar, 1989, p.xiv.

239. S.B. Dasgupta, 1962 (2nd ed.), *Obscure Religious Cults*, Kolkata: Firma K.L. Mukhopadhyay, p.xxxiv, cited in D. Desai, 1985 p. 114.

240. G. Feuerstein, 1998, pp. 123, 126.

241. *Kula Arnava Tantra* 1.16.27, cited in G. Feuerstein, 1998, pp. 53–54.

242. *Yoga Vasishtha* 4.23.18–24, cited in G. Feuerstein, 1998, pp. 57–58.

243. *The Yoni Tantra*, cited in P. Varma and S. Mulchandani, 2004, pp. 166–72.

244. P. Jayakar, 1989, pp. 41, 46.

245. G. Feuerstein, 1998, pp. 62–66.

246. *Kula Arnava Tantra* 2.68, cited in P. Jayakar, 1989, p. 14.

247. *Kaulavalinirnaya* VIII, 56 ff, cited in D. Desai, 1985, pp. 118–19.

248. D. Desai, 1985, p. 123.

249. D. Desai, 1985, p. 117.

250. S.B. Dasgupta, 1962 (2nd ed.), *Obscure Religious Cults*, Kolkata: Firma K.L. Mukhopadhyay, p.xxxiv, cited in D. Desai, 1985 p. 113.

251. G. Feuerstein, 1998, p. 136.

252. G. Feuerstein 1998, p. 135.

253. C. Chakravarti, 1963, *The Tantras: Studies on their Religion and Literature*, pp. 51, 32, Kolkata: Punthi Pustak, cited in D. Desai, 1985, p. 123–24.

254. D. Desai, 1985, pp. 132–33, 135.

255. From Aryadeva's *Cittavisuddhiprakarana*, pp. 24–38 (AD 7), cited in W.T. De Bary, 1958, pp. 194–96.

256. A.L. Basham, 2004, pp. 282–83.
257. D. Desai, 1985, pp. 112, 126.
258. N.N. Bhattacharya, 2005, p. 136.
259. D. Desai, 1985, pp. 124–25.
260. W.T. de Bary, 1958, pp. 360–61.
261. D. Desai, 1985, pp. 40, 70, 137.
262. D. Desai, 1985, p. 141.
263. D. Desai, 1985, p. 93.
264. D. Desai, 1985, p. 74, cites temples at Ambernath, Badoh, Bagali, Belgamver, Bhubaneswar, Khajuraho, Nagda, Modhera, Menal, Ramgarh, Roda.
265. D. Desai, 1985, p. 74 (cites temples at Modhera and Roda).
266. D. Desai, 1985, p. 99.
267. D. Desai, 1985, p. 73 (cites temples at Ambernath, Badoh, Bavka, Belgave, Delmal, Dwarka, Kakpur, Kiching, Kiradu, Khajuraho, Konark, Malwa, Modhera, Motap, Mysore, Nagda, Ramgarah, Sanchi).
268. D. Desai, 1985, p. 80.
269. D. Desai, 1985, pp. 72, 73 (cites temples at Bagali, Delmal, Ellora, Halebid, Kakpur, Kandariya, Khajuraho, Konark, Nemavar, Modhera, Padhavli, Puri, Ramgarh, Sinnar, Vishwanatha).
270. D. Desai, 1985, pp. 76, 94, 95, cities temples at Ambernath, Bagali, Belur, Bhubaneswar, Chhapri, Demal, Halebid, Konark, Khajuraho, Sonepur.
271. S.B. Dasgupta, 1962 (2nd ed.), *An Introduction to Tantric Buddhism*, Kolkata: University of Kolkata Press, p. 80, cited in D. Desai, 1985, p. 123.
272. Carl Gustav Jung, 1965, p. 276.
273. H.G. Coward, 1985, pp. 109–11.
274. E. Goldberg, 2002, p. 8.
275. R. Conner et al., 1997, p. 67.
276. P. Mitter, 2001, p. 46.
277. E. Goldberg, 2002, p. 8.
278. E. Goldberg, 2002, p. 8.
279. Z. Jaffrey, 1996, pp. 35–36.
280. P. Jayakar, 1989, p. 82.
281. W.T. De Bary, 1958, p. 265.
282. Mammata in *Illumination of Poetry*, *Kavyaprakasha*, ch. 1, 4, cited in W.T. De Bary, 1958, pp. 265–68.
283. Bhasa, 1993 (A.N.D. Haksar, trans.), p. vii.
284. Bhasa, 1993 (A.N.D. Haksar, trans.), p. i.

285. Kalidasa, 1989 (Chandra Rajan, trans.), p. 29.
286. Bhasa, 1993 (A.N.D. Haksar, trans.), pp. v, vi.
287. W.T. De Bary, 1958, p. 256.
288. Kalidasa, 1989 (Chandra Rajan, trans.), p. 34.
289. ITC Sangeet Research Academy.
290. Ashok Da Ranade, 2002, pp. 5, 30, 34, 37.
291. A. Daniélou, 1994, p. 121.
292. Bhasa, 1993 (A.N.D. Haksar, trans.), p.vii.
293. P. Mitter, 2001, pp. 19–20,
294. W.T. De Bary, 1958, pp. 259–65.
295. W.T. De Bary, 1958, pp. 261–62.

296. Metallurgy also evolved in conjunction with architecture and sculpture. The Iron Pillar of Mehrauli, a single piece of iron over seven metres high which has been transplanted to Delhi, is almost 1700 years old—although it does not contain any alloy, the iron has not yet rusted, a scientific puzzle that awaits a suitable explanation.

297. Ayurveda, the science of formal medicine that had already been institutionalized as early as in the Buddhist times, too made advancements of great magnitude that influenced the way twenty-first-century medicine is practised. Some of the most distinguished medical compendiums of this period were written by the teachers of medicine Susruta and Caraka. Indian surgeons had already perfected techniques that were centuries ahead of medicine in other parts of the world—they could perform caesarian sections, reset broken bones and operate for cataracts and gall bladder stones. Most remarkable were the skills of the plastic surgeons of this period: they had perfected skin grafting and could reconstruct mutilated ears, noses and lips. Their techniques are still used in modern medical textbooks and are known as the 'pedicle graft'. The instructions for surgery gave detailed descriptions of the types of damages that may be observed; for instance, sixteen ear lobe malformations have been listed, together with the step-by-step procedure for the repair of each. Many of these techniques would be observed in practice and translated from the original texts by German and British doctors more than a thousand years later, in the eighteenth century, and introduced into modern European medical practice.

298. From the astronomers of this period came a determination of the number of days in a solar year, and the hypothesis that the earth spins on its own axis and casts a shadow on the moon during eclipses.

299. There was the discovery of the zero, infinity and the decimal system, the concept of the atom (*anu*) as the smallest unit of matter, and the calculation of pi=3.1416.

300. A.L. Basham, 2004, p. 67.
301. S. Mukerji, 1969, pp. 21–24.
302. R. Thapar, 1990, pp. 145–47.
303. R.E. Svoboda, 1993, p. 11.
304. A.L. Basham, 2004, p. 166.

THE COLONIAL PERIOD

1. S. Mukerji, 1969, p. 195.
2. S. Sen Gupta, 2001, pp. 30–31.
3. Sukracharya cited in D.L. Eck, 1985, p. 51.
4. R. Thapar, 1990, p. 114–15.
5. Sarangapani's 'A Married Woman's Complaint', cited in P. Varma and S. Mulchandani, 2004, p. 316.
6. R. Thapar, 1990, p. 247
7. R. Thapar, 2002b, pp. 423–24.
8. N.N. Bhattacharya, 2005, p. 119.
9. R. Thapar, 2002b, p. 422.
10. D. Desai, 1985, pp 161, 163, 177.
11. D. Desai, 1985, p. 172. (She refers to the books *Prithviraja Raso* and *Prabandhachinitamani* as the source.)
12. B.P. Majumdar, *Socio Economic History of Northern India*, p. 359, cited in D. Desai, 1985, p. 172.
13. R. Thapar, 1990, pp. 239–40.
14. R. Thapar, 1990, p. 253.
15. R. Thapar, 1990, pp. 241–51.
16. R. Thapar, 2000, pp. 27, 31, 34.
17. D. Desai, 1985, p. 158.
18. R.M. Eaton, 2002, pp. 76–77.
19. S.C. Dube, 1992, p. 21.
20. R. Thapar, 1990, p. 232.
21. S. Lane-Poole, 1997, p. 18.
22. S. Lane-Poole, 1997, pp. 137, 142.
23. S. Lane-Poole, 1997, pp. 137, 170.
24. R. Thapar, 1990, pp. 272–80.
25. W.T. De Bary, 1958, p. 502.
26. R. Thapar, 1990, p. 271; S.C. Dube, 1992, p. 25.
27. Shaikh Hamadani in his list of conditions in *Zkhirat ul-Muluk*, folios 94a–95a, cited in W.T. De Bary, 1958, p. 481–82.
28. R. Thapar, 1990, p. 290.

29. Barni, Fatawa-i-Jahandari, folios 58a–58b, 130a, cited in W.T. De Bary, 1958, pp. 502, 509, 510.

30. R. Thapar, 1990, p. 298.

31. *Memoirs of Babur*, vol. 2, J. Leyden and W. Erskine (trans.), L. King (ed.), Oxford University Press, 1921, p. 241, cited in P. Spear, 1990, pp. 25.

32. *Bhagavat Purana*, cited in W.T. De Bary, 1958, p. 334.

33. Q. Ahmad, 1999, pp.xv–xix.

34. P. Spear, 1990, pp. 17, 31.

35. Iqtidar Alam Khan, 'Akbar's Personality Traits and World Outlook: A Critical Reappraisal', in Irfan Habib (ed.), 2000, *Akbar and His India*, New Delhi: Oxford University Press, p. 84.

36. Iqtidar Alam Khan, 'Akbar's Personality Traits and World Outlook: A Critical Reappraisal', in Irfan Habib (ed.), 2000, *Akbar and His India*, New Delhi: Oxford University Press, p. 88.

37. M. Athar Ali, 'The Perception of India in Akbar and Abu'l Fazl', in Irfan Habib (ed.), 2000, *Akbar and His India,* New Delhi: Oxford University Press, p. 220.

38. W.T. De Bary, 1958, pp. 431, 442, 447; *Encyclopaedia Britanicca*, 1981, *Macropaedia*, vol. 9, 15th ed., p. 378.

39. W.T. De Bary, 1958, pp. 431, 442, 447.

40. Hobson-Jobson, 2002, p. 517.

41. Barni, Fatawa-i-Jahandari, folios 12a, 119a–20b, cited in W.T. De Bary, 1958, pp. 480–81.

42. Niccolao Manucci, *Storia do Mogor* (Mogul India, 2 vols), William Irvine (trans.), London: John Murray, 1907, vol. 2, pp. 5–6, cited in H.K. Kaul, 1997.

43. Barni, Fatawa-i-Jahandari, folios, 10b, 121a, cited in W.T. De Bary, 1958, pp. 472–73.

44. A.H. Sharar, 2001, p. 63.

45. W.T. De Bary, 1958, p. 193.

46. W.T. De Bary, 1958, pp. 335–57.

47. F.E. Keay, 2003, p. 66.

48. A.H. Sharar, 2001, pp. 77, 78, 116.

49. R. Vanita and S. Kidwai, 2001, pp. 191–93.

50. S.C. Dube, 1992, p. 106.

51. A.H. Sharar, 2001, p. 180.

52. R. Nath, 2005, pp. 52–56.

53. Z. Jaffrey, 1996, p. 55.

54. R. Thapar, 1990, p. 302.

55. S. Tharu and K. Lalita, 1997, p. 103–07.

56. *Digha Nikiya* of the Pali Cannon, iii, 181ff, 'Address to Sig la', cited in A.L. Basham, 2004, p. 288.

57. R. Vanita and S. Kidwai, 2001, p. 109.

58. M. Mujeeb, 1967, pp. 206–07.

59. William Bruton, 1638, 'News from the East Indies or a Voyage to Bengalla', London, cited in C.R. Wilson, 1895, p.13.

60. James Tod, *Annals and Antiquities of Rajasthan*, vol. 2, 1829, reprinted 1884, pp. 45, 315, cited in Hobson-Jobson, 2002, p. 19).

61. R. Thapar, 1990, p. 292.

62. P. Jayakar, 1989, pp. 131–33.

63. D. Kinsley, 1998, pp. 90, 94.

64. R. Thapar, 1990, pp. 328–29.

65. A.H. Longhurst, 1982, p. 26.

66. P. Mitter, 2001, pp. 93–94.

67. *Encylopaedia Britannica*, 1981, *Macropaedia*, vol. 9, 15th ed., p. 377.

68. Kakolee Chakraborthy, 2000.

69. S. Tharu and K. Lalita, 1997, p. 57.

70. S. Tharu and K. Lalita, 1997, pp. 79, 81.

71. R.H. Major, n.d., pp. 138, 141, cited in R.M. Eaton, 2002, pp. 80–2.

72. R.M. Eaton, 2002, pp. 82–83.

73. A.H. Sharar, 2001, pp. 116–17.

74. A.H. Sharar, 2001, p. 77.

75. S. Lane-Poole, 1997, pp. 144–47.

76. A.H. Sharar, 2001, pp. 34–35; V.T. Oldenberg, 2001, p. 135.

77. K.C. Tarachand, 1991, *Devdasi Customs, Rural Social Structure and Flesh Markets*, New Delhi: Reliance Publishing House, p.xi, cited in Kakolee Chakraborthy, 2000, pp. 30–31.

78. Mirza Hadi Ruswa, 2006.

79. S. Tharu and K. Lalita, 1997, p. 64.

80. A.H. Sharar, 2001, p. 63.

81. R. Vanita and S. Kidwai, 2001, pp. 108–24.

82. Francis Robinson, 2000, pp. 233–36.

83. R.M. Eaton, 2002, pp. 194–8.

84. R. Vanita and S. Kidwai, 2001, p. 115.

85. Bruce B. Lawrence, 1993, p. 37.

86. J.N. Bell, 1979, *Love Theories in Hanbalite Islam*, Albany: SUNY Press, p. 143, cited in R. Vanita and S. Kidwai, 2001, pp. 115–16.

87. A.H. Sharar, 2001, p. 54.
88. W.T. De Bary, 1958, p. 393.
89. Irfan Habib, 2002, pp. 205, 209.
90. W.H. Moreland and P. Geyl, 2001, pp. 54–57.
91. P. Spear, 1990, pp. 44, 46, 47.
92. Irfan Habib, 2002, pp. 240–43.
93. Irfan Habib, 2002, pp. 376–78.
94. P. Spear, 1990, pp. 65, 68, 83, 97, 104–15.
95. T. Bowrey, *A Geographical Account of the Countries Round the Bay of Bengal 1669 to 1679*, Sir Richard Temple (ed.), Hakluyt Society, second series, XII (1895), p. 24, cited in Lawrence James, 2001, p. 56; J. Forbes, 1834, *Oriental Memoirs: A Narrative of Seventeen Years Residence in India* (3 vols), vol. 1, p. 242–43, cited in Lawrence James, 2001, p. 56.
96. J. Forbes, 1834, *Oriental Memoirs: A Narrative of Seventeen Years Residence in India* (3 vols.), vol 1, p. 242–43, cited in Lawrence James, 2001, p. 56.
97. Minutes of J. Farish, 28 August 1938, quoted in B.K. Boman-Behram, *Educational Controversies of India: The Cultural Conquest of India Under British Imperialism*, Mumbai: Taraporevala Sons & Co., 1942, p. 239, cited in S. Tharu and K. Lalita, 1997, p. 62.
98. S. Tharu and K. Lalita, 1997, p. 9.
99. S. Chakravarty, 1991, p. 243.
100. *Hill of Devi and Other Indian Writing*, cited in S. Chakravarty, 1991, p. 243.
101. Abbé J.A. Dubois, 1906, *Hindu Manners, Customs and Ceremonies*, Oxford: The Clarendon Press, p. 631, cited in D.L. Eck, 1985, pp. 35–36.
102. Diogo de Couto, 1616, *Decadas da Asia*, vol. 7, iii, p. 11, cited in Hobson-Jobson, 2002, p. 517.
103. *Letters from Madras 1836–1839*, by Lady Julia Charlotte Maitland, published 1843, p. 156, cited in Hobson-Jobson, 2002, p. 517).
104. A. Hamilton, 1727, *A New Account of the East Indies* (2 vols), Edinburgh, vol. 1, p. 152, cited in Lawrence James, 2001, p. 57.
105. C.F. Bechhofer, 1923, *The Brahmin's Treasure*, London; Basil Mathew, *The Secret of India*, n.d., London, pp. 126–27; Al Carthill, *The Lost Dominion*, pp. 174–75; Aldous Huxley, 1930, *Jesting Pilate: The Diary of a Journey*, London: Chatto & Windus, pp. 158–59; Penderel Moon, *Strangers in India*, p. 198, all cited in S. Chakravarty, 1991, p. 232.

106. F.E. Keay, 2003, p. 126.

107. A. Hamilton, 1727, *A New Account of the East Indies* (2 vols), vol. 2, p. 19, Edinburgh, cited in Lawrence James, 2001, p. 211.

108. John Stuart Mill in *History of British India*, Wilson (ed.), pp. 186, 294, cited in Javed Majeed, 1992, p. 185.

109. Lawrence James, 2001, p. 217.

110. R.M. Eaton, 2002, p. 57.

111. Lawrence James, 2001, p. 46.

112. Horace Walpole's correspondence (48 vols, Oxford 1937–48), W.S. Lewis (ed.), vol 23, pp. 400, 499, 524, cited in Lawrence James, 2001, p. 46.

113. I. McCalman, 1984, 'Unrespectable Radicalism: Infidels and Pornography in Early Nineteenth Century London', *Past and Present* 104: 99, cited in J. Majeed, 1992.

114. Lawrence James, 2001, p. 174–75.

115. George Otto Trevelyan, 1864, *The Competition Wallah*, Macmillan & Co., pp. 3–15, cited in Elleke Boehmer, 1998, p. 4.

116. *British Paliamentary Papers: East Indies*, vol.15, p. 205, *British Parliamentary Papers: Colonies, East Indies, 1804–1874*, 22 vols, Shannonm 1970, cited in Lawrence James, 2001, p. 175.

117. George Otto Trevelyan, 1864, *The Competition Wallah*, Macmillan & Co., pp. 3–15, cited in Elleke Boehmer, 1998, pp. 6, 9.

118. George, Viscount Valentina, 1809, *Voyages and Travels to India* (3 vols), London: William Miller, vol.1, p. 243, cited in H.K. Kaul, 1997.

119. Jeremy Black and Donald M. Macraild, 2003, pp. 213–15.

120. George Otto Trevelyan, 1864, *The Competition Wallah*, Macmillan & Co., pp. 3–15, cited in Elleke Boehmer, 1998, p. 6.

121. J. Leopold, 1974, 'British Applications of the Aryan Theory of Race to India', *English Historical Review* 84: 584, cited in Lawrence James, 2001, p. 158.

122. T.B. Broughton, 1893, *Letter from a Mahratta Camp*, M.E. Duff (ed.), p. 3, cited in Lawrence James, 2001, p. 58.

123. Flora Annie Steel, 1928, *King Errant*, London: John Lane, pp. 272–75, cited in S. Chakravarty, 1991, p. 56.

124. A. Huxley, 1930, *Jesting Pilate: The Diary of a Journey*, London: Chatto and Windus, p. 5, cited in S. Chakravarty, 1991, p. 54.

125. Robert Byron, 1931, *An Essay on India*, London: Routledge, p. 15, cited in S. Chakravarty, 1991, p. 54.

126. C.R. Wilson, 1895, pp. 62–68.

127. J.K. Stanford, 1926.

128. C.R. Wilson, 1895, p. 223.

129. Lawrence James, 2001, p. 508.

130. Lawrence James, 2001, p. 208.

131. Lawrence James, 2001, p. 216.

132. Lemuel Sadoc, n.d., *Zarina: A Romance in India*, London: Arthur H. Stockwell Ltd, p. 42, cited in S. Chakravarty, 1991, pp. 88–89.

133. See C. Younger, 2004, for some biographical accounts of European women who married into Indian royalty.

134. E.W. Savi, *The Devil's Playground*, www.lib.unc.edu/mss/inv/a/A.P.Watt.html, cited in S. Chakravarty, 1991, p. 129.

135. J.K. Stanford, 1926, p. 17.

136. M. Murray, 1934, 'Female Fertility Figures', *Journal of Royal Anthropological Institute* 64: 99, cited in D. Desai, 1985, p. 94.

137. Richard Payne Knight, 1786, 'A Discourse on Worship of Priapus', in *Sexual Symbolism, A History of Phallic Worship* (2 vols), Richard P. Knight and Thomas Wright, New York: The Julian Press, 1961, p. 17, cited in D. Desai, 1985, p. 94.

138. Lawrence James, 2001, p. 207.

139. Lawrence James, 2001, p. 209.

140. Jeremy Black and Donald M. Macraild. 2003, p. 272

141. I. McCalman, 1984, 'Unrespectable Radicalism: Infidels and Pornography in Early Nineteenth Century London', Past and Present: 101, cited in Lawrence James, 2001, p. 209.

142. P. Fraxi, 1877, *Indix Librorum Prohibitoru*, being notes, Bio—, Biblio-Iconographical and Critical on Uncommon Books, p. 380, cited in Lawrence James, 2001, p. 207.

143. R. Hyam, 1990, *Empire and Sexuality: The British Experience*, Manchester: Manchester University Press, pp. 132–33, cited in Lawrence James, 2001, p. 509.

144. Veena T. Oldenburg, 2001, p. 137.

145. K.C. Tarachand, 1991, *Devdasi Customs, Rural Social Structure and Flesh Markets*, New Delhi, Reliance Publishing House, p.xi, cited in Kakolee Chakraborthy, 2000, pp. 30–31; Hobson-Jobson, 2002, p. 296; John Fryer, 1698, *A New Account of East India and Persia in Eight Letters*, London: Folio, p. 152, cited in Hobson-Jobson, 2002.

146. Veena T. Oldenburg, 2001, pp. 137, 141.

147. P. Fraxi, 1877, *Indix Librorum Prohibitoru*, being notes, Bio—, Biblio-Iconographical and Critical on Uncommon Books, quoting Edward Sellon, 1877, p. 380, cited in Lawrence James, 2001, p. 211.

148. *Westminister and Foreign Quarterly* 3(July 1850): 488, cited in Lawrence James, 2001, p. 212.

149. Lawrence James, 2001, p. 212.

150. Frank Richards, 1965, *Old Soldier Sahib*, New York: Harrison, Smith and Robert Haas, pp. 197–99, 303–04, cited in Lawrence James, 2001, p. 509.

151. Lawrence James, 2001, pp. 509–10.

152. Lawrence James, 2001, p. 213.

153. A.D. Harvey, 1978, 'Prosecution for Sodomy in England at the Beginning of the Nineteenth Century', *History Journal* 21: 939–40, cited in Lawrence James, p. 212.

154. R. Hyam, 1990, *Empire and Sexuality: The British Experience*, Manchester: Manchester University Press, pp. 130–31, cited in Lawrence James, 2001, p. 508.

155. Lawrence James, 2001, p. 213.

156. Lawrence James, 2001, p. 211.

157. R. Hyam, 1990, *Empire and Sexuality: The British Experience*, Manchester: Manchester University Press, p. 115, cited in Lawrence James, 2001.

158. Lancereux, 1869, *A Treatise on Syphilis* (G. Whitly, trans.), The New Sydenham Society, pp. 295–96, cited in Lawrence James, 2001, pp. 217–18.

159. Kenneth Ballhatchet, 1976, 'Race, Sex and Class under the Raj 1885–1905', paper read at the European conference on Modern South Asian Studies, Leiden, p. 1, cited in V.T. Oldenberg, 2001, p. 132.

160. Frank Richards, 1965, *Old Soldier Sahib*, New York: Harrison, Smith and Robert Haas, pp. 197–99, 303–04, cited in Lawrence James, 2001, pp. 509–10.

161. Lawrence James, 2001, p. 218.

162. Iltudus T. Prichard, 1869, *The Administration of India 1859–1869* (2 vols), London: Macmillan & Co., vol. 2, p. 283, cited in V.T. Oldenburg, 2001, p. 132.

163. R. Holmes, 2005, p. 490.

164. C.R. Wilson, 1895, pp. 62–63.

165. C.R. Wilson, 1895, p. 68.

166. C.R. Wilson, 1895, p. 206.

167. J.K. Stanford, 1926, pp. 2–4.

168. C. Younger, 2004, pp. 24–27.

169. J.K. Stanford, 1926, p. 4.

170. C. Younger, 2004, p. 28.

171. R. Holmes, 2005, p. 444.

172. R. Holmes, 2005, p. 491.

173. Lawrence James, 2001, pp. 138–39, 218, 220.

174. L. Sadoc, n.d., *Zarina: A Romance in India*, London: Arthur H. Stockwell Ltd, p. 42, cited in S. Chakravarty, 1991, pp. 88–89.

175. Rudyard Kipling, 'His Chance of Life', in *Plain Tales from the Hills*, pp. 77–84, cited in S. Chakravarty, 1991, p. 119.

176. Lawrence James, 2001, p. 219.

177. Rudyard Kipling, 'His Chance of Life', in *Plain Tales from the Hills*, pp. 77–84, cited in S. Chakravarty, 1991, p. 119.

178. J.K. Stanford, 1926, p. 71.

179. Laurence Fleming, 2004, p. 75.

180. E.W. Savi, 1936, *The Glamorous East*, pp. 21, 236, 280, 284, cited in S. Chakravarty, 1991, pp. 31–32.

181. From *Memoirs of a Bengal Civilian*, 1961, cited in E. Boehmer, 1998, pp. 32–38.

182. V.T. Oldenburg, 2001, pp. 52–53.

183. J. Gilchrist, 1800, *The Anti-Jargonist or A Short Introduction to the Hindoostanee Language*, Kolkata: Fort William College, cited in Lawrence James, 2001, p. 159.

184. C. Younger, 2004, pp. 23–36.

185. K. Ballahatchet, 1980, *Race, Sex and Class under the Raj: Imperial Attitudes and Policies and Their Critics 1793–1905*, London: Weidenfeld & Nicolson, pp. 5–6, cited in J. Majeed, 1992, p. 105.

186. R. Holmes, 2005, pp. 453–54.

187. Lawrence James, 2001, p. 510.

188. Rudyard Kipling in 'The Tomb of His Ancestors', *The Day's Work*, New York: Doubleday and McClure Co., cited in S. Chakravarty, 1991, pp. 46–47.

189. John MacKenzie, 1984, *Propaganda and Empire: The Manipulation of British Public Opinion 1880–1960*, Manchester: Manchester University Press, p. 108, cited in S. Chakravarty, 1991, p. 3.

190. Maud Diver's *Desmond's Daughter*, cited in S. Chakravarty, 1991, p. 27.

191. Bithia Mac Croker, 1888, *Diana Barrington: A Romance of Central India*, vol. 3, London: Ward and Downey, p. 63, cited in S. Chakravarty, 1991, p. 24.

192. Anthony Fletcher, 1999, p. 343.

193. Lawrence James, 2001, p. 134.

194. James Mill, 1972 (1st ed. 1817), *The History of British India*, Delhi: Associated Publishing House, cited in S. Tharu and K. Lalita, 1997, p. 46.

195. S. Tharu and K. Lalita, 1997, p. 47.

196. N. Ferguson, 2004, p. 141.

197. N. Ferguson, 2004, p. 141.

198. George Otto Trevelyan, 1864, *The Competition Wallah*, cited in E. Boehmer, 1998, p. 6.

199. J.A. Norris, 1967, *The First Afghan War*, New York: The Cambridge University Press, p. 433, cited in Lawrence James, 2001, p. 98.

200. N. Ferguson, 2004, p. 150.

201. Indira Ghosh, 2002, pp. 200–16.

202. Lawrence James, 2001, pp. 283–87.

203. Lawrence James, 2001, p. 283.

204. S. Tharu and K. Lalita, 1997, pp. 8–9.

205. Mary Hancock, 1999, pp. 148–160.

206. Flora Annie Steel, 1890, *The Complete Indian Housekeeper and Cook*, Edinburgh: Frank Murray, cited in E. Boehmer, 1998, pp. 126–32.

207. J.K. Stanford, 1926, p. 38.

208. S. Gosson, 1596, *Pleasant Quippes for Upstart Newfanlged Gentle Women*, London, cited in Anthony Fletcher, 1999, p. 22.

209. J. Black and D.M. Macraild, 2003, p. 270.

210. J. Black and D.M. Macraild, 2003, p. 272.

211. J. Black and D.M. Macraild, 2003, p. 245.

212. Lord Carver, 1989, *Wellington and His Brothers*, Southampton: University of Southampton, p. 14, cited in Lawrence James, 2001, p. 208.

213. Lawrence James, 2001, p. 209.

214. J. Black and D.M. Macraild, 2003, p. 272.

215. J. Black and D.M. Macraild, 2003, p. 272.

216. J. Black and D.M. Macraild, 2003, p. 247.

217. J. Black and D.M. Macraild, 2003, p. 266.

218. Indira Ghosh, 2002, p. 9.

219. Clarisse Barder, 1925, *Women in Ancient India*, London: Longmans Green, cited in S. Tharu and K. Lalita, 1997, pp. 44–45.

220. M.E. Wiesner, 1993, *Women and Gender in Early Modern Europe*, p. 226, cited in Anthony Fletcher, 1999, p. 47.

221. Anthony Fletcher, 1999, p. 65.

222. K.V. Thomas, 1971, *Religion and the Decline of Magic,* London: Oxford University Press, p. 38, cited in Anthony Fletcher, 1999, p. 63.

223. James Mill, 1972 (1st ed. 1817), *The History of British India*, Delhi: Associated Publishing House, cited in S. Tharu and K. Lalita, 1997, p. 46.

224. Rajul Sogani, 2002, p. 125.

225. Sumanta Banerjee, 1989, 'Marginalization of Women's Popular Culture in the Nineteenth Century Bengal', in *Recasting Women: Essays in Colonial History*, Sudesh Vaid, ed., Delhi: Kali for Women, p. 134, cited in S. Tharu and K. Lalita, 1997, pp. 154–55.

226. Rajul Sogani, 2002, pp. 67, 125, 200, 201.

227. S. Tharu and K. Lalita, 1997, pp. 154–56.

228. S. Tharu and K. Lalita, 1997, pp. 187–90.

229. S. Tharu and K. Lalita, 1997, pp. 154–56.

230. *Report of the Malabar Marriage Commission with Enclosures and Appendixes* of the Malabar Marriage Commission, section 47, Madras Government Printer, 1891; Maria Mies, 1980, *Indian Women and Patriarchy*, Delhi: Concept, pp. 84–90, cited in S. Tharu and K. Lalita, 1997, p. 159.

231. S. Tharu and K. Lalita, 1997, pp. 6, 7, 116–19.

232. S. Tharu and K. Lalita, 1997, pp. 6, 7.

233. S. Banerjee, 2004, pp. 35, 38.

234. J.K. Stanford, 1926, p. 9.

235. F. Parkes, 1850, *Wandering of a Pilgrim in Search of the Picturesque, during Four-and-Twenty years in the East with Revelations of Life in Zenana*, vol. 1, London: Pelham Richardson, p. 60, cited in G. Murshid, 1983, p. 53.

236. R. Chandra, 1863, *Dekhe Shune Akkel Gurum*, Kolkata, pp. 6–7, cited in G. Murshid, 1983, p. 53.

237. G. Murshid, 1983, pp. 98, 112, 113.

238. G. Murshid, 1983, p. 14.

239. *Census of India, 1901,* vol. VIA, Pt II, Bengal Secretariat Press, 1902, pp. 60–61, 100–104, 106–11, cited in G. Murshid, 1983, p. 20.

240. G. Murshid, 1983, p. 21.

241. Kakolee Chakraborthy, 2000, pp. 62–63.

242. *Laws of Manu* IX.94 (W. Doniger, 1992).

243. H.B. Henderson, 1829, *Sketches of Society and Manners in the East*, London: Smith, Elder and Co., p. 298, cited in Lawrence James, 2001, pp. 353–54.

244. H.C. Mackenzie, 1854, *Life in the Mission: the Camp and the Zenana* (2 vols), vol. 1, London: Richard Bentley, pp. 278, 287, cited in Lawrence James, 2001, p. 354.

245. Banani Mukhia, 2002, pp. 20–21.

246. *Report of the Franchise Committee*, 1918, cited in Rozina Visram, 1992, p. 33.

247. Report in *Stri Dharma*, Journal of the Women's Indian Association, August 1928, cited in Rozina Visram, 1992, p. 14.

248. K. Nag and D. Burman (eds), 1977, *Selected Works of Raja Rammohun Roy*, New Delhi: Government of India Publications, pp. 156, 163, cited in Banani Mukhia, 2002, p. 18.

249. Ashok Sen, 1977, *Vidyasagar and His Elusive Milestones*, Kolkata: Ridhi India, p. 60, cited in Banani Mukhia, 2002, p. 20.

250. Banani Mukhia, 2002, pp. 30, 36, 39, 69, 71, 143, 156.

251. M. Borthwick, 1984, *The Changing Role of Women in Bengal, 1849–1905*, Princeton: Princeton University Press, p. 64, cited in Banani Mukhia, 2002, p. 21–23.

252. B. Mukhia, 2002, pp. 21–23.

253. Sarat Chandra Chattopadhyay, *Sarat Rachanavali*, vol. 1, Kolkata: Tuli Kalam, p. 380, cited in B. Mukhia, 2002, p. 21.

254. 'Strishiksha O Stree Swadhinata', *Tattvabodhini Patrika*, November–December 1878, pp. 154–56, cited in Banani Mukhia, 2002, p. 23.

255. Banani Mukhia, 2002, p. 24.

256. G. Murshid, 1983, p. 46.

257. *Bamabodhini Patrika*, July–August 1891, p. 106, cited in G. Murshid, 1983, p. 47.

258. S. Tharu and K. Lalita, 1997, p. 181.

259. Jane Robinson, 1996, *Angels of Albion: Women of the Indian Mutiny*. London: Viking, p. 14, cited in R. Holmes, 2005, p. 446.

260. James Lunt (ed.), 1970, *From Sepoy to Subedar: The Life and Adventures of Subedar Sita Ram*, Delhi: Vikas Publications (Translated and published by Lieutenant Colonel Norgate, Bengal Staff, 1873), p. 24, cited in R. Holmes, 2005, p. 446.

261. Godfrey Mudy, 1832, *Pen and Pencil Sketches*, 2 vols, London: John Murray, vol. 2, pp. 216–22, cited in H.K. Kaul, 1997, pp. 96–97.

262. Lewis D. Wurgaft, 1983. p. 51.

263. Banani Mukhia, 2002, p. 24.

264. Rozina Visram, 1992, pp. 16, 17.

265. Letter written by Gangaben to Gandhi in February 1931, India Office Records, R/3/1/289, cited in Rozina Visram, 1992, p. 29. Gangaben wrote of how the police baton cracked her skull, and even as she bled she did not leave her post of protest and asked the women with her to continue as they were. She was arrested and taken to the police station, but she still assures Gandhi that she felt 'quite fearless' and bore no 'hatred or anger' for her assailants.

266. Zareer Masani, 1987, *Indian Tales of the Raj*, London: BBC Books; Bejan Mitra and Phani Chakraborty (eds), 1946, *Rebel India*, cited in Rozina Visram, 1992, p. 47.

267. Krishna Nehru Hutheesing, 1967, *We Nehrus*, New York: Holt, Rinehart & Winston; Manmohar Kaur, 1968, 'Role of Women in the Freedom Movement 1857–1947', *Amrita Bazar Patrika*, cited in Rozina Visram, 1992, p. 29.

268. Mithan A. Tata, 'Why Indian Women Should Have Votes', in *Stri Dharma*, May 1918, cited in Rozina Visram, 1992, p. 31.

269. Rozina Visram, 1992, p. 39.

270. A. Basu, 2000, pp. 135–137.

271. S. Tharu and K. Lalita, 1997, p. 174.

272. S. Tharu and K. Lalita, 1997, p. 160.

273. *The Letters and Correspondence of Pandita Ramabai*, 1977, A.B. Shah (ed.), Mumbai: State Board of Literature and Culture, p.xxx, cited in S. Tharu and K. Lalita, 1997, p. 160.

274. S. Tharu and K. Lalita, 1997, pp. 190–191, 195.

275. G. Murshid, 1983, pp. 31–33.

276. Nirad C. Chaudhuri, 1976, p. 140.

277. Swarna Kumari Debi, 1899, '*Amader Grihe Antahpur Shiksha O Tahar Sanskar*', *Pradip* August–September, p. 318, cited in G. Murshid, 1983, p. 32.

278. Rokeya Sakhawat Hossein, 1973 (1st ed. 1905–12), *Rokeya Rachanabali*, A. Quadir (ed.), Dacca: Bangla Academy, p. 482, cited in G. Murshid, 1983, p. 32.

279. S. Tharu and K. Lalita, 1997, p. 167.

280. Leslie A. Flemming, 'Between Two Worlds: Self-construction and Self-identity in the Writings of Three Nineteenth Century Indian Christian Women', pp. 81–107, cited in Nita Kumar, 1994.

281. G. Murshid, 1983, pp. 40, 52, 25.

282. A lady from Boalia, 1871, '*Bangladesher Mahilaganer Swadhinata Bishay*', *Bamabodhini Patrika* May–June, pp. 62–64, cited in G. Murshid, 1983, p. 52.

283. G. Murshid, 1983, p. 40.

284. Leslie A. Flemming, 'Between Two Worlds: Self-construction and Self-identity in the Writings of Three Nineteenth Century Indian Christian Women', pp. 81–107, cited in Nita Kumar, 1994.

285. Appendix in Baba Padmanji's novel *Yamuna Paryatan*. The appendix is a first-hand account of a widow's life and is titled '*Hindu Vidhwanchi Dukhit Stithi: Eka Vidhwa Baine Varnilelei*' (The Plight of

Hindu Widows As Described by a Widow Herself), cited in S. Tharu and K. Lalita, 1997, pp. 356, 358–63.

286. Rajul Sogani, 2002, p. 38.

287. S. Tharu and K. Lalita, 1997, p. 191.

288. Lotika Sarkar, 2000, p. 101.

289. Ranajit Guha, 1987, 'Chandra's Death', in *Subaltern Studies V: Writings on South Asian History and Society*, R. Guha (ed.), New Delhi: Oxford University Press, pp. 135–65,156, cited in Rajul Sogani, 2002, pp. 38–41, 126.

290. Rajul Sogani, 2002, pp. 177–79.

291. S. Tharu and K. Lalita, 1997, p. 123.

292. S. Tharu and K. Lalita, 1997, pp. 221–22, 245–55, 237.

293. S. Tharu and K. Lalita, 1997, pp. 216–18.

294. S. Tharu and K. Lalita, 1997, p. 444.

295. S. Tharu and K. Lalita, 1997, pp. 191, 196.

296. S. Tharu and K. Lalita, 1997, pp. 191, 290–93.

297. S. Tharu and K. Lalita, 1997, pp. 424–25.

298. S. Tharu and K. Lalita, 1997, p. 444.

299. S. Tharu and K. Lalita, 1997, p. 240.

300. S. Tharu and K. Lalita, 1997, p. 241.

301. S. Tharu and K. Lalita, 1997, p. 221.

302. S. Tharu and K. Lalita, 1997, pp. 424–25.

303. Kailasbasini Debi, 1865, *Hindu Abalakuler Bidyabhyas O Tahar Samunnati*, Kolkata: Gupta Press, pp. 11–12, cited in G. Murshid, 1983, p. 25.

304. G. Murshid, 1983, p. 25.

305. S. Tharu and K. Lalita, 1997, p. 397.

306. S. Tharu and K. Lalita, 1997, p. 340.

307. S. Tharu and K. Lalita, 1997, p. 160.

308. S. Tharu and K. Lalita, 1997, pp. 162–63.

309. S. Tharu and K. Lalita, 1997, p. 162.

310. *Stri Dharma* 11(12), October 1928, p. 305.

311. Mrinalini Sinha, 1999.

312. P. Spear, 1990, p. 109.

313. *Transactions of the British National in Indostan from the Year MDCCXLV* , 2 vols, 1763, vol. 1, pp. 38, 41, cited in Lawrence James, 2001, p. 1.

314. R.P. Rana, 'Agrarian Revolts in Northern India during the 17th and Early 18th Centuries', in *Land Control and Social Structure in*

Indian History, R.E. Frykenberg (ed.), 1979, cited in Lawrence James, 2001, p. 192.

315. *Annals of the Indian Administration*, 1856–58, M. Townsend (ed.), vol. 1, p.ix, vol. 3, pp. 326–33, cited in Lawrence James, 2001, pp. 192–93.

316. *Gazetteer of the Bombay Presidency*, VII (Baroda), XV, ii (Kanara), Bombay, 1883, vol. 7, pp. 110, 111, 113, 119, 126, cited in Lawrence James, 2001, pp. 192–93.

317. R. Mukherjee, 'Satan Let Loose upon Earth: The Kanpur Massacres in India', in *The Revolt of 1857, Past and Present*, no.128, 1990, pp. 284, 290, cited in Lawrence James, 2001, p. 193.

318. N.N. Panikkar, 1989, *Against Lord and State: Religion and Peasant Uprisings in Malabar, 1836–1921*, Oxford, p. 1, cited in Lawrence James, 2001, p. 192.

319. James Forbes, 1813, *Oriental Memoirs*, 4 vols, London: White, Cochrana and Co., vol. 1, pp. 392–93, cited in H.K. Kaul, 1997, pp. 188–89.

320. Indira Ghosh, 2002, p. 295.

321. Fanny Parkes, 2003, pp. 296–97.

322. Nirad C. Chaudhuri, 1987, *Thy Hand, Great Anarch!,* London: Chatto and Windus, p. 47, cited in Patrick French, 1997, p. 59.

323. Patrick French, 1997.

324. M.K. Gandhi, *The Collected Works of Mahatma Gandhi*, 1958–1980, 82 vols, vol. 42, pp. 223, 433, cited in Lawrence James, 2001.

325. Speech at the First Gujarat Political Conference, 3 November 1917, *Collected Works of Mahatma Gandhi*, vol. 16, p. 116, cited in David Hardiman, 2003, p. 17.

326. *Constitutional Relations between Britain and India: The Transfer of Power, 1942–47* (12 vols), Nicholas Mansergh (editor-in-chief), London: HMSO, 1970–83, vol. 5, p. 43, cited in Patrick French, 1997, p. 185.

327. Speech at Muir College Economic Society, Allahabad, 22 December 1916, *Collected Works of Mahatma Gandhi*, vol.15, p. 277, cited in David Hardiman, 2003, p. 76.

328. M.K. Gandhi, 'About *Navjivan*', *Navjivan*, 14 July 1929, *Collected Works of Mahatma Gandhi*, vol. 36, p. 272, cited in David Hardiman, 2003, p. 68.

329. David Hardiman, 2003, p. 68.

330. M.K. Gandhi, *The Collected Works of Mahatma Gandhi*, 1958–1980, 82 vols, vol. 42, pp. 470–71, vol. 43, p. 224, Delhi, cited in Lawrence James, 2001.

331. Sudhir Kakar, 1991, pp. 90–91.

332. M.K. Gandhi, 1968, 'Yervada Mandir', in *Selected Works*, Ahmedabad: Navjivan, vol. 4, p. 220, cited in Sudhir Kakar, 1991, p. 97.

333. M.K. Gandhi, *Collected Works*, 1927–28, vol. 36, p. 378, 'Letter to Harjivan Kotak', cited in Sudhir Kakar, 1991, pp. 95, 104.

334. M.K. Gandhi, 1943, *To the Women*, Karachi: Hingorani, pp. 49–50, 52, cited in Sudhir Kakar, 1991, p. 95.

335. Robert Payne, 1969, *The Life and Death of Mahatma Gandhi*, London: The Bodley Head, pp. 185–86, cited in David Hardiman, 2003, p. 98.

336. 'Trial of Harilal Gandhi and Others', 28 July 1908, *Collected Works of Mahatma Gandhi*, vol. 9, pp. 15–16, cited in David Hardiman, 2003, p. 99.

337. David Hardiman, 1987, pp. 207–08.

338. M.K. Gandhi, 1968, 'Yervada Mandir', in *Selected Works*, Ahmedabad: Navjivan, vol. 4, p. 220, cited in Sudhir Kakar, 1991, p. 96.

339. M.K. Gandhi, 1968, 'Yervada Mandir', in *Selected Works*, Ahmedabad: Navjivan, vol. 4, p. 220, cited in Sudhir Kakar, 1991, p. 96.

340. Sudhir Kakar, 1991, pp. 102, 107.

341. N.K. Bose, *My Days with Gandhi*, Kolkata: Nishana, p. 189, cited in Sudhir Kakar, 1991, p. 107.

342. M.K. Gandhi, *Letters to Premaben Kantak* (*Kumari Premaben Kantak ken am patra*), Ahmedabad: Navjivan, 1960, pp. 260–62, cited in Sudhir Kakar, 1991, p. 106.

343. M.K. Gandhi, 1927, pp. 209, 501.

344. M.K. Gandhi, 1927, p. 309.

345. M.K. Gandhi, 1968, 'Yervada Mandir', in *Selected Works*, Ahmedabad: Navjivan, vol. 4, p. 223, cited in Sudhir Kakar, 1991, p. 98.

346. M.K. Gandhi, 1927, p. 324.

347. M.K. Gandhi, 1927, p. 324.

348. M.K. Gandhi, 1927, pp. 209, 501; M.K. Gandhi, *Collected Works*, 1927–28, vol. 36, p. 378, 'Letter to Harjivan Kotak'; Vol. 37, 1928, 'Speech on Birth Centenary of Tolstoy', p. 258, cited in Sudhir Kakar, 1991, pp. 99, 101.

349. M.K. Gandhi, *The Collected Works of Mahatma Gandhi* (90 vols), 1969–1984, vol. 86, New Delhi, p. 420, cited in P. French, 1997, p. 18.

350. Patrick French, 1997, pp. 21–22.

351. Patrick French, 1997, p. 20.

352. M.K. Gandhi, *Collected Works*, 1927–28, vol. 36, p. 378, 'Letter to Harjivan Kotak', cited in Sudhir Kakar, 1991, p. 378.

353. Patrick French, 1997, p. 20.

354. David Hardiman, 2003, p. 108.

355. *Young India*, 4 October 1928, in Terchek, *Gandhi*, p. 207, cited in David Hardiman, 2003, p. 108.

356. M. Desai, 1920, p. 262.

357. 'Letter to Gangaben Vaidya', 2 February 1931, *Collected Works of Mahatma Gandhi*, vol. 51, p. 94, cited in David Hardiman, 2003, p. 115.

358. M. Desai, 1920, p. 263.

359. M.K. Gandhi, 'Yervada Mandir', in *Selected Works*, vol. 4, Ahmedabad: Navjivan, 1968, p. 220, cited in Sudhir Kakar, 1991, p. 97.

360. Sudhir Kakar, 1991, p. 89.

361. Sudhir Kakar, 1991, p. 124.

362. Patrick French, 1997, p. 26.

363. Sudhir Kakar, 1991, p. 112.

364. Sudhir Kakar, 1991, p. 112.

365. Sudhir Kakar, 1991, p. 111.

366. Patrick French, 1997, p. 21.

367. Sudhir Kakar, 1991, p. 108.

368. M.K. Gandhi, *Letters to Premaben Kantak* (*Kumari Premaben Kantak ken am patra*), Ahmedabad: Navjivan, 1960, p. 188, cited in Sudhir Kakar, 1991, pp. 109–12.

369. Jawaharlal Nehru, 1936, *An Autobiography*, London: The Bodley Head, pp. 73–76, cited in Patrick French, 1997, p. 56.

370. Hubert Evans, 1988, p. 224.

371. M.K. Gandhi, 1927, p. 24.

372. M.K. Gandhi, *Letters to Premaben Kantak* (*Kumari Premaben Kantak ken am patra*), Ahmedabad: Navjivan, 1960, p. 260–62, cited in Sudhir Kakar, 1991, p. 106.

373. M.K. Gandhi, *Letters to Premaben Kantak* (*Kumari Premaben Kantak ken am patra*), Ahmedabad: Navjivan, 1960, pp. 260–62, cited in Sudhir Kakar, 1991, p. 106.

374. M.K. Gandhi, *Letters to Premaben Kantak* (*Kumari Premaben Kantak ken am patra*), Ahmedabad: Navjivan, 1960, p. 190, cited in Sudhir Kakar, 1991, p. 112.

375. *Bapu's Letter to Mira (1924–48)*, Mira Behn (ed.), Ahmedabad: Navjivan, 1949, p. 141, cited in Sudhir Kakar, 1991, p. 125.

376. Cited in Sudhir Kakar, 1991, p. 127.

377. Madhu Kishwar, 1985, 'Gandhi on Women: Part II', *Economic and Political Weekly*, 12 October, p. 1755, cited in David Hardiman, 2003, p. 103.

378. Sujata Patel, 1988, 'Construction and Reconstruction of Women in Gandhi', *Economic and Political Weekly*, 20 February, p. 378, cited in David Hardiman, 2003, p. 103.

379. Madhu Kishwar, 1985, 'Gandhi on Women: Part I', *Economic and Political Weekly*, 5 October, pp. 1693–94, cited in David Hardiman, 2003, pp. 103–04.

380. David Hardiman, 2003, p. 96.

381. 'Satyagraha in South Africa', *Collected Works of Mahatama Gandhi*, vol. 34, p. 202, cited in David Hardiman, 2003, p. 104.

382. Madhu Kishwar, 1985, 'Gandhi on Women: Part I', *Economic and Political Weekly*, 5 October, pp. 1693–94, cited in David Hardiman, 2003, p. 107.

383. Speech at the Second Gujarat Education Conference, Bharuch, 20 October 1917, *Collected Works of Mahatama Gandhi*, vol. 16, p. 93, cited in David Hardiman, 2003, p. 106.

384. Bharati Ray and Aparna Basu, 2000, pp. 3–4.

THE DEMOCRATIC PERIOD

1. UNFPA (The United Nations Population Fund) 2005 Overview on 'Health and Socio-Economic Indicatiors/Policy Development'. www.unfpa.org/profile/india.cfm

2. Chirdeep Bagga, 2005.

3. K.P. Nayar, 2006; 'A Lesson or Two in Population', *Hindustan Times*, 6 July 2005.

4. Venetia Ansell, 2005.

5. UNAIDS, 2007.

6. NDTV View Poll, 3 December 2004.

7. *Taittiriya Samhita* VI.5. 10.3.

8. L. Visaria, 2000, p. 81.

9. Swami Agnivesh, R. Mani, and A. Köster-Lossack, 2005; G.N. Allahbadia, 2002.

10. P.V.J. Ayyar, 2002, p. 43.

11. Sreemaoyee Piu Kundu, 2004.

12. Gajinder Singh, 2004.

13. A. Lipietz, 1987, *Mirage and Miracles: The Crises of Global Fordism*, London: Verso, cited in S. Corbridge and J. Harris, 2000, p. 164.

14. Yahoo! India Movies, Indo-Asian News Service, http://in.movies.yahoo.com/050926/43/60bez.html

15. BBC News, 7 Februrary 2000. http://news.bbc.co.uk/2/hi/south_asia/634324.stm

16. R. Kidwai, 2005.

17. Janaki Nair, 2005.

18. Sudhir Kakar, 1991, pp. 20–22.

19. *Fire* (1996), director Deepa Mehta.

20. R. Vanita and S. Kidwai, 2001, pp. 214–15.

21. *Telegraph*, Kolkata, India, July 28 2007, www.telegraphindia.com/1070728/asp/calcutta/story_8115947.asp

22. P. Mondal, 2005.

23. Flavia Agnes, 2005.

24. S.C. Dube, 1992, p. 68.

25. Chirdeep Bagga, 2005.

26. L. Sarkar, 2000, pp. 103–04.

27. *Ratanlal and Dhirajlal*: *The Indian Penal Code*, 1987, 26th ed., Nagpur: Wadhwa and Co., p. 478, cited in L. Sarkar, 2000, pp. 103–06.

28. Aparna Bhat, Aatreyee Sen, Uma Pradhan, 2005, pp. 11, 14.

29. *Indian Express*, 9 May 1986, 'Dowry Main Cause of Early Marriage in U.P.'

30. S.C. Jain, 1996, p. 163, cited in L. Sarkar, 2000, p. 107.

31. G. Aravamudan, 2007, pp. 12–13.

32. Infochange Agenda, http://infochangeindia.org/agenda8_02.jsp

33. *Towards Equality*, 1974.

34. L.J. Calman, 1992, pp. 49, 61, 70.

35. WHO, UNICEF, UNFPA, 2000, p. 2.

36. R. Bakshi, 2006.

37. Peter Goma, 2003; and http://azadindia.org/social-issues/maternal-health-in-india.html

38. Anand Soondas, 2005.

39. Flavia Agnes, 2004a.

40. Flavia Agnes, 2004a.

41. Shoma A. Chatterjee, 2004.

42. 'India teams with UN to fight spread of HIV/AIDS among military personnel', UN News Center, 28 April 2005. www.un.org/apps/news/story.asp?NewsID=14119&Cr=hiv&Cr1=aids

43. Anand Soondas, 2005.

44. Flavia Agnes, 2004b.

45. Flavia Agnes, 2004b.

46. Z. Hasan, 2000, pp. 122–23, 126.

47. Janaki Nair, 2004.

48. Fatima Chowdhury, 2004.

49. Tapas Chakraborty, 2004.

50. *Indian Express*, 9 May 1986, 'Dowry Main Cause of Early Marriage in U.P.'

51. A method of extrapolation that Dr Amartya Sen had first applied in 1986, where he compared the actual gender ratio from the census results to what is a normal or expected gender ratio for human populations.

52. S.K. Ramachandran, 2005.

53. B. Miller, 1981, *The Endangered Sex: Neglect of Female Children in Rural North India*, Ithaca, New York: Cornell University Press, cited in R. Patel, 1996, p. 2.

54. G. Aravamudan, 2007, p. 46.

55. Amnesty International reported in 2004 that at least 15,000 women are killed in dowry-related cases in India annually. However, other reports estimate the figure to be as high as 25,000 dowry-related homicides a year. See S. Agnivesh, R. Mani and A. Köster-Lossack, 2005.

56. G. Kelkar, 1992, 'Stopping the Violence against Women: Fifteen Years of Activism (India)', in M. Schuler (ed.), *Freedom from Violence: Women's Strategies from around the World*, New York: UNIFEM/Women, Law and Development, cited in Francine Pickup et al., 2001, p. 91.

57. *Injustices Studies*, vol. 1, November 1997, cited by Amnesty International News Release, 3 May 2004, 'Making Violence against Women Count: Facts and Figures—a Summary', http://news.amnesty.org/index/ENGACT770342004

58. Himendra Thakur, 2007.

59. S. Kishor, 1994, 'Gender Differentials in Child Mortality: A Review of the Evidence', in *India: Risk and Vulnerability*, Monica DasGupta, T.N. Krishnan and Lincoln Chen (eds), Mumbai: Oxford University Press, cited in J. Drèze and A. Sen, 2002, p. 238.

60. CRY, 2007.

61. UNICEF, 2007, p. 14.

62. Monica Dasgupta, 1987, 'Selective Discrimination against Female Children in Rural Punjab, India', *Population and Development Review* 13(1): 77–100, cited in L. Visaria, 2000, pp. 94–95.

63. B. Cowan and J. Dhanoa, 1983, 'The Prevention of Toddler Malnutrition by Home Based Nutrition Education', in *Nutrition in the Community: A Critical Look at Nutrition, Policy, Planning*, New York: John Wiley and Sons, pp. 339–56, cited in K.A. Kendall-Tackett, 2001, p. 110.

64. B.D. Miller, 1987, 'Female Infanticide and Child Neglect in Rural India', pp. 95–112, in *Child Survival: Anthropological Perspectives on the Treatment and Maltreatment of Children*, N. Scheper-Hughes (ed.). Boston: D. Reidel, p. 95, cited in K.A. Kendall-Tackett, 2001, p. 111.

65. R. Patel, 1996, p. 3.

66. Murthy, 1996, cited in Francine Pickup, et al., 2001, p. 89.

67. 'Dumped Baby Eaten by Dogs', *Hindustan Times*, February 25 2005.

68. G. Aravamudan, 2007, pp. 157–59.

69. The idea of legalizing abortion was, of course, to allow women more control over their own bodies. However, in India abortion has become a weapon used against women by their targeted elimination.

70. R. Patel, 1996, p. 5.

71. R. Patel, 1996, p. 6; G. Aravamudan, 2007, p. 3.

72. A. Ramanamma and U. Bambawale, 1980.

73. Scott Baldauf, 2006.

74. G. Aravamudan, 2007, pp.xv–xvi.

75. Convention on the Prevention and Punishment of the Crime of Genocide, the UN General Assembly, 9 December 1948.

76. R. Dube et al., 1999, pp. 73–74.

77. A. Gentleman, 2005.

78. A. Gentleman, 2005.

79. N. Raaj, 2008.

80. Media Report Source: Kaiser network website, 15 August 2001, 'Ads-pitching Sex-Selection Opportunities Target Indian Expatriates in United States'. Service/sci–tech/features/health/sexwise/sw–news/views8.shtml

81. N. Eberstadt, 2006.

82. Lifton, Robert Jay, 1986.

83. Lifton, Robert Jay, 1986, pp. 491–93.

84. G. Aravamudan, 2007, pp. 37–38.

85. Lifton, Robert Jay, 1986, p. 434.

86. P.V.J. Ayyar, 2002, pp. 56–59.

87. Lifton, Robert Jay, 1986, pp. 450–51.

88. R. Dube, et al., 1999, p. 74.

89. D. Rose, 2007.

90. BBC News, 8 March 2006.

91. R. Ramesh, 2006.

92. G. Aravamudan, 2007, pp. 127–31.

93. Archana Jyoti, 2005.

94. 'Raped and Then Sold', *Telegraph*, 6 July 2005, p. 13.

95. Merriam-Webster Dictionary. www.webster.com/dictionary

96. J. Chapman, 1995, p. 98.

97. K. Millet, 1970, *Sexual Politics*. New York: Ballantine, pp. 24–25, cited in D. Stanistreet et al., 2005, p. 1.

98. United Nations, 2004, 'Statistics and Indicators on Women and Men 2004', http://unstats.un.org/unsd/demographic/products/indwm/indwm2.html, cited in D. Stanistreet et al., 2005, p. 1.

99. WHO, 1997.

100. Robert Simon, 1996, *Bad Men Do What Good Men Dream*, Washington DC: American Psychiatric Press, cited in Debra Niehoff, 1999.

101. Robert Simon, 1996, *Bad Men Do What Good Men Dream*, Washington DC: American Psychiatric Press, cited in Debra Niehoff, 1999.

102. BBC World's *Correspondent*, 'Dowry Law', reporter, Adam Mynott, aired in India on 18 December 2003, 7 p.m.

103. P. Menon, 1999.

104. Asha Krishnamurti, 1998.

105. G. Aravamudan, 2007, pp. 20–23.

106. E. Goldberg, 2002, p. 115. Extending Jung's theory, Goldberg equates Jung's archetype of self to the *ardhanari*, but on p. 8 also acknowledges that the lingam–yoni is a symbolic form of the *ardhanari*.

107. *Brihadaranyaka Upanishad* II, iv cited in D. Goodall, 2001, p. 63; and O. Ghosh, 2001, pp. 155–56.

108. S. Slipp, 1993, *The Freudian Mystique: Freud, Women and Feminism*, New York: New York Press, p. 173, cited in D.D. Gilmore, 2001, p. 165.

109. D.D. Gilmore, 2001, pp. 165–66.

110. W.T. De Bary, 1958, p. 191.

111. D.L. Eck, 1985, p. 28.

112. R. Vanita and S. Kidwai, 2001, pp. 65, 104.

113. R.P. Conner et al., 1997, p. 134.

114. R.P. Conner et al., 1997, p. 183.

115. S. Rowland, 2000, p. 246.

116. J. Butler, 1990, *Gender Trouble: Feminism and the Subversion of Identity*, London: Routledge, pp. 47, 146, cited in S. Rowland, 2000, p. 245.

117. R.L. Sell et al., 1995.

118. A. Toufexis and E. Linden, 1992.

119. Mahabharata's 'Santi Parva' II: CCCXXI, cited in R. Vanita and S. Kidwai, 2001, p. 23.

120. J. Drèze and A. Sen, 2002, pp. 337, 338, 402.

121. J. Drèze and A. Sen, 2002, p. 402.

122. Robert O. Blake, 2005.

123. J. Drèze and A. Sen, 2002, p. 402.

124. J. Drèze and A. Sen, 2002, p. 147.

125. J. Drèze and A. Sen, 2002, p. 403.

126. B. Ray and A. Basu, 2000, p.xvii.

127. J. Drèze and A. Sen, 2002, p. 391.

128. A.G. Gold, 2002, p. 187.

129. D. Shea and A. Troyer, 1843, p. 24.

130. S. Rowland, 2000, p. 246.

131. H.G. Coward, 1985, pp. 109–11.

132. H.G. Coward, 1985, pp. 109–11.

133. M. Jacoby, 1992, p. 2.

134. M. Jacoby, 1992, p. 2.

135. E.J. Frattaroli, 1997, p. 174.

136. R. Fiumara, 1992, p. 442.

137. C.D. Smith, 1990, p. 96.

REFERENCES

Abravel, E., and H. Gingold. 1985. 'Learning via Observation during the Second Year of Life', *Developmental Psychology* 21: 614–23.

Agnes, Flavia. 2004a. 'AIDS and the Married Woman', *Asian Age*, 14 December, p.13.

——. 2004b. 'The Apex Court and Hindu Conjugality', *Asian Age*, 20 April 2004 [AIR 1984, Delhi 66; AIR 1984, SC 1562].

——. 2005. 'House of Depravity: Law, Justice and Gender', *Asian Age*, 26 July.

Agnivesh, Swami, Rama Mani, and Angelika Köster-Lossack. 2005. 'Missing: 50 Million Indian Girls'. *International Herald Tribune*, 25 November.

Ahmad, Qeyamuddin (ed.). 1999. *India by Al-Biruni*. New Delhi: National Book Trust.

Alkazi, Roshen. 2003. *Ancient Indian Costume*. New Delhi: National Book Trust.

Allahbadia, Gautam N. 2002. 'The 50 Million Missing Women', *Journal of Assisted Reproductive Genetics* 9: 411–16.

Ansell, Venetia. 2005. 'State of Denial', *Telegraph*, 18 July.

Aravamudan, Gita. 2007. *Disappearing Daughters: The Tragedy of Female Foeticide*. New Delhi: Penguin Books India.

Archer, J. 1988. *The Behavioural Biology of Aggression*. Cambridge: Cambridge University Press.

Ayer, V.A.K. 1998. *Hindu Sastras and Samskaras*. Mumbai: Bharatiya Vidya Bhavan.

Ayyar, P.V. Jagadisa. 2002. *South Indian Customs*. New Delhi: Rupa and Co.

Bagga, Chirdeep. 2005. 'Below 18 and Married', *Times of India,* 28 March.

Bakshi, Roopa. 2006. 'UNICEF Unveils New Tool to Combat Maternal Mortality in India'. The Unicef Press Centre, 6 April.

Baldauf, Scott. 2006. 'India's "Girl Deficit" Deepest among Educated', *Christian Science Monitor*. www.csmonitor.com/2006/0113/p01s04–wosc.html.

Banerjee, Gauranga Nath. 1981. *Hellenism in Ancient India*. New Delhi: Munshiram Manoharlal Publishers Pvt. Ltd.

Banerjee, Sudeshna. 2004. *Durga Puja: Yesterday, Today and Tomorrow*. New Delhi: Rupa and Co.

Barik, Satyasundar. 2004. '615 Women in Orissa Unaware of AIDS', *Asian Age*, 7 February.

Basham, A.L. 2004. *The Wonder That Was India: A Survey of the History and Culture of the Indian Sub-Continent before the Coming of the Muslims*. London: Picador.

Basu, Aparna. 2000. 'Women's Education in India: Achievements and Challenges', in *From Independence towards Freedom: Indian Women since 1947*, Bharati Ray and Aparna Basu (eds). New Delhi: Oxford University Press, pp. 135–57.

BBC World. 2003. *Panorama*, 'Sex and the Holy City'. Aired in India in October. Documentation of the impact of the Vatican's ruling on the condom, on the Catholic populations of the Philippines, Kenya and Nicaragua.

Bell, G. 1982. *The Masterpiece of Nature: The Evolution and Genetics of Sexuality*. London: Croom Helm.

Bhasa. 1993. *The Shattered Thigh and Other Plays*. A.N.D. Haksar (trans.). New Delhi: Penguin Books.

Bhat, Aparna, Aatreyee Sen, and Uma Pradhan (eds). 2005. *Child Marriages and the Law in India*. New Delhi: Human Rights Law Network.

Bhattacharya, N.N. 2005. *History of the Tantric Religion*. Delhi: Manohar Publishers.

Black, Jeremy, and Donald M. Macraild. 2003. *Nineteenth Century Britian*. New York: Palgrave MacMillan.

Blake, Robert O. 2005. Speech delivered at 'DRUM Post Graduate Management Program Launch Event', on US–India Collaboration on Improved Access to Energy. New Delhi, 15 July. http://usinfo.state.gov/sa/archive/2005/Jul/18–426637.html

Boehmer, Elleke (ed). 1998. *Empire Writing: An Anthology of Colonial Literature, 1870–1918*. Oxford: Oxford University Press.

Burgard, Peter J. (ed.). 1994. Introduction to *Nietzsche and the Feminine*. Charlottesville: University of Virginia Press.

Burrow, T. 2001. *Sanskrit Language*. New Delhi: Motilal Banarsidass. pp.380–86. Cited in R. Thapar, 2002, *Past and Prejudice*, p.51.

Burton, Antoinette (ed.). 1999. *Gender, Sexuality and Colonial Modernities*. London: Routledge.

Burton, Richard (trans.). 1993. *The Kama Sutra of Vatsyayana: The Classic Hindu Treatise on Love and Social Conduct*. New Delhi: Penguin Books India

Calman, Leslie J. 1992. *Toward Empowerment: Women and Movement Politics in India*. Boulder, Oxford: Westview Press.

Campbell, Joseph. 2000. *Oriental Mythology: The Mask of the Gods*. London: Souvenir Press.

Carus, Paul. 1995 (1st ed. 1915). *The Gospel of Buddha: Compiled from Ancient Records*. London: Senate.

Chakraborthy, Kakolee. 2000. *Women As Devadasis: Origin and Growth of the Devadasi Profession*. New Delhi: Deep and Deep Publications.

Chakraborty, Tapas. 2004. 'Father Kills Fleeing Pair in New Hate Zone', *Telegraph*, 13 March.

Chakravarty, Suhash. 1991. *The Raj Syndrome: A Study in Imperial Perceptions*. New Delhi: Penguin Books India.

Chapman, J. 1995. 'The Feminist Approach,' in *Theories and Methods in Political Science*, D. Marsh and G. Stoker (eds). London: Macmillan.

Chatterjee, Shoma A. 2004. 'AIDS, War and Women', *Statesman*, 22 December.

Chattopadhyay, Sarat Chandra. 1898. *Sarat Rachnavali,* vol. 1. Kolkata: Tuli–Kalam.

Chaudhuri, Nirad C. 1976. *The Autobiography of an Unknown Indian*. Mumbai: Jaico Publishing House.

Chowdhury, Fatima. 2004. 'When Family Turns to Murder,' *Telegraph,* 20 August, p.18.

Chowdhury, N. 1985. 'Some Haunting Question Marks', *Statesman*, 23 December.

Cockburn, Andrew. 1991. *An Introduction to Evolutionary Ecology*. Oxford: Blackwell Scientific Publication.

Coleman, James William. 2002. *The New Buddhism: The Western Transformation of an Ancient Tradition*. New York: Oxford University Press.

Conner, Randy P., David H. Sparks, and Mariya Sparks.1997. *Cassell's Encyclopedia of Queer Myth, Symbol and Spirit*. London: Cassell.

Convention on the Prevention and Punishment of the Crime of Genocide. Adopted by Resolution 260 (III) A of the U.N. General Assembly on 9 December 1948. Entry into force: 12 January 1951.

Coomaraswamy, A. 1938. 'The Tantric Doctrine of Divine Biunity', *Annals of the Bhandarkar Oriental Research Institute* 19: 179.

Corbridge, Stuart, and John Harris. 2000. *Reinventing India: Liberalization, Hindu Nationalism and Popular Democracy*. Cambridge: Polity Press.

Coward, Harold G. 1985. *Jung and Eastern Thought*. Albany: SUNY Press.

Crooke, W. 1952 (1st ed. 1918). 'Prostitution', vol. 10, *Encyclopaedia of Religion and Ethics,* James Hastings (ed.). Edinburgh: T&T Clark.

CRY (Child Relief and You), 2007. 'Statistics: Indian Children'.

Daniélou, Alain (trans.). 1994. *The Complete Kama Sutra*. Vermont: Inner Traditions India.

De, Sushil Kumar. 1959. *Ancient Indian Erotics and Erotic Literature*. Kolkata: Firma K. L. Mukhopadhyay.

De Bary, William Theodore. 1958. *Sources of Indian Tradition*, vol.1. New York: Columbia University Press.

De Lamo, C. 1997. 'India Killing Girls', *London Times*, 12 March.

Desai, Devangana. 1985. *Erotic Sculptures of India: A Socio-Cultural Study*. New Delhi: Munshiram Manoharlal Publishers.

Desai, Mahadev.1920. *Day-to-Day with Gandhi*, vol. 2. Varanasi: Sarva Seva Sangh Prakashan.

Diamond, Jared. 2002. *The Rise and Fall of the Third Chimpanzee: How Our Animal Heritage Affects the Way We Live*. London: Vintage.

Dondis, Donis A. 1981. 'Signs and Symbols'. In *Contact: Human Communication and Its History*, Raymond Williams (ed.). New York: Thames and Hudson.

Doniger, Wendy (trans.). 1992. *The Laws of Manu*. New Delhi: Penguin Books India.

Dowson, John. 2004. *A Classical Dictionary of Hindu Mythology and Religion*. New Delhi: Rupa and Co.

Drèze, Jean, and Amartya Sen. 2002. *India Development and Participation*. New Delhi: Oxford University Press.

Dube, Leela. 1988. 'On the Construction of Gender: Hindu Girls in Patrilineal India', in *Socialisation, Education and Women: Explorations in Gender Identity*, Karuna Chanana (ed.). London: Sangam Books.

Dube, Renu, Reena Dube, and Rashmi Bhatnagar. 1999. 'Women without Choice: Female Infanticide and the Rhetoric of Overpopulation in Postcolonial India', in *Women's Studies Quarterly: Teaching Women about Violence against Women* 17(1–2): 73–86.

Dube, S.C. 1992. *Indian Society*. New Delhi: National Book Trust.

Dubois-Descaulle. 1905. *Bestiality: An Historical, Medical, Legal, Literary Study*. Paris: Charles Carrington.

Dutt, Vijay. 2004. '15000 Dowry Deaths a Year in India', *Hindustan Times*, 8 March, p.4.

Eaton, Richard M. 2002. *Essays on Islam and Indian History*. New Delhi: Oxford University Press.

Eberstadt, Nicholas. 2006. 'The Global War against Baby Girls'. Speech delivered on 6 December before the United Nations General Assembly.

Eck, Diana L.1985. *Darsan: Seeing the Divine Image in India*. Chambersburg, Pennsilvania: Anima Publications.

Emeneau, M.B. 1951. Review of *A History of Sanskrit Literature. Classical Period*, vol. 1, by S.K. De and S.N. Dasgupta. *Journal of the American Oriental Society* 71(1): 86–87.

Eraly, Abraham. 2002. *Gem in the Lotus: The Seeding of Indian Civilization*. New Delhi: Penguin Books India.

Evans, Hubert. 1988 (1st ed. 1892). *Looking Back on India*. London: Frank Cass.

Ferguson, Niall. 2004. *Empire: How Britain Made the Modern World*. London: Penguin Books.

Festy, Partrick. 2000. 'Looking for European Demography, Desperately?', Expert Group Meeting on Policy Responses to Population Ageing and Population Decline. Population Division, United Nations Secretariat, New York, 15 August.

Feuerstein, Georg. 1998. *Tantra: The Path of Ecstasy*. Boston: Shambhala South Asian Editions.

Fiumara, Romano. 1992. 'The Psychology of the Individuation Process and Group Analysis: The Role of "Pronominalism"', in *Carl Gustav Jung: Critical Assessments*, ed. Renos Papadopoulos, London and New York: Routledge.

Fleming, Laurence. 2004. *Last Children of the Raj: British Childhoods in India*, vol. 1 (1919–39). Oxford: The Radcliffe Press.

Fletcher, Anthony. 1999. *Gender, Sex and Subordination in England 1500–1800*. New Haven, London: Yale University Press.

Frattaroli, Elio J. 1997. 'Me and My Anima: Through the Dark Glass of the Jungian/Freudian Interface', in *The Cambridge Companion to Jung*, Polly Young-Eisendrath and Terence Dawson (eds). pp.164–84, Cambridge: Cambridge University Press.

Freed, R.S., and S.A. Freed. 1989. 'Beliefs and Practices Resulting in Female Deaths and Fewer Females than Males in India', *Population and Environment* 10 (3): 144–61.

French, Patrick. 1997. *Liberty or Death*. London: HarperCollins.

Freud, Sigmund. 1955. *Moses and Monotheism*. New York: Random House.

——. 2001. *Totem and Taboo*. London and New York: Routledge Classics.

Friedlander, Henry. 1995. *The Origins of Nazi Genocide: From Euthanasia to the Final Solution*. North Carolina: University of North Carolina.

Gandhi, M.K. 1927. *The Story of My Experiments with Truth*. Trans. Mahadev Desai. Ahmedabad: Navajivan Prakashan Mandir.

Gaufurd, Q. 1817. *Researches Concerning the Laws, Theology, Learning, Commerce etc. of Ancient and Modern India* (2 vols). London: T. Cadell and W. Davies.

Gentleman, Amelia. 2005. 'India Still Fighting to "Save the Girl Child"', *International Herald Tribune,* 15 April. www.iht.com/articles/2005/04/14/news/india.php

Ghosh, Indira (ed.). 2002. *Memsahibs Abroad: Writings by Women Travellers in Nineteenth Century India*. New Delhi: Oxford University Press.

Ghosh, Oroon. 2001. *Selected Stories and Tales from Indian Classics*. New Delhi: Crest Publishing House.

Gilmore, David D. 2001. *Misogyny: The Male Malady*. Philadelphia: University of Pennsylvania Press.

Gold, Ann Grodzins. 2002. 'Counterpoint Authority in Women's Ritual Expression: A View from the Village', in *Jewels of Authority: Women and Textual Tradition in Hindu India*, pp. 177–202, New York: Oxford University Press.

Goldberg, Ellen. 2002. *The Lord Who Is Half Woman: Ardhanarisvara in Indian and Feminist Perspective*. Albany: SUNY Press.

Goma, Peter. 2003. 'Maternal Deaths Increased in Developing Countries', *Standard Times,*18 November, Freetown. Cited on the website of Peace Woman: International League for Peace and Freedom, www.peacewoman.org.

Goodall, Dominic. 2001. *Hindu Scriptures*. New Delhi: Motilal Banarsidass Publishers.

Gross, Rita. 1992. *Buddhism after Patriarchy: A Feminist History, Analysis and Reconstruction of Buddhism*. Albany: SUNY Press.

Habib, Irfan (ed.). 2000. *Akbar and His India*. New Delhi: Oxford University Press.

——.2002. *Essays in Indian History: Towards Marxist Perception*. London: Anthem Press.

Hancock, Mary. 1999. 'Gendering the Modern: Women and Home Science in British India', pp.148–60, in *Gender, Sexuality and Colonial Modernities*, Antoinette Burton (ed.). London and New York: Routledge.

Hardiman, David. 1987. *The Coming of the Devi: Adivasi Assertion in South Gujarat*. New Delhi: Oxford University Press.

——. 2003. *Gandhi in His Time and Ours: The Global Legacy of His Ideas*. London: Hurst & Co.

Hasan, Zoya. 2000. 'Muslim Women and the Debate on Legal Reform', pp.120–34, in *From Independence towards Freedom: Indian Women since 1947*, Bharati Ray and Aparna Basu (eds). New Delhi: Oxford University Press.

Hester, Marianne. 1992. *Lewd Women and Wicked Witches: A Study of the Dynamics of Male Dominance*. London: Routledge.

Hickerson, Nancy Parrott. 1980. *Linguistic Anthropology*. New York: Holt, Rinehart and Winston.

The Hindu. 1998. 'Female Infanticide Alarming in Dharmapuri'. 2 August.

Hitebeitel, Alf. 1991. *The Cult of Draupadi: On Hindu Ritual and Goddess*. Chicago: University of Chicago Press.

Holmes, Richard. 2005. *Sahib: The British Soldier in India (1750–1914)*. London: HarperCollins Publishers.

Hobson-Jobson: A Glossary of Anglo-Indian Words or Phrases and of Kindred Terms, Etymological, Historical, Geographical and Discursive, eds. Henry Yule and A.C. Burnell. 2002 (1st ed. 1886). New Delhi: Rupa and Co.

Hopkins, Thomas. 1971. *The Hindu Religious Tradition*. Belmont, California: Wadsworth Publishing Company.

The Indian Antiquary, A Journal of Oriental Research in Archæology, History, Literature, Languages, Folk-Lore, &c., &c. Ed. Burgess Jas. Bombay: Thacker, Vining & Co.

ITC Sangeet Research Academy. 'Story of Hindustani Classical Music: The Chronology'. www.itcsra.org/sra_hcm/sra_hcm_chrono/sra_hcm_chrono_300ad.htmlDattilam:gandharvashastra:moving towards raga

Jacoby, Mario. 1992. *Individuation and Narcissism: The Psychology of Self in Jung and Kohut*. London: Routledge.

Jaffrey, Zia. 1996. *The Invisibles: A Tale of the Eunuchs of India*. New York: Vintage Books.

James, Lawrence. 2001. *Raj: The Making and Unmaking of British India*. London: Abacus.

Janis, Irving L. 1982. *Group Think: Psychological Studies of Policy Decisions and Fiascoes*. Boston: Houghton Mifflin.

Janssen-Jurreit, M. 1992. 'Female Genocide', in *Femicide: The Politics of Woman Killing*, J. Radford and D.E.H. Russel (eds), pp. 67–76, New York: Twayne.

Jarman, Francis. 2002. 'Sati: From Exotic Custom to Relativist Controversy', *Culture Scan* 5(5).

Jayakar, Pupul. 1989. *The Earth Mother*. New Delhi: Penguin Books India.

Jung, Carl Gustav. 1965. *Memories, Dreams, Reflections*. New York: Vintage Books.

——. 1976a (1st ed. 1922–41). *The Spirit in Man, Art, and Literature*, Collected Works vol.15 paragraphs 97–132. Trans. R.F.C. Hull. In *The Portable Jung*, Joseph Campbell (ed.). USA: Penguin Books.

——. 1976b (1st ed. 1934–54). *The Archetypes and the Collective*

Unconscious, Collected Works, vol 9. I paragraphs 87–110. Trans. R.F.C. Hull. In *The Portable Jung*, Joseph Campbell (ed.). USA: Penguin Books.

Jyoti, Archana. 2005. '15-yr-old Girl's Abduction Reveals Gender Gap', *Asian Age*, 14 July, p.3.

Kakar, Sudhir. 1991. *Intimate Relations: Exploring Indian Sexuality*. New Delhi: Penguin Books India.

Kalidasa. 1989. *Kalidasa: The Loom of Time, A Selection of His Plays and Poems*. Ed. and Trans. Chandra Rajan. New Delhi: Penguin Books India.

Karkal, Maline. 1985. 'How the Other Half Dies in Bombay', *Economic and Political Weekly*, 24 August.

Kaul, H.K. 1997. *Travellers' India: An Anthology*. New Delhi: Oxford University Press.

Kautilya. 1992. *The Arthashastra*. Ed. and Trans. L.N. Rangarajan. New Delhi: Penguin Books India.

Keay, F.E. 2003. *A History of Hindi Literature*. New Delhi: Rupa and Co.

Kelly, Liz, and Jill Radford. 1996. '"Nothing really happened": The Invalidation of Women's Experiences of Sexual Violence', in *Women, Violence and Male Power: Feminist Activism, Research and Practise*, Marianne Hester, Liz Kelly and Jill Radford (eds). Buckingham: Open University Press, pp.19–33.

Kendall-Tackett, Kathleen A. 2001. 'Victimization of Female Children', in *Sourcebook on Violence against Women*, C.M. Renzetti, J.L. Edleson and R. Kennedy Bergen (eds). Newbury Park, California: Sage Publications, pp.101–13.

Kidwai, Rasheed. 2005. 'Curse Cuts Off Hands', *Telegraph*, 12 May. www.telegraphindia.com.

Kinsley, David. 1998 (1st ed. 1987). *Hindu Goddesses*. Delhi: Motilal Banarsidass Publishers.

Krishnamurti, A. 1998. 'Scanning for Death', *Frontline*.

Krishnaswamy, Revathi. 2005. 'Globalization and Its Postcolonial (Dis) Contents: Reading Dalit Writing', *Journal of Postcolonial Writing* 41(1): 69–82.

Kumar, Nita (ed.). 1994. *Women As Subjects in South Asian Histories*. Kolkata: Stree.

Kundu, Sreemaoyee Piu. 2004. 'Gender Bender', *Asian Age*, 29 February, p.20.

Kusum. 1993. 'The Use of Pre-Natal Diagnostic Techniques for Sex Selection: The Indian Scene', *Bioethics* 7(2/3): 149–65.

Lane-Poole, Stanley. 1997 (1st ed. 1890). *Babar*. New Delhi: Low Price Publications.

Lawrence, Bruce B. 1993. 'The Earliest Chishtiya and Shaikh Nizam-u-din Awliya'. In *Delhi through the Ages: Selected Essays in Urban History, Culture and Society*, R.E. Frykenberg (ed.). New Delhi: Oxford University Press, pp.32–56.

Lifton, Robert Jay. 1986. *The Nazi Doctors: Medical Killing and the Psychology of Genocide*. New York: Basic Books Inc. Accessed online courtesy The Mazal Library and the Holocaust History Project www.holocaust-history.org/lifton/

Llewellyn-Jone. 2001. 'A Fatal Friendship: The Nawabs, the British and the City of Lucknow', in *The Lucknow Omnibus*. New Delhi: Oxford University Press.

Longhurst, A.H. 1982 (1st ed. 1917). *Hampi Ruins: Described and Illustrated*. New Delhi: Asian Educational Services.

Mackenzie, Donald A. 1993. *India*. Myths and Legends Series. London: Studio Editions.

Majeed, Javed. 1992. *Ungoverned Imaginings: James Mill's 'The History of British India and Orientalism'*. Oxford: Clarendon Press.

Mahalingam, T.V. 1967. 'The Cult of Sakti in Tamilnad', in *The Sakti Cult and Tara*, D.C. Sircar (ed.). Kolkata: University of Calcutta Press.

Man, L., J.W. Newton, and J.M. Innes. 1982. 'A Test between Deindividuation and Emergent Norm Theories of Crowd Aggression', *Journal of Personality and Social Psychology* 42: 260–72.

Marshall, Sir John (ed.). 1931. *Mohenjo–Daro and the Indus Civilization*, vol. 1. London: Arthur Prosbesthain.

Matrubhoomi (Indian film). 2004. Released 4 January 2005. Director: Manish Jha.

Mazumdar, Kiran. 2003. From the speech titled 'Women Scientists and Entrepreneurs', delivered on 7 January at the National Fair in Chennai, India.

McCalman, Ian. 1984. 'Unrespectable Radicalism: Infidels and Pornography in Early Nineteenth Century London', *Past and Present* 104: 101.

McCrindle, John W. 1971 (1st ed. 1927). *Ancient India As Described in Classical Literature*. Amsterdam: St Leonards Ad Orientem Ltd, Philo Press.

Menon, Parvathi. 1999. '"Dowry deaths" in Bangalore', *Frontline* 16(17).

Meyer, Johann Jakob. 1989 (1st ed. 1930). *Sexual Life in Ancient India: A Study in the Comparative History of Indian Culture*. New Delhi: Motilal Banarsidass Publishers.

Miller, Barbara Stoler. 1984. *The Gitagovinda of Jayadeva: Love Song of the Dark Lord*. New Delhi: Motilal Banarsidass Publishers.

____. 1986.*The Bhagavad-Gita: Krishna's Counsel in Time of War*. New York: Bantam Books.

Mitter, Partha. 2001. *Indian Art*. Oxford: Oxford University Press.

Mondal, Pronab. 2005. 'Danger Lurks at Home for Girls', *Telegraph*, 14 August, p.10.

Mookerjee, Ajit. 1984. 'Kundalini: The Awakening of the Inner Cosmic Energy', in *Ancient Wisdom and Modern Science*, Stanislav Grof (ed.). Albany: SUNY Press, pp.115–34.

Moreland, W.H., and P. Geyl (trans). 2001 (1st ed. 1925). *Jahangir's India: The Remonstrantie of Francisco Pelsaert*. New Delhi: Low Price Publications.

Motoyama, Hiroshi. 2001. *Theories of the Chakras: Bridge to Higher Consciousness*. New Delhi: New Age Books.

Mukerji, Shobha. 1969. *The Republican Trends in Ancient India*. New Delhi: Munshiram Manoharlal Oriental Publishers.

Mukherjee, Prabhati. 1999. *Hindu Women: Normative Models*. Hyderabad: Orient Longman.

Mukhia, Banani. 2002. *Women's Images, Men's Imagination. Female Characters in Bengali Fiction in Late Nineteenth and Early Twentieth Century*. Delhi: Manohar Publishers.

Mukhia, Harbans. 2004. *The Mughals of India*. London: Blackwell Publishing.

Mujeeb, M. 1967. *Indian Muslims*. London: George Allen and Unwin.

Murphy, Robert F. 1986. *Cultural and Social Anthropology*. New Jersey: Prentice-Hall Inc.

Murshid, Ghulam. 1983. *Reluctant Debutante: Response of Bengali Women to Modernization 1849–1905*. Rajshahi: Sahitya Samsad, Rajshahi University. www.murshid.co.uk/reluctant.pdf

Murthy, R. 1996. 'Fighting Female Infanticide by Working with Midwives: An Indian Study', *Gender and Development* 4(2).

Nair, Janaki. 2004. 'Just Another Anniversary', *Telegraph*, 8 March, p.10.

——. 2005. 'Umbrella Morals', *Telegraph,* 26 July.

Nath, R. 2005. *Private Life of the Mughals of India (1526–1803 AD)* New Delhi: Rupa Publications.

Nayar, K.P. 2006. 'No. 1 in Population Sooner', *Telegraph*, 26 February, p.1.

Niehoff, Debra. 1999. *The Biology of Violence*. New York: The Free Press.

Nietzsche, Friedrich. 1964a. *Joyful Wisdom* (1882). Trans. Thomas Common. In *Complete Works of Friedrich Nietzsche,* Oscar Levy (ed.). New York: Russell and Russel.

——.1964b. *Beyond Good and Evil* (1886). Trans. Helen Zimmern. In *Complete Works of Friedrich Nietzsche,* Oscar Levy (ed.). New York: Russell and Russell.

——. 1969. *Thus Spoke Zarathustra* (1883–85). Trans. R.J. Hollingdale. Middlesex: Penguin Books.

O'Flaherty, Wendy Doniger. 2000. *The Rig Veda: Selection, Translation and Annotation of 108 Hymns*. New Delhi: Penguin Books India.

Oldenburg, Veena Talwar. 2001. 'The Making of a Colonial Lucknow 1856–1877', in *The Lucknow Omnibus*. New Delhi: Oxford University Press.

Okano, Haruko. 1995. 'Women's Image and Place in Japanese Buddhism'. In *Japanese Women: New Feminist Perspectives on the Past, Present, and Future*, Kumiko Fujimura-Fanselow and Atsuko Kameda (eds). New York: The Feminist Press, The City University of New York, pp. 15–28.

Palmer, Michael. 1997. *Freud and Jung on Religion*. London: Routledge.

Parkes, Fanny. 2003. *Begums, Thugs and Englishmen: The Journals of Fanny Parkes*. Selected and Introduced by William Dalrymple. New Delhi: Penguin Books India.

Patel, Rita. 1996. 'The Practice of Sex Selective Abortion in India: May You Be the Mother of a Hundred Sons', *Carolina Papers in International Health* 7. University of North Carolina, Chapel Hill: UCIS Publications.

Piaget, Jean. 1976. *The Grasp of Consciousness*. Cambridge, Massachusetts: Harvard University Press.

Pick, Daniel, and Lyndal Roper. 2004. *Dreams and History*. East Sussex: Brunner-Routledge.

Pickup, Francine, Suzanne Williams, and Caroline Sweetman. 2001. *Ending Violence against Women: A Challenge for Development and Humanitarian Work*. London: Oxfam.

Pike, Albert. 1992. *Indo-Aryan Deities and Worship As Contained in the Rig-Veda*. Whitefish, MT: Kessinger Publishing.

Poddar, Pramila, and Pramod Poddar.1995. *Khajuraho: Temples of Love*. New Delhi: Lustre Press.

Pool, Daniel. 1993. *What Jane Austen Ate and Charles Dickens Knew: From Fox Hunting to Whist—the Facts of Daily Life in Nineteenth Century England*. New York: Simon and Schuster.

Raaj, Neelam. 2005. 'Hearth Break', *Times of India*, 3 July, p.17.

____. 2008. '"Thanks to Asians, US has got a skewed sex ratio"', *Times of India*, 2 April.

Radford, Jill, and Elizabeth Stanko. 1996. 'Violence against Women and Children: The Contradictions of Crime Control under the Patriarchy', in *Women, Violence and Male Power: Feminist Activism, Research and Practise*, Marianne Hester, Liz Kelly and Jill Radford (eds). Buckingham: Open University Press, pp.65–80.

Radhakrishna, G.S. 2005. 'Child Bride Waits for Groom and Divorce', *Telegraph*, 14 July.

Ramachandran, Smriti Kak. 2005. 'Oxfam to Kick-Start Campaign to End Violence Against Women', *Tribune*, 23 April. www.tribuneindia.com/2005/

Ramanamma, A., and U. Bambawale. 1980. 'The Mania for Sons: An Analysis of Social Values in South Asia', *Social Science and Medicine*, 14B(2): 107–10.

Ramesh, Randeep. 2006. 'Jailing of Doctor in Indian Sting Operation Highlights Scandal of Aborted Girl Fetuses', *Guardian*, 30 March.

Ranade, Ashok Da. 2002 (1st ed.1997). *Hindustani Music*. New Delhi: National Book Trust.

Rathus, Spencer A. 1990. *Psychology*. 4th ed. Fort Worth: Holt, Rinehart and Winston Inc., p.272.

Ray, Bharati. 2000. 'Women and Partition', in *From Independence towards Freedom: Indian Women since 1947*, Bharati Ray and Aparna Basu (eds). New Delhi: Oxford University Press.

Ray, Bharati, and Aparna Basu (eds). 2000. *From Independence towards Freedom: Indian Women since 1947*. New Delhi: Oxford University Press.

Raychaudhuri, Hemchandra. 2000. *Political History of Ancient India*. New Delhi: Oxford University Press.

Reddy, Balaji. 2005. 'A Staggering Increase in Gang Rape of Young Girls in India Especially in Collaboration with Police—Is Government Sleeping?' *India Daily*, 5 May.

Reuband, Karl-Heinz, and Eric A. Johnson. 2005. *What We Knew: Terror, Mass Murder, and Everyday Life in Nazi Germany*. Cambridge: Basic Books.

Rhys Davids, T.W. 1903. *Buddhist India*. London: T. Fisher Unwin. Republished New Delhi: Low Price Publications.

Ridley, Matt. 2003. *The Red Queen: Sex and the Evolution of Human Nature*. New York: Harper Perennial.

Robinson, Francis. 2000. *Islam and Muslim History in South Asia*. New Delhi: Oxford University Press.

Robinson, Richard H., and Willard L. Johnson. 1982. *The Buddhist Religion: A Historical Introduction*. California: Wadsworth Publishing Co.

Rose, David. 2007. 'British Asians Aborting Unwanted Girls', *The Times*, 3 December.

Rossi-Landi, Ferrucio, and Massimo Pesaresi. 1981. 'Language', in *Contact: Human Communication and Its History*. New York: Thames and Hudson, pp.21–38.

Rowland, Susan. 2000. 'Imaginal Bodies and Feminine Spirits: Performing Gender in Jungian Theory and Atwood's Alias Grace', in *Body Matters: Feminism, Textuality, Corporeality*, Avril Horner and Angela Keane (eds). Manchester: Manchester University Press.

Ruswa, Mirza Hadi. 2006 (1st ed. 1899). *Umrao Jan Ada*. Trans. David Matthews. New Delhi: Rupa and Co.

Salman, Sherry. 1997. 'The Creative Psyche: Jung's Major Contributions', in *The Cambridge Companion to Jung*, Polly Young-Eisendrath and Terence Dawson (eds). Cambridge: Cambridge University Press, pp.52–70.

Samuels, A. 1985. *Jung and Post-Jungians*. London and Boston: Routledge and Kegan.

Sarkar, Lotika. 2000. 'Reform of Hindu Marriage and Succession Laws: Still the Unequal Sex', in *From Independence towards Freedom: Indian Women since 1947*, Bharati Ray and Aparna Basu (eds). New Delhi: Oxford University Press.

Sell, Randall L., James A. Wells, and David Wypij. 1995. 'The Prevalence of Homosexual Behaviour and Attraction in the United States, the United Kingdom and France: Results of National Population Based Samples', *Archives of Sexual Behaviour* 24(3): 235.

Sengupta, Joy. 2005. 'Parched Villagers Turn to Naxalites', *Telegraph*, 6 June.

Sen Gupta, Subhadra. 2001. *Devalaya: Great Temples of India*. New Delhi: Rupa & Co.

Sewell, R. 1961. *A Forgotten Empire*. New Delhi: Publication Division, Government of India.

Sharar, Abdul Halim. 2001. 'Lucknow: The Last Phase of an Oriental Culture', in *The Lucknow Omnibus*. New Delhi: Oxford University Press.

Sharma, R.S. 1996. *Looking for the Aryans*. Mumbai: Orient Longman.

Shea, David, and Anthony Troyer. 1843. *Dabistan or School of Manners*, vol. 2. London: Allen and Co.

Singh, Gajinder. 2004. 'Girl couple set free', *Telegraph*, 11 December 2004.

Singh, Upinder. 2002. *Mysteries of the Past Archaeological Sites in India*. New Delhi: National Book Trust.

Sinha, Mrinalini. 1999. 'The Lineage of the "Indian" Modern: Rhetoric, Agency, and Sarda Act in Late Colonial India', in *Gender, Sexuality and Colonial Modernities*, Antoinette Burton (ed.). London and New York: Routledge, pp.207–21.

Sivaramamurti, C. 2002. *Indian Painting*. New Delhi: National Book Trust.

Skinner, B.F. 1979. *The Shaping of a Behaviorist*. New York: Knopf.

Smith, Curtis D. 1990. *Jung's Quest for Wholeness: A Religious and Historical Perspective*. Albany: SUNY Press.

Smith, Vincent A. 2002 (1st ed. 1890). *Ashoka: The Buddhist Emperor of India*. New Delhi: Low Price Publications.

Sogani, Rajul. 2002. *The Hindu Widow in Indian Literature*. New Delhi: Oxford University Press.

Solomon, Robert C. 1997. *Living with Nietzsche: What the Great 'Immoralist' Has to Teach Us*. New York: Oxford University Press.

Soondas, Anand. 2005. 'Hearth-break', *Times of India*, 3 July.

Spear, Percival. 1990. *A History of India*, vol. 2. New Delhi: Penguin Books India.

Stanford, J.K. 1926. *Ladies in the Sun: The Memsahibs' India 1790–1860*. London: The Gallery Press.

Stanistreet, D., C. Bambra, and A. Scott-Samuel. 2005. 'Is Patriarchy the Source of Men's Higher Mortality?' *J. Epidemiology. Community Health* 59: 873–76. doi:10.1136/jech.2004.030387 [accessed on jech.bmjjournals.com]

Stern, Robert W. 2003. *Changing India*. Cambridge: Cambridge University Press.

Stri Dharma 11(12): p.305.

Sudha, S., and S. Irudaya Rajan. 1999. 'Female Demographic Disadvantage in India 1981–1991: Sex Selective Abortion and Female Infanticide', *Development and Change* 30: 585–618.

Svoboda, Robert E. 1993. *Ayurveda: Life, Health and Longevity*. New Delhi: Penguin Books India.

Thakur, Himendra. 2007. 'Are Our Sisters and Daughters for Sale? When Will the Horrors of Dowry and Bride-burning End?' *India Together*, 25 September. www.indiatogether.org/wehost/nodowri/stats.htm

Thapar, Romila.1990. *A History of India*, vol. 1. New Delhi: Penguin Books India.

———. 2000. *Narratives and the Making of History: Two Lectures*. New Delhi: Oxford University Press.

———. 2002a. *The Past and Prejudice*. New Delhi: National Book Trust.

———. 2002b. *Early India: From the Origins to AD 1300*. New Delhi: Allen Lane.

Tharu, Susie, and K. Lalita. 1997 (1st ed. 1993). *Women Writing in India*, vol. 1, *600 BC to the Early Twentieth Century*. New Delhi: Oxford University Press.

Tirrel, Lynn. 1994. 'Sexual Dualism and Women's Self-Creation: On the Advantages and Disadvantages of Reading Nietzsche', in *Nietzsche and the Feminine*, Peter J. Burgard (ed.). Charlottesville: University of Virginia Press, pp.158–84.

Towards Equality. 1974. Report of the Committee on the Status of Women in India, New Delhi.

Toufexis, Anastasia, and Eugene Linden. 1992. 'Bisexuality: What Is It?' *Time* 140(7): 49.

Tripathy, Ajit Kumar. n.d. 'The Real Birth Place of Buddha: Yesterday's Kailavastu, Today's Kapileswar', *OHRJ (Orissa Historical Research Society Journal)* 47(1): 3, 7, 8.

UNAIDS. 6 July 2007. '2.5 Million People Living with HIV in India'.

UNICEF. 2007. 'State of the World's Children, 2007', South Asia Edition.

Uttam, Kumar. 2005. 'Naxals Butcher 9 of Landlord Army', *Asian Age*, 15 November.

Van Der Hoop, J.H. 1999. *Character and the Unconscious: A Critical Exposition of the Psychology of Freud and Jung*. London: Routledge.

Vanita, Ruth, and Saleem Kidwai. 2001. *Same-Sex Love in India*. Delhi: Macmillan India.

Varma, Pavan K., and Sandhya Mulchandani. 2004. *Love and Lust: An Anthology of Erotic Literature from Ancient and Medieval India*. New Delhi: HarperCollins India.

Venugopal, Ayswaria. 2005. 'Girl Child Shame for Delhi', *Telegraph*, 5 February, p.5.

Visaria, Leela. 2000. 'Deficit of Women in India: Magnitude, Trends, Regional Variations', in *From Independence towards Freedom: Indian Women since 1947*, Bharati Ray and Aparna Basu (eds). New Delhi: Oxford University Press, pp.80–99.

Visram, Rozina. 1992. *Women in India and Pakistan: The Struggle for Independence from British Rule*. Cambridge: Cambridge University Press.

Waite, Geoff. 1996. *Nietzsche's Corps/E*. Durham: Duke University Press.

Watson, John B., and R. Rayner. 1920. 'Conditioned Emotional Reactions', *Journal of Experimental Psychology* 3: 1–14.

Weart, Spencer R. 1988. *Never to War: Why Democracies Will Not Fight One Another*. Connecticut: Yale University Press.

Wilson, C.R. 1895. *The Early Annals of the English in Bengal,* vol. 1. London: W. Thacker & Co.

WHO (World Health Organization). 1997. *World Health Statistics Annual, 1997*. Geneva: WHO.

WHO, UNICEF, UNFPA. 2000. 'Maternal Morality in 2000: Estimates Developed by WHO, UNICEF and UNFPA'.

Wrangham, Richard, and Dale Peterson. 1996. *Demonic Males: Apes and the Origins of Human Violence*. New York: Mariner Books.

Wujastyk, Dominik. 1998. *The Roots of Ayurveda: Selections from Sanskrit Medical Writing*. New Delhi: Penguin Books India.

Wurgaft, Lewis D. 1983. *The Imperial Imagination: Magic and Myth in Kipling's India*. Middletown, Connecticut: Wesleyan University Press.

Younger, Coralie. 2004. *Wicked Women of the Raj: European Women Who Broke Society's Rules and Married Indian Princes*. New Delhi: HarperCollins Publishers.

INDEX